THE SOUL OF LOVE

E.X. ALEXANDER

11TH MUSE PUBLISHERS

Cover design by Wicked Smart Designs

Content Warnings: This book contains some scenes with mild violence, sexual situations, and references to suicide and miscarriages. Reader discretion is advised.

Digital ISBN: 978-1-955599-00-9

Print ISBN: 978-1-955599-01-6

Created with Vellum

For my parents, without whose love and support this would not have been possible.

PROLOGUE

Before the dawn of man and gods, there was nothing; a disordered and timeless dark void, a universe without form, without sound, without light, without life, or love.

For untold eons, the universe passed in this state of nothingness, until the birth of the primordial ones. Powerful beings, they were the first—and most primal—generation of gods.

These gods rose out of Chaos with powers and abilities unrivaled by any. They created the universe—the planets, the stars, and the cosmos—but they had the power to destroy it all. What they created they could tear asunder.

These primordial beings were volatile with raw emotions. Balance was needed to temper these emotions of greed, anger, jealousy, and hatred. They were cold with the powers they wielded. Lone wolves who thought only of themselves, they needed a flame to warm them, to balance them, to make them use their powers for good instead of for selfish want.

It was love that saved them.

Love created all that followed Chaos. Light conquered

night, order was brought to disorder, the void was filled, and life beyond the primordial ones began with a single primordial being. Known by many names—Eros, Thesis, Phanes, Protogonus—they were the primordial god of Love, Sex, Creation, and Procreation. Though other primordial gods were powers in and of themselves, they were the most powerful, and the most beloved of them all. Phanes filled the other primordial gods with love, desire, compassion, and the burning need for one another.

Tall and muscular, Phanes was a hermaphroditic god with golden wings, and a beauty that rivaled anything in creation. Male and female, hard and soft, cruel and kind, Phanes was embraced by the first serpent—Ophioneus—who became a constant companion.

It was through Phanes that humanity—and all the successive generations of gods—were born. Phanes created life through love and sex: powerful humans, with two heads, four arms, four legs, and three sexes. These humans were complete, happy, and they gladly worshipped and laid sacrifices to the primordial gods—Phanes especially.

But the gods of later generations became jealous and fearful, and each new generation fought to overthrow their predecessors. They even feared and hungered for the power of the primordial gods. For a power they had no hope of controlling, one that threatened the very existence of the universe if the primordial gods fell.

War came. The Primordialomarchy was the first war between the gods. Factions formed. Allies became enemies. Lovers became rivals. Enemies became uneasy allies, and the primordial gods disappeared, yet they were fated to return and upset the balance of power.

Wars were waged against the primordial gods and Phanes was betrayed by those they trusted. They fought, but they were ripped to shreds. Cut into two—forever separating them into two bodies—male and female—they fell to earth where Eros—their male form—disappeared beneath the sea, while Thesis—their female form—vanished. Eros lay broken in both body and spirit for untold years, while rage over his betrayal festered in his heart. So he waited. Biding his time, he vowed to be reunited with his other half, and to take his vengeance against his betrayers.

Ophioneus fell, too, joining Eros in their watery tomb, transforming as their blood mingled beneath the waves, changing in unforeseen ways as they plotted their return.

The betrayers of Phanes, in a rage at being thwarted in their power grab, took their wrath and punished the mortal creations of Phanes, splitting the humans in half and scattering the former pairs far from each other. The poor humans were left to wander, always yearning in their search of their other half: their soul mate.

And so it was during another betrayal that Eros and Ophioneus made their way back to the world of gods and mortals. Rising out of the water with the birth of Aphrodite, they returned to the world of men and gods.

CHAPTER 1

Aphrodite stalked into the Olympic home of Eros looking for him. Anger rode her as she pushed through the door of his private chambers, overriding common sense. "Eros! Where are you?" she yelled, suddenly seeing his sleeping form, strode over to him and grabbed his shoulder, shaking him. "Wake up, I need you."

Springing up with a growl, Eros cut off her words, pinning her to the wall, her throat in his hard grip. Aphrodite struggled to free herself as his fingers tightened and a frighteningly vicious growl rumbled from deep within his chest. Clawing at his arm as his grip tightened in warning, she choked as she struggled to breathe. She tried using her powers against him, but they had no effect on him at all, which frightened her even more. Eyes narrowed, Eros leaned in close as he inhaled the scent of fear coming off Aphrodite. His inner predator was almost completely in control. His eyes flashed to the swirling molten colors of red, yellow, and blue, that marked the presence of the ancient predator that lived within him. It drew back and crouched down, ready to spring free and bring to ground the prey it scented in Aphrodite.

"Eros, please!" she choked out as she struggled to breathe.

Hearing the fear and pleading in her voice penetrated the red haze that clouded his mind as nothing else could, allowing him to take back control of the beast that lived within him. While they would viciously tear apart an enemy with no feelings of guilt, harming a woman—even Aphrodite—was another matter entirely. Letting go and stepping back a pace, Eros reined in his inner beast. He eased back as his eyes returned to normal and the beast finally retreated. Seeing the fear that Aphrodite struggled to hide, he stepped back to the dimly lit portion of the room to better conceal his beast's presence from her.

Sending a negligible wave of his power at Aphrodite, he clouded her mind and removed the memory of all that she had seen that could have led her to the discovery of his true nature and identity. He also healed the injury he had caused her with his beast in control. Blinking in confusion, Aphrodite slowly came out of the haze that had enveloped her mind. Needing to distract her from what he may have inadvertently revealed about his true nature, Eros scolded her in a manner guaranteed to get her angry. An angry Aphrodite was a forgetful one. "That was a stupid thing to do. You know better than to come up behind me, Aphrodite. Especially when I am sleeping. Have you no regard for your own safety?" he asked, sneering.

Stepping away from the wall, her cheeks flushed with anger at his words, Aphrodite quickly forgot about the haze that clouded her mind. "How dare you, Eros! Do not think that because I am the Goddess of Love that I do not know how to fight? I have more than enough power to strike you down."

His beast's snorting in contempt at her words helped to

rein in his temper. Scorn for her delusions of power filled him. She had no inkling what true power was, but soon she would learn. They *all* would learn. Letting her think she had won this round cost him nothing. With a grumble and a hard look, Eros growled, "What is so important that you must disturb me at this hour?"

Looking at him, Aphrodite could not help but reluctantly admire the rugged beauty of Eros. With the sunlight glittering off his golden locks and pure white wings, his cobalt-blue eyes still hazy from his slumber, she could not prevent the lustful thoughts she had about him, especially when he proved difficult. She had always lusted after him, but she had never been able to seduce him into her bed. Her failure to tempt him, to add him to her list of conquests, to taste his dark passions, made her even more spiteful towards him.

"I need your help dealing with a distasteful situation. My temples have been abandoned, and the people have forsaken me to worship a mortal imposter. I will not tolerate this insult."

Sighing, Eros walked over to the balcony to put some distance between him and the oftentimes irrational goddess. He felt the predator that lived below the surface of his skin begin to bristle and claw at him. It was becoming harder and harder lately to rein him in. His growing impatience was dangerous, and Aphrodite's jealous rant did nothing but incite the beast's temper.

"Why are you coming to me with this?" he snarled. "Anteros would be a better choice to deal with this, and you know it."

Aphrodite put her hand on his arm. The touch of her hand infuriated him. There was only one whose touch he would welcome, and she was not that woman. "I need your specific skill set, not your brother's. I want *you* to punish this girl for her insolence. Make her life a misery by having her fall in love with the lowest of men, a beast, one who will treat her ill and who others would feel shame for belonging to one such as him."

Eros gave her a cold stare filled with venom and shrugged off her touch. "You are viciously jealous of a mere mortal," he said, smirking at her. "My, how the mighty have fallen, Aphrodite, to wish such a fate on a simple girl. Don't tell me your capricious nature has finally driven away your acolytes," he taunted.

Her face red with fury, Aphrodite said, "Don't take that tone with me. Your own contrary nature has caused no end of trouble for the pantheon. *You* have caused strife between lovers, broken up marriages, caused even the gods to make themselves act the fool over mortals and immortals alike, and have helped to create demigod children. You are in no position to judge."

Eyes hard, Eros turned to face her. Her accusations were all true, but even she did not grasp the true motivation behind his behaviors of late. His endgame was all that mattered to him. Nothing and no one would stand in his way. Aphrodite did not see him as a powerful god struggling to contain his nature by his fingernails, his control nearly shredded, but as an inferior being that she thought to control. Fool that she was, she could not see the danger that stared her right in the face. Now she wanted to tempt the fates and have him punish what he was sure was an innocent, all in the name of her wounded pride and vanity.

Seeing the anger in his eyes, Aphrodite quickly realized she had chosen the wrong tactic and changed her approach, becoming more cajoling and conciliatory. "Don't look at me that way. You know I don't deal well with rejection, and the thought of all the mortals worshipping another in my place is unbearable. Please, just be a dear and help me in this one matter. It's just a little thing that I ask for, a few moments of your time," she simpered.

"No."

Seductively, she leaned against him, sensuously pressing up against him. "Do this for me, and I will make it worth your while," she whispered.

Grasping her hips, he brought her closer. Her body was pliant as he ground his hips against her. He felt her nipples harden as desire filled her. Leaning in, Eros whispered into her ear, "Really, Aphrodite? Seduction tactics? Since when have I ever given you the impression that I would welcome one such as you in my bed?"

Eyes flashing with anger, she wrenched away from him, raising her hand to strike him. Grabbing her hand before she could slap him, he pulled her to him, keeping a firm grip on it as she tried to pull away. "Never think that I will ever fall for one of your cheap seduction tricks, Aphrodite," he said, his voice cold. "I will never bed you. Not now, not ever."

Pulling free and stepping back, her cheeks flushed from both desire and anger, Aphrodite snarled, "You can't resist me forever, Eros. I can *feel* the hunger in you. It eats at you, a hunger you can never satisfy. It rides you mercilessly, doesn't it?"

Eros stilled at her words, the predatory stillness that only he—and Anteros—could affect. It sent a shard of lust and fear through Aphrodite. It was an aphrodisiac to one such as her, and it goaded her to push him further, to strip him of the control he held over his passions.

"Poor, poor Eros. Always looking for a new lover, but always left unsatisfied. No matter how many women you take to bed, not a one has quenched that fire. How could they?" Seeing his anger-filled gaze focused solely on her, she tauntingly pressed her point, "Deny it all you want, but you know only one woman will ever satisfy the raging lust you try so hard to hide."

"And you think *you* are that woman, don't you?" he mockingly demanded.

"Oh yes, Eros. I *know* I am. You will come to me to quench your hunger eventually, and when that time comes, I will make you crawl and beg. Your hunger is slipping past your control, and sooner than you know, you will be in my bed."

A vicious look of disdain passed across his face. "I value my cock too much to chance contaminating it by sleeping with you."

Gasping in outrage, she screamed, "You miserable, wretched beast! How dare you?"

He laughed cruelly, for she had no idea how true that statement was. "I dare because I am a beast. Never forget that."

Her cheeks flushed with anger again, and that only added to her allure. "Then I hope it falls off, you miserable cur."

The contempt that Eros felt for her rankled only slightly more than the veneration of Psyche by the mortals. It drove her to find a way to punish both of them for the insult they both leveled at her. Psyche for being worshipped in her stead, and Eros for rejecting her sexual advances. Knowing how Eros was so protective of mortals, Aphrodite was determined to force him to harm the girl as punishment for his vicious rejection of her. "As you will not help me, I will take care of Psyche myself. Killing her will get rid of the problem just as well. Moreover, I know many ways to make her death a warning to other mortals."

When she turned to leave, Eros gripped her arm to stop her. He was fully aware of her manipulation tactics, but knowing the viciously cruel torture that Aphrodite reserved specifically for women, he could not allow an innocent to suffer such a fate. The only saving grace was that he could at least see that the girl did not suffer too greatly from Aphrodite's vanity.

Cursing himself a fool, he knew the only way to stop her from harming the girl was to concede to her demands, but he would get something in return for his troubles. "Fine, I will fly out and see what havoc I can cause her, but you will owe me a debt. Swear on the River Styx that when I call in your debt, you will pay it without protest or hesitation. But know this: You may not like the results of this day's mischief," he warned.

Frowning, Aphrodite was reluctant to give him such a vow. To swear by the River Styx was an unbreakable vow when given by the gods. To do so would bind her to whatever he demanded as his debt. She would be compelled to pay, but her desire to see Psyche punished was stronger than her wariness, as was her desire to force Eros to do her bidding. "I swear by the River Styx that I will owe you a debt when you make Psyche fall in love with a beast. And when you call in this debt, I will pay it without protest or hesitation."

"So be it."

Clapping her hands happily, she kissed him and whirled away to pursue other matters. Dancing merrily out of the room, she left a lingering scent of the sea in her wake.

Eros stood in the middle of the room for long minutes after her departure, cursing himself ten times the fool for ever agreeing to her childish demands. Gathering his bow and arrows, he left to perform the distasteful duty he had obliged himself to complete.

CHAPTER 2

King Andronikos, along with his trusted advisors, were sitting in the throne room listening to the captain of the guards' latest report with alarm. His youngest daughter, Psyche —and a potential suitor—had almost been trampled to death by a crowd in the market square that very morning.

"My king, it is too dangerous for the princess to leave the palace grounds again. My men and I were barely able to keep the crowds at bay long enough to get her out this time. Even so, several people were nearly crushed to death in the ensuing madness. If Prince Alexander's bodyguards had not been there to provide reinforcement, we would have been overrun."

"Captain, what exactly happened?" demanded the king.

"The princess was heading to the temple of Hera to make an offering. She was accompanied by her chaperone and Prince Alexander. There were visitors from neighboring city-states present, and when they caught sight of the princess, they were awestruck. We have seen this happen before, and we thought we were prepared. Unfortunately, there was a foreign priestess among them this time. She approached Psyche as if in a trance, declaring to everyone in the agora that as a high priestess of Aphrodite, she had traveled to see if the rumors were true. She then fell to her knees, declaring loudly that Psyche was the goddess Aphrodite herself. Then the crowd went wild and rushed to the princess, begging and praying to her."

Pausanias, one of the king's oldest friends and advisors, sat forward. "I heard that there was a strange occurrence, as well. Is it true that after the princess commanded them to stop, the crowd froze in place?"

The captain nodded. "Yes. It was the only reason we were able to escape."

"How long did the crowd remain frozen?"

"Until the princess was out of the agora."

Pausanias nodded. "What do you make of this?"

"I believe it was the shock of being spoken to by the goddess that caused their strange reaction," the captain replied.

"Psyche is not a goddess!" the king snapped.

The captain of the guards flinched and dropped his eyes. "Of course, my king. I misspoke."

After the king dismissed the captain, another council member spoke up. "I am afraid there is more bad news. The priestesses of Aphrodite have sent a formal complaint. People are no longer worshipping at the temple; instead, they have been coming here to worship outside the palace walls, calling for the princess to appear to them. Every day, more and more people are making the journey. The priestesses have threatened to take action if something is not done soon. We are being overrun with pilgrims, and we cannot take much more."

Before the king could respond, a royal messenger arrived.

"Yes, what is it?"

"Your highness, I have a message from Prince Alexander," the messenger replied, before handing over the document.

The king opened it and read it silently. Then he crumpled it and cursed, angrily dismissing the messenger. "Prince Alexander has departed. He has withdrawn his offer of marriage to Psyche and has decided to make an offer to marry another, though he still wishes to keep the alliance between us."

Zeno shook his head. "Not a wise move on his part. He needs us more than we need him, especially with the alliances we were able to forge with the marriages of Aikaterini and Emilia. But that still leaves us with Psyche."

The king's two oldest daughters, while not as beautiful as his youngest, had made advantageous marriages into the royal families of neighboring city-states. Psyche was now in her early twenties, and still unwed. It was unheard of.

Dismissing the council save for Pausanias, the king then pulled him aside to speak privately with him.

Striding into the throne room just then, Queen Eleni stopped and surveyed the scene until she spotted her husband. She walked purposefully to the men with a tight smile. "With your leave, I need to consult with my husband on an urgent matter." With a respectful bow, the adviser took his leave of the royal couple. It was only when they were alone that she stated the reason for the interruption to her husband.

"Something must be done, Andronikos. Our daughter cannot even leave the palace grounds anymore. She nearly died today, and now the priestess of Aphrodite has informed me that the people no longer worship the goddess as they should. Instead, they now worship our daughter, and no good can come from this."

"I know, my love," sighed the king. "That was what Pausanias and I were just speaking about. I have decided to increase Psyche's dowry and to hold a feast to see if a marriage can be made for our youngest. I would see our daughter settled with a good man who will provide her a home—and the gods be willing—children. I can't bear to see her grow evermore lonely and isolated."

Her eyes glazed with unshed tears, the queen asked, "When are you planning this feast?"

The king took his wife into his arms to give her some measure of comfort. "In one month's time. Many young men of good, noble families will be here for the harvest festival. It will be the best time to make this announcement."

"I hope for all our sakes that your plan works. If not, I do not know what else to do. Our time grows short, and I fear we may leave our child to fend for herself."

* * *

PREPARATIONS WERE MADE for the feast that the king would hold in a last-ditch effort to find a husband for his daughter. All he wanted was to see her future settled. The king and queen's greatest fear was to leave the world before all their children's futures were established. With their elder two daughters safely married, they focused their combined energy and worry on the future of their youngest. They did not want to leave her with no one to stand between her and the dangers a woman alone faced in their world.

The invitations were sent and the feast was held at the end of the month. The king had invited all the eligible men to the feast, where he planned to make it known that he had doubled the dowry of his youngest in the hopes of receiving a viable offer of marriage. He was determined to find a suitor who would follow through and marry her, unlike the several previous ones, who had broken their word after seeing the attention Psyche's beauty attracted.

After the guests had gathered in the great hall, partaking of the excellent feast provided by the royal family, he stood and waited until the crowd quieted down. King Andronikos walked to where Psyche sat with her mother, drawing her to her feet, and brought her with him to stand beside him on the dais. "Honored gentlemen, let me present my youngest daughter, Psyche, to you all. She is of marriageable age, has a sweet disposition, and she brings with her a dowry of fifty golden drachmas."

Gasps and quiet murmurings of sheer disbelief could be heard among the gathered crowd at the staggering amount of her dowry. The queen turned a shocked gaze to her husband. Even Psyche was surprised at the lengths her father was willing to go to. Fifty golden drachmas was more money than even the most prosperous noble families saw in several years. Several men filled with envious speculation turned to the desperate royal family, and some contemplated the offer laid at their feet.

Psyche turned back to the crowd, schooling her features into a serene mien, letting none of her thoughts and fears appear on her face. Inwardly, though, she worried that the assembled men would become ruled by the greed such an amount could arouse in them, and she braced herself in fearful anticipation to see if this would lead to a fight among the potential suitors.

She continued to stand silent under the combined stares of the crowd, and silently wished for the floor to open up and swallow her whole—for that was how uncomfortable and humiliating she found the whole affair to be. Heat flooded her face, and she tried to keep the tremor that seized her body under control. As her gaze travelled over the crowd, she witnessed the greed that had entered the eyes of some of the men, the pitying stares of others, and the jealous envy of many of the women present. Finding not a friend among the sea of faces only increased her embarrassment and feelings of isolation. She felt like a prized sow brought to market, waiting to be bid on. She silently cursed and wished for the evening to be over with, but her father was not done with his unintentional humiliation.

"Whoever wishes the hand of my daughter will find her a most agreeable wife," he continued. "Should you wish for her hand in marriage, you need only present yourself at any point during the evening."

With that final announcement, Psyche walked with her head held high, trying to ignore the cruel whispers that accompanied her as she went back to her seat. She tried to hide the tremor in her hands by holding on to her gown.

Conversations suddenly erupted all throughout the room, with wagers quietly sallying back and forth among the crowd on whether she would finally receive an offer of marriage by evening's end—or whether she would end the eve as a maid still.

Psyche tried to ignore it all, but soon the volume of the room became too loud for her to tune out. As snippets of conversations reached her, she could not help herself and began to listen to the gossip about her.

A group of noblemen from a neighboring city-state were gathered off to her left. Psyche recognized several of them from past visits. They were currently engaged in a heated debate, trying to keep the topic of their conversation surreptitious, but their volume increased in direct proportion to the wine they consumed, and soon, their topic—and their opinions—reached her ears.

"Eh, Polyx," slurred one of the men. "That girl is a fine piece. Never seen such a lovely package. Bet she'd be able to keep even *you* at home," he said, with a lecherous look that left no doubt as to his meaning.

"But there must be something wrong with her," wondered

another, "her not being wed at her age and all. What do you think is wrong with her?"

"Well, just look at her," exclaimed Polyz. "She's too beautiful. Entering into a marriage to Psyche is to invite trouble such as Menelaus had when he wed Helen, and only a fool would court such trouble. Better a plain and impoverished wife, then all the trouble such riches and her beauty would cause a man. That is why every suitor she has ever had has begged off marrying her after seeing the trouble her beauty causes. It has gotten so bad that she is even being worshipped in place of Aphrodite. Can you imagine being married to a woman like that?"

The others mulled this over for some time before one by one, the men all agreed that marriage to Psyche would be more trouble than it was worth—even with the financial incentive. They then turned to other topics of conversation, their drinking and feasting escalating.

Turning her face away from the men, Psyche blinked rapidly, fighting the tears that flooded her eyes. The pain caused by their words were daggers in her chest. It was as real as any physical wound she had ever suffered as a child.

Unwillingly, her gaze traveled to the one corner of the dining hall she had studiously avoided looking at all evening.

He had come, as well, and he was not alone. Alexander had brought his new bride with him.

Seeing him with his wife hurt her more than all the viciously cruel talk going on all around her. Psyche cursed herself for caring about what could have been. Alexander was the one suitor who she had allowed herself to believe in when he said he would marry her. He would not be like the others, who had all forsaken her.

He had sworn to her that he would marry her. That he cared for her.

Liar.

After nearly being trampled to death in the agora, he had told her he could not deal with her being thought of as a goddess by the masses. He wanted a *real* woman, not a curiosity.

Now look at him, she thought to herself, married to another and coming here to join in as a spectator to watch her humiliation, for there was no other reason to come here tonight. He was just like all the others before him.

Turning away from him, Psyche called on her years of hiding behind the mask she had learned to wear to protect herself from such cruelty. Pride kept her from allowing anyone to know how her heart and soul bled from such cruelty.

The feast continued well into the evening. Men could be heard admiring Psyche for her beauty, yet none approached the king. Most of the guests stayed late, each waiting and watching in gleeful anticipation to see if any of the men would make an offer for Psyche's hand in marriage, Alexander and his bride among them.

Psyche sat with a heavy heart as she— and her parents— slowly came to the realization that there would be no offer. While she was greatly admired for her beauty, no one dared to approach her father about marriage.

When it eventually became apparent to the guests that not one of the men in the crowd was going to offer for her, they slowly trickled out of the palace. Many were eager to go home to spread the gossip of the night's events.

* * *

AFTER THE FEAST, the king and his queen retired to their bedchamber, distraught over their failure to secure Psyche's future.

"Enough is enough, wife," said King Andronikos as he

prowled around the bedroom in restless anger. "I am sick of seeing our daughter become a shut-in, unable to live as a woman should, with a husband and children by her feet."

"What can we do?" the queen asked despondently, her head in her hands as she cried. "You heard the whispers as well as I did. No one wants our daughter because they think she is too beautiful; that she will be nothing but trouble. There is no sum of money that can overcome that belief, not since Helen herself caused so much trouble."

Hearing the heartbreak in his wife's voice, the king walked over and gathered her into his arms and pulled her down into the bed. They lay there for some time, the king stroking his hand over her bronze hair lit with silver. The silence stretched out between them, each lost in their own thoughts.

Several long minutes passed, and only one solution came to the king's mind. "I see no other option for us. I have decided to make the journey to Delphi to seek the council of the Pythia. She is our only hope in resolving the matter of our daughter's future. I will leave on the next tide."

Queen Eleni fearfully agreed with her husband's decision to seek the council of the gods, but her heart raced with terror. The Pythia would give an answer to their dilemma, the queen had no doubt of that, but it was the possible answer that she feared most.

CHAPTER 3

Psyche could not sleep after the feast. She paced around her room, waiting for the palace to quiet so that she could escape to her private sanctuary. The humiliation of the night's events weighed her spirit down.

After the moon had risen, she wandered out into the inner courtyard to the garden. Taking a deep breath and letting all her hurt emotions out with that single breath, she sat in silence, tears gently slipping down her cheeks, letting her mind wander for a time in numb acceptance. As she sat looking out over the garden that she had helped plant as a child, a small butterfly danced over the blooms in a haphazard waltz. It flew in a lazy flutter over her head and landed on her left shoulder. Smiling sadly at the little creature's antics, she said, "Hello there, little one. Come to keep me company?"

Fluttering its wings in what Psyche took as a yes, she sat in comfortable silence with her little companion.

"Did you know that I helped to plant the flowers in this garden?" she asked the little butterfly. "My sisters are much older than I am, so I didn't have any playmates as a child. It was rather lonely,' she reminisced sadly. "But there was an old blind woman who had a gift when it came to flowers, and Father had her create this garden for my mother, and the old woman let me help her."

The butterfly walked across her shoulder, as if it wanted to get closer to her face, as if it was interested in hearing more of her story.

"I loved working in the garden with her. It was one of the few times I could be myself. Stefania couldn't see my face. She judged me based on my character, and her blindness allowed her to see me in a way no one else ever has," she said softly. "Now, all anyone sees when they look at me is this pretty face. No one ever bothers to look beyond the surface to who I truly am."

While Psyche poured her heart's pain to the little butterfly, she was unaware of the presence of another being silently listening to her tale.

Eros stood behind Psyche, invisible to the eyes of mortals. He had come to her home, prepared to follow through on the promise that he had made to Aphrodite, but the haunting beauty of her voice mesmerized him as she told her story to the butterfly on her shoulder.

The beast inside him was quiet as it listened to her, just being in her presence was soothing to him, and the never-ending rage inside him was held at bay for once. That alone gave him pause. His heart seized in pain at the sound of her sad loneliness, and all he wanted to do was spirit her away and protect her. The desire was so uncharacteristic of him that he stopped to mull over the unsettling need. Not liking the power this girl seemed to have over him, he pulled out his bow and arrow to carry out his mission.

He drew back, but the part of him that lived in the abyss refused to let him release the arrow. Long moments passed as he struggled with himself. Fists clenched in anger, he put down his bow and arrow and silently berated himself. He had never shirked from his duty before, and his uncharacteristic behavior set off alarms in his head. The thought that this mere slip of a girl could have this kind of effect on him activated his primal instincts.

The pull of her voice drew him closer, and he wanted to get a better look at her. He moved to stand in front of her, still unseen to her human eyes. Her head was turned slightly away from him, so that he could only see her profile, but what he could see was enough to seize his interest. Thick tresses of dark brown hair that almost appeared black in the moonlight—save for the hidden fire it held—fell in long waves to the small of her back. Her skin was the color of the purest cream, with hints of blush on her cheek. Her nightgown revealed a body lush with curves made to tempt even the gods with lust, but as he watched her, he was struck by the beauty she carried within. Her outward appearance was nothing more than the reflection of the beauty of her soul. It spoke to him and tugged at a long-forgotten memory.

Psyche turned her head toward where he stood. Her gaze unknowingly swept over him, and as her tear-filled hazel eyes sparkled in the moonlight, their eyes locked. In that fleeting moment, everything in him stilled. Yet his heart raced as recognition ran through him with crushing awareness.

It was *her*, he roared in silent triumph. *Thesis.*

Standing there in stunned disbelief, Eros looked at Psyche in wonder. All these eons he had spent searching for his other half, never knowing where she had hidden herself. Since rising from the sea after the betrayal, he had spent every waking moment scouring the world for her. Every thought, action, and scheme he had engaged in was in the pursuit of finding her.

Now she had finally returned, but as a human. He had

never thought to look amongst the mortals for her. But even this form could not hide who—or what—she truly was. The danger of discovery of her true nature by other immortals caused his beast to rise to the surface in violent protest of her fragile mortal form. The need to protect her grew until it became a burning inferno that brought a snarl to his lips and threatened to unleash the primal beast that lived within him.

No one would harm her and live.

But as he continued to gaze at her profile, a more earthly feeling seized him. His body hardened painfully, and he was consumed with a violent lust for her, such that he could barely hold himself back from taking her right there and then in the garden. Reining himself in, he stood guard over her as he plotted on how he would make her his.

She was not escaping him again.

As dawn approached, Psyche made her way wearily back to her room, the butterfly still upon her shoulder. Eros followed, unable to bear having her out of his sight for even a moment. She carefully removed the butterfly and gently placed it on one of the flowers that was by the foot of her bed. "Good night, little friend. Thank you for the pleasant company," she said. Shaking her head at the absurdity of carrying on a conversation with a butterfly, she got into her bed and quickly fell into an exhausted sleep.

Eros approached the bed on silent feet and gazed down at her. He looked at the butterfly that seemed to be standing guard, protecting the fragile heart of the lonely princess. Unable to resist touching her, he gently threaded his fingers through the soft dark silk of her hair, before trailing them along her face to her jawline, finally circling her throat with his hand. He leaned down until their breaths mingled in a kiss. Then he whispered "mine," before gently pressing a soft kiss against her lips. The taste of her sent flames coursing through his blood and threatened to drive him past the point of no return.

Not trusting himself, he straightened and forced himself to walk away from the temptation to make her his right then and there. His mind raced with the plans he had for Psyche; for now that he had looked into her soul and recognized who and what she was to him, he had no intention of releasing her. The thought of another touching her brought a scowl to his face and his hand tightening around his dagger with violent intent. It was fortunate no one had made an offer for her hand in marriage; else he would have been forced to gut the man who thought to take Psyche from him.

Smiling grimly, he leapt into the air from her balcony, and flew in the direction of Mount Olympus. As he flew, his thoughts turned to the promise he had made to Aphrodite. The goddess would get her wish. Psyche would wed a beast—just not a mortal one.

CHAPTER 4

As Eros flew back to his home on Mount Olympus, he sent a mental call to those he needed to help him carry out his plans—ones who owed him a debt and who could be trusted to remain silent—with the right incentive.

Zephyrus. Khloris: I have need of your services. Meet me at my home in an hour.

After receiving their answer, he continued on his way home.

Landing on the balcony, Eros was not surprised to see his brother Anteros waiting for him. To look at his brother was to see a reverse image of himself. Where Eros was fair, his brother was dark. Black hair framed a face that was a mirror image of his own, wings the color of the night, and Anteros' eyes were so dark a brown they appeared black.

Now those eyes were trained on Eros with a concerned look, as if he already knew the trouble that was brewing. "Where have you been?"

Knowing the reaction that he was going to get from his brother, Eros braced himself for the fallout his words would bring. "Dealing with a situation concerning Aphrodite and her petty jealousies."

Anteros rolled his eyes at Eros' reply. "You know better than that, O adelfós mou, to be sucked into one of her petty intrigues. What possessed you to agree to help her?"

"I've found her," Eros said in reply to his brother's demand.

"Found who?"

"Her." Seeing the knowledge of just who he was speaking of enter his brother's eyes, Eros turned and put away his bow and arrows. The pull to return to Psyche's side was a gnawing pain in his gut, but he forced himself to remain in the room and to put his plan into motion, to ensure not just her safety from Aphrodite, but their future, as well.

"Thesis? Are you sure?"

Eros saw the tension in his brother's stance. "Yes, I've finally found her. In this life, her name is Psyche, and she has been reborn in a mortal body. The irony is that I have Aphrodite to thank for it, but I must also protect Psyche from that spiteful goddess."

After Eros explained the situation and his plans fully to his brother, the concern that had gripped Anteros at his announcement turned to a savage fury, and the promise of blood filled the air.

Before his brother could say anything, Zephyrus and Khloris arrived.

Zephyrus' wife was tucked protectively at his side. "Eros. Anteros." Zephyrus nodded his head in greeting to the twins. Khloris smiled in amusement at the jealous possessiveness of her husband, his body placed slightly in front of her, as if to protect her from the brothers' sight.

"Zephyrus, Khloris, thank you for coming so soon," Eros said. "I need to avail myself of your special talents."

"And your discretion," warned Anteros softly.

His eyebrows lifting at the subtle threat, Zephyrus was about to make a cutting remark when his wife elbowed him in the ribs. "Behave," was her hissed response. He gave her a heated look that promised a sensual revenge once they were alone. Smiling down at her as he rubbed his ribcage, where she had scored her hit, Khloris turned to face the twins. "You too," she warned them, giving them a gimlet-eyed glare when they turned innocent faces to her. Then she shook her head at them and asked, "Now, what do you need?"

Smiling at her, for he had always had a soft spot in his heart for the sweet-natured former nymph turned goddess of flowers, Eros said, "I need you to go to my island and create a garden paradise, but leave huge parts of it incomplete. The island is to become the home of my future bride. Psyche loves to garden, so she must be able to put her personal stamp on it, and she must have something to fill her days with when I cannot be there with her. But make sure not to include any plants that could cause her any harm, for she is mortal, and I would not have her injured in any way."

Khloris was unable to hide her shock, for she knew of the girl he spoke of, and the hatred that Aphrodite held for Psyche. Khloris looked to her husband to gage his reaction to Eros' revelation, finding the same stunned disbelief reflected on his face. She turned back to Eros. "I will leave right away and get it done." Turning and pressing her hand to her husband's, she left the men alone. Her mind already planning out a garden sure to make the mortal girl happy, but she was nevertheless frightened of the precarious situation she and her husband now found themselves in.

Watching his wife until she was no longer visible, Zephyrus turned back to look at the solemn visage of the brothers. He was about to reprimand Eros for placing him and his wife in the middle of a grudge match when he chanced a glance into Eros' eyes. What he saw was so unexpected that the words died on his tongue before they had a chance to leave his lips.

"Yes," Eros said softly, answering his friend's silent question. "Psyche is to me what Khloris is to you. Did you really think that I would involve you in this if she wasn't the one?"

Hearing the truth in his words, Zephyrus sighed and shook his head in weary resignation. "Very well. What do you need me to do?"

"I need you to escort Psyche safely from her home in Pylos to my island. She will be brought to Sfaktiria and left there, per the orders of the Pythia. Once she is alone, take her to her new home, but tell her nothing of who her new bridegroom is. Then leave her in the dark as to what awaits her."

"Have you suffered a head injury?" Zephyrus demanded, sarcasm dripping off his every word. "You mean to tell me you plan on having that poor woman left abandoned on that rock, like some sacrificial lamb, after you've taken her away from the only world she knows, and keep her ignorant and isolated?"

Eros took an aggressive step forward, but Anteros put a restraining grip on his arm and pulled him back. *Easy, remember you need his help. Also, you wouldn't want Khloris after you,* his brother teased through their shared link.

Taking a deep breath, Eros reined in his temper long enough to command, "Just do as I say."

"Fine. But you need to rethink this plan of yours. Nothing good will come of it." And with that piece of advice, Zephyrus spread his wings and took off.

Shrugging off his brother's hand after their friend's departure, Eros gave him a surly stare and warned, "Don't" before stalking off to the balcony.

Following him out, Anteros leaned against the door, watching his brother in silence for several minutes. "What is it you are not telling me? Why did you not bring Thesis here with you? Why is she masquerading around as a mortal, drawing the attention of Aphrodite? And why this charade about preparing the island for your bride with Zephyrus and Khloris? Has she rejected you? Tell me what is really going on. Surely she is not blaming you for what happened?"

Eros refused to turn around, "We have debated over what really happened that night thousands of times. We both have searched for her, and the others, always ending in failure. What we didn't realize was what happened to Thesis after she sacrificed herself for us. Now I think I know. My soul mate must have used up almost all of her powers to save us, to give us the time needed to heal, evolve, and grow even more powerful. To become who we are today. But it wasn't until last night that I learned that in order to accomplish that, she must have paid an unimaginable price."

Anteros frowned. "What are you talking about? What price? She had to have evolved and grown as well, after all these eons. Yes, she hid and locked our brethren away to provide us cover so that we could reemerge hidden in plain sight and prepare for the final war among the gods when the primordials returned. "

Eros shook his head. "She was so weakened that she must have gone into a kind of stasis; that can be the only explanation for why it has taken her so long to return, and in a mortal vessel, at that. She only has fragments of power clinging to her now. No mortal body could ever contain the kind of power we have. She didn't just lock away the memories and powers of the primordial gods before scattering and hiding them away. She must have done the same to herself, with what little powers she had left in order to survive. Without her abilities or her memories, we have no way of finding and identifying them in their new incarnations. The ancient gods—Thesis included —have no knowledge of who they are, and cannot be found and released until the seal binding their souls and memories is broken."

"By Ouranos' balls. How can this be?"

"I do not know. It is a miracle that I finally found her. By locking away herself, she has developed into an entirely different person, just as we have. Psyche is the key, but we cannot force her to remember, not in her fragile human state. She is locked inside a mortal's body. Nor can I reveal my true self to her while she is without her powers. A mortal cannot be in the presence of a god in their true form. I fear even a shadow form like the one used by the gods when they visit mortals could be too much. My powers would kill her. She will not be another Semele. No, in order to unlock her memories, she must learn to love, but more importantly, to trust me. The *new* me. Just as I must learn to love and trust her in her new form. Only then can our souls be reunited, and hopefully that will set her and the others free. For that, I must hide my new identity as Eros, the god of love, from her."

"And what about her human vessel? Will she regain an immortal body once she reunites her soul with yours?"

"I do not know."

"I do not like this. Zephyrus is correct. If your plan fails and she rejects your love, I will be forced to punish her."

Without turning, Eros growled. "As if I would even let you live long enough to ever let you harm her," he warned. While he loved his brother and would lay down his life for him, in this, they could well become blooded enemies if Anteros ever tried to harm Psyche.

After rising from the sea, Anteros had transformed into the god of unrequited love. His specialty was punishing anyone who rejected true love. Eros knew his brother's nature was as predatory as his own, that his inner beast would not rest until he fulfilled his duty and punished

Psyche for not returning his love and trust. It was a dangerous game they all played. But in this, he would always choose Psyche over any familiar bonds.

"You know that you are placing yourself in danger," hissed Anteros in frustration. "You are the true god of love—not that pathetic Aphrodite as everyone thinks—in the Greek Pantheon. If Psyche rejects your love and refuses to reunite your souls together, you may not be able to recover from that rejection. I have no wish to see you hurt. For all our sakes, rethink your plan on keeping Psyche in the dark about who and what you really are to each other."

The pleading in Anteros' voice moved Eros as nothing else could—save for one other—but he knew that his course was set. "She must love me for me, not my godhood, or our past, and you know that. As a mortal, she has been raised to worship, obey, and revere the gods. That is not true love, or trust, and you damn well know that, too. She needs time to learn to love the real me, without the added distractions of who I am, or what I've become. Speak to me no more on this, O adelfós mou," Eros warned his brother.

Seeing that his words fell on deaf ears, Anteros gave in to his brother's demands, for the moment, at least. Seeing Eros spread his white wings in preparation for flight, Anteros stopped him with one last demand. "Where are you off to now?"

"I am off to speak with the Pythia. I need to confer with her about the message that she will give to King Andronikos when he arrives at Delphi." With that, Eros flew off, leaving Anteros behind to mull over the revelations of the past few minutes in worried agony. "I fear this will not go as smoothly as you plan," he said to himself.

CHAPTER 5

King Andronikos waited outside the temple of the Oracle at Delphi, having been granted an audience with the Pythia shortly after his arrival the night before. As he sat waiting for the priest to bring him in, his mind wandered over how quickly he had made the sea journey to Delphi. It was as if Zephyrus, the god of the west wind, had had a hand in getting his ship swiftly and safely to the shores of the holy site. Not to mention how quickly the head priest had placed him in front of all the others who had come to seek the advice of the Pythia. *Surely,* he thought to himself, *the gods were showing him their favor.*

He then heard footsteps, and the head priest of the Oracle came up to him and bowed. "King Andronikos, if you will follow me, the Pythia is ready to receive you now."

He rose and followed the priest through the temple until they reached the inner sanctum of the Oracle. There, he saw the high priestess sitting on a stool in the middle of a barren chamber. He could barely make out the features of the pretty woman still in her prime through all the haze and distilled light in the chamber.

"Ask your question," whispered the priest.

King Andronikos took in a deep breath to steady his nerves. "Pythia, I have come to ask on the fate of my youngest daughter, Psyche. What must be done to ensure her marriage?"

The Pythia began to sway slightly, the temperature seemed to drop by several degrees, and the sudden change in the air raised the hackles of the king, for it was an unearthly sensation that filled the chamber. It was as if the god Apollo himself was in the tiny room with them.

When the Pythia's response came, it raised the hair on the back of his neck and crushed his heart into a thousand pieces.

"In a fortnight's time, prepare this girl for dreaded wedlock, O King of Pylos, and leave her on the lofty mountain-rock of Sfaktiria. Surender all hope for a mortal son-in-law. No male of human seed shall wed your daughter, but a fiery-winged serpent for her there will be. One who is destined to rain death and destruction on the world. He is a beast soaring on wings in the sky, who makes all things burn, who afflicts each living thing with bow and arrow. The sky weeps, the earth shudders, and the dark realms tremble below. The gods and goddesses show their terror for him. Even the king of the gods fears him. This the gods decree as punishment for the crime of taking the place of the goddess Aphrodite.

Staggering out of the temple into the light of day after receiving the Pythia's prophesy, the king bent over, trying to hold back the rage and tears inside him that sought to break free. He had come for an answer to his daughter's dilemma, thinking that when he left he would be planning a celebration when he returned home. Only now, instead of a wedding, he must go home and inform his wife that they would be planning a funeral.

* * *

Psyche was sitting among the flowers in her mother's garden when she heard the sound of the horn announcing the return of her father from his journey to Delphi. With her heart racing in anticipation, she quickly ran up to her bedroom to change out of her dirt-stained peplos and into a fresh one.

"Hurry your highness," said her maid, bucketing hot water into the wash basin. "The queen is already with your father in their receiving chamber. You must be ready when they call for you."

With that said, she helped Psyche strip down, and after a quick bath, was quickly fixing her hair into a simple bun when a knock sounded at the door.

Leaving her side with a few choice words for the interruption, the maid hurried to see who it was. When she pulled it open, she let out a gasp, for the king and queen both stood in the doorway, the shattered expressions on their faces leaving no doubt that the news of the Pythia was not to be welcomed.

"Leave us," said Psyche's mother, her face pale, tear tracks lining her cheeks.

After closing the door behind her, her mother came to Psyche's side and pulled her into a tight, trembling hold. It soon proved difficult to breathe, but Psyche made no move to extract herself from her mother's hold. It was as if her mother believed that if she just held on tight enough, it would keep her daughter from any harm.

After a few moments, Psyche reluctantly pulled herself from her mother's arms, wiping at the tears that silently slid down her own cheeks. Then she turned to look at the helpless rage that filled her father's face. "What did she say?" Psyche quietly asked, trying to brace herself, but nothing could prepare her for the words her father spoke.

Taking in a shuddering breath, the words tore out of him in a dead voice. "You are to be left on Sfaktiria in two days' time, to be wed to a beast even the gods fear, for the crime of usurping the goddess Aphrodite."

Struck dumb for a time, and feeling terror stab through her body like frozen shards of daggers, Psyche sat in stunned silence as her mother let out a heartbreaking wail and her father collapsed to his knees beside her, too overcome with grief. All Psyche could do was sit there in disbelief as her parents clutched her in their embrace.

CHAPTER 6

Psyche opened her eyes and rolled over in bed. It was still early, the dawn's light just barely breaking in her room. As it moved throughout her chamber, she watched the shadow play along the walls. But instead of a lazy few minutes resting in bed before the day's work was to be done, she lay there in mourning. The day of her wedding had arrived.

The past few days since learning of her fate were a hazy blur in her mind. The pain she felt over the agonizing self-blame of her parents had kept her from screaming and lashing out at the injustice of it all.

Not able to stay in bed a moment more, she rose and took a look around her barren room. The day before, she had gathered all her belongings that marked the various stages of her life, and she had donated most of them to the temple to be passed out to those less fortunate. A few mementos she had passed out to the various servants. The cherished ones she had saved for her family.

Sighing, she looked out over the gardens as the sun rose,

and she could hear the first stirrings of life in the palace. The day promised to be a beautiful one.

A knock came at the door, and taking a deep breath, Psyche called out, "You can come in! I am awake."

Several women from Psyche's extended family came into the room, each holding a piece of the garments and jewels that she would wear. Her mother was in the lead, barely holding on to her composure. "It is time, Psyche. We must prepare you."

Holding back her own tears, Psyche bravely gave the women of her family a watery smile and rose to follow them to the bathing chambers.

For the next several hours, she was prepared as any bride would be on her wedding day. She was bathed, rubbed down with sweetly scented oils, and her hair was put into an elaborate topknot. Her veil was held in place by a golden headband. While the women prepared her, the men of the family made sacrifices to the gods.

Her peplos was black—the color of mourning—with gold *herakles* knot pins at both shoulders that matched the gold girdle of her peplos. Her jewelry consisted of two golden snake armbands, a necklace, and earrings.

Back in her bedchamber, looking into the mirror, what she saw was a macabre mockery of what the day should have meant. Speaking to her gathered women folk, she asked, "Please leave me. I promise that I will join you outside in the courtyard. I just need a moment."

With sad looks, the women silently left and closed the door gently behind them.

Looking to make sure that she was truly alone, Psyche walked over to the bed and knelt down in front of it. Reaching down to feel under the bed, she pulled out a small leather sheath and dagger. She quickly pulled up the hem of her dress and strapped it to her upper left thigh. She tightened and secured the strap, and then quickly stood back up, dropping the hem of her dress to conceal it. Checking to make sure that there was no visible line to reveal that she carried a weapon, she took a steadying breath. A calm acceptance settled over her. One way or another, it would end today.

With that thought in mind, Psyche walked out of the room to join the waiting wedding party. She stepped out into the courtyard. Seeing her parents' grief-stricken faces, she hurried over to them and clasped them into her arms.

"Why are you both making yourselves ill?" she demanded. "I love you too much to see you waste away with grief. Please, I don't want my last memories of you to be of you grieving to the point of madness," she pleaded.

Drawing back from her parents, Psyche then turned to address the gathered crowd of curious onlookers and mourners. "Take heed of my fate," she warned. "I am being punished for impious envy. This is the result of angering the gods. I have always honored them, and I have always tried to live up to the virtues of my gender, to bring honor and pride to my parents, to my city-state. And where has that led me?"

Anger erupted within her soul at the malicious glee that she spied in the eyes of some of the female onlookers in the crowd, and she lashed out at them. "All of you who called me the new Aphrodite, be of cheer. You will now have a new tale to tell to spread about me. Only now do I see that my one undoing was not that I was too pretty, but of the title and honors you threw at me. But beware, what has happened to me can easily happen to you."

Many in the crowd turned their gaze away from Psyche and her parents in guilt. Some crossed themselves in fear that they too would be punished.

Feeling like she had lanced an infected wound in her soul, the resulting poison drained out of her, along with her anger.

"Escort me to Sfaktiria, where the fates have said I must go. I want to behold this fearsome husband of mine. Why should I delay in meeting the being who is destined to destroy the whole world?" And with those words, the wedding procession began the long walk from the palace, through Pylos to the waiting docks.

Her parents led the way, with Psyche following. Music played throughout the city-state, and all the inhabitants lined the streets to say goodbye to their youngest princess. Once the wedding procession walked by, the citizens followed, carrying torches and lighting their way to the harbor.

The procession wept and wailed for the fate that awaited Psyche. To be doomed in marriage to a monster even the gods feared was a fate unbearable to fathom. To be the innocent victim of an envious and vengeful goddess for the crime of beauty was beyond mortal limits of understanding.

What good was this beauty? thought Psyche to herself. *What sorrows and suffering had she borne due to an accident of circumstance?*

Once at the harbor, the populace stayed behind, while only the royal family boarded the ship that sailed out to the rocky island of Sfaktiria.

Once there, the three of them walked up the carved stairway until they reached the top of the island. There, they planted the torches into a semicircle facing out to the Ionian Sea. With one last tearful goodbye, Psyche's parents left her on the island and went back to their palace, to shut themselves in and mourn for the daughter that they had loved the most, but lost to fate.

CHAPTER 7

Now left on the top of the hill of the island of Sfaktitia, awaiting her fate, Psyche—driven to her knees in despair and exhaustion—succumbed to the waiting arms of Hypnos and to his brothers, the Oneiroi, who filled her fretful sleeping mind with unsettling images that had no rhyme or reason. She lay slumbering on the hilltop, unaware of the passage of time when a gentle breeze slowly and carefully roused her from her sleep. Pulling back the cobwebs that clouded her mind, Psyche slowly became aware that she was no longer alone.

When she slowly rose into a crouch from her prone position, a shadow fell across her face, blocking her view. Blinking rapidly for several seconds, her vision finally cleared, and Psyche beheld the smiling face of a beardless male with grey eyes the color of the sky during a storm. He had dark brown hair. With the setting sun behind him, his light grey wings captured her attention. They reminded her of the crest of the many doves that came daily to her bedroom window.

"Hello there. I am Zephyrus and I've been tasked to take you to your groom."

Psyche trembled in the presence of the god of the west wind, for he had the power to rend her limb from limb with a single breath. His words also terrified her, for it meant her groom was powerful indeed to be able to send a god as an escort for a lowly mortal. "I thank you for your kindness and hope you were not waiting too long for me," she said, trying to settle her nervous awareness of the sheer power that emanated from the otherworldly being.

Zephyrus held out his hand, pulled Psyche to her feet, and said, "Not at all. Now hold on tight." With that said, he pulled her back against his front, wrapped his arms around her, and took off into the air. He kept rising into the sky until they were blanketed by the clouds. She was petrified as she saw the ground became smaller. She clutched at his arms in fear that he might drop her. As they rose into the sky, the air became colder and her thin peplos was not enough to keep her warm.

Feeling despair at leaving the only home she had ever known, she cried out, "Wait! Please let me say my last goodbye."

Zephyrus folded his wings in and they dropped like a stone into water. She let out a short scream as they plummeted straight down below the cloud cover. Then he snapped his wings out at the last moment and began to beat them until they hovered high over Sfaktitia. With her heart racing, she clutched at the arms holding her. Then Zephyrus turned them so that they faced Pylos. "Say your farewell, little mortal. Burn the memory into your heart and mind, for you will not be the same girl should you ever return to this shore after today."

Psyche craned her head back to take one last look at her home. In the distance she could see the lights beginning to dot the land as dusk slowly approached. It made the city-state look like a cluster of stars. Silently saying goodbye to her loved ones, she also mourned the death of the life she had led before that momentous day when the oracle's prophesy forever changed her fate. Tears silently welled up and slipped down her cheeks as she took in what she was sure would be the final sight of her home. She made an effort to commit this last glimpse to her memory. With a heavy sigh, she whispered, "I'm ready to leave now."

With a snap of Zephyrus' wings, they rose above the clouds again, turned away from Pylos, and headed out toward the open sea. Flying in a direct line away from the land, they stayed high in the sky until the clouds disappeared as they chased the sun as it traveled toward the west. She was secretly thrilled with the unexpected flight. Turning her head to look up at Zephyrus, she asked, "Where are you taking me?"

He answered with a rueful chuckle and a wink. "I'm taking you to your new home, princess. Don't worry, your groom may be a beast, but he'll be *your* beast." With that, he winged his way across the sea for several more minutes. The speed at which they traveled was faster than any chariot Psyche had ever driven. They traveled for a time over the water with no land in sight as far as the eye could see.

In the distance, a speck of land came into view. It slowly grew larger. After a few more minutes, it became apparent that they were heading toward the island. The closer they came, the more the fear that she had been holding at bay returned with a vengeance. Before she could stop herself, Psyche burst out with a torrent of questions. "Can you tell me anything about my intended? Is what the oracle said true? Is he a monster that even the gods fear? Do you know what he intends to do to me?"

As the island grew closer, her anxiety continued to

increase at the silence that met her questions. Why would Zephyrus not answer her? The only thought that came to Psyche was that the answers to her questions were ones he thought she could not handle. It meant her fate at the end of this journey was one as horrible as the oracle had hinted it would be. After a few more minutes of flight, Zephyrus landed in a field of wildflowers. He gently disentangled her grip from his arms and stepped back from her once he was sure she could stand on her own two feet.

She took a moment to get her bearings and glanced at her surroundings. There was a stillness to the air that was only broken by the sound of the waves crashing on the shore of the island, which seemed to echo her rapidly beating heart. She could feel the oppressiveness of her isolation as a physical weight that threatened to drown her in a sea made of her fears.

She turned to her one hope for escape and tried to save herself from this horrific situation in which she found herself. "Please don't leave me here alone. I do not deserve to be punished for something that is not my fault. Please take me away from here," she pleaded.

Zephyrus let out a sad sigh. "Psyche, I can't interfere with your fate. The only thing I was allowed to do was to escort you to your new home. Even if I should take you somewhere else, there is no place that you can hide from your intended. He will find you." With that, he began to rise in the air.

"Can you at least tell me anything about him? Please!"

Zephyrus stopped and hovered just above her head, with an indecipherable look to his face. "Your intended is indeed feared by the gods for the power he wields over them. He can be a valued ally or the most treacherous of adversaries, so few cross him. However, I will say this, little mortal: You may be the only one to tame this beast. Continue to hold fast to your courage and you may come out of this changed for the better." Then he flew off into the distance and disappeared from sight.

Psyche sat there for a few moments in stunned disbelief. Taking several deep breaths, she stood up and looked around, finding herself alone, as expected. As she took in her surroundings, she happened to see a smaller island off in the distance. It appeared to be within easy reach. The sea was calm and tranquil for once, the direct opposite of her emotional state. Formulating an escape plan, she looked around and saw a beach close by. If she could get to the nearby island, she might be able to find someone there to take her as far away as possible. Looking at her wedding jewelry, she knew she could easily sell or trade them to pay for her passage. Moreover, should the island prove to be deserted, she could at least hide out there until she could come up with another plan of escape.

"Where there is water, there must be a boat," she reasoned out loud. With that thought in mind, she ran to the beach and began to follow it at a quick pace.

After several moments, she let out a happy yell as she spotted a small fishing boat resting on the beach. Running up to it, she quickly looked it over. It seemed to be in good shape, and there were two oars resting in it. Smiling in relief, she went to the bow and grabbed the mooring line. Then she slowly began to drag the boat the precious few feet she needed to get it into the sea.

Arms straining, her face dripping with sweat from her exertions, she finally got the boat in the water. She dragged it until the water was thigh high, then went to the side and climbed in. After settling herself, she grabbed the oars and started to row toward the island in the distance.

After putting several yards between her and the larger island, the boat suddenly came to an abrupt stop. It was so sudden and unexpected that it sent her tumbling forward off her seat onto the floor of the boat. Thinking she might have hit a rock, she scrambled up and looked around the boat.

There was nothing but clear water. Within seconds of that realization, the boat started heading toward the shore on its own, as if an invisible rope was pulling it back. Scrambling up, she grabbed the oars and vainly tried to stop the backwards momentum of the boat.

"Please, stop. No!" she cried.

No matter how hard she rowed, nothing stopped the small boat from going backwards. It hit the shore and gently slid along the beach until it was back in the original position she had found it.

Psyche jumped out and tried to drag it back out to sea, but it would not budge at all. Finally giving up on it, she sat down to catch her breath.

Looking out to the other island, she made a quick calculation of the distance. *Perhaps the boat was enchanted,* she thought to herself. If that were the case, maybe she could swim out to the island instead. She *was* a fairly good swimmer, and with the sea so unusually calm, she stood a real chance of at least making it to the other island. And if not, well, better to not think of the alternative.

Standing up, Psyche took a fortifying breath and walked to the water's edge. After getting in deep enough, she started swimming in the direction of the island, setting an easy pace for herself so as not to tire too quickly.

After several minutes of swimming, she reached the point where the boat had abruptly been stopped. When she hit that point, she felt something disturb the water beneath her. The sea surrounding her suddenly erupted in a churning mass of swirling currents and air. It moved around her like a whirlpool, gaining speed and momentum with every passing second, closing in on her until she was surrounded by a wall of water.

Screaming in fright, Psyche stopped swimming and began to tread water, fearing she was about to get sucked down into the depths of the sea. As it churned around her, she found herself being lifted onto a bed of air that rushed up from below.

It carried her back toward the island, taking her back to the spot where Zephyrus had originally left her, and then gently set her down on the ground.

Knees buckling, Psyche collapsed. She lay there for some time in stunned disbelief. She was trapped. Terror and despair took hold of her. Thoughts raced through her mind about what she was left to face alone. The oracle's words played over and over, like a drum beating her down until she could not think straight. Her teeth began to chatter as cold dread fill her limbs.

She quickly ran through every other conceivable escape, but every plan ended in disaster, and finally she ran out of options—save one. Knowing that escaping the island was impossible, she slowly pulled out the knife that she had hidden in the sheath strapped to her thigh. She raised it and steeled herself to plunge it into her heart, but as she prepared to make the only escape she thought left to her, she felt her body freeze. As she struggled to plunge the knife home, a soft breeze gently wrapped itself around her and a strange sense of peace filled her. She suddenly found that she could no longer keep her eyes open, yet she struggled against losing consciousness. If she fell asleep, she could not carry out her plan to at least save herself from a fate worse than death. In the end, she lost her battle. The knife fell from her hand and dropped harmlessly to the ground beside her. She slowly sank back and fell into a restful sleep, surrounded by the wildflowers.

CHAPTER 8

Zephyrus began to wing his way back to Mount Olympus after leaving Psyche in the field of wildflowers. As he flew away, he could not help but feel troubled. The more distance he put between himself and the island, the stronger the sensation became. Deciding to delay his return, he flew back to the island to see what was causing his unease.

Making sure that he was invisible to the human eye, he watched as Psyche headed for the beach. Her attention was focused on a spot out at sea. Looking out toward what had caught her attention, he spied the island of Antipaxos in the distance. Intrigued, he followed her as she turned away from the island and traveled along the beach. It was when she tried to take the fishing boat out to sea that he realized her plan.

"Clever girl," he murmured to himself.

He watched as Psyche made her way toward the island, and he could not help but feel a stab of sympathy for the little mortal when she hit against the natural barrier that protected the island. It became apparent that Eros had set up the boundary to prevent Psyche from escaping the island.

Zephyrus shook his head as he watched her struggle against it, sure that she would now give up.

It was when he saw her try to swim out that she won his respect. She had courage, and was determined to escape. Knowing she was doomed to fail again, he watched when she again triggered the island's defenses. However, before he could intervene, he watched as she was gently lifted out of the water and transported back to where he had originally put her. He had to admit that Eros had thought of everything in his preparations for her arrival.

Looking back at the island of Antipaxos, Zephyrus felt better knowing that she had not made it there, where he knew the cantankerous goddess that lived there would not have been welcoming to Psyche.

He turned to look back and watched as she collapsed to the ground. With the sunlight glittering off the knife she had somehow hidden, her intent became clear and panic filled him. Cursing, he stopped and pulled a small pouch from his belt. With a thought he froze her body before she could plunge the knife into her heart. He called up the west wind and sent a small portion of it back toward the lone figure, and as it traveled toward Psyche, he sprinkled some of the sleeping powder from the pouch into it. The wind and the sleeping potion encircled her, and when it became clear that she had fallen under its influence, he released his hold on her and allowed her to slip down into a restful slumber.

He then flew back to Psyche and landed beside her. After checking to make sure she had not harmed herself, he tossed the fallen knife away.

"Little innocent fool. Death is no escape, and one as young as you should not court it." Pity for the girl who reminded him of his own wife wrapped itself around him, and before he could decide his next move, he realized that he could not leave Psyche unattended in her current state of mind.

Looking at the wildflowers that bore the touch of his wife, he called to her to join him. Smelling the scent of dew-kissed roses, Zephyrus looked up to see her standing off to the side of Psyche with a frown on her face. "She truly is a beauty. No wonder Aphrodite bears her such a grudge."

"Outwardly, yes. However, her *true* beauty shines from within, and that is what caused the mortals to worship her in place of Aphrodite. It is what captured Eros' heart, as well. She is not at fault for that."

With one last quick search to make sure Psyche carried no other weapons with which to harm herself, he stepped up to his wife and pulled her into his arms, gripping her auburn hair in his fist as he kissed her with a starving passion. "My lovely wife, I've missed you. It seems you have been very busy here while I have been away. This island is your best work yet. Trying to impress that little archer, are you?" he teased with mock jealousy.

Wrapping her arms around his waist and pressing up against him, Khloris pinched his backside with a reproving look in her doe-colored eyes. "None of that now. My efforts were for that poor girl, who captured his fancy, as well you know."

Zephyrus laughed at the reprimand. "Just making sure you remember which of the winged brotherhood you belong to, love." He nuzzled her neck and spent the next few minutes whispering into her ear what his plans were for her once they returned home. Breathless, and with cheeks rosy from lust, she broke away from him and stepped back. "You don't play fair," she accused.

"Never," he growled. "Stay here and watch over her until she wakes up. I must report to that fool Eros what happened here."

"Be careful," she warned with a troubled frown. "This is a precarious situation. Aphrodite will not be happy with either of us thwarting her desire to punish this poor girl."

"I know. However, I have never seen Eros like this before. He may actually have found in this girl what I found with you."

"And that is?" she asked with a sly smile.

"My other half."

CHAPTER 9

After leaving Psyche in the care of his wife, Zephyrus flew back to Mount Olympus. All the while, the anger he felt at Eros and Aphrodite for the harm they'd caused the little mortal churned in his gut. After landing on the balcony of Eros' home, he tried to rein in his anger, but the west wind swirled around him, causing the house to shake. It threatened to rip it off the very mountain, a testament to his ire. Then a noise warned him that someone had joined him on the ledge. Taking a deep breath, Zephyrus finally gained enough control to lessen the impact of his powers on the structure.

Turning, he saw Anteros leaning against the door behind him, studying him with a quizzical stare. "What's happened to get you all in a rage?"

"Your fool of a brother is what happened," snapped Zephyrus. "Not to mention that jealous shrew, Aphrodite."

"Careful there, they might hear you. You wouldn't want them to interfere with your marriage to Khloris, now, would you?" asked Anteros.

"As if they could," Zephyrus sneered. "You know even *they* cannot interfere with soul mates."

"True. But that wouldn't stop them from having others fall in love with you or your wife. Could get very tiresome being chased or fighting off immortal suitors, wouldn't you say?" Anteros stated with a quiet chuckle.

With a lifted brow and a look promising severe pain to any who dared, Zephyrus stalked into the room to await the arrival of Eros. Anteros followed him in and sprawled on the chair beside the bed. His relaxed pose didn't fool Zephyrus in the least. Anteros was a warrior who missed nothing. It was only a fool who didn't see the dangerous glint in his dark gaze, one that could freeze lesser men with one look. Anteros was a predator in a handsome package. He was vicious in his defense of those he considered his, and it was only his love for his brother Eros that allowed him to be one of the few who could challenge him and survive. Zephyrus did not like being the bearer of the message he was about to deliver.

He waited impatiently for Eros to arrive. With each passing second, his patience eroded even more. He wished to get back to his wife and son and to forget the role he had played in the sordid mess he found himself in. With the embers of his anger still smoldering, he chose to wait in silence rather than to chance losing his temper again.

Both men were comfortable with the silence that stretched out between them as they waited for Eros. Fortunately, they did not have long to wait before his arrival.

He walked in and took in the scene before him. Seeing the strained expression on Zephyrus' face and the almost militaristic pose that he held himself in, he knew that the news would not be to his liking. However, it was the look in his brother's eyes that concerned him the most. The predator that lived in them both was too close to the surface. If one did not know the two men, it would appear that they were at odds with one another, but that was most certainly an illusion. "Did all go as planned, Zephyrus?" asked Eros.

"Did everything go as planned? Why yes, I took a terrified girl from her home, swept her out to a deserted island to await the 'monster' she is to be wed to, and left. What could possibly have gone wrong? Oh, but did I mention the part where she was so terrified that she tried to take her own life with a knife she had hidden after failing to escape several times?"

Both Eros and Anteros tensed at that piece of information. Anteros leapt up from the lounge and went to stand next to his brother. Standing shoulder to shoulder, the twins faced Zephyrus with identical thunderous expressions that did not bode well for this particular messenger. The hairs on the back of his neck rose as he felt the volatile powers of the twins begin to rise. Chancing a glance into their eyes revealed the predators that lived in both of them staring out at him with violent intent. A dangerous quiet filled the room. "What did you just say?" Eros quietly demanded.

"I said the poor girl was so terrified that she tried to take her own life. She begged for my help to escape. Eros, this is not right. You cannot think that this will end well for either of you. Fear such as that will doom the both of you. Let her go before she suffers any more damage," pleaded Zephyrus.

Eros took an aggressive step forward. "You left her there in that state?"

"Don't take me for a fool," Zephyrus snapped, affronted. "I stopped her from harming herself, and then put her into a forgetful sleep. My wife stands watch over her even as we speak, and will remain there with her until another can take over the watch to ensure that Psyche does not try to harm herself again."

Eros stood silent and motionless for several moments. After reining in his temper, he managed to respond with civility to Zephyrus. "My thanks to you and your wife for your help in this matter. For now, you may take your leave and retrieve your wife. The island caretakers will watch over Psyche. Stay close, though, for I may still have need of your skills in this matter." Giving Zephyrus a curt nod, Eros then stalked out of the room onto the balcony, leaving the two other men behind.

"You did well, Zephyrus. But speak to no one of this matter," warned Anteros.

"As if I want to be reminded of the role I played in this tragedy. But I warn you, this girl may never be able to return Eros' love, and then you may well be tempted to punish her. For everyone's sake, try to convince your brother to rethink this plan of his." After giving his last warning, Zephyrus departed.

Anteros waited until he was sure he and his brother were alone before he joined his twin on the balcony. Eros was lost in thought, and it was several moments before he turned to his brother with a determined look in his eye. "You heard what Zephyrus said before he left," murmured Anteros, "and you know he speaks the truth. If Psyche rejects your love, I will punish her for it."

Whirling around in a rage, Eros grabbed Anteros by the throat and shoved him up against the wall. Snarling and shoving his face so close that barely a whisper separated them, he warned, "Touch her, and we will no longer be brothers."

Eyes just as rage filled, Anteros grabbed Eros, and with a move too fast for the eye to catch, had him pinned face down on the ground, with his knee pressed into his back to keep him in place. "Listen to me," growled Anteros. "You would become sick and weak, making it easy for our enemies to strike out at you if she rejects your love. And you damn well know it. Do you really think that I would want to hurt your beloved? Or to lose you, again? But you know I cannot fight my nature any more than you can. I say this plan of yours to only let her see and know part of you—not *all* of you—will end in a tragedy that can be prevented."

Using his wings, Eros bucked his brother off of him and sprang to his feet, tensed and ready to fight his brother should he attack. Anteros leapt back, breathing heavily, but made no move to counter attack.

"Just as you cannot fight your nature, neither can I," said Eros. "She must love *me*, not my godhood or our past. That is the only part of myself that I will keep from her. Later, when I know that her love for me is true, then, and only then, will I reveal the rest."

Seeing that Eros would not be swayed from the path he had chosen, Anteros sighed sadly. "Very well, we will try it your way. Though I pray I am wrong, I will support you in any way that I can. But if you fail, I will do what is necessary to protect you."

Nodding his head, Eros turned and flew in the direction of the island that Psyche was even now exploring.

CHAPTER 10

Psyche slowly came awake. The sun was overhead and she shaded her eyes, trying to determine how much time had passed. The last she knew, it had been night in Pylos. "I must remember not to drink wine that has not been watered down again," she muttered. Giggling at herself, she rolled over intending to sleep a few more minutes when she realized that she was not in her bed, but on the ground. Startled into full wakefulness, she tried to remember how she had gotten there to begin with. Fragments of the previous day flittered through her mind, with pieces missing like an unfinished mosaic.

Then, with the speed of a galloping horse, enough of the previous day's events came back to her in a flash. Gasping in alarm, she looked around her, seeing no one and nothing that looked familiar. She swallowed her sudden panic, and sitting up, she realized that she was no longer on Sfaktitia.

"Hello!" she called. "Is anyone here?" Receiving no answer and realizing that there was no one around, she settled down, trying to determine her next move.

After some time had passed, she rose up from the ground

and looked around at her surroundings. She was in the middle of a field of wildflowers, and beyond that was a grove of various fruit trees. Turning, she looked to the sea for signs of passing ships. Seeing none, Psyche sighed and turned back toward the grove. She blinked her eyes several times, not believing what appeared before her.

Beyond the grove of trees was a palace of unearthly beauty. It was apparent that no human hands could have created a palace of such splendor and magnitude. It was a home fit for a god. "Well, I might as well try to see if anyone is at home. There must be a caretaker who can help me figure out where I am," Psyche said aloud as she began to make her way to the palace.

As she walked through the grove, she looked around at the manicured lawn and how there were marble statues in the shape of various creatures—a chimera, a hydra, a griffon, and a hippocampus—that seemed to be guarding the palace in various poses. They were so lifelike it appeared they would move at any moment.

But there were whole sections of the gardens that were incomplete; as if someone had started on it, only to then abandon it, only to repeat the pattern in other sections. She forced herself to turn away from the temptation of the garden and made her way to the main building in the middle of the grounds.

She approached the door to the palace, steeled herself with a deep breath, and using the bronze knocker, she knocked loudly several times in a row. The door opened on its own. She gingerly entered the palace.

Gathering her courage, she called out, "Hello! Is anyone here?" After waiting several minutes, she repeated herself and again received no response.

The sight that she beheld inside rivaled the outside splendor. She was so struck with the opulence and beauty of the place and she could not decide where to look as each pass of her gaze proved more wondrous than the last. The coffered ceilings were made of citron wood and stone, and were supported by large, white marble ionic columns. The brightly painted walls were embellished with gold and silver, and filled with scenes from nature.

Even the floors were exquisite, with mosaics made from precious gems. Everything—the rooms, colonnade, and even the massive doors—were made from expensive materials. The craftsmanship only a god could afford and produce lured Psyche into exploring further. She wondered if Hephestian himself had had a hand in the creation of all the various metal work that she found. As she moved further into the palace, she discovered storerooms filled from floor to ceiling with gold, silver, and priceless jewels; others were filled with fragrant spices and aromatic oils. There was no treasure the home lacked. What astonished Psyche even more was the seemingly lack of concern for guarding such a tempting treasure. No guards or locks could be seen anywhere.

Psyche continued to look in awe at her surroundings, and thinking herself alone as no one had answered her as she continued to call out, she was suddenly startled by a voice behind her.

"My lady, why are you so surprised by all that you see? All that you gaze upon is yours."

Psyche frantically looked around to find the person who had spoken to her, but could not see anyone. "Where are you? Show yourself."

"My apologies, my lady, but no mortal eyes can see us," replied the feminine voice apologetically.

Looking around and seeing nothing, not even shadows to betray the invisible being, she looked to where she believed the voice was coming from. "How many are there of you? And what do you mean, everything here is *mine*?"

"There are many servants here, my lady. We take care of the island and all that you see. It will be our pleasure to take care of the bride of our master."

At the mention of her yet unseen husband, Psyche felt her legs tremble and she gripped the wall behind her for support. "Where is my intended?" she asked, unable to hide the tremor in her voice.

"He returns this night, and he bade us to take care of you. Anything you desire is yours, except for leaving the island. You have only to ask, and it will be provided to you. Please do not fear, the master is a good one, and he only wishes to make you happy."

Taking some measure of comfort from the servant's words – for if her husband was truly a monster, then why go to the trouble of providing for her every need –she felt a little better.

"What is your name?" inquired Psyche.

"Rhea, my lady. You must be tired from your journey, please allow us to take care of you."

With those words, a torch carried in unseen hands appeared. Using that as a guide, Psyche followed Rhea to the great hall, where a small feast had been prepared. Sitting down, she watched in amazement as plates of food were carried in by invisible servants and placed on the table before her. Taking an olive, she moaned in pleasure as the tart juices exploded in her mouth. Realizing how famished she was, she ate from the various plates that were brought for her enjoyment. Washing it down with a sweet wine, she slowly felt the tension leave her. A lyre played by itself; a mellow tune filled the room while she ate.

It is a strange wedding feast, thought Psyche. Under normal circumstances, there would be a feast attended by many, not just her and the invisible servants. Even her mysterious husband had not joined her, driving home just how alone she truly was.

Pushing back from the table, she settled back against the chair and lazily drank from the wine goblet that refilled as soon as she emptied it. It was much stronger than she was used to, and it was not long before she began to feel its slumbering effects.

Smiling for no apparent reason, she hummed along to the lyre's tune. Her mind slightly muddled from the effects of the wine, she slowly got up from her chair, grabbing the goblet to take with her. She walked out to the inner courtyard to wander along its perimeter in a rambling stroll. Sipping the wine, she sat on the marble bench after a time, content under the lone olive tree. Leaning her head back, she enjoyed the feel of the sun's rays caressing her face. Losing track of time, she relaxed in the courtyard as the sun traveled overhead.

Suppressing a yawn, Psyche gave a start as she felt a hand land on her shoulder. "My apologies, mistress, for startling you, but I thought you might like to have a bath and then take a nap."

Psyche smiled her thanks. "I would love to, and a nap would be wonderful. I'm afraid I am not used to the strong wine," she said ruefully.

"Please follow the torch and I will bring you to the bathing chamber," said Rhea.

Psyche followed the servant to the chamber, where a hot bath awaited her. The room was a fairly large one, with several different sunken pools of water scattered about. In the center of the back wall was a beautiful waterfall that emptied into the central pool of water. The room was decorated in a soothing blend of different shades of sandstone taupe, with sea foam green accents done in a continuous wave pattern that bisected the walls into two halves. Running along on two sides were various types of seating, with thick rolled cloths to dry oneself with. The air was perfumed in various scents that teased her nose. It was at once beautiful and inviting to the senses.

"Rhea," she called hesitantly, for it still seemed strange to speak to someone who she could not see. "What are all these pools for? Surely they are not all for bathing?"

"No mistress, they are not all for bathing. They each have a different function and purpose. Let me show you each of them, and then you may decide which ones you wish to try." And with that, the unseen Rhea—carrying a torch to lead Psyche through the room—walked to the nearest pool.

"This one is a hot pool; the water is heated to a high temperature to loosen tense and aching muscles and to help chase away the chill of a cold day."

Psyche bent down and ran her hand through it, enjoying the luscious heat of the water.

Standing, she followed the torch to the next one.

"This is a cold pool, my lady. When the heat becomes too much you may cool off in this one."

Psyche felt how cold the water was and a little shiver ran through her.

Walking to the next pool with the waterfall, Rhea said, "This pool is filled with warm water and is used for bathing. You may lie in the water or stand under the waterfall, whatever is your pleasure. The water is continually cleansed and replenished so there is no need to empty it after every bath."

"Amazing," murmured Psyche, in awe over the inadvertent power display of her husband.

The final pool that Rhea led her to resembled the Mediterranean Sea during a storm; it swirled and bubbled as steam rose from the water like the spray of the sea as it crashed against the shore. It looked inviting. "This is the hot springs pool. The water is warm and the motion of the water is quite soothing. It is meant to relax you after a trying day."

Psyche dipped her hand in the hot springs and felt the slight tug the motion of the water made on her hand. She was definitely intrigued with trying out this particular pool.

The air was moist and warm, such that Psyche felt a thin droplet of water run down her throat and across her breast till it disappeared beneath her gown. Looking down at herself, she realized that she carried faint traces of the earth on her person.

"I would like to bathe, and then I would like to soak in the hot springs for a while, if that is possible."

"Very well, my lady." And with that, unseen hands began to take down the remains of her topknot. Psyche was then stripped of her soiled wedding garments and jewels and led to the bath. Seeing the steps leading into the pool, she stepped carefully into it and waded over to stand under the waterfall. The warm water reached her waist. It washed over her, and once she was thoroughly wet, she spied a bench that circled the interior of the pool. She sat down on the one nearest the waterfall and stretched out her legs. Then she let loose a sigh as the heat of the water loosened her tense muscles, and she found herself slowly relaxing.

Psyche watched in wonder as jars of aromatic oils floated in the air, tipping. The oils were added to the bath and the room filled with a pleasant flowery fragrance that she couldn't identify. Shifting around, she sat back, and with her eyes drifting close, she laid her head back on a cushioned headrest as hands began to gently wash her hair. The soothing massage on her scalp felt good. Rinsing her hair under the waterfall, she shifted back and waited to see what would happen next.

A pair of sea sponges appeared at the top of each of her shoulders and began a gentle glide down her arms, to her fingertips. Once done, they went underwater to her feet and traveled over her calves to her upper thighs.

Drifting and lulled into a restful doze, Psyche slowly became aware of the sea sponges traveling over her breasts, and as the sponges tenderly scraped over her nipples, her sensitive peaks hardened into hard nubs. The pleasure this aroused in her body traveled down her stomach until it reached her sex.

One of the sea sponges continued over her stomach and explored further down while the others lazily traveled over the rest of her body. Psyche became slightly embarrassed by her body's response, but when nothing was said, she closed her eyes and let the pleasure slowly travel through her.

After several more minutes, she opened her eyes. She stood up and leisurely walked to the steps leading out of the bathing pool. A drying cloth unrolled itself and wrapped around her body. Taking a moment to pat at her skin, Psyche walked to the hot springs pool. Unwrapping the drying cloth and letting it fall to her feet, she stepped gingerly into the pool until she reached the bottom. Feeling something in front of her, she discovered a reclining bench in the middle of the pool. Turning, she slid back onto it and rested. The feel of the warm bubbling water was a delicious sensation against her skin.

Lifting her legs to brace her feet on the seat, she felt the swirling motion of the water in the pool glide over her sex. Feeling the languid pleasure from the bath return, she closed her eyes and enjoyed the sensations that the water aroused in her body. She drifted in pleasurable silence for several moments; the only sounds that broke the silence of the bathing chamber were of the movement of the water and her own breath. After a few moments, she opened her eyes, aware that there was a presence in the room with her. Thinking it was Rhea, she called out to her, but when no reply came, she thought she was mistaken and closed her eyes again and relaxed into a lazy haze.

Feeling hands gently grip her ankles, Psyche held her breath as her legs were drawn slowly further apart; pushing her legs open till her most intimate area was exposed. A whisper of a touch slid over her sex, adding to the pleasure she already was experiencing. The strange sensation that swirled low in her stomach that had begun while her breasts were scraped by the sea sponges in the bath returned; only instead of lessoning, the pleasure continued to build in strength and intensity.

Lulled into acquiescing by the wine and the warm bath water, Psyche could not summon a protest to the new sensation. Her sex was spread open while ghostly fingers cupped one of her breasts. She felt the gentle tugging of her nipples and arched her back as pleasure raced through her. The rhythmic tugging and pinching had her gasping and letting out little moans of pleasure. Hands floundering, she gripped the sides of the tub as she panted.

The fingers at her sex rubbed up and down her slit, spreading the moisture that had gathered there, before gently rubbing the secret little pleasure nub at the top of her sex. Ecstasy increasing in waves at this new caress, Psyche panted, unable to do more than grip the edge of the hot springs pool, drowning in the intense sensations.

She felt the slow push of a finger into the heart of her sex. Moving in and out of her in a steady rhythm, the pleasure only intensified. Before she could catch her breath, a second finger joined the first and began to thrust in long, firm strokes. Unable to stop herself, she began to rock her hips in concert, letting out a chorus of gasps and moans. Feeling a circular caress around the little bundle of nerves at the top of her slit, she panted as her muscles tightened. Pleasure raced from her sex to her nipples. Heat radiated out of her core and spread all over her.

Suddenly, without warning, her body locked up and her back arched, and a long cry of pleasure ripped from her throat as an explosion erupted from deep within her and spread throughout her body. Long moments passed as ripples of pleasure washed over her in little aftershocks that left her weak and breathless.

Slowly petting her through the little aftershocks, the ghostly touch slowly receded. Slumping back against the headrest, Psyche sat in stunned disbelief over what had just occurred in the hot springs pool before sated exhaustion pulled her into a light sleep.

Eros sat back, his cock threatening to burst at the site of Psyche's orgasm. Knowing he would not last long, he gripped his cock in oil slicked fingers and firmly rubbed up and down his shaft in a swift motion. His gaze never leaving Psyche, he quickly found his release. Biting back a moan, he eased his grip and sat back, making sure to stay hidden from her sight.

Seeing her stunned little smile, Eros felt himself harden again. Not wanting her first time to be in the bathing pool, he quickly rose—and gathering a bath sheet—lifted her up in his arms. He carried her over to one of the reclining chairs and laid her down on it. Covering her, he stepped back and gazed down at his little bride. His body tightening even more, he was fiercely glad that he had decided to start her education in the pleasures of the flesh prior to the wedding night. Her orgasm in the bathing chamber would help ease her fears of the marriage bed.

Hungering to finish what he had started, he turned on his heel and walked out of the room, calling out to Rhea as he went.

The nymph hurried to answer his summons, and as he

rounded the corner to the passageway that led to his sleeping chamber, Rhea appeared, carrying the sleeping gown with the Herakles knot girdle. Seeing the symbol of his marriage to Psyche, he was gripped with a vicious satisfaction in finally having her in his home, and soon, in his bed.

Coming to a halt in front of him, Rhea bowed slightly. "You called for me, sire?"

"Yes, allow Psyche to sleep for a few more minutes before you awaken her. Once you have prepared her, take her to my bedchamber and make sure the room is shrouded in darkness. See to it that the other nymphs do not disturb us for any reason."

"Yes, sire." Heading down the corridor to enter the bathing chamber, Rhea turned to speak to Eros before he left. "If I may say, sire, your bride is a lovely, kindhearted thing. Please be assured that all the island nymphs will watch over her and make sure no harm befalls her while she is in our care."

Eros smiled slightly. "Thank you, Rhea."

Returning his smile, Rhea entered the bathing chamber and quietly closed the door behind her.

CHAPTER 11

Rhea looked around the chamber until she spotted Psyche lying down in a daze. With her face flushed and her eyes pleasure glazed, it was not hard to fathom what had occurred in the bathing chamber when Eros had arrived and silently ordered all the servants out of the room.

Walking over to the girl, she knelt down and gently shook her awake. "My Lady, let me prepare you for bed."

Psyche sat up, embarrassed and confused by the events of the past few moments, and the possible knowledge among the unseen servants of the events of a little while ago. Saying nothing, she rose and allowed Rhea to prepare her for bed.

Rhea led her to a chair and spent the next few minutes brushing her hair out until, dry, it fell down her back like a shining waterfall. Leaving it down, she then helped her into a soft white nightgown that skimmed her ankles and left her arms bare; around her waist went her Herakles knot girdle that her new husband would break as a symbol of their marriage.

Finished, Rhea took hold of a torch and led Psyche out of

the bathing chamber and took her a short distance down the hall to a large double door. Opening it, Psyche walked in and stopped in astonishment at the sight before her. An enormous bed, easily the span of her entire room back at her parents' home, stood in the center of the chamber. Flanking the bed on either side were small tables that held oil lamps. At the foot of the bed were a set of small stools. A dressing table with a tall bronze mirror took up one wall. Wandering over to the vanity table, Psyche opened and sampled the various creams, smelling some of the various oils, then she closed the jars and walked to stand in front of the full-length mirror.

The reflection that stared back at her revealed a woman much different from the one who had walked out of her own bedroom the day before. Her hair fell around her shoulders to the small of her back in flamed-tinged brown waves, her hazel eyes sparkled in the light, and her skin glowed with a healthy flush to her cheeks.

Turning away from her reflection, Psyche wandered out to the balcony, leaning against the rail. She looked out over the moonlit-bathed garden. She thought about how different her wedding day had been. She apprehensively waited for the arrival of her husband, but after a while she gave up the vigil after exhaustion gripped her.

She walked over to the enormous bed and stopped. Frowning at it, she muttered, "Who needs a bed the size of a chamber?"

Shrugging off that thought with a yawn, she climbed into the center of the bed and settled down on her side facing the balcony. After struggling to stay awake, she soon fell into a restless doze.

Sometime later, Psyche slowly woke from her sleep and became aware that she was no longer alone. She heard the soft footfalls of someone making their way to the bed. Then the covers were lifted and the bed dipped as someone climbed into it behind her.

She held her breath and stayed as still as possible as her heart raced in fearful anticipation. Before she could move, she felt a large, warm body press up against her back. A heavy leg slid over her legs, pinning them down. Strong arms encircled her upper body, one around her waist and the other wrapped around her upper chest, with a hand gently gripping her throat. With her body pinned to the bed and a hard male body pressed all along her back, she began to tremble uncontrollably.

"Easy, little butterfly, I mean you no harm," whispered a deep, husky voice as her husband nuzzled her ear.

Several minutes passed, and when he made no further advances, her trembling slowly subsided. "There we go," he crooned. Releasing his grip on her neck, he slowly brought his hand down and gripped the belt at her hip. Then he broke the clasp, and pulling the belt from her, he threw it across the room.

"My Lord, I…"

"Shh, it is all right. Now we are truly wed. There is no need for you to fear me. You are my bride, and I protect what is mine, Psyche." Letting his words sink in, he casually brought his hand to the shoulder ties of her gown and began to undo them.

"What do I call you, my Lord?" she asked nervously. The neckline of her gown quickly loosened and was pulled down, revealing her breasts to the moonlight. She looked down. She was somewhat assured by the appearance of her husband's hand. It was a strong hand, but nonetheless a human one.

"You may call me Phanes," he murmured against her skin, kissing her neck.

"Phanes, will you please light an oil lamp?" she implored.

She immediately felt the sudden tension that gripped her husband. Then he pulled slightly away from her.

"Psyche, for now, you may not gaze upon me. I can only come to you at night, and I must leave before the dawn. You must promise me that you will never attempt to see me when I am with you."

"I don't understand. Why can't I look upon my own husband? Why will you only be with me at night?" she demanded.

"I have my reasons."

"But—"

"Psyche,' he interrupted, "it is for your protection that I must ask this of you. One day you will be able to gaze upon me, and when that day comes, there will be no restrictions on the time we can spend together. But that day is sometime in the future. Now promise me that you will not try to look upon me."

Psyche mulled over his words for a few minutes. As she thought, she felt the tension that had gripped her husband at her request for light increase at her continued silence. She thought of the words that the oracle had said of her husband; that he was a beast that even the gods feared. But there was nothing monstrous in the body that pressed up against her. She then compared that to the words that Zephyrus and Rhea had spoken about her husband; that she was safe with him. But it was the care that Phanes had shown her that was the most compelling evidence. She, better than anyone, knew that words were cheap, but that actions spoke the greatest truths. "I promise that I will not try to look upon you when you are with me," she finally said.

As she gave her vow, the tension drained out of his body. "Good. It will not be forever, butterfly." Cuddling her closer, he pressed light kisses across her neck. Nibbling on her ear, he said in a teasing tone, "Now where were we? Ah yes, our wedding night." He pulled her upper body back as he reclined so that she was resting her back on his chest, freeing both his hands to further explore her body.

Slowly, so as not to frighten her any more then he already had, he rubbed his hands along her stomach as he gentled her to his touch. A warm feeling started to spread out from her core, and it brought back some of the pleasure she had felt in the bathing chamber. After a few strokes, he brought his hands up to cup her breasts, gently gripping her nipples between his fingers. Then he lightly pinched and pulled them until they hardened in pleasure.

Gasping, Psyche arched into his touch as his fingers played with her breasts. Daringly, her hand slid into his hair and grabbed hold as the pleasure streaked through her body. Kissing his way from her neck to behind her ear, he continued to play with her breasts, learning what brought her the most pleasure.

"Please," begged Psyche, "I need…"

"I know what you need," he growled, "and I'll give it to you, just like I did in the bathing chamber."

Startled, Psyche gasped out, "That was you?"

Feeling the predator within him rage at the thought of another touching her, he lost control of his temper at her words. Letting go of one of her breasts, he shackled her neck in his grip and snarled into her ear, "Do you think I would allow any other to touch you, pleasure you?" he demanded. He then released her breast and gripped her nightgown, ripping it. He flung it away from her, and then cupped her sex. "No one else will ever touch you and live."

Frightened by the sudden violence of his actions, she began to struggle, trying to break free. "Let me go," cried Psyche fearfully.

Cursing himself for frightening her, he tightened his hold on her and made a soothing whisper into her ear as he gently rocked her. "Forgive me," he murmured, "I did not mean to frighten you. My temper got the better of me. I forgot this is all new to you."

"Please, my lord, I would never betray you like that. I am untouched!" she cried out.

"I know that, Psyche. Even if you allowed another male to touch you, I would never harm you in any way." Sighing deeply in regret, he knew that he had to convince her of his sincerity or the damage of his jealous actions would cause irreparable harm to their relationship, but he could not lie to her, either. "I will never lay a hand on you in anger or to cause you any harm, even if you betray me," he vowed solemnly.

Seeing her calming down as she listened to him, he gave in to the need to warn her, as well. "But know this, if any male lays a finger on you in lust, I *will* kill him. I will never share you," he promised darkly. "But I will vow this to you—on my honor—I will never betray you by allowing another female to lay a hand on me. I belong to you just as much as you belong to me. I will never betray you or dishonor you in any way."

Hearing the sincerity in his voice, she lay still in his arms, thinking over what he had vowed to her. Her parents' marriage aside, she knew how preciously rare his vow of fidelity was, and she was stunned by his commitment to her. But as she would not be with him during the day, she had no way of knowing if he would keep his word to her.

Seeing the indecision on her face, Eros sighed. "I know you have no reason to believe me right now, Psyche. Once we get to know each other better, you will see the truth of what I say."

She lay still in his arms, allowing the heat from his body to lull her back into a semi-relaxed state. When he made no move to resume the intimacy of their wedding night, she turned slightly toward him.

Burying his head in her hair, he breathed in her scent as if committing it to memory. "I will leave you alone if that is your wish. We can wait until you are ready to consummate our marriage." Feeling a heavy sorrow at the thought of leaving her, he nonetheless did not want to cause her any more turmoil. He would wait, even as it threatened to dim the joy he felt at finally having her back in his life.

He pressed a kiss against her temple and released her. As he turned away and made his way out of the bed, Psyche was gripped with fear at the thought of him leaving her. It was so strong it overwhelmed her with a desire to keep him by her side in spite of her reservations.

Not understanding her reaction to his departure, she cried out, "Wait!" Reaching out to stop him, she was shocked to discover what her hand was gripping. "You have wings," she said in startled amazement.

Eros stopped and shuddered at the touch of her hand on his wing. It was the first touch she initiated between them of her own volition, and it devastated him. Holding still, for he did not trust himself, he waited to see what she would do.

Psyche was too stunned to do anything but hold on to his wing for several moments. When he did nothing to repudiate her touch, she slowly slid her hand down his wing, marveling at the soft texture and heat. Repeating the caress, she inched closer and brought her other hand to press against his other wing. Feeling emboldened by his continued silence, she pressed against his back and continued to stroke his wings.

Then Psyche laid her cheek against the center of his shoulder blades, where his wings grew out of his back. She continued her slow caress. The feel of his wings seemed strangely familiar, as if she had run her hands over them hundreds of times. Frowning, she tried to remember, the memory teasing along the edges of her mind, but no matter how hard she tried, the knowledge danced away from her. Before she could chase the phantom memory, she was distracted by the hiss of pleasure that her new husband released at her touch.

Eros could barely restrain himself from turning around and pinning her to the bed as lust consumed him. The feel of her bare breasts pressed against his lower back sent shards of pleasure directly to his groin, where he tightened painfully as she continued to pet him. But it was her breath teasing the sensitive nerve endings of where his wings emerged from his back that was his undoing. When she started to nuzzle him, Eros knew he had to warn her before he lost total control. "Psyche, make your choice now. I only have so much control, and I have waited so long for you that I cannot continue to let you touch me without taking you. So choose, do I stay or do I go?"

Psyche stilled at his words. Faced with the power to control even a small part of her destiny gave her courage. Feeling that something fragile and precious would be lost if she allowed him to leave this night, she made her decision. "Stay."

CHAPTER 12

Eros released the breath that he had been holding as she made her decision. He had been sure that she would send him away. The courage she had displayed humbled him and made him all the more determined to bind her to him with pleasure.

He rose up and turned around in the bed to face Psyche. Thrusting his hand into her hair, he hauled her against him and wrapped his arm around her waist as he dragged her up his kneeling body so that she straddled him. Feeling her wet heat against his cock sent him into a frenzy of vicious need. Needing her, he lifted her up so that he could reach her mouth. Fastening his lips over hers, he groaned at the taste of her.

Wrapping her arms around him, pleasure ripped through Psyche as he explored her mouth. His tasted of wine and honey, and she was soon addicted to his taste and touch. She was startled when his tongue slipped past her lips and began to explore. Hesitantly, she met his with hers. Groaning at her response, he let her set the pace and they began a gentle duel. But before long, the primal need to dominate rode him hard, so he took over the kiss, unable to rein in his aggressive desire for her. Releasing her lips with a groan, he pulled back her head as he made his way across her throat, leaving hot, open-mouth kisses in his wake. His beast roaring in his head, he soon started giving her little love bites across her throat, determined to leave his mark. He couldn't resist before returning to her lips. Their breaths mingling, he ravaged her mouth. Over and over again, he repeated this pattern until they were both breathless and in almost painful need.

The feel of his naked body sent shivers throughout her body. She could feel his manhood pressed up against her lower belly, and she was intimidated by the sheer size and hardness of his member. It felt like a long, thick dagger looking for its sheath. While she was an innocent, she knew what was expected in the marriage bed, but she feared that her body would not be able to handle the invasion of his.

Before fear could set in, Eros distracted her by lifting her up and fastening his mouth on her nipple. Gasping, Psyche arched back, groaning with pleasure as his mouth laved at her nipple until it was hard. He then kissed his way to her other breast and paid it the same attention. He became more aggressive in his caresses, and he nipped her nipple with his teeth, giving her a bit of pain. Moaning, Psyche gripped his hair in a tight fist, torn between trying to get closer and shying away from the intensity of the pleasure he was giving her. Licking away the sting, he continued to alternate between pleasure and pain until she was begging and withering against him as a chorus of "oh please" fell from her lips. Each small bite of pain sent bolts of pleasure racing through her body straight to her sex, which contracted in pleasurable waves.

Eros lowered her back against the bed until she was spread out on it. He made his way down her stomach, licking and tasting her as he eased down her body to slowly sit back on his heels. His gaze traveled over her, and the sight of her in his bed threatened his control. Pulling back hard on the urge to plunge into her and sate his need in her body was proving to be a real struggle. The only thing holding him back was that his need to protect her was stronger than even his craving for her. He would guard her against any harm—even a threat from himself.

Her lips swollen and wet from his kisses, Psyche lay panting from her pleasure. Opening her eyes, she could see the outline of Phanes in the dim moonlight. Even with the limited visibility, what she could make out was impressive. The sheer size of him was immense. With his wings spread out behind him, it gave him the impression of a colossal statue come to life. The edges of his wings seemed to glitter in the faint moonlight, as if they had been dusted in gold. The power and presence he commanded was both terrifying and beautiful to behold, especially when all that raw power and intensity was focused solely on her.

On that thought, she became aware of how her body was splayed out before him as he crouched between her legs. She moved to cover herself, but when he hissed out his displeasure, she froze. He gripped her inner thighs and forced them further apart, until her knees were pressed against the bed, fully exposing her to him. "Don't, little butterfly. Every part of you is mine to look at. Mine to touch. To pleasure. To taste." Before she could guess his intent, he leaned down and fastened his mouth over her sex.

"What are you doing?" she cried out. Shocked at the intimacy of this act, she fisted her hands into his hair—whether to pull him from her or to urge him closer—she knew not. But it soon didn't matter. The pleasure that ripped through her from his clever mouth had her incoherent.

Eros slowly licked his way across her mound, taking his time to explore every fold. Groaning in hunger at the taste of her, he refused to rush, and so he took his time exploring her, learning what drove her mad with pleasure. Taking her labia into his mouth, he gently nipped her, giving her a little bit of pain before quickly soothing it away with his tongue. Over and over he repeated this pattern, nipping and flicking his tongue around her clitoris without ever directly caressing it, until Psyche was shaking with painful need, gasping and pleading in desperation, unable to orgasm. Thrusting his tongue into the heart of her, he set up a rhythmic pattern mimicking the ones his fingers had taken in the bathing chamber. Soon her hips were thrusting in concert with his tongue, but release still hovered just out of her reach.

Frustrated, with tears streaming down her face from being in such painful need, she cried out, "Phanes! Please help me."

Hearing the tears in her voice, he pulled back slightly. "What do you need, my love?" Seeing her struggle to ask for what she needed, he took pity on her. "Do you wish to orgasm?"

"What?" she asked in confusion.

Cursing, he reined himself in at the innocence of her question. It violently reminded him of how sheltered she truly was, to not even know what she was asking for. Having forgotten how all of this was new to her, her question sent a wave of tender amusement through him. "Do you wish to find your pleasure like you did in the bathing chamber? Do you wish for release? To orgasm?"

Understanding dawning on her, Psyche nodded her head, too shy to ask such a thing out loud. But Eros would have none of that. Both the man and the beast in him wanted her to acknowledge her need and desire for only him, and the pleasure only he could give her. "Tell me," he demanded.

Shaking her head, she refused to answer. Determined to win this battle of wills, Eros smiled darkly, and shifting his hands to grip her under her thighs, he pulled her closer. Fastening his mouth over her clitoris, he swirled his tongue around the little nub, sending waves of pleasure pulsating out from her core. Just before she reached climax, he stopped. Pulling back, he blew softly over her clitoris, keeping her on the edge. Leaning in again, he swirled his tongue over her until she hovered on the brink of orgasm, only to stop yet again. Over and over he did this, breaking down her resistance.

Sobbing in need, Psyche twisted and pulled on his hair, trying desperately to get him to send her over the edge, but he wouldn't comply. Finally, he pulled back and demanded harshly, "Tell me, Psyche, or I will continue to torment you all night and leave you wanting in the morning."

Hearing the truth in his words, and needing release so badly it hurt, she finally broke down. "Damn you. Fine, please, I need to orgasm," she snarled in frustration.

Chuckling in wry humor—for he was in no better shape—Eros couldn't help himself from teasing her, for he found her bad-tempered response amusing. "Of course, my love. All you had to do was ask."

Psyche felt a need for violence at the amusement in his voice, but before she could give in to the urge to hit him, he fastened his mouth over her clitoris again, swirling his tongue over it, building her pleasure until it spread throughout her entire body. Racing toward completion, she stopped at the edge, struggling to let go, afraid that he would stop again. Crying out in frustration, she thrashed beneath him, trying to get him to give her the one caress that would send her over the edge. Sensing her struggle, Eros lightly grazed her clitoris with his teeth, pushing her over the edge into a firestorm of sensation. Crying out at the intensity of the pleasure that tore through her, Psyche arched back, feeling like she was coming apart at the seams. Eros kept licking her gently throughout her orgasm, slowly bringing her down. With one last lick, he pulled back to look at her. The sight of her lying limp with pleasure brought a snarl of satisfaction to his lips. The need and the demands of his own body urged him forward.

Rising up to cover her with his body, Eros pinned her as she slowly calmed down from the intensity of her climax. Fisting her hair in his hand, he took her mouth in a voracious kiss. Tasting herself on his mouth, Psyche gasped at the eroticism of the kiss, their tongues dueling as he settled himself between her thighs. Gripping his cock in one hand, he slowly began to enter her. Pushing in just an inch, he suddenly came to a stop. Trembling from the need to plunge in and sate himself with her, he held back instead, refusing to cause her anymore pain then necessary. Pushing his way in another inch, and then another, he came to a stop when she began to whimper against his lips and showed some signs of distress. Releasing his cock, he entwined his fingers with hers and held her hand against the bed.

Feeling a slight burn at the stretching as she tried to accommodate his massive size and girth, Psyche tensed slightly. Breaking their kiss, she gasped out his name in question.

Need was riding Eros hard, so he pulled back slightly. "Wrap your legs around my hips."

She did as he told her, and some of the tension eased. Making a quick decision, he flexed his hips and pushed past the tight muscles. Pushing all the way through until he was sheathed in her wet warmth. Psyche cried out at the sudden invasion, so he came to a stop and held himself still, giving her time to adjust.

"Shh, my love, the worst is over," murmured Eros soothingly.

Breathing through the slight discomfort, Psyche was soon

slightly shocked that she felt some of her earlier pleasure return. She thought that he had rung every possible drop from her body, but it appeared she was wrong. Sliding her free arm around his waist, she began to move restlessly beneath him, wanting to see what possible pleasures still awaited her.

Pulling back from her until he almost pulled free from her body, he pushed back in, setting a strong and steady rhythm. Slowly he rode her, stroking the embers of her pleasure until she was crying out again in need.

Stroking his tongue over her lips, he then thrust his tongue into her mouth, matching the rhythm with his hips. Over and over again, he kept a tight leash on his passion. Fighting to make sure she was with him every step of the way.

Thrusting deep, he ground his hips in a swirling pattern against her mound, and sent shock waves of pleasure rippling out from her core. Psyche broke their kiss on a cry of ecstasy, her hand raking down his back, leaving a trail of scratches.

Seeing her wild abandon, Eros let loose the reins of his passion and began to drive into her over and over with wild abandon. Every time he slammed into her, she met him with equal passion.

Throwing her head back, she came again, crying out his name as her climax took hold of her body. Feeling her contractions as she came sent him into his own climax. Shouting in pleasure, he collapsed on her, struggling to catch his breath. Fearing that he would crush her, he pulled out of her and sprawled beside her as they both tried to recover from their earth-shattering orgasms.

* * *

PSYCHE LAY PANTING on the bed, too sated and tired to move. Long moments passed, and the only sound was their breaths as they slowly came back down to earth. Before long, Eros rose and walked to the other side of the room. After a few minutes, he returned to the bed.

A warm, wet cloth was pressed against her, slowly and gently wiping away all traces of their passion from between her legs. Psyche was too tired to be embarrassed, though if she were honest with herself, she found his tender care of her touching. After he finished, he threw away the washcloth and climbed into bed behind her. Protectively curling himself around her, he pulled the covers over them and wrapped his arms around her. Pressing a light kiss to her hair, he whispered, "Sleep, little butterfly."

Unable to keep her eyes open any longer, she quickly fell into a dreamless sleep in her husband's arms.

Petting her, Eros spent much of the night just holding Psyche, watching over her as she slept. He still couldn't quite believe that after all the eons he had spent searching for her that he had finally found her. Knowing the dangers would only intensify once the truth came out, he made his plan to keep her safe and away from the prying eyes of other immortals until they were truly reunited. Once it became known that he had joined with his soul mate, their enemies would stop at nothing to destroy not just them, but the others, as well. That he could not, *would not* allow. This time, he would be cruelly vicious in defense of those he considered his. There would be no mercy for his enemies.

Dawn approached faster than he wished. Slowly getting out of the bed, he stared down at his beloved. She bore the marks of his passion, and he was violently pleased that all who saw her would know that she had spent the night in his bed. She belonged to him, and no one—not even Psyche herself—could deny the ardent passion she alone aroused in him. Knowing he had been rougher than he would have liked to have been for her first time, he quickly checked to make sure she would not be feeling any ill effects from their night together. Sending a small amount of his powers into her body, he noted that while she was a little sore, there was no real concern that he had hurt her in his passion. Pulling back, he decided not to ease her soreness. He wanted her to *feel* his possession of her—and truth be told—he wanted her to carry a physical reminder of their wedding night, to reinforce the knowledge of whom she belonged to.

Leaning over, he pulled the covers over her more securely. Pressing a kiss where her shoulder met her neck, he nuzzled her for a few stolen moments, inhaling her scent and steeling himself for the long hours he would have to spend away from her, going about his subterfuge, before he could finally join her again this evening. Straightening, he took one last look at her.

Forcing himself to turn and walk away, he went in search of Paxos—the primordial goddess of his island—to ensure her cooperation in her protection of Psyche. Walking out onto the terrace, he spread his wings and took off to the other side of the island until he was skimming the waters of the Ionian Sea. Then he circled back and flew to the cave, where he was sure Paxos waited for him.

Entering the sea cavern, he landed and called out, "Pax! I need to speak to you."

Water began to swirl several feet in front of him, until it spewed out like a geyser. From the center, Pax sprang out of the water draped in a short sea foam green gown. Pushing her wet, honey-gold locks back from her face, she smiled mischievously in greeting. "Eros, you're looking quite… relaxed this morning. To what do I owe this visit?"

Shaking his head at her, he took a moment and sent his powers out to surround them, not wanting any prying eyes, or ears, to hear their conversation. Once he was assured of their privacy, he spoke what was on his mind. "Pax, still a troublemaker, even after all these years," he scolded. "You know why I am here."

Using her powers to dry herself, she crossed her arms and looked him over. Lifting a hand to her face, tapping her finger on her chin, and affecting a befuddled expression, she mused, "To wax poetically about your new bride? No?" Pausing in dramatic fashion, she snapped her fingers as if the answer had just occurred to her, and with her eyes opening wide in pretend shock, she exclaimed, "Oh, I know! You came here to brag about what a—"

"Pax!" he snarled. "Can you be serious for just a moment?"

Laughing at his expense, she couldn't stop herself from needling him. "If you want serious, Eros, you are talking to the wrong twin," she smirked. "Seriously."

Rolling his eyes, Eros struggled to stop himself from laughing at her antics. Shaking his head and finally giving up the struggle, he chuckled and opened his arms. Giving a little cry of joy, she jumped into them and hugged him tight. She was happy for him in a way few could understand, and given their history, she thought of him as her brother.

Her blue eyes glowed with humor. "Hmm, so you came to see me right after the wedding night. I'm flattered, but really, you should still be with your bride, Eros, not seeking out another woman so soon. Though I know I'm completely irresistible to the male sex, and that you can't resist me, you simply must." she teased.

Giving her a squeeze and slight pinch to her waist that had her breaking off with a laugh, he let her go and set her from him. Seeing his expression close down as his thoughts turned serious, Pax stopped her teasing, as well. "I am so happy you finally found her, Eros. And I can guess why you sought me out. You know I will shield and protect her while she is here. I won't fail you, not again."

Shaking his head in rejection of her statement, Eros admonished, "No, Pax, you did not fail me; you and your sister *saved* me. Saved us." Giving her a reproving look at the doubt on her face, he warned, "I had better never hear you say that you failed us ever again."

Smiling sadly, for he would never convince her of that, she let it go. There were more pressing concerns that needed to be addressed. The past was the past, and could not be changed. There was no use in rehashing old wounds. Protecting Psyche from Aphrodite, and the others, while she was still mortal and vulnerable, was the main priority, and Pax was determined to do it right this time.

"I know you will protect her, Pax, but I also need you to be her friend. She will be lonely—even with the nymphs—and she will need your friendship again. I know she is not who she once was, nor does she remember—"

"Eros," she said sternly, "you don't have to ask me that. You know I will be there for her in any way she needs me. Yes, she is different in this form, but the heart and soul of her remains the same. I have missed her also. We all have. I want to get to know her all over again. To be friends again."

Relieved, he still had to give her one final warning. "Remember, you cannot tell her anything about our past history. She must remain in the dark about me until the time is right."

"Eros, I am not a fool. I know what is at stake, and I will not tell her anything that you don't want her to know. Trust me in this," she assured him.

Flaring out his wings, preparing to leave, he nodded and took off in the direction of Mt. Olympus.

CHAPTER 13

Psyche slowly came awake from her deep sleep, memories of the previous day's events flooding her mind, causing her to sit up and look around the bed chamber. Her mysterious husband was nowhere to be found. It was only after determining that she was alone that she realized that she was naked underneath the sheets and startled by the unfamiliar sensation.

Heart pounding, she took several deep breaths, trying to calm down. "I'm alive," she whispered to herself. "Naked, but alive." And with that ironic thought, she began to giggle in crazed relief.

Falling back onto the bed, one arm flung over her eyes, she lay there until she could stop her slightly hysterical laughing. Lifting her arm off her eyes and turning her head to where her husband had last been, she saw two flowers tied to a scroll resting on the pillow beside her.

Sitting up, she reached over and carefully picked up the roses: one was a deep red, the other pure white. Bringing them to her face, she was enchanted by their sweet fragrance. After releasing the flowers from the scroll, she turned her attention to it. Slowly, she read the message left by her husband:

Good morning, my beautiful bride. I trust this note finds you well. Last night was a pleasure unlike any that I have experienced and I look forward to being with you again tonight. Garden, read, do whatever your heart desires while the sun is out. The days and the island are yours. Do with it as you please. However, the nights—and you—are mine.

Psyche reread the note several times. Looking out the window, she saw that it was late morning. Realizing that she had slept well past her normal hour, she was at a loss for a moment about what to do. If she were at home, she would have already been up and about her duties, helping her mother about the palace. But that was not an option here. Thinking about home brought tears to her eyes. She missed her parents, her mother, especially, and wished that she could hold her, talk to her, and seek her advice, but that was impossible at the moment.

Sighing, she put away such useless thoughts and slowly made her way to the edge of the bed. The moment she tried to stand she felt the aches in her body. She was slightly sore from her husband's lovemaking, and as her gaze swept over her body, she could make out the faint marks of his passion. Seeing them brought back memories of the night before. She was shocked at the things he had done to her, the pleasure he had wrung from her. She sat there, reliving their evening of passion, and knowing that he planned to repeat the night's events sent a shudder of nervous anticipation through her.

Standing, she looked around for something to wear when she spotted a robe lying across the foot of the bed. Slipping her arms into it, she belted it tightly, enjoying the glide of silk across her skin. She walked over to open the door in search of the bathing chamber when it opened on its own.

Remembering the invisible servants from the day before,

Psyche came to a stop. "Hello?" she called out hesitantly.

"My lady, how may we serve you today?" came the disembodied voice of Rhea.

"Oh, hello, I was hoping to use the bathing chamber before breakfast, but it seems I overslept," she said apologetically.

"My lady, you have missed nothing. You have only to tell us what you desire and it is yours. The island runs according to your rules and wishes, and no one else's."

"But what about my husband, what about his wishes, his rules?" she asked. Even at home, though her mother ran the palace, she still deferred to her father in most matters. Psyche did not want to run afoul of her new husband by countermanding any of his rules.

"My lady, the only rule that the master has is that you cannot leave the island. That is all. He was quite clear that you would command and control not just the palace, but the island, as well."

Stunned, Psyche could barely wrap her mind around the thought of having such power. It was unheard of for a woman, even a highborn one, to have such freedom and control. Resolving to leave that thought for another day, she decided that she would go about getting her bearings around the palace first before she set her mind to the island.

"All right, then. I would like to bathe, have breakfast, and spend the rest of the day learning the layout and running of the palace."

"Very well. Please follow me."

Seeing the absurdity of that statement, Psyche asked, "Rhea, how can I follow you when I cannot even see you? Is there any reason why I am not allowed to see you all?"

"I am so sorry, my lady, I forget. Mortals cannot see us without our powers affecting them, usually in a negative fashion," Rhea said apologetically.

Psyche thought about that for a moment, and quickly devised a solution to the problem at hand. "Well, if I can't look upon you, then how about if you all wear a necklace made of some type of bell that I can see and hear when you move? With each of you having a unique sound that I can use to identify you with?"

"I think that is a wonderful solution." A necklace suddenly appeared floating in front of Psyche, making it easy to 'see' and hear Rhea in front of her.

Following behind, Psyche felt a little surge of triumph over gaining a little control over her new life on the island. Entering the bathing chamber, she was delighted to see that there were several different necklaces floating about, each uniquely different in both style and lyrical tone.

Rhea turned to Psyche. "My lady, would you like to soak in the hot springs pool first? It will help to relax you, and it will also provide you with some relief. Once you feel more relaxed, you can bathe, and—if you wish—have a massage?"

Cheeks red with embarrassment, Psyche could only nod her head. Walking over to the hot springs pool, she was suddenly shy about disrobing, not wanting the other women to see the marks left on her body from her wedding night.

Seeing the discomfort and indecision on Psyche's face, Rhea came to her side and whispered quietly, "Please don't feel embarrassed, my lady. We have all experienced the morning after our first time with a man. It is nothing to feel shy about, especially not with your husband. Please, let us take care of you."

Moved by the kindness and understanding in Rhea's voice, Psyche slowly untied the knot of her robe, allowing it to open. Then she felt it being tugged from her body to be carried away by one of the servants. Gingerly, she stepped into the hot springs pool, slowly lowing herself onto the reclining bench. Feeling the warmth seep into her, it quickly helped to ease some of the soreness from her wedding night. Sitting there, feeling the water swirl around her, brought back the memories of what had happened the night before with her husband. As she thought about what Phanes had done to her, she felt a return of that same pleasure. The more she thought about it, the heavier her body became. Opening her legs slightly, she felt the water pulse over her sex, reawakening her nerve endings. Her nipples hardened and her breathing quickened. The pleasure ebbed and flowed, but it never reached the level that she had enjoyed the night before.

Feeling slightly frustrated, she rose up and stepped out, then went to the bathing pool, where several of the servants waited quietly. Stepping down the few steps until the water reached her waist, she went to stand under the waterfall. A set of sea sponges slowly and gently moved over her, cleaning her. A servant came up behind and poured some warm cleansing oil onto her hair, gently massaging her scalp.

Feeling the sponges scrape along her sensitive nipples, she shuddered, pleasure slowly spreading throughout her body. But again, it stayed at a level that never reached past the point to push her over into a climax.

Once she was done bathing, she was dried by the servants and led to the massage table, where for the next hour, every tense muscle not loosened by the hot springs pool and the bath was slowly worked into a relaxed state.

After, the servants dressed her and led her to the dining room, where breakfast had been laid out for her. Suddenly famished, she sat down and ate a huge portion before sitting back.

Feeling much better than she had since the day her father had brought back the Pythia's prophecy, Psyche rose from the table—and after thanking the servants—went to explore her new home in earnest.

CHAPTER 14

Flying back to Mt. Olympus, Eros thought back over the night he had spent in Psyche's arms. Smiling smugly, he knew that he had made some strides with her by giving her so much pleasure on their wedding night. Realizing that she was a match for his passions, he could hardly wait until their next encounter.

Landing on the terrace outside his home, he was not surprised to see Aphrodite waiting impatiently for him. Feeling a tiny flicker of gratitude that her petty jealousy had enabled him to find Psyche, he was in an indulgent mood this morning. However, even his gratitude would only buy her a few minutes of his patience, for she still represented a real threat to Psyche, albeit a small one.

Turning at the sound of Eros landing behind her, Aphrodite looked him over. There was something slightly different about him, but she could not quite put her finger on what that something was. He had the beginnings of a strange aura about him, and his wing tips looked as if they had been dusted in glittering gold.

Seeing her slightly puzzled look, Eros realized that he

was already showing signs that he was becoming whole again after spending just a few hours in Psyche's presence. Pulling back on his powers, he projected what he wanted the pantheon to see: an Olympian god.

Giving Aphrodite a hard look, he leaned back against the wall, crossed his arms, and waited for her to speak. Fortunately, he didn't have long to wait.

Glaring at him, she demanded, "Well, did you take care of that little imposter for me as you promised?"

Raising an eyebrow at her shrill tone, he replied, "Of course, I did. Psyche is married to a beast even as we speak."

Smiling maliciously at the thought of the girl suffering such a fate, Aphrodite could not keep the glee from her voice as she inquired, "Well, tell me. Who did you make her fall in love with? Where is the little wretch, and how is she being made to suffer?"

Hearing the venom directed at Psyche had his beast rising up in a sudden rage, ready to tear Aphrodite into shreds. Struggling to contain his predatory nature—his beast having almost slipped beyond his control more than once recently—he fought to control his need to strike out, to kill.

Biting back a growl, he swept a contemptuous glare over Aphrodite. "Psyche is no longer your concern. I did as you asked. She is married to a beast, and she is shut away from the world. Your temples are safe and you can go back to being worshipped as the goddess of love and beauty. Now that you have what you wanted, you can leave and forget she ever existed."

"That is it? That is all you have to say to me?"

"There is nothing more to be said. Forget her; she will not trouble you again."

Recognizing the look in his eye, Aphrodite knew the discussion was at an end. And really, what did she care now that the mortal had been taken care of, anyway? "You're right, I will forget about that pathetic girl. I have wasted enough time on this." Sweeping out past him, she left his home.

Sighing in relief as the tension from containing his beast slowly drained from his body, he walked into his bedroom, aware that another waited for him.

Knowing his home was impenetrable to the spying of the other gods, he nonetheless reinforced the shields surrounding his bedroom so that he and his brother could speak freely. Feeling the familiar buzz of his brother's power, he knew Anteros had reinforced his shield as well, determined to protect their secret.

Anteros stood by the window, looking out over the clouds that circled Mt. Olympus. Knowing that his brother was not really seeing the view, but was lost in thought, Eros waited for him to speak.

Anteros looked over at him. Seeing the languid satisfaction in Eros' stance spoke volumes as to how his first night with his bride had went. The relaxed look in Eros' eyes was so rare as to give him pause. Eyes narrowed, he looked more closely at his brother, seeing what had almost tipped off Aphrodite—that something was not quite right—and he shook his head at him in warning. "You need to be more careful, Eros. Just being with Psyche for a short time has already begun to change you. You need to keep your nature under better control; now more than ever."

Eros nodded ruefully. "I know. I will be more careful."

Accepting his word, Anteros demanded, "Good, now you might as well tell me, what is she like?"

Eyes going distant, it took a few moments for Eros to answer. "She is everything that I remember and nothing at all. She is unique; her own person. She has evolved, as well; her outer shell can barely contain her inner beauty. But

Anteros, she not only holds part of my soul, she may also have some of my lost powers."

Shock spread across Anteros' face, and Eros thought back to the night before, to all the little signs of the powers that Psyche still had trapped within her. "She has a gift for creation. The garden she helped create as a child? Many of the plants should never have taken root, let alone thrive. I could feel the power in that garden, subtle though it was."

Anteros turned back to look out the window. Silence stretched out between them, and he mulled over what Eros had just revealed. Walking over to stand by his brother, Eros waited to reveal an even bigger secret. Knowing the demons that tortured his brother, he waited before revealing the potentially damning information to Anteros. The secret had the potential of setting off the predator that lay hidden in him. The damage he could wrought if he lost control would be devastating on a global scale.

"Tell me what you are holding back," demanded Anteros.

"She can communicate with animals, even control them. Though she doesn't even seem to be aware of it."

Whipping around with a low growl, his eyes flashing to silver slits, Anteros tensed as he fought his instinctual need to eliminate the potential threat that Psyche posed.

Feeling the power ripple around his brother, Eros reached out and gripped his shoulder hard. "Easy, she is no threat to you. Remember, she is part of us."

Shrugging off his hand, Anteros grew angry at his brother's blindness to the danger that Psyche presented to them, overriding his control. "So was that traitorous bitch, and look what happened to us. We trusted then, too. If she can control our beasts, then she *is* a threat," he hissed in a rage that heralded the emergence of his beast.

His rage incited the drakons that lived within them, threatening to unleash their fury and power. Eros called on his own abilities and attempted to contain and shield the distinct signature of their powers as each fought for control of the other. Energy swirled between them as Eros' beast rose up in challenge and defense to the threat to Psyche. Each fought the other for dominance in a dangerous dual. The backlash of their matched abilities threatened to tear apart Mt. Olympus itself.

"Anteros! Eros! Enough!"

Both turned to glare at Zephyrus, who stood braced against the power swirling around them, watching them with wary anger. "Are you two trying to reveal yourselves, or are you both so caught up in your pissing contest that you just don't care?" he yelled over the thundering sound of their power as they twisted and twirled around him in a chaotic dance that threatened to explode out of control.

"Leave," snarled Anteros in a bestial voice. "This does not concern you."

"By Tartarus, it does. Chaos take you both," he cursed them. "This is neither the time nor the place for this. Stand down before our enemies get wind of your return. You know it is not yet time to reveal yourselves."

Hearing the reminder of their mutual enemies helped to rein in their beasts as nothing else could. The desire to spill the blood of their enemies was too powerful an enticement to the beasts that dwelled in each of them, and it was the burning need for the vengeance that they would unleash that finally tipped the scales back to the twins. Anteros and Eros were finally able to completely rein in their inner beasts. Both were left breathing hard from the physical exertion of trying to control their drakons, but they nevertheless got them contained. Barely.

Eyes going back to brown, Anteros stepped back from Eros and nodded his thanks to Zephyrus before stalking off to stand on the balcony. Arms braced on the railing, he stared off into space, lost in the memories that haunted him.

Zephyrus turned to Eros and demanded, "What has gotten into both of you?"

Turning away from the sight of his brother with a sigh, he answered, "Psyche is my true soul mate, reborn, with no memories of her previous life. She is also the key to freeing the others, and it seem she has some of my lost abilities, including the power to control beasts."

Zephyrus paled at the news. "Are you sure? Eros, if she truly has returned, then that means—"

"Yes, it means that the time of the second Primordialomachy is upon us. War is coming, and this time, we will not fail." Glancing over at Anteros, Eros continued. "Once she and I are truly reunited, the others will awaken, though we must continue to remain in the shadows and prepare for their return. It will not be long before our enemies make an appearance of their own."

Turning back, Eros briefly outlined the rest of his plan to win back Psyche. Zephyrus was more troubled then assured that the plan was a sound one, but he kept his thoughts to himself when he saw the black look that passed between the twins. It would seem that there was more discord between them over this, and he did not want to stir up more strife that could lead to their enemies being tipped off to the impending return of the primordial gods. Soon after, Zephyrus departed.

Walking over to stand next to Anteros, Eros waited for his brother to speak his mind.

Their earlier conflict was still unresolved between them.

"Eros, be careful. You know that I will stand by you only so long as she poses no real threat to you. Remember my vows. But know this: She poses a very real threat to us. She is weak, and that weakness can be used to harm you. Even you cannot deny the near-fatal outcome should she refuse to reunite her soul with you. All will be lost without your guidance and leadership. Better to just take back what is yours and be done with her. Her weakness will be the ruin of us all."

"If I do that, it will kill her mortal form, and I will never harm her, not even to save myself." Shaking his head in sadness, Eros understood all too well the bitterness that poisoned his brother against Psyche, and women in general. "She is not her, Anteros. Her weakness is not hers."

Eyes narrowed in rage, Anteros glanced sideways at his brother before he hissed, "They are *all* weak. Never forget that. *Never.*" Spreading his wings, he flew off, leaving behind a troubled Eros.

CHAPTER 15

Psyche was feeling a level of satisfaction as she sat in the dining hall, waiting to be served the evening meal. It had been a very productive day. She had explored and learned the layout of her new home. The sheer size and scale of it gave her a headache when she thought about navigating it on her own, but she felt she had made a dent in learning the main rooms and passageways for now.

As day turned to dusk, she wondered when her husband would arrive. All day she had vacillated between wanting to discover more about him and fearing that his kindness was just an illusion to hide a more sinister side. She had been fooled before, and she did not relish the thought of being fooled again.

She still harbored the fear of the unknown, and her husband was the greatest unknown of her life. His power was unimaginable, especially the power he wielded over her body. All day she had felt the effects of her wedding night—both in the slight soreness that still lingered, and the various shards of arousal that would strike at the oddest moments. It was as if a long-dormant part of her that she had not been aware of was waking; a sensual creature that had the power to make her behave in a way that was alien to her. It unsettled her.

Remembering her wedding night, a languid warmth slowly travelled up her body from her core, making her shift in her seat as desire made her grow slick and sent her pulse racing. Lost in her memories, she was unaware of the passage of time, until the hairs on the back of her neck rose in warning that she was no longer alone in the dining hall.

All of a sudden, all the oil lamps went out, leaving the room swamped in darkness, blinding and leaving her with just vague shadows cast from the dim moonlight. Caressing hands gripped her shoulders before her mysterious husband spoke from behind her. "Ah, little butterfly, the scent of your arousal is a welcome homecoming, indeed."

Gasping in embarrassment, and her cheeks red with the thought that her husband could smell her arousal, Psyche gripped the edge of the reclining chair in a white-knuckled grip. The knowledge that her husband was no ordinary being was a sharp reminder of her precarious situation. "My lord, I did not expect you back so early this evening."

Eros slid up behind her and pulled Psyche against him until her back was pressed up against his chest. Propping his head on his hand, he wrapped the other around her waist. Feeling her tense against him, he nuzzled her hair and took a deep breath, inhaling her unique scent. "You are so tense. What is wrong?"

At her continued silence, his beast prowled to the surface at the sign of her obvious distress, and he couldn't help the growl that entered his voice. "Has someone done anything to upset you? Tell me, and they will never trouble you again."

Trembling at the leashed violence in her husband's voice, Psyche blurted out, "Is it true? Can you truly smell my desire?"

Rearing back from her, his shocked relief that she was unharmed had him chuckling. After the conflict earlier in the day between Anteros and himself over her, his drive to protect her was a vicious need that goaded him to eliminate anything that threatened her. The thought of her being upset was enough to set his drakon in a vicious state, though the cause was just another reminder of her inexperience. "That is what has you so troubled? Psyche, my sweet little innocent, I am no mortal. My powers and abilities are beyond the understanding of mortals."

Sensing her continued embarrassment, he pulled her closer to him and pressed a kiss behind her ear. "Psyche, you belong to me. The rules of your old life no longer apply. It is my pleasure and duty to teach you all that you need to know to thrive in your new role."

The reminder of the life that she left behind sent a stab of pain in her heart. She wished that her mother was near so that she could speak with her, and be held by her. The need for something familiar from her old life was a sharp reminder that she was truly alone in this new, alien world. A tear slid down her cheek after a wave of sadness swept over her.

Seeing the tear on her face and feeling the pain that wounded her as if it were his own, he raged at himself for his thoughtless words. The knowledge of how sheltered she had been prior to their marriage was both a curse and a blessing to their union, but the loneliness that filled her made it obvious how truly isolated she was on the island. Sheltered though she had been in her parents' palace, she had had her family to lean on, and here she had no one.

Gathering her to him, he turned her so that she was nestled against his chest with his wings curved protectively around her, creating a cocoon-like feeling. Running his hand in a slow caress up and down her back, he sighed as he tried to mend some of the pain he had caused with his thoughtless words. "Forgive me, Psyche. Your husband can be an insensitive fool at times. I did not mean to hurt you with memories of your life before our marriage. I know the pain and heartache that missing a loved one can cause, and I do not like that I must cause you this pain, even if it's for your own protection."

Psyche was stunned at how attuned he was to her feelings. Very few people were able to discern her true thoughts behind the mask that she showed the world, but it would appear that her mysterious husband could see past it, even in the darkness. "How did you know that I was feeling pain, my lord?"

"Phanes, not 'my lord.' Say it."

After a slight pause, she said, "Phanes…how did you know?"

Wanting to tell her the truth, Eros knew that to reveal all to her at this point would only cause problems between them, but he was loath to lie to her. He settled on giving her as much of the truth as he could without letting her know who, or what, she was dealing with. "It is my duty and privilege as your husband to ensure your happiness. Therefore, if you are feeling hurt, or lonely, than I will make it so that you no longer feel that way."

Smiling a little at the arrogance of his statement, Psyche gathered her courage to ask another question. "Phanes, if you truly wish to take my pain away, would you allow me to see my family?"

A feeling of foreboding filled Eros at her request. It set both him and his beast snarling in denial, because all they wanted was to keep Psyche safe. A part of him that he was not proud of wanted to eliminate all competition for her love and affection; coveting all of her love and loyalty for himself and his beast. Both wanted her to come to trust and depend on them for all her needs. In this moment, both man and beast were in agreement in wanting to guard her away from any and all who could take her away from them.

Eros looked into Psyche's eyes to deny her request and saw the yearning sadness in them, and he knew that he could not deny her need to see her family forever, though he would for now, until he was more sure of her devotion to him and their union. He needed their bond to be firm before he allowed anyone from her past to have any access to her. He also needed to weaken the bonds that tied Psyche to her old life first, though he realized a complete severing might never happen.

"I will allow you to see your family, Psyche. But," he paused, as he saw hope fill her eyes, "not until we have spent more time together. It is too soon. You must rid yourself of your need for them and learn to be completely loyal to me before I will allow you to see your family again. Do this, and I will eventually allow you to see them, but not before I feel that your bond to me is stronger than your bond to your family."

"I don't understand. We are married; there is no power that can undo that. I know where my duties lie, and my loyalty is to you. Seeing my family will not change that. The thought of their suffering, not knowing my fate, is so painful for me. Please, at least let them know that I am alright," she pleaded.

Shaking his head, he said in a hard tone, "That is not possible right now. Aphrodite wants you punished, and should she find out that you are unharmed, she will strike out at your family to punish them in your place. You are beyond her reach here on the island, but your family is not. Your parents would never be able to hide their relief if they were to learn the truth. Better for them to suffer a little over not knowing your fate than to have them tortured and killed by that jealous bitch."

Knowing he spoke the truth, she was still shocked at the venom and contempt in his voice when he spoke of Aphrodite. The disdain that he held the goddess in was blindingly obvious to her, and she was fearful of what Aphrodite would do in retaliation if she ever found out. The goddess wanted her tortured and punished for the simple crime of being worshipped for her physical beauty, but what would she do to her husband for his more damning crime of disrespect to the gods? Covering his lips with her fingers, she whispered fearfully, "Phanes, please do not speak like that. The gods have ears everywhere. They would punish you for your words."

Eros nipped her fingers gently with his teeth, and his lips curved up into a smile at her concern for his wellbeing. Holding her hand, he said, "Don't worry, little butterfly. Remember the words of the Pythia: 'Even the gods fear my wrath.'" Seeing her frown at the reminder of his predatory nature, he continued. "Enough with all this unpleasantness. Let us focus on more pleasurable things for the rest of the evening."

Gently, he nibbled and licked at the pad of her fingers before slowly working his way down to the pulse in her wrist, where he pressed his lips in a kiss. Feeling her pulse race, he was pleased to sense the return of her desire. "That is better. You smell much more appetizing than the evening meal."

At the reminder of his ability to smell her desire, Psyche felt her cheeks flush as she ducked her head, sure that if he could smell her, he could surely see her in the pitch black of night that enveloped the dining area.

"Enough of that," he said sternly. Seeing that she was listening to him, he pressed his point. "The scent of your desire is a pleasure to me. It pleases me to know that I am providing for you in all things. Never be embarrassed or ashamed of your desire. Pleasures of the flesh are your right. It pleases me to know that I am satisfying you."

Realizing her old life still held her in its grip, Eros used his powers to bring their evening meal to them and set it down within arm's reach. He made sure that none of the servants would disturb them. The plan he had to further break her of the constrictions of her previous life had his body stirring to painful life. He looked forward to tying her more fully to him.

"I've sent the servants away. It will be just the two of us tonight."

Picking up the goblet of wine, he held it to her lips and watched as she took a sip. Tilting it a little more, a few drops overflowed from the cup, landing on her chest.

"How clumsy of me, spilling the wine on you. Here, allow me to clean up the mess I made." Pulling the cup back, Eros leaned forward and caught the drop of wine with the tip of his tongue as it slowly made its way toward her breast. Hearing her gasp, he followed the path of the wine to the top of her breast. The taste of her was headier than the wine itself, threatening to rend the control he had over himself. Stopping when he reached the top of her gown, he forced himself to pull back. Leaning back, he took a drink as well, making sure to place his lips over the same spot where she had taken hers. Putting the cup back on the table, he grabbed a handful of grapes.

Holding one to her lips, he murmured, "Open up, my love."

She took the grape in her mouth, and he slowly fed her the rest. Squeezing one, he watched as the juice squirted over her lips and down her chin. "Pardon my clumsiness," he said in a teasing tone. "Allow me."

He slowly licked his way across her mouth, lapping up all the juice. Gently tracing her lips, he slipped his tongue between them when she opened her mouth to catch her breath. He explored her leisurely, tasting the wine and grapes. Shyly, her tongue brushed against his, tasting him, as well. Groaning at her touch, he dueled with her by teaching her how to kiss him. After spending some time doing that, they broke apart, both panting as they tried to catch their breath.

"Now it is your turn to feed me. The plate of food is behind me," he murmured.

"Can you please hand it to me?" she asked.

Eros smiled wickedly. "No, little one. That is not how we play this game."

"Game? What kind of game are we playing?" she asked in confusion.

"The best type of game."

Psyche could hear the teasing tone in his voice; it reminded her of when he got her to beg him to help her reach her pleasure on their wedding night. Shying away from the memories, she waited for him to speak. When she received no response to what he considered the 'best type of game,' she finally demanded, "What is this 'game' called, Phanes?"

"Copycat."

"Copycat? I have never heard of it."

"Really?" he asked, chuckling wickedly. "I am surprised, Psyche. It is such a fun game to play."

Suspicious of his tone, she was sure there was something she was missing. Her husband—she was learning—had a devious side. "What are the rules to this game?" she inquired.

Enjoying their banter, Eros decided to tease her a little more. The more comfortable she became around him, the more she allowed her true self to shine through, and he liked what he saw, especially the temper she tried to hide from him. "The rules of copycat are simple," he said. "We each take turns doing the same thing to one another. I fed you, so now you must feed me. At the end of each turn, we see based on our response what the most pleasurable part was, and which was not."

"That is it? I don't see the purpose of this game."

"Psyche, my dear, where is your sense of fun? The purpose of this game is twofold: to learn more about each other; and to have fun. One can learn a great deal about a person from the way they play a game."

She mulled over his explanation, and she had a sneaking suspicion where this game of his would eventually lead to, but she was curious and wanted to get to know him better. "And then? Will there be a winner? And if so, what does the winner get as a prize?"

His eyes shimmered with a wicked gleam. "The winner can demand from the loser that they perform a carnal act."

Flashbacks of their wedding night flooded her mind. Her cheeks flushed and her memories sent a stab of desire low in her belly. Deciding to play along, she said, "Alright, I will play this game with you."

"Very good. Now, you may begin."

Psyche carefully reached over her husband, but her lack of sight hampered her ability to find the tray that held their dinner. After blindly searching, she realized that the food was out of her reach in the position that she was in. The only way that she would be able to get to the food was if she got on top of Phanes' body and reached over. It would put her in a wanton position, and she realized that was his intention all along. Fuming at the deviousness of her husband, she allowed a small smile to curve her lips as she decided to pay him back in kind. "My dear husband," she said in a soft voice, "do I have to copy everything exactly as you do, or can I adjust the game a little? After all, you are so much bigger than me, and your reach is at least double mine."

"I think a few accommodations can be made to even the playing field."

"Thank you," she said demurely. Slowly, she slid her leg over his thighs and shifted over him until she lay on top of him. Hands on his chest, she pushed back, straddling his thighs as she pushed herself into a sitting position.

Eros gripped her thighs and groaned softly. His beast tested his control as it fought to regain the dominant position, but he pushed it back, liking the sight of Psyche as she was.

"Are you alright? Would you like me to get off of you?"

"No, stay as you are. I like to look at you. Your beauty truly is a sight to behold. It is a pleasure that I plan in indulging in as much as I can while we are together."

She frowned at him. She did not like to be reminded of her physical appearance. Then she thought of how his words revealed his ability to really see her, even in the pitch black of the dining room. "Can you see me?"

"My night vision is perfect. I can see you as if it were day. Now, let us get back to our little game, shall we?"

Psyche carefully reached out and felt her way to the table. Phanes tightened his grip on her thighs to prevent her from falling, as she had to stretch to reach the side table that held their food. Feeling her way over the plates, she took hold of the wine goblet and brought it to his lips, allowing him to take a sip. Pulling back the goblet, she tilted it, allowing several drops to spill onto his chin and chest. Leaning forward, she delicately lapped up the wine. She could taste the dangerous essence that was her husband. It was a combination of the richest wine and forbidden fruit. She knew she could quickly become addicted to his taste.

Forcing herself to stop, she went to put the goblet back

on the table when he stopped her. "No, no little one. You did not copy me completely. You missed a step. Now you must pay a forfeit."

Startled, she said, "What do you mean? I did exactly what you did."

He shook his head and smirked at her; she had fallen neatly into his trap. "I took a drink of the wine before I put it back on the table. You didn't."

"But I can't see in the darkness. You can. How was I to know that you took a sip?"

"You have other senses, Psyche. Touch, taste, smell, hearing...intuition. Your eyes can all too often deceive. Use your other senses."

Mustering up her courage, she dared to argue with him. "You agreed to give me some accommodations, and shouldn't my inability to see in the dark be taken into account, since I am not allowed to see you?"

"No."

"No?"

"No. Your other senses are strong and can more than compensate for your lack of sight. Learn to use them, and you will be all the more powerful for it."

Psyche thought over what he said. There was a hidden message behind this game, she was certain of it. But what? It was as if he was trying to tell her something, but couldn't—or wouldn't. Shaking her head, she let that thought slide away to be examined at another time, for now she had a far more pressing concern. Eyes narrowed, she demanded, "What do you mean I now owe you a forfeit? You never mentioned that."

Eros laughed at her little show of temper. "You never asked. All games such as copycat have rules and a point system, so that each player can gain or lose points. This is how a winner can be determined. Remember, to the winner goes the spoils; and I plan on winning this particular game."

"And what does the winner get?" Psyche dared to ask.

"Hmm, that is the question, is it not? What will I demand as my winnings?"

The confidence in his voice combined with his conclusion that she would be the loser of their game irritated her. Especially as it seemed he was not above cheating to win by withholding vital information from her. "You seem very sure of yourself, my lord. I can still win this game you know," she bit out.

It was only after the words left her mouth that she realized how she had let her temper get the better of her judgment. Her thoughts on his attitude were apparent in her tone. She blanched in fear at his reaction. She also braced herself, fully expecting that she had angered him and that he would punish her for it.

Eros saw the blood drain from her face and the fear invade her eyes after she had rebuked him. It immediately set his temper on fire. That she still feared him angered not just him, but his beast, as well. It raked at him, wanting to get out. It goaded him into responding to her fear in a harsher manner than he meant to. Snarling, he rose up and got right up into her face. "Never," he growled, "be afraid to show me your true self. Rail against me, curse me, but never be *afraid* of me. Your fear is repugnant to me. No male of any worth would ever harm those who belong to them."

Dipping his head, he then kissed her, nipping her lips in reprimand before releasing her and settling back down. He waited for his words and actions to penetrate her fear. She *had* to get over it, or they were both doomed.

Psyche touched her lips, the slight sting quickly fading as she waited. When he said nothing more, she breathed deeply, letting her racing heart settle back into its normal pattern. "Forgive me, I—"

"Did I ask you to apologize?" he snapped.

"No, but—"

"Psyche," he warned in a stern tone, "I know you are still afraid of me. It is natural to feel that way in a new situation, but this visceral fear you have toward me is not good. It has the power to destroy us both."

The anguished look on her face cut Eros to the bone. They had been enjoying themselves, and he wanted to recapture the playful mood from their game; to show her that she had nothing to fear from him. "Now, enough with your stalling. You still owe me that forfeit."

Startled out of her dark thoughts with the sudden change in subject, she asked, "Forfeit? You still want to continue to play our game?"

"Of course. I still mean to win and collect my winnings. Though you may try your best to win, I will warn you: No one has ever beaten me in this game. So don't feel bad when you lose. I promise not to laud my victory over you too much."

Tilting her head to the side, Psyche tried to see his expression, though it was a vain attempt in the darkness of the room. Realizing she was totally blind in the pitch black—for even the dim light of the moon had faded—she thought over his advice to use her other senses. An idea on how to win this game suddenly came to her, and she was determined to make him eat his words. Smiling sweetly at him, she asked, "What is my forfeit?"

Raising an eyebrow at the mischievous expression on her face, Eros was fiercely glad to see the return of her playful mood. He was intrigued to see how this would play out, since he could see the hints of a competitive streak within her.

Deciding to see how far he could push her, he said, "Undo the pins of your chiton. Let me see more of you."

Smiling shyly, Psyche slowly reached up to unclasp the pins at her shoulders that held up her gown. She undid one, letting it fall before she undid the other one. Dropping the pins to the floor, the top of her chiton fell to her waist, held there by her belt. Lifting her head, she looked over to where her husband was sitting silently with a triumphant mien.

He growled in annoyance. "You are wearing a *strophion*."

Battering her lashes, Psyche replied in a honey-sweet voice, "Why yes, of course, Phanes. How else can I support my breasts under my gown?"

"Take it off," he demanded. "I want my forfeit."

Psyche shook her head in mock sadness. "No, my lord, that is *not* how we play this game."

Glaring at her, Eros was slightly shocked that she dared to tease him. But his shock quickly faded at the playful look on her face. Grinning at her show of spirit, he was immensely pleased to see this lighthearted side of her personality reveal itself to him. He decided to push her harder to see just how far he could take their exchange. "What do you mean, that is not how we play this game? I won the forfeit, and my forfeit was to see your breasts. Now take off your s*trophion*," he demanded gruffly.

Psyche schooled her features into a serene mask. "No."

"No?"

"No. Your forfeit was only for me to undo the top of my dress so you could see me," she reminded him.

"And see your breasts," he added.

"You didn't specify that, but in any case, you can still *see* my breasts. My strophion does not cover them completely," she countered sweetly.

"I meant to say your naked breasts," he argued back.

"Ah, but you did not say that when you asked for your

forfeit," she gently reminded him. Shaking her head, she tapped her chin with her hand, all the while giving him a mock considering look. "However, I may be willing to grant your request, if you are willing to pay a forfeit in kind."

Eros thew his head back as laughter erupted from his chest at her clever maneuver. He was immensely pleased with his clever little bride.

Psyche broke out in an answering grin, pride filling her at being the cause of her husband's joy. Unable to help herself, she joined her husband in his laughter.

"Clever, devious, little butterfly," Eros scolded her in a voice still imbued with the remnants of his laughter. "To be able to gaze upon your lovely breasts, I will gladly pay any forfeit you demand. So tell me, what do you wish?"

Psyche gave in to the sensual creature that seemed to have taken up residence in her. Right now it urged her to act in an uncharacteristically bold and wanton manner. "A fair exchange only, my lord. As I am blinded by darkness in my interactions with you, I must rely on my other senses, just as you said. Touch...," she whispered, running her hands over his chest in a caress, "...smell..." she continued, as she leaned over his chest, pressing her nose to his sternum, softly inhaling his delicious scent, "... and taste..." Then she ran her tongue leisurely up his chest, pressing a kiss over his racing heart before she rose back up to a sitting position. "It is only fair that you yourself must be as blind as I am, forced to only rely on the same human senses that I am bound by." Hearing the ragged breathing of her husband, she reveled in her new power over him.

His grip tightened on her thighs as his body hardened painfully from her teasing. "So what do you propose?" he inquired, his voice rough with lust.

"I will take off my *strophion* and use it to blindfold you. You will get to gaze upon my naked breasts, but for a few moments only. As part of your forfeit, you must play the rest of the game limited to the same senses that I have as a human. And no cheating."

Seduced by her sensual play, Eros was willing to give her just about anything at that moment, just for the pleasure of her. She, who was the innocent, was proving to be a quick study of the sensual arts, and he was a very good teacher. "Very well. I agree to your terms. But on one condition."

Her eyebrows rose in question. "And that would be?"

"Take it off slowly."

Nodding, she reached behind her and slowly pulled at the knot that held her *strophion* in place. Loosening it, she dragged it down, the rough silk rasping over her nipples, turning them into hard points and sending pleasure throughout her body. Her breasts felt heavy from wanting. The need to have him touch her there was an ache. Moaning softly at the sensation, she lowered her arms, displaying her breasts for the pleasure of her husband.

Eros feasted on the visual bounty in front of him. Her nipples were hard, and he hungered to lick them, caress them, and bite them. Clenching his hands on her legs, he fought to allow her to continue to play their little game.

Psyche slowly leaned forward, bringing the *strophion* with her. "Close your eyes." Then she wrapped it around his head. Hunching over him as she secured the cloth with a knot, she moaned when Eros latched onto her nipple with his mouth, nipping and licking it in a hungered frenzy. Clutching him to her, she arched into his mouth as she ground her hips against him, helplessly giving in to her lust. Letting go of her nipple, he latched onto the other one and ministered to it in the same manner. Crying out, Psyche gripped his hair, pulling him off her as she scrambled back. Breathing hard, she tried to reclaim control over herself. She was determined to win, and she could not afford to be distracted.

She felt his arousal, his rigid length pressed against her core, and her answering wetness a sign that she was just as affected by their sensual game. "I am counting that as you turn, my lord. Now it is my turn again."

Struggling to control himself, he wanted to pin her beneath him and sate his lust, and it was proving to be more and more difficult. It took several attempts before he was able to trust himself to continue their contest. The only thing he wanted more than sex was her trust and love, and he was determined to gain both. "I believe we will call it a draw at this point. Now, I believe you still must feed me some grapes."

She reached out and grabbed a handful. Slowly she fed them to him, making sure to purposely squeeze one so the juice fell onto his lips. "Your clumsiness must be contagious. Allow me to make up for it."

"What a lucky man I am to have such a dutiful wife," he teased.

Psyche slowly licked across his lips, groaning at the need riding her, and soon she deepened their wine-soaked kiss. Eros let her explore his mouth for a few seconds before he took over and dominated the kiss.

Breaking apart, both were breathless.

"Very good. You are a quick learner. My turn now."

Selecting a stuffed grape leaves, he held it to her lips. Wrapping her hands around his, she slowly brought it to her lips and took several small, delicate bites. Feeling wicked, she gently nipped the pads of his fingers, licking them clean of the juice that had run down his hand from the dolmades. Hearing the change in his breathing and feeling the tensing of his muscles underneath her, Psyche felt a little thrill go through her at the signs of the effect she was having on him. This went on until she pushed his hand away. "Enough."

Reaching out, she grabbed a dolmades, then held it out to

his lips. Releasing his grip on her thigh, he wrapped one of his hands around hers and slowly ate, nipping and licking as he went about consuming it. He took his time, savoring every lick of her flesh. The way he licked and nipped her fingers was reminiscent of the way he had feasted on her more tender flesh the night before. The memory of it sent a shiver through her, and heat spread from her core, making her ache with need.

After finishing the last dolmades, he sat back. The control he had over his passions was quickly unraveling as a result of their sensual play. His hunger for food had been replaced with a hunger to taste more tempting fare.

"I believe I am winning this game of ours," she murmured.

"And what makes you think that?"

"You did not copy me exactly. I used both hands, you used one."

He took one of her hands and held it up against his, easily dwarfing it. "You have soft, tiny, delicate little hands. Mine are easily twice the size of yours, so I only *needed* one."

Lacing his fingers through her hand, he brought it to his mouth, where he placed a kiss on the back of it before pressing it over his heart, holding their clasped hands there. A wicked thought entered his mind as he came up with a new level to take their game to. He relished his role as her guide and teacher in exploring her sexuality, and he had a very special lesson in mind for her.

"Still hungry?" Her voice a husky rasp.

Smiling at the desire in her voice, he said, "Yes, but not for food. What do you hunger for right now, Psyche? Food, or something else?"

Shifting slightly on his lap, she thought of how throughout the day she had been feeling waves of arousal: at times a gentle pull, and at others, a dull ache. Gathering her courage, she confessed softly, "Something else."

Lust surged in him at her admission, and Eros sat up, ripped off the blindfold, keeping their clasped hands between them. "Game over. You win. Now, what does my lady claim for her prize?"

Laughing at his disgruntled tone, she nevertheless was secretly pleased at winning their game, though she could not resist teasing him a little. "Really? You concede? I am a quick study, my lord, admit it."

The wicked idea that had occurred to Eros during their game took root with her words. She was a quick study, indeed, and he was determined to see just how quickly she would master her next lesson. "You are. I freely admit it. Now, about your prize...what is my lady's pleasure? Jewels? No? What about a special perfume just for you? No? What does my lady desire?"

Psyche shook her head, for the prize she truly wanted she knew she could not have—at least right then—so she asked instead, "Must I give you an answer right now, or may I have some time to think about what I want as my prize?"

"You may have all the time you want. Now, since I still owe you a forfeit, I have a proposal for you. As my forfeit, I will teach you the art of self-pleasure."

Frowning, Psyche was not sure what her husband meant exactly by the 'art of self-pleasure,' although she had a feeling it was not something a proper woman of her station would be familiar with. But what was expected of her in her old life was not —so it seemed—what was expected of her in this new life. "I don't understand what you mean by that."

Eros took possession of both of her hands and brought them behind her back, where he held her against his chest. Dipping his head to her throat, he pressed fleeting kisses along her neck. Her nipples scraped along his chest, causing a shudder of pleasure to travel throughout her body. "Do you feel the pleasure my touch is giving you, Psyche? Remember how you climaxed in my arms, writhing and screaming in pleasure? I could teach you how to achieve such pleasure on your own, so you would be able to give yourself an orgasm whenever you desired, day or night, with or without me. Would that not be nice, to be able to relieve that ache of desire, that need that I scented on you when I first came to you this evening?"

Shuddering at the duel sensation of his lips and his words, Psyche was shocked at his proposal. Cheeks flushing as much from mortification as from the passion that his kisses were arousing in her, she said, "I could never do that."

Licking behind her ear, he whispered, "Why not?"

Angling her head to the side to allow him to continue his caress, her eyes drifted close as she stammered, "Because… because it would not be proper."

"According to whom? Who is to tell you or me what is proper and what is not between us?"

Her thoughts scattered, Psyche was unable to come up with a reply, too caught up in the pleasure of his touch. Moaning in protest when he pulled back from her, she realized he was waiting for her attention to return to him and their conversation. Eyes opening, she focused her gaze on where she thought his eyes were, blind though she was in the dark.

Seeing her attention on him, he said, "Psyche, I will not allow you to limit yourself to the expectations of a world you no longer belong to. You are free here on the island. Free to experience all the world has to offer. Anything you desire, you may have. Anything you wish to experience, I will provide. There is no one here to judge you."

She thought over his words, but the restrictions of her upbringing would not so easily be forgotten. "But what about the servants?"

"What about them?"

Eyes downcast, she whispered, "I don't wish to do anything that would bring shame on you. That would cause them to speak ill of me."

Eros' eyes flashed in anger, for her painful whisper spoke of a past where she had obviously been made to feel shame. "Never. Say. That. Again. Nothing you do will ever bring shame on me, Psyche. *Nothing.*"

Wanting to tear apart the ones responsible for causing her to question and doubt herself, he forced himself instead to focus on her needs, and not on seeking to destroy those who had hurt her. He sought to make her understand instead. "You have so much to learn and experience. And I mean to push your limits. To push you beyond your comfort zone. How else are you to learn what pleases you and what does not? To become the woman you were always meant to be? Stretch your wings, and don't be afraid."

Taking a shuddering breath, she asked, "Do you..."

"Do I what?" he coaxed when she faltered.

"Do you do that?"

"Yes, Psyche," he assured he., "I am an expert in the art of self-pleasure, though the word you are looking for is masturbation. It is quite pleasurable, and I would teach you."

Trembling from need and desire, she thought over his logic and reasoning. Part of her clamored for the forbidden knowledge. The need was so powerful it overrode her inhibitions, pushing her to accept his shocking suggestion for his forfeit. "Teach me," she whispered.

Capturing her lips in a swift kiss in a salute to her courage, he spent several minutes caressing her, gentling her. Releasing her, he then pulled back and swiftly lifted her off of him and spun her around until she was facing away from him. He pulled her fully on him, forcing her legs open with his own until she lay spread open on top of his body.

With a mere thought, Eros stripped them both bare.

Wrapping his hands around her waist to keep her steady, he nuzzled the top of her head with his chin. Lifting his eyes to the ceiling, he created and positioned a mirror so that he could feast on the wanton view of her spread out on top of him. The sight of her sent a painful stab of pleasure through him, and he mindlessly thrust his hips against her before he ruthlessly clamped down on his own desire. He refused to cheat them both of the pleasures this lesson held in store for them.

"Now, think back to yesterday. To everything we did in the bathing chamber and in our bed. What brought you pleasure when I touched your breasts?"

Psyche lay on top of Phanes, embarrassed from being so spread out on top of him, so utterly exposed to anyone who might enter the room. She could scarcely believe that she had agreed to his outrageous proposal for his forfeit. The thought of learning how to pleasure herself, to touch herself, was both intimidating and strangely freeing. It was if by giving herself permission to be bold, to be daring, she was breaking down one of the bars to the cage that held her captive. She had always felt as if she was trapped, and the desire for freedom was now too tempting to resist.

She shifted slightly, trying in vain to close her legs, only to have her husband force her legs further apart with his own. She covered her sex with her hand in alarm. Phanes took her hands and placed them on her breasts, leaving her utterly exposed. She was grateful the room was draped in darkness. She could feel him growing harder—if that were even possible—against her backside, and she felt her sex spasm, needing to fill the aching emptiness.

"Now, I believe I spent a great deal of time worshipping your breasts. They are quite sensitive to the slightest touch. I want you to cup them. Do it now."

Slowly, she shifted her hands so that she was cupping

them. They felt heavy, and her slight touch sent a pleasurable shiver through her. Rolling them in her hands, she alternated the amount of pressure, first squeezing them, and then releasing them. She did this for several moments, learning what gave her pleasure, and what didn't.

"Very good, Psyche. Play with your nipples, and remember what brought you pleasure." At the first brush of her fingers, her nipples hardened, which sent pleasure streaking directly to her core, causing her to become even wetter. Tightening her fingers, she pinched them, then slowly tightened her grip. The harder she held them, the more pleasure she felt. When the pressure became a small shaft of pain, she felt an answer spasm in her sex. It seemed she liked a little bite of pain with her pleasure.

"Now, slide your hands down your body."

Slowly, she released her breasts and slid her hands down her stomach. Pausing before she reached her sex, she hesitated to go any further.

"Don't stop now, Psyche. Touch yourself. Slide your fingers across your sex, and coat them with your arousal. Remember how I touched you there. Explore and experiment, and see what brings you pleasure."

Slipping her fingers through the folds of her sex, she gathered the moisture that coated her inner lips and spread it around her clitoris. She rubbed in a circular motion, sending waves of pleasure throughout her body. She varied the pressure and the speed, learning what made her feel good. Soon she was panting, her hips restless.

"That's it. By the gods, you are beautiful," he growled. "Now put your finger inside you. Pretend it is my cock and thrust in and out."

She did as he ordered, sliding a finger inside her sheath. She pumped it in and out, all the while continuing the caress on her clitoris. But it wasn't enough. She added a second finger, increasing the speed and strength of her thrusts, mimicking how Phanes had taken her.

Pleasure spread like molten lava through her, leaving her breathless and gasping as the pressure built. Hips undulating, she came suddenly, arching her back as a cry was torn from her. Wave after wave of aftershocks coursed through her body, causing tiny little spasms that would have sent her tumbling to the floor if Phanes did not have such a firm hold on her. The pleasure slowly receded, leaving her lying in a boneless heap, floating in a sea of satisfaction. She should be feeling appalled at her behavior, but instead she was still aroused. Her climax had ignited a deeper desire, and while it had taken the edge off, she yearned for her husband to fill her, to take away the feeling of emptiness that she still felt.

Eros was in agony. Watching Psyche pleasure herself in the mirror was sweet torture. The sight of her hands touching herself, and seeing the pleasure suffuse across her face as she orgasmed made his cock harden painfully. It was a sight he would never forget, and he was fiercely glad for it, even though it tested his will mightily to see this through to the end. Impatient now to ease his own suffering, he widened his stance further and maneuvered her into a better position on top of him. All the while, his eyes locked on their image in the mirror.

Lust urging him on, he reached down and grasped his cock, guiding it to her entrance. With a quick thrust of his hips, he entered her, wringing a groan from her. Wrapping one arm securely around her waist to keep her in place, he seized her hand and guided it to her sex. "Touch yourself until I tell you to climax again," he ordered.

Fondling her breast with his free hand, he watched in fascinated wonder as she touched herself, both her sex with one hand, and her breast with the other. Her earlier inhibitions ripped to shreds.

Hips pounding, he set a long, hard pace, drawing out the pleasure for both of them. The feel of her tight, wet sheath threatened to cut short their lovemaking. Eyes riveted to the sight of their coupling in the mirror, to the erotic sight of Psyche writhing on top of him as pleasure took her over, Eros fought to hold off his own climax. He was determined to draw out the pleasure until they were both weak from it.

"Phanes...please..." Psyche gasped pleadingly.

"Now," he commanded.

Letting out a soft scream, her orgasm tore through her, the rippling effect of her climax felt like a hand rhythmically squeezing him. Arching up, she thrashed as wave after wave of pleasure crashed through her.

Eros roared as his own orgasm sent him over the edge of sanity. The pleasure and pain of it a bittersweet release to him. It left him dazed and satisfied as the intense grip of Psyche's orgasm left him limp and sated. It took several moments to catch his breath, and opening his eyes, he let out a rough chuckle at what he saw reflected in the mirror above them. Psyche was passed out on top of him, her orgasm leaving her unconscious, sprawled all over him in limp gratification.

Gathering her body more tightly to him, he thought of their bedroom, and seconds later, they were falling into the soft folds of their bed. Eros arranged her until his body sheltered hers to his satisfaction, and then he fell into an exhausted sleep.

CHAPTER 16

Psyche looked around, dazed and confused, wondering where she was. A dull throbbing pain beat at her temples, reminiscent of that one time she had indulged in too much wine at the harvest festival. The discomfort and slight nauseous feeling made her vow to never drink so much wine ever again. Had she overindulged at dinner? She had no idea how she came to be standing in the middle of a field at night. At least, it looked like it was nightfall. And come to think of it, she was not quite sure it was a field she was standing in; at least not one she had ever seen before. A heavy fog clung to the ground, and it seemed to move in a sluggish crawl, clinging and swirling in a lazy dance all around her. It pulsed with various shades of grays and white, lightning illuminating the odd patch here and there.

The last thing she remembered, she was with Phanes in the dining room, playing his game of copycat. Blushing at the memories, she took another look around. Seeing nothing familiar, she tried to see if she could hear anything. Just because she could not see anyone did not mean she was alone, after all.

Twirling around, she called out, "Hello? Phanes? Is anyone here?"

Nothing.

In the distance, she could hear a low rumble, the kind that one heard across the sea, foretelling of a storm brewing in the distance. The fog seemed to take on a life of its own, swirling faster as ominous shapes formed in the distance. The closer they came, the more sinister they appeared. She could make out faint whispers coming from the shadows, though she could not make out any real words. Her hair rising on the back of her neck, a sudden sense of foreboding filled her.

Gathering the folds of her gown in one hand, she started to quickly walk away from the shadowy figures. Glancing behind her, she saw that they were closer, and abandoning all pretense, she started running as fast as she could.

Panting from exertion, she dared to look over her shoulder again, just as the shadow figures seemed to reach out, intent on grabbing her. Then she let out a scream of pure fright.

* * *

PSYCHE WOKE UP WITH A CRY, her body quaking and covered in a light sheen of sweat. She sat up in bed and frantically looked around. It was well past dawn, and sunlight flooded the room.

Taking a few deep breaths, her heart slowly settled into a more regular beat. "Just a nightmare," she murmured to herself. Dropping her head into her hands, she rubbed at her temples until the slight ache went away. She stayed that way until she heard the jingle of the bell that signaled that Rhea was entering the room, a tray of food floating in the air.

"Good morning, my lady. I have brought some food for you to break your fast."

Sighing, Psyche looked over at the food that Rhea had brought in. The tray was placed beside her on the bed. "Thank you."

"My lady, are you not feeling well? You look pale."

Psyche turned her head away from the food. "My head aches, and I feel slightly nauseous."

Rhea placed her hand on Psyche's forehead. "You are not feverish. Do you have any other ailments?"

Shaking her head, Psyche lay back down. Closing her eyes, she tried to breathe past the nausea.

"My lady, drink this. It will help settle your stomach, and it will sooth away your headache."

Opening her eyes, Psyche saw a steaming cup floating next to her. She rose up, took the cup, and drank. Bracing herself for the unpleasant taste of a medicinal elixir such as the ones her mother made, she was pleasantly surprised to find the cup contained chamomile tea laced with some spices that she could not identify. Draining the cup, she handed it back to Rhea and settled back down in the bed. "Thank you."

Very quickly, the nausea and headache caused by her nightmare disappeared. Feeling like her old self again, she thought of what she wished to accomplish for the day. She looked over at the food, then realized just how famished she actually was.

"How are you feeling now, my lady?"

"Better. Thank you so much, Rhea. The tea worked wonders. I hardly ever get sick, and I wonder why I felt so ill this morning."

"Forgive me, my lady, for being so bold, but with all that has happened to you in the last few days, it is a wonder you haven't sickened before now."

Mulling over Rhea's words, Psyche saw the wisdom behind them, and the last of her worries disappeared along with the memory of her nightmare. "You're right, of course. The stress of the last few days must be the cause."

Rhea slid the tray closer to Psyche. "Now, I think you should eat before you do anything else, my lady."

Picking up some bread with honey on it, Psyche quickly ate a few slices. Then she turned to the goblet and quickly drank the pomegranate juice. Feeling full, she pushed the tray away and slid out of bed. Almost immediately, a chorus of chimes sounded, heralding the arrival of more servants. Quickly, the room was set to rights. After bathing, Psyche dressed in a work gown. She gathered a few more things and then set out to spend the rest of the day properly exploring the island.

CHAPTER 17

Psyche stepped out into the sunlight of the late-morning sun. The heat was a welcome sensation on her skin. Lifting her face towards it, she closed her eyes and savored the warmth. Inhaling deeply, she lowered her head and stepped onto the path leading away from the main house towards the stables in the distance. Bending down and grabbing a basket that had been left forgotten, she stopped and pulled some apples from a tree that grew alongside the path. Once her basket was filled, she continued on her way.

Psyche took a better look around the island, mentally listing all the locations of the buildings, the layout of the gardens, and all the work that still needed to be done to complete them. The closer she got, the sounds of the horses grew stronger. In the distance, she could make out a small herd. She entered the stables and made her way to the stalls. All were empty save one for a lone horse.

The familiar scents sent a stab of loneliness through her. She had spent many an hour in her family's stables back home, and the familiar setting reminded her of all she was missing on the island. Pushing away thoughts of home, for she refused to shed any more tears, she was determined to make the most of this new life of hers, so she walked up to the first stall and peered in. In the back corner stood a black horse; it was too dim to make out its gender. It turned restlessly in the stall, occasionally kicking the sides, snorting in anger and frustration at being penned in.

Stepping closer to the stall door, Psyche made a soft cooing sound, so that the horse became aware of her. Ears laid back, whirling around in a rage, the horse charged at her, causing her to stumble back in fear, drop the basket, and fall against the opposite wall. Bracing herself and throwing up her hands in a feeble attempt to protect herself, she yelled, "Stop!"

The horse came to an abrupt stop, mere inches from the stall door. It stood trembling and breathing heavy, a taut mass of muscles barely leashed. Stomping the ground, snorting and flinging its head back, the beast's anger and frustration were clearly visible. The danger of the horse breaking through the stall door and trampling her was very much a possibility. It froze her in place, her heart racing in fear and her mind focused on not triggering the horse to any higher levels of violence.

Psyche stayed as still as a statue, waiting to see what the horse would do. When it just stood there trembling, as if held back by an invisible force, she slowly relaxed.

Cautiously, she pushed herself off the wall, making sure her movements were slow so as not to set the horse off again. Carefully, she took a small step toward the horse. Slowly bending, she reached down to the ground, plucking one of the scattered apples from the floor where they had fallen out of her basket. Rising, she picked her way through the maze of fallen apples, not wanting to trip and set the horse off again with any quick movements. "Shh, my beauty. I mean you no harm," she murmured soothingly.

Freezing in place when the horse stomped and pawed at the ground, Psyche waited until the horse settled back down. When its ears came forward, she approached it again, until she came to a halt before the stall door. "Easy there, my beauty. What a beautiful horse you are. There is no reason to be mad. I only want to be your friend."

She stood still as the horse cautiously lowered its head, sniffing her, its intelligent eyes never leaving hers. The power of the horse evident in its muscular chest, it could easily maim or kill her if it wanted to, but she knew somehow that it would not harm her. Why she was suddenly sure of her safety, she could not say; she just knew that she could handle this particular horse.

Sniffing her hair, the horse lowered its head, working its way down her body until it suddenly thrust its head against her, nuzzling against her chest. Speaking softly, Psyche lightly stroked her hand down its neck, caressing and murmuring softly to the horse, gentling it to her touch. Once she was assured that the horse was completely calm, she brought up her hand that held the apple to the horse's mouth, allowing it to take it from her. It chomped down on it, working the juicy flesh from the core.

While the horse ate the apple, Psyche ran a critical eye over the beast, noting that it was a stallion of the Andravida breed. It was pure black, only a few years old by the looks of him. After the horse finished the apple, it dropped the core to the ground, whinnying softly. The stallion looked over to the scattered apples on the floor, its desire for them evident. Psyche laughed softly. "Typical male, always wanting to be fed. I bet you want all the apples for yourself, don't you? You probably don't even want to share with any of the other horses, do you?"

The stallion shook his head, as if he understood her words. Nodding his head toward the apples, he then looked over at Psyche as if to say "please feed me more."

"Well, I don't know. I'm not sure if I should give you any more apples, greedy one. What did you do to be locked up in the stable all alone, anyway? Is it that temper of yours, maybe?"

"That is exactly right. He hurt the last person who tried to ride him. Not to mention his penchant for biting," said a feminine voice behind her.

Turning around, Psyche looked around for the owner of the voice, seeing no one. Then she gave herself a mental kick, as she was still not used to having invisible people speaking to her. She looked for a necklace, and seeing none, she frowned, for she had no idea where the woman was that spoke to her. Looking to where she thought the voice came from, she asked, "Who are you?"

"My apologies, Psyche. I did not mean to frighten you. My name is Pax."

Hearing the friendliness in her tone put Psyche immediately at ease. "Hello Pax. Are you one of my husband's servants?" she inquired.

The musical notes of laughter filled the stables, calling forth an answering smile from Psyche. The joy of Pax's laughter was contagious. "Heavens, no. Me, a servant? Don't be absurd. I am a *goddess*. This is my island, and I am its guardian and protector."

Her hair rising on the back of her neck, Psyche was momentarily distracted from her fear by Pax claiming of the island. "What do you mean, you are the guardian of the island? I thought the island belonged to my husband."

Pax laughed kindly. "Men. I let him *think* he rules the island, but that will be our little secret. I am in fact the goddess of the island. Your husband and I share dominion over it. Though truth be told, it has been a while since he spent any significant time here in recent years. It is good to see him back."

Turning fully to where the voice was coming from, Psyche felt terror at being in the presence of a goddess, and she braced herself. Knowing the capricious nature of the gods, she was on the alert to any change in Pax's demeanor. The threat of Aphrodite still fresh in her mind, Psyche had no way of knowing if this Pax was a friend of Aphrodite sent to harm her further, or if not, perhaps she would try to harm her anyway to curry favor with the vengeful goddess.

Psyche was well aware of the scheming side of the female gender, and she could not chance another goddess aiming to harm her.

Seeing the blood drain from Psyche's face as fear filled her, Pax cursed. She had forgotten how it was a goddess' envy that had brought her to the island. "Be at ease, Psyche. I mean for us to be friends. I would never knowingly harm you. I swear by the River Styx that all I say is true."

Psyche's eyes went wide. For Pax to swear by the River Styx was an unbreakable oath. That she would so easily give such a vow spoke volumes of her sincerity. Finally relaxing, Psyche thought over her offer. "I would like a friend," she said wistfully.

Reaching out to grasp her hands, Pax laughed. "Good. Now that that is settled, let us get to know one another."

"Well, since you are not a servant, is it possible that I may see you? It is so strange to speak to invisible people."

Pax kept her grip on Psyche's hands as she thought over her request. She could not be sure that Psyche would recognize her once she saw her, which would go against the vow she had given Eros concerning their shared history. She was about to deny her request, but the haunting loneliness in

Psyche's eyes tugged at her, causing her to change her mind. She would reveal herself—at least enough of herself that a mortal could handle. Eros would just have to deal with it; besides, it was not as if he had forbidden Pax from allowing Psyche to see her. "Alright, but I can only show you a shadow of my true self. A mortal cannot look upon the true form of the gods without causing death," she warned.

"I understand. Thank you, Pax."

The space in front of Psyche shimmered and swirled. It was as if a shade from the realm of Hades was slowly being made into flesh and bone before her eyes. Slowly, a woman came into sight before her.

Having never seen a goddess in real life, Psyche felt sure that even among the gods, Pax was a unique and extraordinary being. Honey-gold locks of hair fell like a waterfall down her back. They were shiny and full of waves, like the sea. She was dressed in a scandalously short chiton of deep green that left most of her legs bare. The color of her dress brought out and complimented the color of her eyes, a dark forest green, and they crinkled in humor that looked out of a pale face. If ever Psyche were to meet an Amazon, she was sure they would look exactly as Pax did, for even with her stunning beauty, the stamp of a warrior was clear to see on her face.

Smiling broadly, Pax asked, "There now. Is that better?"

Nodding her head in agreement and looking over Pax again, Psyche felt a familiar tug. A wisp of a memory teased at the edges of her consciousness. Before she could pursue it, the stallion neighed, trying to draw their attention back to him. He had a pathetically pleading look in its eyes as he tried to reach the apples that lay scattered on the floor. Laughing, Psyche and Pax shared a look, then they both reached down to pick up an apple. They spent the next few minutes quietly feeding and petting the stallion, who ate almost half of the apples that Psyche had brought with her to the stables before he was satisfied. "Well, greedy one, you certainly were hungry," laughed Psyche.

"Yes, he seems more like a member of the pig family then a member of the equine one," Pax snickered. The stallion snorted at her, as if it understood the insult Pax had leveled at him.

"Well," mused Psyche, "he does need a name. Maybe 'Piglet' would be a good one if he hasn't already been given one."

"He hasn't chosen a name yet, but I like Piglet." Turning to face the horse, Pax said to him, "Well, does Piglet sound like a good name for you?"

Shaking his head in apparent disgust, the stallion turned up his nose at Pax and leaned against Psyche instead, seeking a scratch behind the ears. Obliging him, Psyche thought over other names that would suit the stallion, discarding one after the other until only one remained. "Fury."

"Fury? He does have a temper. I suppose it does suit him, though I still like Piglet."

Smiling, Psyche pulled back to look into the stallion's eyes, the intelligence there undeniable. "Well. What do you think? Do you like the name Fury?" She smiled as the stallion nodded its head in agreement. "Then Fury it is."

Clapping her hands together, Pax looked over at Psyche and Fury, an idea coming to her that she was sure would help build the foundations to their budding friendship. "Now that we have that settled, how about I show you around? We can take our new friend here; nothing compares to seeing my island on horseback."

Stunned, Psyche turned around to look at Pax. "I don't know how to ride. It is not considered proper behavior for a woman to ride."

"Then it's a good thing that you no longer have to listen to such stupid rules. I'll teach you how to ride, and before you know it, you will be riding like an Amazon."

Walking over to the stall door, Pax opened it and stepped back, allowing Fury out, a saddle and bridle suddenly appearing on him. Grabbing hold of the bridle and looking directly into the stallion's eyes, Pax demanded, "Now you be a good boy and help me teach Psyche how to ride." Fury nodded his head as if in agreement.

Casting a critical eye over Psyche's attire, Pax waved her hand, and Psyche's gown shortened to match Pax's gown. "That's better."

Embarrassed, Psyche tried in vain to pull down the helm of her gown. The sudden exposure of her legs from the scandalously short gown was unnerving. "I don't think this is a good idea. I don't think that my husband Phanes would approve of any of this."

Concerned at the fear she heard in Psyche's voice, Pax had to stop the immediate protest that almost left her lips. The idea that Eros would harm Psyche—or any woman for that matter—was repugnant to her, but Psyche would not know that. "I promise you, Phanes will not be angry with you. He would not have left the horses here if he did not want you to ride them."

Pax kept her expression sincere as she lied through her teeth. Psyche did not need to know that the horses on the island were immortal, or that Eros would spill the blood of said beasts if Psyche came to any harm.

Psyche needed to break free of the hold her upbringing had on her, for all their sakes.

Psyche looked longingly at Fury. She had always loved horses, and had yearned to learn how to ride them. To have a secret desire that she thought had been an impossible dream only a few days ago suddenly become a reality was almost too much to comprehend. As if understanding her indecision, Fury stepped up to her side and nudged her toward the saddle. Psyche suddenly came to a decision. "It seems that I am going to learn how to ride after all."

CHAPTER 18

Pax and Psyche returned to the stables just before sunset. The day had flown by. Learning how to ride and then spending time exploring the island had been a thrilling adventure. After settling the horses back in the stables, they spent time grooming the horses and settling them down for the evening, making sure they had plenty of food—and apples—before leaving.

"I must be off. I truly enjoyed spending the day with you; it has been ages since I had such a wonderful day."

Smiling and nodding her head in agreement, Psyche inquired, "Will I see you again soon?"

"You may count on it," Pax replied, and then she disappeared before Psyche's eyes, and she was left alone.

She made her way back up the path from the stables, torches lighting the way. She had spent the day riding Fury around the island with Pax, seeing all that the island had to offer. After Pax spent an hour teaching Psyche the basics of riding, Pax had then gotten her own horse and they had spent a very fun day together. Smiling over some of the outrageous comments Pax had made throughout the day,

Psyche chuckled to herself. She liked Pax and was happy to finally have a friend.

Lost in her thoughts, she was unaware of the passage of time. Suddenly the lights from the torches went out, leaving her in complete darkness. The moon was also hiding behind the clouds on this night. Startled, she stumbled and would have fallen, but she was caught from behind.

"Easy there, Psyche. I don't want you to hurt yourself."

The sound of her husband's voice sent a shiver down her spine before he swept her up into his arms. He kissed her ravenously, leaving her breathless and clinging to him. Snapping his wings out, he then rose into the air, never breaking their kiss.

Wrapping her arms tightly around him when she felt them leave the ground, Psyche finally broke their kiss. "Don't be afraid, I promise I won't drop you," Eros assured her.

As the clouds drifted pass the moon, he made himself invisible. Psyche looked at him, and seeing nothing, clutched him tighter in fear. He thought to distract her from her fright until his eyes traveled over her body, and seeing her fully for the first time, he growled, "What are you wearing?"

Psyche ducked her head. She had forgotten how short her gown was after spending the day with Pax. Since Pax had worn an identical gown, it had gradually become natural to wear such a revealing outfit. Psyche had forgotten about it as the day had progressed, but hearing her husband's question brought back how bare she really was in it. Shame filled her. Feeling exposed, she went to tug the gown down in a vain attempt to cover her legs.

"Stop."

Freezing at the command, Psyche waited fearfully in anticipation of the scolding she was sure to receive from her husband for her scandalous outfit.

"Where did you get that gown?"

"I went riding with Pax, and my gown was too long, so she changed it so that she could teach me how to ride." Psyche rushed through her explanation, but stopped when she felt him tense up. She could feel the anger radiating off him.

"Do you mean to tell me that you went riding on one of the horses of the island?" he demanded, fear for her safety gripping him, making him speak more harshly then he meant to. "Which horse did you ride?"

She took a steadying breath. "I rode Fury."

"Fury?" Eros asked.

"The stallion in the stable. We didn't know his name, so we came up with one. I don't know if he already has a name," she explained nervously.

Terror gripped him. The stallion that she spoke of was a demon on four legs with a vicious temper. The thought of her being anywhere near such a beast sent him into a blinding rage. It made him struggle with his inner drakon; it was ready to kill any threat to her. She could have been maimed, or worse. Her fragile human form could so easily be destroyed. He had just found her; he did not intend to lose her again. Her soul lost to wander. After the fight he'd had with Anteros over her, his protective instincts were in overdrive. The need to destroy any threats to her safety rode him hard.

"PAX! What in blazes were you thinking? You let her ride Arion's colt? She could have been killed," he snarled, using their mind link so Psyche would not be privy to their argument.

"As if I would ever allow her to be harmed. She is not as fragile and powerless as you would like to believe," Pax sniffed in disdain. *"She already had the stallion well under control when I arrived. She has power, and she uses it without any conscious thought. She had him eating out of the palm of her hand within minutes."*

"That is besides the point. She is mortal, easily killed by that beast. What were you thinking?"

"I was thinking she wanted to go riding, so I taught her. You did say she had the run of the island, didn't you?" Pax reminded him. *"Now stop being an ass and reassure her that she has done nothing wrong. I can feel her fear, and I don't like it."*

Pax abruptly broke off, leaving Eros snarling in frustration. Turning his attention back to Psyche, he eased his hold on her, not wanting to bruise her. Eying her pale face, he took a deep breath, pushing his terror to the side. "I'm not angry at you. I simply fear for your safety. Why did you go to the stables, Psyche? Do you even know how to ride? Tell me the truth."

"I have always loved horses. I used to go to the stables and feed them when I could. I swear to you, I only went to feed them some apples. But then…well, I met Pax. Please don't be mad at her. She offered to be my friend and to teach me how to ride. No one has ever offered to teach me, but it was my decision to learn. So please, don't be angry at her. I deserve your anger, not her."

Hovering over the ground, Eros could hear the longing in her voice when she spoke about Pax, and the horses. It made it very clear what her life had been like before her arrival on the island. Along with the fear for her safety, pride filled him as she defended her new friend. That she was willing to face her fear and suffer his judgment filled him with joy. She deserved to have anything that made her happy, and he was determined to give her anything she asked for, within reason.

With that thought came an unexpected pang of jealousy. He was envious of the time she had spent with Pax. Desire to have Psyche all to himself, to not share her affection with anyone else, was a hard knot in his gut. He wanted to be the one to teach her new things, to guide her and watch her grow and spread her wings. To be everything and anything for her. It was irrational, and he knew it. The limited time he could spend with her was already grating on his nerves. Pushing aside his jealousy, he asked, "So did you enjoy riding...Fury, was it?"

Nodding shyly, she whispered, "I did, very much so."

"Then I will get you a proper mount. One that is more suited to a young woman. That horse is too dangerous for you."

Psyche stiffened.

He was shocked at the wounded pride that flittered across her face before she lowered her eyes. He had insulted her, he realized with a start. He tried to think of a way to make her understand. She was too precious, too fragile, too mortal. He —who had never had to explain himself and his actions to anyone—had found himself struggling with the need to explain himself to his wife. The thought that he had unintentionally hurt her was unacceptable to him.

However, she surprised him by speaking first.

"I'm sure you know what is best, my lord," she said stiffly. "Though I would point out that I spent the entire day riding Fury without any mishap. He was perfectly well behaved."

"You were also with Pax, who would have prevented any harm from coming to you, and who most likely kept that beast under control," he pointed out.

"Then I'm sure she would vouch for me when I say that was not the case. I was feeding him an apple when Pax first arrived, so he was already behaving himself," she countered back.

The terse tone she used on him should have stroked his temper, not his lust. He found it perversely arousing when she took him to task over whatever had set her temper on edge. The predator that shared his body moved closer to the surface, enjoying being in her presence and silently laughing at the thought of her taking them both to task over their protective nature.Needing to stay in control, Eros lowered them back to the ground. Setting her down on her feet, he started walking them back to the stable. His desire to make her happy warred with his need to keep her safe. Unfortunately, the only way to do both was to put her to a test. He did not like the idea of placing her in a position where she could fail, but he saw no other option.

"Well then, let us see how well you control this animal. If I think that you will be in no danger, I will allow you to continue to ride him. But know this: If I feel like you could lose control of him at any moment, I will get rid of him and all the others before I will allow you to be harmed. Do I make myself clear?"

Shuddering in fear at the warning in his voice, Psyche stopped and turned to him. "Please, do not hurt them. I would rather never go near them again than chance having you destroy them on my account."

Eros stopped and gathered her into his arms, tilting her face up to his. Even though she could not see him, he wanted her full attention to be on him and his words. He also desperately wanted her to *know* him, to *trust* him. "Destroy them? Psyche, you misunderstood me. I would never harm an innocent creature. I did not mean that I would hurt the horses, only that I would remove them from the island. They are immortal and dangerous. I only want you to be safe. They could easily maim or kill you."

Psyche heard the truth of his words. She could also hear the pain behind them. The idea that she had somehow hurt him troubled her. She did not like knowing that she had caused another pain, especially her husband, who had shown her nothing but kindness.

Her feelings for him were just in their infancy, but she already felt the beginnings of affection for him. When she was not afraid, she did not feel the need to hide her true personality from him, as she had had to do when she lived with her family. She could be herself with him, not the shadow that she presented to the world. He seemed to like the fact that she had a temper and was willing to stand up to him.

Sliding her hand up his chest until she cupped his cheek, she stroked it gently. His body trembled slightly at her touch, and he turned his face into her hand as he pressed into her caress. He seemed just as starved for affection as she was, she realized with a start.

"I'm sorry, Phanes. I did not mean to hurt you," she murmured softly.

Kissing her palm, he drew her closer. "The only way you could hurt me is if you reject me. As long as you are willing to talk to me, we can overcome anything."

He tenderly held her to him. Laying his head on top of hers, he closed his eyes, enjoying just being in her presence. The peacefulness of the moment seeped into him, giving him a measure of tranquility that he had not felt in centuries.

Slowly drawing back, he said, "Now, my lady, let me see how you handle the other beast you tamed."

"Other beast? What beast did I tame besides Fury?"

"Me."

Laughing, Psyche shook her head at him. "I am not sure you *are* tame, my lord. You seem too headstrong to ever be considered such. "

"Oh, I wouldn't know about that. Wave the right incentive in front of any male and you will have them eating out of the palm of your hand."

Tilting her head to the side, she said, "Well, Fury likes apples. What would I have to feed you?"

"You," he purred.

Shocked at his outrageous suggestion, she shook her head at him. "You are incorrigible."

Chuckling, he tucked her more securely by his side, strolling along the path back to the stables. "Only for you."

Upon reaching the entrance, Eros opened the door and lit the torches, casting a warm glow over the interior. Putting her hand on his chest, Psyche turned to stand in front of him. "Please let me go to him first. I want to prove to you that I can handle him. Will you please stay here while I go to him?"

"Alright, we will do this your way. But I warn you, any threatening move on Fury's part and I am sending him away immediately."

Relieved that he was giving her a chance to prove herself, Psyche gave into the need to thank him in some small way. She stretched up on her tiptoes, and after finding his face, kissed his cheek.

Eros lifted her up and proceeded to kiss her senseless before he set her back down and turned her in the direction of the stall that held Fury. Leaning down, he pressed a quick kiss behind her ear and murmured, "See, I told you. All I need is to feed on you. Now go on. Show me how well you have tamed another beast besides me."

Taking several breaths to ease the rapid beating of her heart, Psyche walked over to Fury's stall. Calling out softly to him, she stopped a few feet from the door and waited. Almost immediately, Fury thrust his head out and whinnied softly to her in welcome. Walking over to him, she gently scratched behind his ears while he nuzzled against her.

Whispering endearments to him, she smiled when the stallion started making the noises she had learned he made when he wanted to be fed an apple. "I'm sorry. I don't have any apples with me right now, greedy one."

Before she could finish speaking, a basketful of apples appeared next to her. Sending a grateful smile in the general direction of where she thought her husband stood, she bent down and picked one up, feeding it to Fury. "There you go. I think we need to seriously reconsider calling you Piglet," she said laughingly.

"Piglet?"

Startled at the sound of her husband's voice coming directly behind her, she turned to face him as Fury snorted at him disdainfully. "Pax and I debated on what to call him. She thought Piglet would be a good name since he devoured all the apples I had brought with me."

Chuckling, Eros inquired, "So how did you come up with the name Fury, then?"

Worried, Psyche thought over how to answer him without setting off his protective instincts.

Seeing her frown, he narrowed his gaze at the stallion. "Psyche, remember what we spoke of earlier. We need to be honest with each other; it is the only way we can build trust between us."

Knowing he spoke the truth, she still needed to warn him. "I know, but please hear me out first before you do anything rash."

"Psyche, I want to know what you obviously don't want to tell me. I will hear you out, but do not leave anything out, even if you think it will anger me."

"Alright, but please remember that Fury is quite well behaved. You can see it for yourself. I have no problem controlling him. I'm perfectly safe."

"Stop stalling and tell me."

Leaning up against Fury, Psyche recounted how the horse had charged at her and how she had slowly gotten him to accept her touch before Pax had arrived.

As Eros listened to her, he could not help his instinctive need to remove the horse from the island. His beast rose to the surface, and his eyes changed to swirling red as his beast looked out and glared at the stallion. Fury snorted and glared back, unafraid in the presence of the drakon, silently challenging him. Then Fury gently moved Psyche out of the way, surreptitiously nudging her toward the apples.

When she bent to pick up another one, she froze when she heard a low growl coming from behind her. Quickly looking around, she realized the sound had come from the direction of where Phanes stood. The hair on the back of her neck rose, and she could feel the dangerous presence of a beast. Fury snorted in challenge, his muscles straining as he prepared to launch himself, his eyes focused on where she knew Phanes stood. She realized with a start that the stallion could see her husband.

"Phanes?" she whispered.

The inhuman growl that answered her sent shivers of fear through her. Unsure of what she was facing, Psyche kept very still, trying to think of what she should do.

Thinking of her conversation with Phanes, she slowly reached toward the ground, grabbing two apples. Rising, she inched her way towards the two combatants. Placing herself between them, she whispered soothingly to the both of them. Nonsense words, anything to break the precarious standoff between the two of them.

Freezing at the sounds both of them made when she stepped between them, she took a deep breath and turned to face Fury, trusting that whatever rage had gripped her husband, he still had enough presence of mind not to hurt her. She desperately wanted to diffuse the situation, not wanting to see either one of them injure the other.

Bringing one of the apples to her mouth, she bit into it loudly, drawing the attention of both of them. Chewing slowly, she brought the other apple up. "Fury, look what I have. Come on, you know you want the apple," she murmured coaxingly.

The low growl behind her sent a shiver through her, and immediately she was drawn back, arms wrapped tightly around her. It felt like her husband's body, but her instincts were screaming at her that it was not him. It was as if something had taken possession of him. When he did nothing more than hold her, she slowly relaxed. It was a struggle, but she gradually relaxed her body into his arms, allowing more of her weight to rest against him.

Taking another bite, she offered the apple to Fury again. "Come on. Please eat the apple for me. I want us all to get along."

Fury shook his head. Slowly he took the apple from her hand, his eyes never leaving the fixed space behind her. As he worked the apple in his mouth, she felt a blast of warm air above her head before she felt the face of her husband nuzzle her hair. He drew a deep breath, as if drawing her scent in, much as the horse had done when they first met. The comparison raced through her mind, giving her the courage to slowly turn around in his arms to face him. Bringing up the apple she had bitten, she offered it up to him, silently praying for the return of her husband.

CHAPTER 19

The beast looked down at Psyche, drawn to her. Taking a deep breath, he drew in her scent, committing it to memory. He would always find her now.

Bending down, he sniffed at the apple before taking a bite. Chewing softly, he watched her take a small bite of her own before offering it up to him again. Together they shared the apple in silence, slowly eating it until only the core remained. Nipping her fingers until she let go of the apple, the beast then drew her fingers into his mouth, soothing the slight sting. Tasting her.

"Phanes?" she inquired softly.

Shaking his head, the beast let go of her fingers and growled out, "No, not Phanes."

Feeling the sudden tension and trembling that gripped Psyche at his words, the beast laid his head over hers and murmured, "No. No scared. Never hurt you."

"Who are you?"

"Yours."

Gathering her up into his arms, he took her out of the stables and into the night. Rising into the air, he flew them away from the stables and headed toward one of the sea caves that dotted the west coast of the island. Winging his way toward one of them, he landed on a small outcrop of rocks inside one with an opening in the ceiling that let the moonlight in. It danced along the seawater, creating the illusion of glittering jewels that reflected along the cavern's walls, a kaleidoscope of colors.

The beast allowed Psyche to sink down on the rocks. Once he made sure she was safely seated, he let go and jumped into the sea, transforming into his drakonian form as he hit the water. She let out a shriek as she was completely soaked by the huge splash he made. Sputtering, she swept her wet hair out of her face, desperately trying to clear her eyes of the saltwater.

Rising above her, the beast shook himself, showering her again with seawater. Then he let out a laugh as he watched her sputter and make aggravated sounds as she struggled to wipe the water out of her face and eyes. He found her outrage amusing. Lowering his head, he gently blew warm air on her to help dry her off. Once she could see, he drew back, waiting and watching.

Looking around, Psyche could make out the dim outline of the sea cave. The moonlight created a shadow play along the walls of the cave. Focusing her eyes in front of her, where the warm air had originated from, she saw the huge shape of a sea serpent rising up out of the water in front of her. Fearfully following the blue-scaled torso up, past the bat-like wings and the arms with their razor-sharp talons, she met the glowing, flame-filled eyes of the serpent.

"Hello."

Screaming in terror, Psyche shrank back, kicking her legs out as she tried to get away. As she did, the serpent bent down toward her, its mouth lined with dagger-like teeth. Saltwater splashed into the face of the serpent as she kicked back, entering his nose, causing him to draw back in a sneezing fit.

Frozen in fear, her heart pounding so hard it felt like it would tear itself from her chest, she watched the serpent sneeze for several minutes, saltwater streaming out of its nostrils.

Hopeless and fearing for her life, she prayed that her death would be quick, for here was the beast of the prophesy. Her husband truly was a beast. Tears streaming down her face, she silently screamed over and over, knowing she had no hope of escape.

The beast finally stopped sneezing. Looking down at Psyche, he smiled, which caused her to let out a whimper as she hunched into herself. Smelling the terror coming off her in waves, the beast lowered itself further until his head rested next to her.

"No. No scared. Friend."

Hearing the beast's voice in her head, Psyche feared for her sanity. Surely, her terror was making her imagine that the beast was actually speaking to her in her mind.

"I speak."

"You can hear me?" she gasped.

"Yes."

"Are you going to hurt me?"

"Never. Friends."

Psyche's eyes widened in shock. "You want to be friends?"

"Yes."

Unsure what to make of the beast, she tensed up as he moved closer to her, moving his head until he rested against her. Closing his eyes, he let out a sigh as he relaxed.

"Touch. Please."

"You want me to touch you?"

"Yes. Like Fury."

Psyche looked over at the drakon. His head was so large he could easily swallow her whole. Iridescent scales in various shades of blue and gold covered his body from snout to tail. He was crowned with a pair of wicked horns that grew out the back of his head. Huge fins topped with a sharp spike ran down the length of his body. He was truly a fearsome sight to behold.

Extending her arm slowly, she cautiously laid her hand on top of his head, near his snout. Surprised at the smooth texture of his scales, the heat radiating off of him was strangely soothing. Slowly she stroked his head, freezing when he made a rumbling noise.

"No stop. More. Please."

Stroking him again, he resumed making rumbling noises that sounded suspiciously like the purr of a cat. The sound echoed off the walls of the cave, drowning out all other sounds. Turning toward him slightly, she used both hands to pet him. When he did nothing more than close his eyes and let out a contented sigh, the terror slowly faded from her as she continued to touch him.

Eyes closed, the beast wallowed in her touch, content to let her explore him at her own pace. Turning his head, he arched his neck slightly, encouraging her to caress him further. Nothing was said between them.

Feeling the weight of Psyche gradually increasing as she rested more of her body against him, the beast opened his eyes. *"Awake?"*

"Yes, I'm awake," she murmured, as she continued to stroke him.

"Tired?"

Frowning, she shook her head, "Strangely, no."

Both lapsed into silence once more before she couldn't stop herself from asking softly, "Phanes?"

"Not Phanes. Other."

"Who are you then, if you are not Phanes? And where is he?" she asked, desperate to understand what was happening.

"Beast. Yours. Sleeping"

"I don't understand."

The beast thought for a moment on how to answer her. *"Phanes sleeping. Inside me. Share body. Me here. You mine, me yours."*

"You share my husband's body? Both of you together?"

"Yes."

"But you're a..."

"Drakon."

Mulling over his answers, Psyche thought over his other revelations. "And what am I to you, then?"

"Mine. Mate. Protect you. Kill for you."

Horrified, Psyche drew back from the beast. "Mate? How is that even possible? We can't be mates. I'm human, and you're a drakon."

"Yes, mates. Share Phanes body," he hissed in pain at her rejection of him. Agitated, the beast pulled back to look at her.

Shrinking back, Psyche cursed herself for angering him. Trying to remain calm, she tried to reason with him. "But aren't there any female drakons? Surely you must want someone of your own species?"

"Want no other. Want you. Both of us mated to you. You mated to us."

Seeing the rejection on her face, the beast let out a piercing howl of pain, causing Psyche to cover her ears. Hunching over to protect herself, she waited for him to strike her down. Long moments passed. When nothing happened, she cautiously looked up, meeting the eyes of the beast. Sucking in a breath, she was shocked at the gut-wrenching pain in them, his head hanging down in defeat.

Then she felt the snap of a connection form between

them, and all his emotions poured down through it, straight into her. She was unprepared for the storm of his feelings. His pain reached out to her, and it felt as if it were her own. A stab so sharp it felt like her heart was being torn from her chest drove her to her knees, leaving her clutching at her chest, tears streaming down her face. Unimaginable loneliness, fear, and pain—all his emotions—poured into her mind. How could one being exist with so much sorrow and despair bottled up inside and still live was beyond her understanding. It tore through her, threatening to drown her. It nearly drove her mad. Then, abruptly, it stopped, and she was left gasping, trying to catch her breath.

She felt sick. Her stomach rebelling, she leaned over to retch, until nothing remained. Wiping her mouth with the back of her hand, she looked the beast in the eyes.

He shrunk back from her. *"Never hurt you. Send you back. Will leave."*

Turning away, he was about to send her back to the palace when he felt her scramble up and reach out, grabbing hold of his wing.

"Wait. Please don't go. I'm sorry. I didn't mean to hurt you."

The beast shook his head. *"Will leave. Never bother you again."*

Psyche clutched his wing harder. "No. Please. Stay. I want..."

"What?"

"I want...no...*need* you to stay. Please," she begged.

The beast stayed absolutely still, neither rejecting nor accepting her request. Waiting for her to finish what she had to say. Needing her to accept him.

"I...can we not get to know each other first? Please? Like I am getting to know Phanes? So many things have happened so fast, and I need time. Can we not take it slowly? I'm not rejecting you."

Closing his eyes to the pain in her voice, he lowered his head until it was level with her. Stumbling forward, she wrapped her arms around him, clutching him tightly, and crying softly.

"No cry. Please. Will not leave. Give you time. Promise."

Whispering "sorry" and "thank you," she slowly calmed down. Pulling back, she locked eyes with the beast. "What is your name?"

"Name?"

"Yes, your name. Shouldn't I know your name? You know mine, don't you?"

"Yes. Psyche. Mine."

"Yes, so what do I call you?"

"Yours."

She chuckled. "Alright, but what other name should I call you besides 'mine'?"

His eyes laughed in wicked delight. *"Eros."*

A startled laugh broke from her lips. "The god of Love? You want to be called by the god of Love's name? Seriously?"

"Yes."

Psyche shook her head. "Alright. It's settled, then. Eros it is."

Suddenly feeling weak from all the day's events, Psyche sat back down on the rock shelf, her stomach rumbling. Now that her nausea had subsided, she ached with a gnawing feeling of emptiness. Clutching her stomach, she looked up at the beast.

"Hungry?"

Grimacing, she tried to remember when she had last eaten. "I'm not sure. I haven't had anything since this morning. I don't feel quite well."

Bending down, the beast needed to make sure she was

alright, not liking the idea that she was unwell. He sent some of his powers through her, settling her stomach and removing all evidence of her being sick. Satisfied that she was not hurt, only ill from the stress of the night's events and hunger, he pulled back. Sliding slightly past her, Eros presented his wing to her so that she could climb onto his back, a saddle suddenly appearing between his wings. *"Feed you. Get on."*

Looking at the saddle, she asked incredulously, "You want me to ride you?"

"Yes. Safe."

Secretly delighted, Psyche climbed onto his wing and made her way to the saddle. She was startled when she felt straps tie her down to it.

"Safe. No fall. Hold on."

Then he launched into the air, grinning at her delighted laugh. Winging his way out of the cave, he took to the sky.

Rising higher into the sultry night, the wind gently blowing, Eros carried Psyche out over the water. The light from the full moon fell along the sea, creating a water dance. The flickering backlight of the stars added even more dancers.

Closing her eyes and lifting her face up to the moonlight, the wind blowing through her hair, Psyche let out a sigh of pleasure. The undulating motion of their flight was reminiscent of the gentle swell of a boat on the sea.

"Play?"

Pulled out of her musings, she opened her eyes and lowered her head. "Play? What do you mean?" she asked suspiciously.

He smiled at her tone. *"Play. Fun."*

Frowning, she asked, "What kind of fun?

"Surprise. Fun. Promise."

Smiling at his teasing tone, Psyche could not help but be

intrigued at discovering what his idea of fun truly was. It seemed both Phanes and Eros liked to play games. "Alright."

As soon as the words left her mouth, he made a sharp turn, taking them out over the sea. Spying a school of dolphins, Eros dove down until he was alongside them, racing with them. The dolphins were leaping into the air, and their grey bodies looked like shadows against the sea. Tucking his wings in against his body, Eros made a quick twisting motion that turned them upside down before snapping his wings out again.

Crying out in joy, Psyche looked down, and reaching out, her fingers barely skimmed the water. One of the dolphins leapt out right between her outstretched hands. Her palms slid down the length of the dolphin's body before it reentered the water. She was in awe. She loved the feel of the dolphin's smooth skin running through her hand. It was so much fun, she found herself laughing so hard it hurt. Before she could become lightheaded from being upside down for so long, Eros made a slithering motion that turned them right side up.

They followed the school of dolphins for several miles before they moved on.

Eros and Psyche continued flying over the water. Banking left, he turned them around and headed back toward the island, but before they reached it, he suddenly shot upward, climbing high into the scattered night clouds until they were enveloped by them. Creating a shield to keep prying eyes from spying on them, they left the protection zone that covered the islands that made up his family's home. Then he sent a cocoon of warm air to circle Psyche, keeping her warm in the cold. Rising even further, Eros flew over the clouds, skimming them as he had the sea below.

Psyche leaned forward, the better to look out over the night sky. At this height, the moon was so much larger in appearance; it looked like a glowing orb sailing through the sky.

"Fun?"

Laughing in delight, she said, "Yes, this is *so* much fun!"

"Hold on."

With that warning, Eros arched up as he came to an abrupt stop. Hovering in midair, in a slithering motion, he pointed himself toward the sea, and tucking in his wings, dived toward it in a straight line.

Screaming as the sea raced up toward them, Psyche was sure they were about to crash to their deaths. Right before they would have hit, however, Eros snapped his wings out and arched upward, forcing them up into the sky. Using the speed of their quick descent, he made a sharp turn to the right. Flapping his wings, he then increased their speed, racing over the sea.

Heart pounding, knuckles white from their tight grip on the saddle that had increased in size until it encircled her high up to her waist before their dramatic drop, she let out a shaky breath. Excitement coursed through her veins. She loved the thrill of their ride.

"Can we do that again?"

CHAPTER 20

Landing in the field next to the orchard, Psyche carefully got out of the saddle and hopped to the ground. She took a few steps away from Eros before she slid down, lying on the soft grass. Spreading out her arms and legs like a starfish, she gazed up at the sky, enjoying the quiet of the evening after the exhilarating ride over the sea.

Eros settled down next to her. They lay there, in companionable silence, gazing at the stars and letting the peacefulness of the night seep into their consciousness. The sound of their breathing and heartbeats lulled her into a light slumber. She drifted in and out of sleep, waking when she heard a loud rumble.

Slowly opening her eyes, she turned her head and glanced over at Eros. Hearing a slight rumble again, a small smile curved her lips, for this time the rumble came from her.

"Hungry. You?"

"Yes, I'm hungry."

In an instant, several torches appeared a short distance away, surrounding several tables heavily laden with a huge feast. A soft breeze brought the aroma of the food to her, making her mouth water. She got to her feet and hurried over, Eros following her. Watching him out of the corner of her eye, she marveled at how graceful his movements were, with such long front and hind legs. His serpentine body was as graceful on land as it was in the sea and in the air.

Reaching the table, she looked over the vast amount of food. There was easily enough food to feed the entire hoplite army of her home city-state. She pulled out the lone chair and sat down.

"Eat."

Looking over the various foods, Psyche made her selections. Placing the food on her plate, she was about to dig in when she realized that Eros had made no move to eat. Looking up at him, she was entranced by the intensity of his unblinking stare, and it left her fidgeting in her seat. "Why are you looking at me like that?"

"Pretty. Proud."

Ducking her head, she fiddled with her drink, not liking the reminder of her cursed beauty. She loathed her looks, hating the effect they had on others, and how it made her an outcast. She was sick of no one seeing her, of no one ever really knowing who she *really* was.

"Psyche. Why sad?"

Plastering a smile on her face that did not reach her eyes, she looked up at Eros, refusing to meet his gaze. "It's nothing. My, this is a lot of food. I hope you are planning on eating most of this, for I surely cannot. I would hate to see it all go to waste."

"Hurting. Why?"

Not wanting to admit what was bothering her, she tried to distract him. "Don't mind me. We should eat before the food gets cold."

"Stop. Tell me. Truth."

Freezing at the hard tone in his voice, she sat back, trying to come up with something to say without revealing what was truly bothering her. She had no desire to ruin the moment. Eros must have seen something in her face though, because he leaned over, looked directly into her eyes, and commanded, *"Tell truth."*

Sighing, she was unable to keep the hurt out of her voice. "Is that why you both want me? Because of the way I look?"

The beast drew back, hating the pain in her voice. *"No. Pretty inside."*

"I don't understand," she said, puzzled. "What do you mean?"

"Loving. Kind."

"How can you possibly know that? Neither one of you really know me. It has not even been a week since we all met."

"Saw it. Before. Loving to parents. Kind to animals."

"You saw me before you met me?"

"Yes. Loving. Kind," he reiterated.

Shaking her head, she was about to question him further, but he shook his head. *"Watch."*

Turning her head toward where he indicated, she saw a large kylix filled with wine. She watched as scenes from the last few weeks of her life prior to the wedding played out in the reflection of the wine.

Psyche watched in awe as scene after scene played out before her eyes. In one she could be seen comforting her parents after receiving the news from the Pythia. She watched as she dried her mother's eyes, assuring her that everything would be alright.

In another, she was sitting with her father in the garden. She held his hand as he struggled to contain his anger and despair over her fate.

The next scene was of her in the garden, helping several of the servants prepare it for new plants. Creating a space for her parents to go to so they could find some peace and comfort. Feeding the house cat several bites of her meal.

Various images appeared of her feeding and caring for the animals of the palace: bringing treats to the horses, petting and cuddling the cats and dogs.

Her at the temple giving out her belongings before her wedding. She watched as she knelt down to speak quietly to a crying child, giving the little girl the doll that had been her favorite toy as a child herself. She watched as the child clutched it to her chest, a small smile on her face as the toddler reached to softly touch her cheek in thanks before turning back to her mother.

She watched as he showed her hiding little notes throughout the palace for her parents to find and read after she was gone: letters expressing her love for them and her desire that they not grieve for her, but instead, to remember all the good times. Her sending letters to her sisters, as well.

"Brave. Stubborn."

Then the images suddenly switched to her arrival on the island. Her various attempts to escape the island played out before her: pleading with Zephyrus to take her away; rowing the boat out; attempting to swim to the next island; and lastly, trying to take her own life.

She watched as she learned how to ride Fury. Never giving up until she had the basics.

She watched herself standing up to Phanes, trying to diffuse the situation between Fury and her husband in the barn.

"Temper."

She saw herself lashing out at the malicious bystanders on her wedding day. Taking her invisible husband to task on their wedding night, and as they played their game of copycat.

"Lonely. Sad."

She saw the night of the feast. The shattered look in her eye as the night progressed. Her in the garden afterwards, pouring her heart out to the little butterfly. Every image shown was of her always set apart from others, there but never a true participant.

"Fun."

She watched their ride throughout the night. Their wild antics in the air as they played. She saw how she slowly opened up to Pax, finally sharing in her humor and shyly joking with her, causing her to laugh hysterically at something she said.

"Sensual."

Blushing, she watched as images of their intimate moments played before her, always with her husband invisible to the naked eye.

"We see you. Know you."

As the cup went back to simply holding wine, Psyche lifted her head to gaze at the beast, a lone tear sliding down her face.

Bending down, Eros gently nuzzled against her. She clutched him to her, holding on to him as if her life depended on it. For several long minutes, they sat there in silence, the only discernable sound their heartbeats.

Finally pulling back, Psyche was about to say something when a loud rumble filled the air. Laughing, she looked up at Eros.

"I think we should eat."

"Better?"

Her heart was filled with happiness and the beginnings of what could be love in her heart, so she could honestly say, "Yes, much better. Thank you."

CHAPTER 21

With dawn barely on the horizon, Eros woke with a start. Blinking rapidly, he was at first confused, for he was not in his bedroom. Shifting slightly, he realized he was in his drakon form in the middle of a field. Alarmed, he began to lift himself up when he felt a slight form pressed up against his side. Lifting his wing, he was shocked to see Psyche.

Terrified by how still she was, he quickly shifted back. Fragments of memories from last night came rushing back to him, and as he rolled her over, he prayed that he had not hurt her. He ran his hands over her, looking for any injuries. Seeing none, he was about to use his powers when he heard a soft sound.

Staying perfectly still, he heard it again. She was snoring. Dumfounded, he could only stare at her as she continued to snore softly. Sitting back on his hunches, he was relieved to see that she was safe, and apparently enjoying a good dream if the small smile that curved her lips was any indication.

Exhaling the breath that he had been holding, he tried to piece together the events of the previous evening. The last thing he remembered clearly was being with Psyche in the barn. Then his beast had risen and taken hold of his conscious mind, wrestling control from him.

What happened last night? he demanded. His drakon was sleepy, lazy in his slumber. The contentment coming from him was so unusual that it gave Eros pause.

"Had fun."

Images flooded through his mind like a play. Scene after scene of Psyche and her various reactions to the drakon set his teeth on edge. Her fear tore at him, and seeing the physical effect on her when their minds connected for a brief moment made him clench his fists. He could hardly stomach the fear and pain it had caused her; the weight of his emotions too much for her to bear.

He was about to call a stop to it but his attention was caught by how she treated the drakon after getting over her initial shock. He watched in awe at her courage when she reasoned with his beast, at the acceptance she gave them, and at how she loved the drakon's idea of fun. He couldn't help but smile when she asked if they could do the freefall again. She was beautiful in her delight.

"Eros! What in Tartarus' name are you doing?"

Swinging around to face Anteros, he asked, "What are you doing here?"

"What am I doing here? You are sleeping out in the open in your drakon form with Helios almost upon you, and you dare ask me that?"

Ignoring his brother, Eros picked Psyche up from the ground. Cradling her against his chest, he was glad to see that she still slept deeply. Spreading his wings, he rose into the air and headed back toward their bedchamber. Anteros followed closely behind.

Landing on the balcony, Eros walked to their bed and gently lowered her into it. Tucking her in, he smoothed back her hair from her face and placed a kiss on her forehead. He chuckled as she continued to snore softly. He would have to remember to tease her about that.

Straightening, he motioned for his brother to follow him out. He was halfway across the room when he realized that Anteros was not following him. Looking back, he saw him standing beside Psyche, an indecipherable look on his face as he gazed down at her.

"Anteros," hissed Eros menacingly. "What are you doing?"

He answered without taking his gaze from Psyche. "She is not as I remember. I can see what you mean when you say she is everything and nothing as she once was. How did she handle your drakon?"

Returning to stand beside Anteros, Eros joined his brother and they both watched Psyche as she slept. Eros thought she was adorable as she continued to snore softly, oblivious to the two of them speaking in hushed tones right next to her.

"I have no words. She was terrified of him at first, but after they briefly connected, she was so accepting and loving. My drakon loves her and views her as his mate. I have no fear that he will reject her, quite the opposite."

Anteros mulled over his words. "She still needs to accept both sides of you and commit fully to both of you. None of us are as we once were. Can she handle that?"

Eros took his time choosing his words before responding, because he was painfully aware of the demons that tormented his brother. Eros was not offended by the doubt in Anteros' voice, knowing the dual meaning behind his question. "I believe so. She is proving to be much stronger than I first thought. I know it will not be easy, but then again, nothing of value ever is."

"You need to be more careful. We were lucky that you woke before you were discovered, but it cannot happen again, Eros. For all our sakes.' Mistakes such as that one cannot become a habit."

"I know."

"Now, we need to talk about some of the issues that have come up since you have been spending so much time here on the island."

Nodding, Eros motioned for his brother to follow him. We can discuss this over breakfast."

With one last look at Psyche, they both left the room. Closing the door behind him, Eros sauntered toward the great hall, where the servants had left a feast for them.

"I will say this, your bride still has the most delicate snore that I have ever heard coming from a female. At least that has not changed," Anteros stated with a smirk.

CHAPTER 22

After discovering a major secret about her husband the previous night, Psyche needed time to wrap her mind around the reality of Phanes' duel nature. Gardening had always been her solace, and now the ordinariness of physical labor helped to ground her.

She headed out to the garden that encircled the farthest building away from the main palace. It was the smallest, and from the unkempt state of it, the most neglected section of the gardens. It looked lost and abandoned, a sad little patch, and she decided it would be the first site she would start putting her touch on the island.

Setting her basket with the tools she needed on the ground, she looked around the enclosure, surveying and cataloguing in her mind what needed to be done, and what she ultimately wanted the garden to look like.

In the center of the small garden was a tholos, a circular temple with Doric columns creating a colonnade surrounding an inner chamber. It was almost completely hidden, covered in vines that clung to it. She could not see anything about the state of the building, whether it was in need of repair or not, just that it was of a fairly decent size. She also saw a door peeking out between a small gap in the foliage. Around the base was a disheveled flower bed, overrun with weeds that had a stranglehold on the available soil. The flowers that had been there had long since disappeared.

After taking another look around and spying a sundial that stood off to one side, Psyche realized that it was already well past noon, and that she only had a few hours before nightfall. A shiver of anticipation ran through her at the thought of spending more time with her mysterious husband. She wondered what lay in store for her this evening. Shaking her head, she banished such thoughts for later, determined to start working on the garden while she still had the light.

Deciding that she would begin by freeing the tholos, she took out a sharp dagger and inspected the vines, grateful that no sharp thorns could be seen anywhere. Kneeling down, she cut the vines at the root, slowly working her way around them until they were all cut. Standing up, she grabbed a handful of the vines and began to pull them off. It took some effort; many of the vines were so tightly wrapped around the columns that she had to use the dagger to cut away the ones that were stuck. And the vines fought her, acting like guards protecting a great treasure, refusing to give up their secrets.

Sweat dripping down her face, Psyche refused to give up, however, and she fought the vines until they finally gave way, slowly coming off the columns. She did not even think to call the servants to help, determined as she was to have this time for herself.

Finally, the only ones left were the ones clinging to the lattice grille style doors. She made several precision cuts before setting aside the knife. Grabbing the plants in both hands, she pulled and tugged, loosening the vines, though they stubbornly clung to the doors. Giving one last hard tug, the vines suddenly gave way, causing her to fall onto her backside. Savoring her victory, she looked over at the freed doors of the tholos. Pushing back her hair and wiping away the sweat from her brow, she took a moment to catch her breath.

Standing up, she walked over and unlatched the door before pushing it open and stepping inside. Then she came to an abrupt halt, for what she saw took her breath away.

The setting sun flooded the interior room with light, illuminating a massive sculpture in the center of the building. It was a tragedy cast in stone. She walked around the statue, deciding that whoever the artist was, they were a genius. She was struck by the poignant pain and suffering that the mysterious artist had been able to capture in the scene before her.

In the center was a winged being; it was beautiful and terrifying at the same time. Wrapped around the androgenous figure—from one angle it was clearly a male, but from the other it was a female—was a fearsome serpent. The statue was of the two in a fierce struggle, falling to the earth. There was also a pool of water under the statue. It hovered in the air, and there were no visible ropes or anything to keep the statue suspended that she could see. Taking a closer look, she realized that the pool of water was a map. Tiny islands jutted through the water in a strangely familiar pattern. Looking back up to the faces of the statue, she was in awe and heartbroken by what she saw.

Both had expressions of agony, their pain clear as day. Circling around to get a better look, she gasped at the wound that bisected the two. It looked like a massive sword had tried to cut them in half; the sorrow and agony of the two was clearly visible in the rigid line of the two bodies as they fell. The wound itself was vicious and brutal to behold. Whoever the sculptor had been, they had captured the agony and impotent fury of the two in their defeat.

Tears running down her face, Psyche felt an answering pain in her chest, as if she too had a sword cut through her body. Though it made no sense, she wanted to gather the two to her; to protect and shelter them from their suffering. Anger flooded her veins on their behalf. Surely this was a statue of the two creatures in the last throes of death. Whoever had attacked them had meant to cause them intense pain before they died. Seeing the two of them entwined, she felt some small gratitude that they did not perish alone; that they at least had had each other in the end.

Tearing her gaze away from the heartbreaking scene, she looked around the rest of the room, trying to see if the artist had carved who— or what—had attacked the pair. The sudden desire to avenge them was a visceral need, but she could find nothing in the gloom of the tholos to indicate who had harmed them. Giving herself a mental shake, she was stunned to find herself so disturbed by her own thoughts. It made no sense that she felt that way. It was just a statue, after all.

"Horrible, isn't it?

Startled, Psyche whipped around; she had thought herself alone. "Phanes? Is that you?"

"Yes, Psyche, it's me."

She frowned at the guarded and weary tone in his voice, for it was so unlike the commanding husband she had come to know. Looking in the direction of where his voice had originated from, she waited for him to come to her as he always did. However, after several silent moments, he made no move toward her.

Taking matters into her own hands, she slowly walked in his direction, extending her hand out in front of her. Reaching him, her hand landed on his chest and she could feel the tension that gripped him. Worried that something was wrong, she moved closer and wrapped her arms around him, resting her head against his chest, right over his rapidly beating heart.

As soon as she wrapped her arms around him, it was as if he had been released from some invisible prison, and he let out a groan, fisted his hand in her hair, and wrapped his other arm tightly around her waist, crushing her to him. They stood there for several long moments, neither of them saying anything, both taking solace from the other.

Psyche gently stroked his naked back, trying to comfort him. Closing her eyes, she inhaled his familiar scent and rubbed her cheek against his chest.

Eros laid his head on top of hers and released the pent-up breath that he had been holding. "What is the matter?" she inquired softly.

Shuddering in relief that she was in his arms and not running from him in terror or disgust from his dual nature, Eros pressed a kiss to her forehead before answering. "I did not know if you would welcome me after what happened last night."

Pulling back from him, she looked up at him, even though he was invisible. "What exactly did happen last night, Phanes? One minute we were in the stable, and the next, I sensed that you were gone. I mean you were there physically, but it was not *you*. I do not know how I knew that. And then I saw the drakon. It's you, isn't it? The drakon is you. I have thought about it all day."

Feeling the tension come back into his body, Psyche pleaded with him, "Please, tell me."

"I will tell you, but not here." Gathering her up in his

arms, he walked out of the tholos and spread his wings, flying them back to the palace. Landing in the center courtyard, he gently put her down. Once he was sure she was standing, he let her go and walked over to pour two cups of wine from the table that the servants had left for them. Quickly draining his cup of wine, he refilled his before he turned and gave Psyche her cup.

She took the floating cup and took a sip of the wine. Taking a seat on the bench under the olive tree, she waited for him to speak.

"I know you must have questions. And I will explain what I can, Psyche, though there are some things I still cannot tell you as of yet."

"But—"

"Please. I swear there is a good reason why I must still keep some things from you. I swear it is for your own protection. Someday I will be free to tell you, just not today."

Hearing the stress and agitation in his voice made her back down. It was clear he was struggling with what had happened last night, just as she was. Taking a deep breath, a small spark of fear still lingered in her at his words. How many more secrets could he possibly have? "Fine. I will not press you for more than you can share. Please tell me what you can about Eros."

Spinning around to face her, he was shocked at what she had just asked. "What did you just say?" he asked in a strangled voice.

Psyche smiled ruefully. "I know. The drakon told me his name was Eros. Apparently he has a sense of humor."

Running his hand through his hair, Eros took another fortifying drink of the wine. *Sense of humor, my ass,* he thought. "The drakon. He lives inside of me. He is his own separate sentient being, though we share one body. He can manifest himself, though last night was the first time he has ever emerged without my express permission—or knowledge."

Psyche was shocked at the uncertainty that colored her husband's voice. She thought of him as all-powerful, masterful; to hear him speak so hesitantly revealed a side to him that she had not thought existed. He had a weakness after all, just as she did. She was sensitive to how her beauty influenced the way people perceived her, and therefore treated her. He had the same vulnerability as she did, she realized with a start, as his beast most definitely affected how people treated and perceived him, as well. It made her feel a certain kinship with him. Maybe their strange relationship was not so imbalanced, after all.

"So do you remember anything that happened last night?"

"Only bits and pieces. Eros…has told me his version of what happened last night. Though I would like for you to tell me what happened, as well."

He listened as she recounted the events of the previous night. He at turns became angry and incredulous as he listened to her version.

"I will not lie to you; I was terrified at first, when I saw your beast. He is truly a frightening sight, but while he definitely has a fearsome nature, he has a sweet and gentle side, as well." Smiling as she remembered their wild ride, she added, "He also likes to have fun, much as you do, my lord. I find that I quite like your beast."

"Psyche, make no mistake. He *is* extremely dangerous. Do not fool yourself into thinking he is as tame as a house cat. He could have easily hurt you," he gently admonished her.

Turning away from him, she rose and walked to stand in front of some of the flowers of the courtyard, her back to him. "I am not stupid, Phanes. I know he is dangerous, but he is still a part of you. Besides, you married me knowing that I might someday be confronted by him. Or did you plan on never telling me?"

Hearing the pain in her voice made Eros feel even more guilty then he already did. He hated hurting her, and his beast raked at him in punishment for causing her to become upset. In that, at least, they agreed. "I do not think you are stupid, Psyche. I know the razor-sharp mind that you think I do not see. It is just your nature to want to see the good in others, and that is what scares me. You could so easily be hurt."

Coming up behind her, he pulled her back against him, holding her close because he could not bear even the slightest separation from her. "How can you not be disgusted with what you have learned about me? Even the gods would be appalled and frightened that such a beast shares my body."

Psyche hesitated before answering, "I will not say that I'm not shocked; but remember, the Pythia said I was to marry a beast that even the gods fear. I thought she meant that my husband was a beast, not that he had a beast inside him. Will you tell me how you came to have him locked inside of you? Where did he come from? Will you finally tell me who and what you are, as well?"

Taking the empty cup of wine from her hand, he set it back to rest on the table. Turning her around, he cupped her face and kissed her. Nipping her lower lip, he pulled back slightly. "I cannot tell you just yet what I am, though it should not come as a shock to you to know that I am an immortal being. I *can* tell you that the drakon has been with me since my birth, though it has only been recently that he has become a true part of me. That is all I can say for now. Please do not ask me anything else tonight."

"Alright. I will not press you for more this time."

Laying his forehead against hers, he murmured, "Thank you. It has been a long day for both of us, and I think it would be best if we had something to eat, bathed, and went to bed."

"I think that is a good plan."

Eros smiled wickedly. "Good, because I definitely need your help washing my back."

CHAPTER 23

Eros and Psyche slowly strolled to the bathing chamber after dinner. Holding her hand in the crook of his arm, Eros led her through the hall until they reached the door. Pushing it open, he allowed her to enter first, and then locked the door behind them. Leaning against it, he watched as she walked over to the center bathing pool with the waterfall.

"It will be just the two of us tonight, Psyche. I have given the servants the rest of the evening to themselves. Do you wish my help with your clothing?"

"No, I should be alright."

Eros stayed quiet and shuddered in anticipation as she raised her hands to her left shoulder and began to unclasp the pins of her peplos, first one shoulder, then the other. Her gown fell to the floor, leaving her standing only in her strophion and perizoma. Tugging at the knot between her shoulder blades, she pulled the strophion off, letting out a small sigh of relief as she dropped the garment to the ground. Bringing her hands to her breasts, she cupped them and gently rubbed the skin under them that bore the marks of the strophion, soothing the slight ache.

Eros struggled to stay where he was, determined to watch Psyche while she disrobed. The sheer eroticism of her innocent act of disrobing caused him to harden painfully. Shifting slightly, he watched as his wife took off her perizoma, leaving her finally naked. Stepping away from her clothes, she made her way to the waterfall. Walking down the steps into the heated water, she went to stand under it.

Unable to stay where he was by the door any longer, Eros quickly stripped off his clothing and entered the heated pool behind her. Picking up a sea sponge infused with soap and essential oils, he gathered her hair and placed it over her shoulder, leaving her back bare to him. Running the sponge across her skin, he gently bathed her.

Before long, the simple act of bathing became a sensual exploration of Psyche's body. Feeling the now-familiar ache of desire filling her, she put her hands over his, stopping him. "Phanes?"

"Yes?"

"Can I do anything for you?"

Pausing, Eros asked, "What do you mean?"

"Well, you said you needed my help with washing your back. I want…"

"What is it you want, my little butterfly? I have said you can have anything your heart desires; all you have to do is ask and it will be yours."

Turning around until she was facing him, she said, "I want to touch you. I want to learn what gives you pleasure. Will you let me touch you, and pleasure you to my heart's content? Will you teach me?"

Eros froze at her softly spoken request, the raging desire slamming through him leaving him painfully close to spilling his seed right there and then. Never before had any of his other bedmates ever cared for learning what pleased him; they only focused on the pleasure that he could give them, never what they could provide for him in return. It had never really mattered to him one way or the other. The fact that Psyche wanted that knowledge was unbearably arousing to him, testing his control. That she desired to learn both excited and humbled him.

He forced himself to release her, since he knew if he continued to touch her, he would be unable to grant her wish, so he took a moment to get himself under rigid control. "I would love for you to learn what gives me pleasure, Psyche. I promise that I will allow you to hold the reins this night for as long as you wish."

Giving him a shy smile, she turned and lathered her hands with the soap. Taking it with her, she walked slowly with her hand outstretched in front of her, stopping when her hand landed on his chest.

"Will you please hold this for me, Phanes?"

Intrigued, he took the soap from her, holding it so that she could use it to find him in the bathing pool.

"Thank you."

"You are quite welcome. Tell me, how do you—"

Placing a finger against his lips, Psyche shook her head. "No, Phanes. You told me that my eyes do not always reveal the truth, that I would be all the stronger if I learned to use my other senses. I wish to do that tonight. Since I cannot see you with my eyes, I wish to see you with my other senses, so please, all I ask is that you do not touch me while I learn what pleases you. Do not hold back your feelings on what I do. I want to see and judge your responses for myself, so I ask that you give me your honest reactions."

Smiling against her finger, Eros gently nipped it before leaning back. "Alright, my love, we will play by your rules. I will not touch you for as long as you wish, and I will be honest in my responses."

Silently, he watched as she drew her hand down from his lips, eager to see what she had in store for them this night.

Slowly dragging her hands over his torso, exploring his heavily muscled chest. She spent a good amount of time caressing the many ropes of muscles that he sported. Eros could not hold back a soft groan as her hands brushed his nipples, and he watched as a shy smile spread across her face. "Hmm, it would seem that you are as sensitive as I am," she murmured.

Leaning forward, she ran her tongue over his nipple before gently nipping it with her teeth. Eros shuddered in painful pleasure, and he grabbed hold of the edge of the pool to prevent himself from prematurely putting an end to her fun. She repeated the same caress to his other nipple, only this time, she nipped him a little harder, causing him to growl his pleasure. "It would seem you like a little pain with your pleasure, my lord husband."

"You have no idea."

Laughing at his rueful tone, she could only guess at how much pain he was in, for he was so hard it felt like a dagger was pressed up against her.

Dragging her hands down his chest, she paused at the scar that cut across it. She traced the entire length of it, returning to it again and again. He was shocked that she was able to feel it. It was so well hidden that no one—save for Anteros—even knew of its existence and history. That she was able to feel it spoke volumes. Leaning down, she kissed it, as if to sooth away the pain of it.

Standing up, Psyche then took a step back. "Spread your wings."

Eros let go of his death grip and turned to face the edge of the pool. Spreading his wings, he took a deep, fortifying breath. "The inner part of my wings is the most sensitive."

Tilting her head, she silently regarded him. His voice had a strained quality to it, revealing that he was barely holding on to his self-control. "I can hear the strain in your voice. You are having a difficult time keeping yourself from taking back control right now, aren't you?"

"Have no fear, I will keep my word to you," he growled. The painful arousal and strain was still heavy in his voice.

Stepping to the side, Psyche quickly ducked under the water and came up behind Eros. "I want you to step forward and hold onto the edge of the pool. Do not let go until I tell you to."

A rough chuckle escaped as he complied. "You have become a demanding little thing, haven't you? Where is my shy little bride?"

Pressing herself against his back, she wrapped her arms around him before she answered in a soft, teasing tone. "She has a husband who demands that she learn to appreciate the pleasures of the flesh, and she does not wish to disappoint him."

Eros laughed roughly, for her teasing helped him to regain some control over himself. "He sounds like a very intelligent man, I would—"

Abruptly, he was unable to finish his thought when Psyche boldly pressed up against him and took a hold of his cock. She had him firmly in her hand, sending painful shards of pleasure to course throughout his body. She then compounded the pleasurable sensation by dragging her tongue across his back, between his wings. The dual pleasure left him on the verge of spending far too quickly.

Thrusting helplessly in her hand as he arched back, he was unable to catch his breath. He was devastated by her. Unable to stop himself, he closed his hand over hers, showing her how hard and rough he needed to be caressed. Letting go when she complied, he shuddered uncontrollably as pleasure ripped through his body. Letting out a roar, his body contorted in painful release. His hips thrusted wildly into her hand, and he spent his release. She wrung every bit of pleasure from him.

Sagging forward as his orgasm left him feeling surprisingly weak from languid satisfaction, Eros pressed his forehead to the edge of the pool, desperately trying to catch his breath. Little aftershocks continued to course through him.

Psyche chose that moment to slip under him. Coming up between him and the edge of the pool, she cradled his head in her hands, softly kissing and petting him until his breathing returned to normal.

Eros looked into her eyes as a lustful grin spread across her face. "My turn."

CHAPTER 24

The sun was high in the sky overlooking a deserted beach, save for Psyche and Pax racing along the shore. Psyche took the lead astride Fury, looking like a black comet leaving a trail of sand dancing through the air in her wake. Soaring through the sky, Fury barely seemed to touch the ground before he was off again, making only a soft squishing sound as his hooves crushed the soft white sand.

Coming to the end of the beach, Psyche and Fury easily made the turn and thundered back the way they came, passing Pax and the roan stallion that she rode. They easily won their impromptu race, with several lengths between them.

Psyche took a deep breath, tasting the clean salty air as she waited for Pax to join her. Her cheeks red from Fury's mane whipping them from their race, she leaned forward and gently stroked his lathered foamed neck.

"Good boy," she murmured to him.

Then she leaned back in the saddle, watching as Pax finally caught up to her. Smiling while she stroked Fury's neck, Psyche secretly laughed as she heard Pax grumble about how she must have cheated in their race across the beach.

Seeing the sour expression on her friend's face, Psyche laughed in open delight. "Really, Pax, how could I have cheated when you were the one who challenged me to a race and then got a head start on me?"

Flinging back her braid, Pax gave her a mock scowl before answering. "Well, you *are* riding one of the fastest horses in the world, so technically you *did* cheat."

Psyche leaned forward and stroked the stallion's glistening neck. "What do you say, Fury? Did we cheat?"

Shaking his head, Fury threw back his head with a snicker of disdain, leaving the women in no doubt as to his answer to that question. "Well, that settles it," Psyche said.

Pax wiped away a trickle of sweat that had made its way down the valley between her breasts, then wrinkled her nose in distaste at the oppressive heat of the day. "Well, I don't know about you, but I think a swim to cool off is in order."

Looking out over the crashing waves on the beach, Psyche could not help but remember the events of the first day of her arrival on the island. She was unsure whether the power that had prevented her from leaving the island would allow her the simple pleasure of swimming in the sea. "I think I'll just sit in the shade while you take a swim."

Pax turned to look at Psyche, a puzzled look on her face. She heard the slight hesitation and longing in her friend's voice, so her declining to join her made no sense. "What is the matter? If you do not know how to swim, we can just wade in the water. Or better yet, I can teach you."

Instead of answering right away, Psyche busied herself with dismounting and quickly taking off Fury's riding gear. Pax followed suit, and within a few moments, both horses were free of their gear and turned loose to wander along the beach to rest and cool off.

Shading her eyes as she looked out over the sea, Psyche took a deep breath as she remembered her fear and desperation the first day she had been brought to the island. "When I first arrived here, I tried to escape on this very beach. I took a small fishing boat that I found and tried to paddle out to the small island, but when I reached a certain point, it brought me right back. Then I tried to swim, and the water somehow picked me up and sent me back to shore. I was so terrified. All I heard running through my mind were the words of the Pythia over and over again: that I was fated to marry a beast that even the gods feared. I was so desperate to escape my fate that I tried to..."

Shuddering, Psyche wrapped her arms around herself, unable to continue as the terror of that day came back to haunt her.

Seeing Psyche struggling with her emotions, Pax wrapped her arms around her, holding her. "It's alright; you don't have to tell me anything more if you do not want to."

Leaning into Pax, Psyche took a few moments to compose herself. It helped that Pax was giving her time, not demanding anything of her. She was grateful for the friendship that she shared with her, something that she had never really had in her old life. "No, I want to tell you. I was so lost and terrified that I tried to take my own life. I thought being a shade was a better fate than to be married to a beast."

"By Ouranos' blood," cursed Pax. "So that is why you have been so reluctant to come back here? I am so sorry Psyche. I did not know."

Shuddering as faint traces of her fears from that day sent cold shards throughout her body, Psyche pulled out of Pax's embrace and walked several feet away from her to look out over the water. "I do not like to remember how desperate I became that day. I have no wish to harm myself, but the fear that I felt was so all-consuming that I could see no other way out."

"You do not carry that fear with you still, do you?"

Psyche shrugged, keeping her eyes on the sea and refusing to turn around. "I still have odd moments of fear and panic. It comes out of nowhere. There is no real rhyme or reason to it. I just know that I have no wish to end my life."

Concerned over the fact that Psyche was still experiencing moments of fear and panic, Pax walked up to stand next to her before gently asking, "Have you told Phanes about your fears?"

"No, what good would it do? I cannot leave the island, nor can I see my family, and I still have a goddess who wishes to punish me for an accident of birth. All of you have been wonderful to me, but I still do not truly know who or what my husband is. He shows me only bits and pieces of himself, and I have to ask myself why that is. Why all this secrecy behind his identity? No, Pax. Until I truly know him, and the threat of Aphrodite is gone, I do not think this fear will ever let go of me."

"He has his reasons for what he does. He cares deeply for you and only wants to protect you. Please believe that if nothing else."

Dropping her head forward, Psyche closed her eyes as weariness filled her. "I know that, Pax. It is just that I am confused. I feel so much for him, but I'm afraid. I have never felt so much for one person before. I live for the nights when I can be with him, and I mourn during the daylight hours when we are separated. I feel truly alive when we are together, and this strange half-life that we share...it's not enough. I want more, Pax."

They stood watching the sea, each deep in thought, the

silence stretching out between them broken only by the sound of the wind whispering over the waves.

"Then tell him how you feel, Psyche. Tell him what you need from him and he will do his best to give it to you. Tell him everything that we have spoken about. Do not make the mistake of keeping this to yourself; it will only hurt him. Be honest with him, and you may be pleasantly surprised."

Sighing, Psyche turned to look at her friend. "You think it will do any good?"

Pax met her eyes before answering. "Yes, I think this is something that needs to be addressed between the two of you, so be brave and tell him."

"Very well. I will speak to him tonight."

"Just make sure you talk to him while the both of you still have all your clothes on, or else the only talking you will be doing is screaming his name over and over again," Pax said with a knowing smirk on her face.

"Pax!"

Laughing at her shocked tone, Pax ran toward the water when Psyche tried to smack her for her impudent comment. The two of them spent the rest of the day running in and out of the waves as they splashed each other, each trying to soak the other. Laughter filled the air as they played, and they were soon joined by Fury and the roan as they waded and splashed in the water with them. It was one of the best afternoons either of them had ever had.

CHAPTER 25

Eros quickly flew his way back home, eager to spend as much time as possible with Psyche. He resented the time that he was forced to spend apart from her. The days dragged and the nights seemed to end with the blink of an eye.

Landing on the balcony outside of his bedchamber, he was disappointed to find it empty. Striding quickly through the room, he went in search of Psyche. He smiled when he heard the tinkling of the bell that belonged to Rhea. The ingenuity of his little bride never failed to bring a smile to his face. Seeing Rhea carrying a basket full of threads, he hurried to her side; surely she would know where his wife was. "Do you know where I might find Psyche?"

Surprised, Rhea turned around, almost dropping the basket full of threads. "My lord, you startled me."

Taking the basket from her, Eros was curious to see that it held more than just needles and threads. Arching a brow in question at Rhea at its contents, he adjusted the heavy basket to his side as he gestured for her to proceed to where she had been heading to before he had stopped her. "Dare I ask what these are for?"

Laughing, Rhea shook her head. "I was just bringing the basket to Psyche, my lord. She is working on a tapestry in the western sunroom."

"I gathered that was what the threads and needles were for, though I am more curious as to the other items in the basket."

Trying to hold back her laughter, Rhea could not stop herself. "Well, I have been told that the other items work well for lonely wives."

"Rhea—"

"Since you are heading to see Psyche yourself, will you be so kind as to bring her the basket while I finish some other work? Thank you so much."

Eros watched in stunned disbelief as Rhea scurried off, barely able to contain her laughter, leaving him holding the basket of questionable materials for his wife.

Shaking his head, he hurried to the western sunroom, eager to see his wife *and* to appease his curiosity.

After traveling through several corridors, he stood outside the closed door to the sunroom, making sure he was invisible. He was about to enter when he heard Psyche laughing and speaking to someone.

"Now now, what do you think you are doing, greedy one? Don't you know that pleasure is much greater when it is shared?"

Eros froze at her words.

"Stop licking me, you fiend," she said, laughing. "Ahh, *now* you want to be stroked. Well sir, you need to wait your turn. I only have two hands, and there are four of you all wanting some loving."

Seeing red, Eros narrowed his eyes in growing rage. His

beast was raking at him to kill whoever was in the room with his wife.

"Now look at what you have done! You have made little tears in my peplos. This is the third garment you have damaged pawing at me."

Temper unleashed, Eros surged through the door, ready to kill. Entering the room, he saw Psyche sprawled on the floor, lying down on several pillows. It was who she was talking to that brought him up short.

* * *

SHE WAS SLOWLY DRAGGING a piece of yarn on the floor as four tiny kittens clumsily tried to catch it. At four weeks old, they still had difficulty with their coordination skills as they crawled onto her lap while she sat on the floor, playing with them as she waited for Rhea to return. Their tiny, high-pitched cries were cute, though it did signal their desire to be fed.

Psyche let out a startled cry when the door suddenly crashed open. The kittens instinctively snuggled up to her. Protectively sheltering the kittens in her lap, Psyche looked to the doorway. Seeing nothing, she leaned forward, trying to figure out what had caused the door to suddenly open so violently. Spying the basket that Rhea was bringing on the floor, its contents spilt, Psyche hurriedly placed the kittens in their bed and stood up, sure that Rhea or one of the nymphs must have fallen and were lying on the floor injured.

"Rhea? Can you hear me? Have you fallen?"

Moving swiftly to where she believed Rhea must be lying on the ground, Psyche was unprepared for the impact of the invisible form that she ran into, causing her to fall back. Letting out a cry, her fall was cut short as she was quickly hauled back into the familiar arms of her husband. "Phanes?"

"Yes, Psyche."

Eros wrapped his arms more securely around her, preventing her from leaving his side. "Phanes, we must see who is injured. Rhea must have fallen—"

"No one is injured. It was I who opened the door and dropped the basket. It is just the two of us."

Stilling at his words, she could feel the tension that gripped his body. Concerned, Psyche brought her hand up until she cupped his face. He immediately nuzzled her hand, the tension slowly leaving his body while she petted him. She had become quite adapt at reading his moods over the past few weeks.

"What is wrong, my husband?"

Closing his eyes as she stroked him, Eros let out a sigh. "It is nothing. I'm sorry for scaring you."

The tension in his voice bothered her, and it was clear that something was not right. "Phanes, please tell me what is the matter. I can tell you are upset. Maybe I can be of some help?"

Pulling back from her touch, he said sharply, "No, there is nothing you can do."

Stunned at his harsh words, a stab of pain pierced Psyche at his rejection of her offer of help.

"My apologies, I did not mean to intrude where I am not wanted."

Pulling out of his arms, Psyche went around him to pick up the scattered items on the floor. Bending down, she tried to hide the pain that his words caused her, quickly gathering the items and placing them back in the basket. Standing, she schooled her features, walked back into the room, and kept as much distance between them as she could as she skirted around him. Then she went to the bed, holding the kittens. Kneeling down, she quickly put together the bottles that she had designed to help feed the orphaned creatures.

Filling the hollow bull's horn with a mixture of goat's milk and several other ingredients, Psyche kept the stopper on the pointed end in place as she stretched the sheep's intestine over the top and halfway down the horn, preventing the mixture from spilling out the other end. She repeated the process until all four horns were ready. Pulling a large cloth over her lap, she took one of the kittens, pulled off the stopper and replaced it with a nipple, and then began to feed the kitten its evening meal, all the time ignoring her husband.

The rustling of feathers alerted her to his approach. Sensing him at her back, she continued to ignore him while she fed the kitten. She saw out of the corner of her eye one of the horns lifting into the air. It was turned this way and that, and it was apparent that her husband was examining her invention. She was about to speak when one of the kittens was lifted from the bed. It floated in midair before it too was soon being fed.

"This is quite an ingenious device. Who taught you how to make such an item?"

She was unable to keep the bite out of her words. "No one taught me. I saw a problem and I came up with a solution. I do have some intelligence, my lord. You do not have to do that. I will finish with the kittens shortly, and then I will join you in the dining room, if it pleases you."

The little kitten finished his meal. Putting down the milk horn, Psyche picked up one of the wet rags and gently wiped down the kitten, paying careful attention to his belly and hindquarters.

After several minutes, she put him back in the bed, where he promptly curled up and fell asleep. Picking up the next kitten, she began feeding her.

"Psyche, forgive me. I hurt you, and that was not my intention. I did not mean to insult you. I know you are intelligent. It is one of the things about you that I value and treasure."

She glanced up, watching as Phanes copied her movements with wiping down the kitten. Waiting to speak until he placed the kitten on the bed and picked up the last one, she turned back to the little one in her lap. "I find that hard to believe. You hurt me on more than one level."

Eros frowned, not liking the pain in her voice, or the guilt it inspired. "What do you mean?"

She took her time before answering him, thinking over how she would respond. Sighing, she threw caution to the wind and spoke from her heart. "You say that you respect and value my intelligence, that you wish for me to grow into my strength and abilities, to shed the shackles of my upbringing, but you do not always act as if you truly want that. I know that there are things that we cannot discuss right now, but you also shy away from speaking to me on various other matters. I know that it is normal for a married couple to live separate lives, with the wife's sole duty to provide children and take care of the home. If that is what you desire, I would rather you tell me now, and I will endeavor to fulfill my role."

When he stayed silent, she took that as her answer. Heartsick with disappointment, she drew on her years of hiding her emotions behind a wall, not willing to let him know just how much her heart bled from the pain of his rejection. He did not want her as a helpmate, just someone to warm his bed. The prospect of her future life on the island made her want to weep in despair.

Psyche concentrated on finishing feeding the kitten, wiping her down when she was done, and then placing her in the bed with her siblings. She watched as all four of them curled up together, sleeping in blissful ignorance of the tension in the room. Wishing she could be as content as the kittens, she began gathering the items to be cleaned for the next feeding time. She would have to make sure that Rhea or one of the other nymphs fed them later in the evening. She was sure her husband would be occupying her time then, having her perform the only wifely duties he seemed to truly want from her, she thought bitterly.

She was startled out of her thoughts when Phanes knelt behind her and gently—though firmly—wrapped his arms around her, preventing her from moving. He pulled her tightly against him, caging her with his body. His breath on her neck sent little shivers through her.

"My lord, if you wish to retire to the bedchamber, I will—"

"Stop."

She fell silent, waiting.

"I must be doing a piss-poor job at being a husband if you feel that I only want you to warm my bed at night, Psyche."

Closing her eyes at the strain in his voice, she kept silent, unwilling to let herself hope that she had misinterpreted his silence.

He let out a sigh as he held her. "I do not want you only for sex. If I only wanted you for that, I would have bedded you and left you. I would not have married you, or brought you to my home. I have bedded many women. I tell you this not to hurt you, but for you to understand. I have never brought them to my bed, or my home. I have always had sex in their beds, never mine. That is reserved solely for you, and no other. I want you, and no one else. Nor do I want a broodmare. If we are blessed with children, I will rejoice. If not, I will count myself blessed for I have you, and *you* are enough. You are the only woman I want or need in my life."

Trembling at the truth she heard in his voice, she could not help the doubt that refused to leave her. "Then why did you reject me when I asked you what was wrong?"

Eros paused before answering. "It was because I was ashamed of myself. I did not want you thinking less of me for what I thought when I heard you speaking before I entered the room."

Puzzled, Psyche thought back to what she had been doing prior to his arrival. Her eyes widened in shock. "You thought that I was with another man? That I was cuckolding you?"

She struggled against his hold, angry at him for thinking that she would ever cheat on him. When he refused to let her go, she elbowed him in the gut, and was satisfied when she heard his grunt of pain. "Let me go. I cannot believe you. As if I would bed another man! And where would this man come from? On an island full of nymphs? Need I remind you that you are the only male here? Hades take you!"

She spent the next few minutes cursing. Her anger was so powerful that she forgot all decorum as she let him know exactly what she thought of his misinterpretation of the situation. It took a while before she was done raking him over the coals for his stupidity.

Finally exhausted from her tirade, she slumped back against him. Phanes had refused to let her go while she had railed at him, listening to her and not interrupting. "Well? Do not just sit there. What do you have to say for yourself?"

* * *

EROS SAT IN SHOCK. He knew his bride had a temper, but by Chaos, he had no idea just how bad a temper she had! It rivaled even his own, which said much. Though if truth be told, he was perversely aroused by her anger. All that passion was an aphrodisiac to him. Struggling to get control of his body, he was tempted to settle their argument in another fashion, but judging from his little butterfly's actions, she would not welcome his amorous advances at the moment.

"I am sorry. I know that I was wrong. My fear of losing you overrode my better judgment. It will not happen again. Though in my defense, I would like to point out that the gods —particularly Zeus—have been known to disguise themselves in a variety of ways, even to taking on the form of the husband."

Psyche turned and glared at him. He found it unbearably sensual and he could not stop himself from kissing her. Ending it before it turned to something more sexual, he pressed his forehead to hers. "Forgiven?"

"It depends. How do you see our relationship progressing? Will I stand at your side, or be kept on a pedestal?"

Eros took her hand and placed it over his heart. "As my wife, Psyche. This I swear to you. I want a helpmate, not a toy."

"Very well. I will forgive you this one time. However, I would advise that you do not make a habit of misinterpreting something you hear out of context. Next time, simply ask me. Do not make assumptions," she scolded.

"Yes, dear," he said solemnly.

Unable to keep a straight face, she let out a laugh. Eros joined her, smiling in relief that she had forgiven him. His fear of losing her had almost cost him their relationship, and he would not make that mistake again. "Now, tell me about the kittens."

CHAPTER 26

Psyche turned around and settled against her husband as she looked down at the sleeping kittens. The two little boys and the two little girls were all curled up against one another. She smiled as one of the kittens made a soft little mewling sound in its sleep. "I was working out in the garden by the tholos when I heard the most pitiful cries. I found them behind some bushes. They were starving and it appeared that they had been on their own for a day or two at least. Their mother was dead a few feet away. I couldn't just leave them, for they would have died, so I brought them here."

Eros rested his head on top of hers. "No, you couldn't leave them to die," he said, pride lacing his voice. "When did you find them?"

"I found them about two weeks ago. They have gained weight and grown steadily since. At first, they slept most of the day, only waking for a few hours at a time when they needed to be fed or cleaned. They needed a lot of care, so I have kept them close as I started working on the tapestry. However, they have become more rambunctious these past few days. I find myself spending more time with them instead working on my tapestry."

Psyche looked over at the unfinished needlepoint. It was a compulsion lately to work on it, especially after having another one of her unsettling dreams where she was lost in the mists, being chased by shadow creatures. The memory of those dreams sent a shiver down her spine. She always woke in a panic from those nightmares, the fear fresh in her mind. If she could put her fears into the tapestry, however, maybe she could make sense of them and conquer her dreams.

She was glad that only the outer edges were complete, that the images that would soon be going into it were still not visible to the casual observer. She did not want her husband, Pax, or the nymphs to see it. Why she felt that way, she could not say, only that she needed to keep this to herself as she tried to make sense of her recurring dream.

"Will the kittens be alright for the rest of the evening?"

Smiling, Psyche nodded. "Everyone has taken turns taking care of them during the evening hours. They have all been so wonderful. I usually drop them off in the kitchen before you arrive, and one of the nymphs cares for them while I am with you."

"Good. Now since I was a complete ass, I would like to make it up to you. How would you like to take a small journey off the island? There is something I want to show you."

Twisting in his arms so that she could look over her shoulder at him, she could not keep the look of delighted disbelief from her face. "You want to take me off the island? Where? Will it be safe? What do you wish to show me? Should I change? Will—"

Laughing, Eros captured her lips in a kiss, cutting off her line of questions. Then he broke off the kiss before they could get carried away. "It is a surprise. And yes, you will be safe."

Flowing to his feet with her cradled in his arms, he sent out a small burst of power, gently lifting the basket of kittens into the air. It floated away from them, heading toward the kitchen, the kittens sleeping peacefully, blissfully unaware of any movement. Sending a message to Rhea to expect the kittens, he strode out of the room and toward the nearest exit.

Once they were outside, Eros made a vertical takeoff, carrying them into the night sky. He made sure that as they left the protective boundaries of the island, they were invisible to the eyes of mortals and immortals alike, Psyche's protection paramount in his mind.

"Phanes?" she asked hesitantly.

"Yes?"

"I wanted to speak to you about something important. Can we talk about it on the way to wherever you are taking me, or should I wait until we arrive at our destination?"

Eros looked down at his wife, the seriousness in her voice alerting him to the gravity of whatever the issue was that concerned her. "We have time before we reach our destination. What is it that troubles you?"

Pausing for a moment as she gathered her thoughts, Psyche took a deep breath. "I have been with you for some time now. I know I cannot leave the island without you, but I wish to see my family. I miss them. I understand the dangers, and I know you are powerful, but could you not use your powers to ensure that the gods do not find out about it?"

Tension gripped Phanes at her request, so much so that she was sure that a denial was forming on his lips, spurring her to further press her case. "Please. The pain from missing my family is slowly tearing me apart. It is as if a piece of me is missing. It haunts me. Can you not understand how that feels? Have you never been separated from a loved one?"

Eros knew that pain all too well. It was the torture he had suffered from all these eons being separated from her, yet he could not tell her that. It killed him that she was suffering because of him. He would do almost anything to spare her.

Taking a deep breath, he slowly let it out before answering her. "I understand your pain all too well. I wish with everything in me that I did not have to cause you such pain in the first place. However, I also know the pain that guilt can cause. If anything happened to the person you loved because of your actions, the pain and guilt would drive you to the brink of insanity. I would rather you never know that sorrow, for it is much worse."

Her heart breaking at the anguish in his voice, she raised her hand to his cheek, cradling his face. Pressing soft kisses along his jaw, she pressed her forehead to his. "Please, is there no way we can solve this?"

When no answer came, Psyche closed her eyes in sorrow. He would not change his mind. Trying to push back her grief, she settled against him, her head resting on his shoulder as they continued to fly. Looking out over the sky, she concentrated on the stars overhead, losing herself in their flickering beauty. They traveled for several miles in silence, the only sound the rustling of feathers as they flew over the sea.

* * *

EROS WAS LOST in thought while he mulled over Psyche's request. His first reaction was to deny her. He wanted to keep her away from any and all harm; the thought of her being exposed to the dangers of Aphrodite's wrath were still all too real. He was intimately familiar with the sadistically cruel ways that she could hurt Psyche. And the best way to hurt her was through her loved ones. He would not put it past Aphrodite to punish her family in place of Psyche. It would be the best revenge she could ever devise, if truth be told.

Though if he were being honest with himself, he also wanted to keep Psyche all to himself. He was viciously possessive of her, wanting her to need and want only him. It shamed him to admit that he was even jealous of the time she spent with Pax and the nymphs. The eons spent without his other half had turned him into a possessive beast, and it was a struggle sometimes to give his wife the freedom she deserved.

As he gazed down at her, he felt the weight of the guilt he carried for separating her from her loved ones. He knew the pain that forced separation caused, and he cursed himself for doing to her what he vowed would never be done to them again. Though she had no memory of their time before the fall, he remembered all too well the madness that had seized him when she had been ripped from him. He had become a monster. The scars from that night would never go away. He understood that it was the fear of losing her again that made him act in such an irrational manner at times, but he could not seem to stop himself from being overly protective. It was part of his nature.

Seeing the pain she was trying to hide cut him to the bone, however. The fact that she did not argue with him, that she felt she had no recourse, filled him with shame. He was failing in his most basic duty to see to her happiness. It gave him little choice in the matter.

"Psyche, what if I could arrange for you to see your parents? I cannot let you go to your family; it is too dangerous. There are too many people who would betray that you were there. But I can bring your parents to the island under the cover of darkness. Would that make you happy?" he asked softly.

Unshed tears filled her eyes, the joy in them arresting the small amount of dread that threatened to overtake him. He feared that she would not want to remain on the island with him once she was reunited with her family. She clearly loved them; on that he had no doubts. It was her regard for him that caused his uncertainty. He was insecure about the depth of her feelings for him. He knew she cared for him, though how much was the question he still had no answer for. How would she react when she would have to be separated from them for a second time? Why would she willingly go back to their half-life together when she could have a full one with her family? She still did not even know his true name, for Chaos' sake.

He was pulled out of his dark thoughts when she threw her arms around him and enthusiastically pressed kisses across his face, with soft thanks interwoven between each kiss.

"Phanes, thank you. When can we see them?"

His heart tightened at her words. That she included him was a balm to his troubled thoughts. It meant she viewed them as a team, which gave him hope that they were closer to achieving the true unity he needed from her. "I need two days to make the arrangements. I want to make sure that both you and your parents can safely meet."

"Will you not be meeting my family, as well, Phanes? I want you to meet them. They will be so happy, and I want them to see that my husband is a wonderful man—not a beast like the Pythia said."

Arching a brow, Eros could not stop the smirk that lit his face, grateful for once that she could not see his expression, for he was sure he would be in for another lecture. "Little butterfly, I *am* a beast, remember?"

Rolling her eyes at him, Psyche haughtily lifted her head. "You *have* a beast; that does not *make* you a beast. There is a difference, my lord husband."

Tossing his head back in laughter, Eros cuddled her closer to him as she joined him in merriment. "Excellent point, my dear. And on that note, we are here."

CHAPTER 27

Psyche could barely see where they landed. She had no clue where her husband had taken them. After being set down on her feet, she took a moment to orient herself. They were in some type of forest. The air was heavy with the many scents of the vegetation. She could hear the sound of water cascading gently down in the distance. With the moon as her only source of light, she could barely make out a path through the trees. "Where are we?"

"I will tell you when we get to the spot further down the path." Eros took hold of her hand and began to lead her down the trail. He was careful to make sure that she did not trip as they walked further into the forest. With the trees overhead, it prevented much of the light from the moon from penetrating, keeping much of the path shrouded in darkness.

The stillness of the night was broken only by the sounds of the forest. It lent a subtle melody to the evening. Before long, they reached a section of the path that led down to a valley.

"Allow me, my lady." Before she could take a step, Eros

picked her up, and with a quick burst of speed, had them at the bottom of the valley.

Laughing, Psyche pulled back slightly. "Well, my lord husband, you are quite fast and efficient when you have a destination to reach."

"Only in certain things, my dear. I definitely like to take my time when I am making love to you. The journey is as pleasurable as the destination, I can assure you," he murmured wickedly.

Heat stained her cheeks as she blushed. She knew that tone in his voice. Her husband was in a particular mood, and she looked forward to whatever new delights he was of a mind to show her this evening.

Psyche could see a small lake fed by a waterfall a few yards away. The moonlight danced over the surface, creating a dazzling display. Here by the lake, there was a smoky scent of frankincense mixed in with smells of the forest, such as one would smell in a temple. She felt like she was in a sacred grove, one that had been dedicated to the worship of the gods of old, the primordial ones. It lent a reverent tone to her voice. "Oh, Phanes, it is beautiful. This is a wonderful surprise."

"While I agree it is beautiful, this is not the surprise."

"It's not?"

"No. Look to the shore."

She looked around until she spotted the outline of a small pleasure barge. A soft glow from oil lamps that dotted the ship came to life, revealing a large pallet strewn with bedsheets and animal furs. Beside it was food and drink, enough to feed a small dinner party. Smiling as she spied several of her favorites, she was reminded of the night when she and Phanes had played the game of copycat.

They headed to the boat, and after getting in, he settled them down on the bedding. Phanes placed her between his legs so that she rested semi-reclined against his broad chest. Within seconds after he wrapped his arms around her, the boat traveled to the center of the lake, and then came to a gentle stop. It stayed in that position, not moving an inch, even though the water lapped gently around them as it swirled and ebbed with the flow of the waterfall.

Psyche watched as a goblet of wine floated to her. Taking it, she took a sip and settled back, her head tucked under her husband's head.

"Comfortable?" he murmured.

"Yes."

"Good. Now for your surprise. Look to the trees in front of you."

Turning, she watched in awe as light slowly rose from the water. It turned the surface of the lake into a mirror image of moonlight. It bathed the forest around them in light, revealing thousands of tiny wings of brown, cream, and splashes of orange that clung to every inch of the trees, flowers, rocks, and plants around them. The tiny winged insects blanketed the entire forest, creating a visual feast.

She leaned forward, looking all around as she took in the sight of so many butterflies. "Phanes, are we on Rhodes?" she whispered, afraid to speak any louder for fear she would startle the little insects away.

"Yes, we are in the Valley of the Butterflies. I thought you might enjoy seeing them as this is the perfect time of year for them. "

A smile of pure pleasure graced her lips as she looked over her shoulder at him. "Thank you. I love my surprise. I have heard stories about them since I was a child. I always wanted to come here and see them for myself. How did you ever guess that?"

"I have my ways. Now, I suggest you settle back and watch the show."

Music began to play in the distance. As the tempo of the lyre gained strength, it had a curious effect on the butterflies. They began to move their wings in a pattern, as if they were dancing to the music. It was not long before they took flight, filling the air with thousands of wings as they fluttered above the boat. They moved in a rhythmic pattern, twirling and dancing above them. The night sky was overtaken with them.

As the music swelled, the butterflies dipped and twirled, creating patterns like star constellations. First a drakon, then a butterfly, then Pegasus. The images seamlessly transformed from one to the next. "Oh Phanes, it's wondrous! How are you doing this?"

"Little butterfly, where would be the fun be if I told you all my secrets?" he said in a teasing tone. Taking the forgotten goblet of wine from her, he set it aside. "Now, give me your hand."

Once she had placed her hand in his, Eros cupped it, turning it so her palm was facing up. Within seconds, a pair of butterflies landed on her hand. Their delicate little legs felt like the soft touch of a kitten's whiskers across her skin. They performed an intricate dance, sending tiny shivers across her skin. Psyche watched them, fascinated and transfixed by their choreographed movements. Slowly they circled one another, coming closer with each twirl. "What are they doing?" she inquired.

Eros rested his head against hers, watching the pair. "They are doing the mating dance. Tonight, they will mate, and the female will go off to lay her eggs. Both will soon perish, as this will use up the last of their energy."

Psyche's heart tightened. "That is so sad. Will they be harmed by their performance?"

"No. I have made sure that they will not have used up any of the energy they need for this last stage of their life. Though they will be more…vigorous and fruitful…in their mating, they will not suffer any ill effects from tonight's performance."

Blushing, Psyche watched the pair for a few more seconds before several branches of the sweet gum tree appeared in a small pithos beside them. Eros brought her hand over to one of the branches and carefully set the butterflies on one of the leaves so that they could complete the final steps in their dance before they began to mate. Psyche looked around and saw that all the butterflies had landed. They were in the final steps of their dance, and before long, the pairs were in an intimate embrace.

Rolling them over, Eros had her on her stomach, pressed down to the bedding before she realized his intent. Easing back on his haunches, he placed a hand on the small of her back, keeping her in place. She felt her clothes disappear, leaving her naked. With the unnatural light from the water dimming slightly, it lent an air of sensuality to the evening.

After arranging her to his liking on the bed, Eros straddled her. "Stay still," he softly admonished her when she made to move. "You will enjoy this, I promise."

Smiling, Psyche settled back down, intrigued to see what her husband had in store for them. She felt Phanes shifting to the side away from where her head rested on her crossed arms, and turned to look at the waterfall at her left. Her mind drifting, she was startled out of her thoughts when she felt warm oil drip down her spine. The heat caused her to jump a little as it warmed her skin, almost to the point of pain. It spread down her sides liked molten honey, leaving trails of cruel pleasure. Before long, Phanes began to massage her back. The hot oil and his massage was a sweet pleasure/pain. Moaning in delight, she felt herself go limp under his expert hands.

"Like that, do you?" he murmured. His voice filled with a dark sensual promise. It sent shivers through her. It was responding to his touch, and she felt herself grow wet with her arousal. Her sex tightened as he continued to work her body, lingering caresses to the back of her neck and inner thighs, sending tendrils of pleasure to wash over her. The heat of the oil being dripped over various parts of her body was a sweet torment. One she came to crave every time he drizzled more of it on her, anticipating the burn as it hit her skin. Before long, she found it nearly impossible to stay still, as involuntary little shudders racked her as she move restlessly.

Eros had her turn over on her back. When she tried to draw him down to her, he pulled back, refusing to give her what she desperately needed. "Hold still. I have plans for you. You will have to hold on a little longer before I give you what you want."

"Phanes,' she pleaded, "I need you. Please..."

She felt so empty inside, and she needed him with a need bordering on pain as her sex spasmed. When she tried to pull him down to her again, he shackled her hands above her head, keeping her pressed down on the pallet. "At least let me touch you," she pleaded.

"No. I will not release you until I am ready. Now be a good girl and stay still, or I will be forced to deny you your reward."

Reclining beside her, Eros plucked one of his feathers, a wicked smile on his face. He dipped a feather in the pot of hot oil. Slowly, using the tip, he traced her lips, leaving them wet. Psyche let out a soft gasp when she felt its touch. Licking her lips, she tasted the almond and honey flavor of the oil.

He painted little patterns on her skin, and with each pass of the feather, her skin became more sensitive. Her senses heightened, so that with each new pass, her arousal grew.

Psyche struggled to stay still with her hands held down,

keeping her from touching him, as she wanted. It was driving her slowly mad. Her need was building with every pass of the feather. Phanes dragged the feather down her sternum to her naval, leaving a hot trail of oil. Teasing her. The heat was arousing, but never quite enough to push her to the release her body was demanding. Never giving her the stronger touches she craved. As the feather made its way back up, he teased the underside of her breast, circling it. With each pass, he came closer to her nipple, though he made sure to never quite graze it. Panting, she watched as the feather was dipped in the pot of oil before it made its way to her other breast, dripping as it traveled over her skin, heating, grazing, circling, but never caressing her nipple.

"Phanes, please," she cried out as he pulled the feather away at the last minute when she arched up, never letting it even touch her nipple as she so desperately wanted. It made her frantic, wild.

"Spread your legs now," he ordered harshly.

Sobbing in need, she did as she was told, praying he would soon show her mercy and quench the fire that burned in her. "Wider. Drape your leg over mine. I want to see your arousal coating your sweet lips."

Moving her legs, she positioned herself as he wanted. The warm breeze teased her exposed sex, ramping up her desire. Her arousal dripped down her thighs. Unable to stop the soft undulation of her hips, she waited—breath bated—to see if he would finally touch her as she craved.

The feathered hovered over her, and with a quick snap, it sent streams of hot oil across her chest, striking her nipples, causing them to harden painfully before it dipped between her legs to tease her clitoris. The heat stimulated her sensitive nerve endings, causing her to cry out as she orgasmed.

Tears streamed down her face, but even with the orgasm,

it was not enough. She needed more. She begged him to take her, to sate the painful arousal that refused to leave her.

Phanes quickly rolled her onto her stomach. He slid a bolster under her hips to raise them up for him. Straddling her legs, he laid down on top of her prone body, pinning her down with his weight. It was a delicious pleasure to her to be surrounded by him, but before she could beg, he was sliding into her, though the position made it a struggle to accommodate him at first. Clutching the bed furs in pleasurable agony, she tried to spread her legs so that he could slide in easier.

"No, you will take me this way," he growled in her ear as he prevented her from moving.

Straining with the control needed to keep himself from plunging into her, he slowly pushed his way in. Before long, he slid his entire length all the way in, causing a sweet pleasurable pain as her body fought to accommodate his enormous size. This new position made him seem all the larger. Her sex spasmed as another small orgasm ripped through her, but still it was not enough.

He began to move, thrusting into her slowly at first. Before long he was driving himself into her, riding her hard. Pleasure rippled through her, driving her mad with need and desire. She urged him on. "Please...harder..." she gasped.

Fisting his hand in her hair, he pulled her head back, capturing her mouth in a savage meeting of lips and tongues, both animalistic in their need for the other. Psyche felt the building of her pleasure as it spread out from her core, the strength of it frightening in its intensity. Crying out against his lips, she screamed as she felt the explosion of her orgasm rip through her. Black spots appeared in her vision before she lost consciousness as the pleasure left her in a senseless heap on the bed.

It was several moments before she was aware of her surroundings. As she slowly remembered where she was and what she had been doing, a smile spread on her lips as she tried to stretch, languid and content in her afterglow. It was then that she realized that her husband was still inside her, harder than before, if that was even possible. Confused she turned to him as she said, "Phanes, what is the matter? Did you not find your pleasure as I did?"

"No," he said, a savage note in his voice. "I wish to show you another way to find pleasure. It will be cruel pleasure to be sure, but one I believe you will ultimately find pleasure in. However, it will be your choice alone if you wish to try it. If you do not wish to, I will make love to you again as we did this night, and I will find my release within your sweet sex."

Psyche heard the dark need in her husband's voice, the one he did not think she heard as he tried to keep his dominant nature at bay. His beast was riding him this night; she could hear it in his voice. Whatever this new pleasure was, he wanted it with a desperation bordering on madness. She did not believe she could find release again, her body too well used and relaxed from the night's activities. However, she would not be averse to indulging him, for even though she doubted she would find release, it would still be pleasurable for them nonetheless.

Curious to see what he wanted to try, she lifted her upper body off the bed. When she shifted back, it pushed him further into her, causing them both to moan in pleasure. Perhaps she spoke too soon, she thought. "What is it you wish to do?"

Sitting back on his haunches and making sure to keep himself inside her, Phanes slid his hand down her spine, stopping when he reached the base. Slipping his hand between the cheeks of her backside, he pressed his finger against her entrance. "I want to take you here."

CHAPTER 28

Momentarily struck speechless by his request, Psyche could only stare at the space where she knew her husband to be. "You want to take me there?"

Phanes gently stroked her backside. The foreign caress felt strange as new sensations slowly spread from where he touched her. The taboo nature of his request both frightened and intrigued her. "Yes, Psyche. I want to introduce you to this form of lovemaking. I promise you that if it's done correctly, it will bring you a new type of pleasure unlike any you have experienced so far."

Frowning, she thought about his request. She would be lying if she said she had never heard of this type of bed play before, but she had only caught faint whispers and snippets of information from the servants of her parents' home. It made her unsure of what to make of her husband's desire for such an act. "But Phanes, would it not be painful for me? I admit, I have heard whispers of such acts, but never about it being pleasurable, only painful. You truly wish to do that to me?"

He continued caressing her as he spoke. "Not *to* you, my

butterfly, *with* you. There is a difference. If you do not ultimately find pleasure in the act, neither will I." He sighed before continuing. "Yes, if done carelessly or with ill intent, it could be extremely painful; however, if done properly, the most discomfort you would feel would be no more than what you experienced on our wedding night, and then you would experience pleasure."

Psyche thought over his words, her hesitation to say yes stemming from her fear of the unknown. It was an act that she had never really given much thought to, and had never conceived of her husband wanting to engage in. The more she mulled over his request, the more curious she became. She found herself wanting to say yes, for the discomfort she had felt the first time they made love was but a faint memory now, easily eclipsed by all the pleasures that she had enjoyed that night, and all their other nights since.

Each time they came together, he lavished so much pleasure on her that she sometimes wondered if her body could take it. He always made sure, even when his needs bordered on giving her cruel pleasure, that she was *with* him, that he never went beyond what she could handle. Truth be told, she was more than a little curious to see what kind of pleasure she could find in such an act. She was inclined to say yes, though she needed some more assurances from him first before she would agree. "Will you stop if I ask it of you, should I find that I am not enjoying it, or if it is too painful?"

Eros stopped caressing her, and leaning slightly forward, he waited until he had her complete attention. "Psyche, I give you my word. If at any time you find yourself feeling as if something is wrong, you will tell me and I will stop. I want you to feel pleasure, not true pain. I never want you to feel that you have to do anything that you truly do not wish to do to please me, either. I will not be happy if you were to agree to do something simply out of fear or pressure. If you do not wish to try it, please say so with no fear that I will be disappointed."

Mulling over his words for few minutes, she finally came to a decision. She would put her faith and trust in him. "Yes, Phanes. I want to try it," she whispered.

He leaned forward, gently kissing her lips before pulling back slightly. "Oh Psyche, you humble me. I promise, before this night is over, you will be greatly rewarded for your courage."

He pulled back and gently began to spread her legs apart, all the while taking care to make sure he stayed locked in her. Once her legs where to his liking, he moved to kneel between them, adding another pillow under her hips to raise them even higher. Satisfied with her position, he resumed making love to her, slowly thrusting in and out, stroking the embers of her passion back to life.

Psyche could not bite back a moan as her body responded to his gentle strokes. She felt the languid pleasure slowly spread out from her core, though his strokes were not strong enough to send her over the edge. They kept her floating along in a pleasurable daze, fixing her in a relaxed state of bliss.

Limp with pleasure, she was startled by the feel of warm oil being drizzled down her backside, the warmth adding to the pleasurable haze. Phanes slowly massaged the oil between her cheeks, adding more before pushing one finger slowly into her. It felt strange at first; there was a slight resistance before her body slowly allowed him in. The pressure was not at all painful, as she had feared. Slowly he pumped his finger in and out of her, matching the rhythm of his hips as he continued to thrust. The dual penetration sent slightly more powerful sensations to radiate out from her core.

"How are you feeling? Tell me," he demanded.

Her sex clenching at the dark tone of his voice, she

murmured, "Good. It felt...strange at first, but it doesn't hurt now."

"It will get better," he promised.

Psyche relaxed, enjoying the new pleasurable sensation. Before long, he poured more oil to coat his hand, and then he carefully pushed two fingers into her. There was a slight twinge of discomfort as he stretched her, but nothing that caused anything close to pain, just some pressure before her muscles slowly relaxed as her body became accustomed to his touch.

The added fullness pushed her arousal higher. She found herself slowly thrusting her hips back, trying to push him deeper inside of her, but he kept his thrusts shallow, never quite filling her as she needed.

Phanes came to halt suddenly, causing her to snarl in frustration. Chuckling darkly, he held her in place, preventing her from thrusting back. "Easy, little one, I am going to stretch you a little more, and then you will be taking me in your backside. Stay still while I prepare you."

He pushed three fingers into her, stretching her. For several minutes he slowly pushed his fingers in and out, spreading them ever so slowly to stretch her further. Waves of pleasure coursed through her, leaving her clutching the blanket with her fists as she tried to stay still. The need to move was driving her mad. The muscles of her sex clenched down on Phanes, ringing a hiss of pleasure from him. Cursing, he pushed in deeper, eliciting a gasp of pleasure from her. Then he began to ride her, pushing his hips in unison with his fingers. Crying in pleasure, she felt her body prepare to climax, but before she could, he pulled out of her completely.

Crying out in need, she begged, "Please come back!"

Before she could move, she felt him pressing against her as he slowly pushed his oil-slicked cock into her. She felt a slight burning as he pushed his way in, stretching her even further. At first her body resisted him, giving her a strange pleasure/pain before it suddenly stopped resisting and he was all the way in. The shock of it sent her senses reeling, leaving her feeling both filled and empty at the same time. Her sex clenched in need. The pressure of his cock was hitting new nerve endings, making her desperate for him to move, to satisfy the cruel need that tore through her. Crying out, she bucked against him, hissing as her arousal increased. "Phanes, please...move...do something..." she panted.

Pulling her back until she was upright on her knees, Phanes wrapped his arms around her, his front pressed to her back as he settled more firmly in her. "Tell me yes or no, Psyche," he demanded.

"What?"

"Are you alright to continue, or do you want me to stop?"

Reaching back, she twisted slightly around as she grabbed a fistful of his hair, dragging his mouth to hers, lust-crazed as she kissed him. Pulling back, she demanded against his lips, "Take me."

Needing no further encouragement, he drew back and began loving her. He set a slow pace at first, letting her body get used to this new way of lovemaking. He continued to kiss her as he brought his hands to her breasts. Cupping them, he tugged at her nipples, causing them to harden in a pleasure that spread down to her weeping sex.

Letting go of her mouth, he pressed his lips behind her ear, leaving a trail of open-mouth kisses down her neck. Stopping when he reached where her shoulder and her neck met, he bit down, holding her in place as he increased the intensity and force of his thrusts, sending her lust spiraling out of control.

In the thrall of the tantalizingly cruel pleasure that was threatening to consume her, she pushed back against him, meeting him thrust for thrust, urging him on. The pleasure/pain took her to new heights of ecstasy. Crying out, she begged him to send her over the edge.

Eros brought one of his hands between her legs, and slipping his fingers deep within her, he thrust up, pumping in and out of her in rhythm with his thrusts.

The duel penetration sent her over the edge. Her back arched as she let out a scream as her orgasm ripped through her body. For a second time that night, black dots filled her vision at the violent intensity of the pleasure crashed through her, leaving her trembling and weak.

Behind her, her husband roared as he found his own release. Emptying himself in her, they both collapsed to the bed in a weak, quivering mass, breathless with the intensity of their orgasms.

It was sometime later before Eros found the strength to gently pull himself out of her. A shudder of latent pleasure ran through her body as he pulled away. With a wave of his hand, he cleansed both of them of the night's passions before covering them in heavy furs to ward off the chill of the evening. Cuddling against her, he petted her as he softly murmured his pleasure and praises as they slowly drifted to sleep under the night sky.

CHAPTER 29

Psyche paced around her bedchamber, restless energy pulsing through her body while she nervously waited for her husband to arrive. Tonight was the night that he promised to reunite her with her parents for a visit. The waiting was driving her mad. Random thoughts of what could go wrong plagued her, keeping her from being able to settle down. It was as if Deimos and Phobos had decided that she would make a perfect whetstone to sharpen their claws on. What if Phanes changed his mind? Could she handle it if he decided that she could not see her parents after all? What would she do? What *could* she do? Pushing that stray thought from her head, she tried to distract herself by keeping busy.

Going over to the bed, she set about fixing it for the seventh time that evening. Smoothing away a nonexistent wrinkle in the covers, she rearranged the pillows before giving up and moving to pace the length of the bedchamber again, the four little kittens chasing after her, attacking the hem of her chiton. Smiling distractedly at their antics, she tried to calm her nerves as she continued to wait.

Moving to stand in front of the bronze mirror, she took in her appearance. Fretting over whether she should change her gown, she looked over at the pile of dresses that she had worn and discarded in her quest to look presentable to her parents. To let them know that she was alright and that they should not fear for her. She shook her head; what she was wearing was one of her better gowns. Turning back to the mirror, she plucked at the golden *anamaschalister* that criss-crossed the top of her white chiton before undoing the strap and retying it again.

Seeing her pale appearance, she lightly pinched her cheeks before smoothing back a stray strand of hair that had escaped her topknot. She glanced down as she felt a tug on her gown, grimacing as she saw that the kittens seemed intent on trying to climb up her dress. Their little claws were sure to leave tiny tears in her gown.

Sighing, she picked up a stray ribbon that was hanging off the mirror and dangled it in front of them, drawing them away from pawing at her dress before they could do any real damage to it. She was also distracting herself as she teased the kittens with it. She chuckled as they clumsily attacked it. As she halfheartedly played with them, her mind wandered as she thought back over the past couple of days. Something in her relationship with her husband had changed since the night they spent in the Valley of the Butterflies. She could not quite put her finger on what it was, though. It was as if her show of faith and trust in him had set off a reckoning of some sort, as if a water clock had begun its final countdown, but to what, she had no clue.

She had a vague sense of foreboding, but with no clear reason for it. However, if she were to be honest with herself, her continuing nightmares were becoming a concern. The fear and dread of those dreams were beginning to haunt her in her waking moments, not just in her sleep. It said something that she was not plagued with these dreams when Phanes slept beside her; that they only seemed to attack her when she was alone in her bed on the island.

Last night her nightmare had been particularly bad. She had spent most of the past two days in the tapestry room, desperately trying to put into threads the visions that tormented her. The images that she wove made her shudder. Thinking back to last night, she became lost in thought as she was drawn back into remembering her dreams.

PSYCHE STOOD in the shadowed field again. The silent stillness of it was suffocating. It had a weight, this unnatural silence. It pressed down on her, like the force of the sea as it crashed into her, slowly drowning her as it sucked her down to its bottom depths, the pressure steadily building, threatening to crush her under its weight.

It was cold in the field. The temperature dropping every minute she was there. She could see her breath, the little wisps becoming a part of the mist, feeding it.

It slowly drove her mad with fear.

Her nightmare always began the same way, her standing in the middle of an empty field shrouded in mists, no end or beginning in sight. An otherworldly light filtering through the shadows, reinforcing how very alone she was. Though it does not stay that way for long, she thought to herself with a shudder.

No matter how many nights she returned to this place, she could never get used to how it could be so alien to her senses, and yet be so familiar to her at the same time. She knew *this place.*

Taking a deep breath, she tried to calm down the rapid beating of her heart. It filled her ears, and it radiated throughout her body, threatening to burst through her ribcage in its ferocity. Putting her hand to her chest, she tried to rub away the chest pain caused by her wild beating heart, afraid that its wild thumping would send her to an early grave.

From the corner of her eye, she caught a movement in the mist. The shadow figures had returned. Dropping her hand, she took a step back, then another one as she tried in vain to distance herself from them. Before long, however, she was surrounded by them with nowhere to run. Low whispers warred with the sound of the beating of her heart, making it difficult for her to hear what was being said by them.

Looking on in mounting terror, she watched in horrified fascination as they took shape, became more solid, more real. Before, they had always been vague in their shape and appearance. Tonight, they became more tangible, more menacing.

Several shadow figures broke away from the rest. Heading toward her, they became bigger with each step closer. She watched as one broke away from the rest; it reached out to her. Then it stalked her, following her every movement, a predator stalking its prey. In its hands, it held what looked like a scythe. The shadow figure raised it up, looking like it was readying to strike her down with it. It crept closer and closer. She could see its lips as it hissed one name over and over again. Thesis. Thesis.

"PSYCHE!"

Snapping back to the present, she blinked in confusion as she was shaken lightly by invisible hands. Tentacles of fear from her nightmare still had her in its grip, making it difficult for a moment to distinguish between what was real and what was not. Still caught in its hold, thinking the shadow figure had her in its clutches, she was about to scream when she caught the familiar scent of musk, sandalwood, and dark spices. It brought her back to reality as nothing else could. Phanes.

Sagging in relief as she escaped the last hold of her nightmare, she wrapped her arms around him, closing her eyes and tightly holding on to him as she breathed in his scent.

Slight tremors raced through her as the last vestiges of the flashback of her nightmare finally left her.

"Psyche, what is the matter? Are you alright?" he demanded harshly as he held her tight. His wings wrapped around her, cocooning her in warmth and safety. His voice shook slightly. It brought her up short that she could hear the fear in his voice. His concern for her well-being made her smile.

He ran his hands over her as he held her against his body, as if checking her for injuries. His body heat quickly chased away the cold dread from her limbs, warming her both inside and out. He cradled her in his arms as he demanded, "Butterfly, speak to me, please."

"I am alright, Phanes. Please forgive me for scaring you," she murmured against his bare chest. "Nothing is wrong."

Eros frowned. "Do not tell me nothing is wrong. You were frozen with fear. I was calling your name for several minutes and you did not even hear me. Now tell me the truth."

She opened her mouth to speak, but nothing came out, something holding her back. No one knew of her nightmares, for she had been very careful to hide the fact that she had them from everyone on the island. Even Pax did not know about them. To admit them to anyone—especially her husband—was something she was not prepared to do.

Dreams were many times portents of things to come. There had to be a reason why she kept having the same nightmare over and over again, especially as it seemed to happen every time she and Phanes made another stride in their relationship. Every significant show of trust on her part was followed by a nightmare soon after. That could not be a coincidence.

Her husband still kept many things from her, his true identity being one of them. She felt that she needed to guard this just as carefully as he guarded his secrets. Her hidden tapestry—the one she worked on surreptitiously behind closed doors—was the only evidence of their existence. Until she figured out the meaning behind her nightmares, she would keep that knowledge to herself. Now she just had to decide on just how much of the truth she could reveal to her husband to satisfy his concerns, all without revealing her secret.

Sighing, she raised her hand to where she knew his face to be. Cupping his cheek, she brought his head down to hers until their foreheads touched. Closing her eyes, she said softly, "I had a moment of panic and I became lost in it. I have been plagued these last few days with fears and doubts. I even dreamed about them, and I was remembering them when you came in."

Phanes tightened his hold on her as he pulled back his head. She could feel his eyes on her. The feeling of being intensely watched was disconcerting as she tried to be truthful. Her husband was no fool; he would know if she tried to lie to him outright. Her only chance was to give him just enough of the truth without revealing too much.

It was ironic that she could always tell when he was watching her, but she had no clue what color his eyes were. After running her hands so many times through his hair, she knew it was soft, with a slight curl, but she did not know its color, either. She knew so many things about her husband. He was passionate, intensely protective of those he considered his, loving, with a wicked sense of humor, and yet, she could not answer such basic questions as what he looked like, or what he was, for that matter.

"What is scaring you? I thought we were past this. I cannot help you if you do not confide in me, Psyche."

Nodding, she said, "I do know that, and I was going to talk to you when you arrived. I have been scared that something will happen tonight, that I will not see my parents, that they will not believe that I am happy and safe with you. That they will ask questions that I cannot give them an answer to, because it may reveal too much, and you have warned me against that."

Psyche felt a small twinge of guilt. While what she told him was strictly the truth, she was still lying by omission by not revealing all that was truly bothering her. She just hoped that he would not probe too deeply, that he would be satisfied with the half-truth that she gave him.

"I know that I have placed you in a difficult position. It is not in your nature to be deceptive. I understand that by holding back some of the truth, you may feel that you are lying to them. I promise you; it is only for their safety—and yours—that it must be so, for now."

Dropping her eyes, she avoided looking at him, instead focusing her gaze on her hand as she stroked the inner part of his wing. Guilt filled her at her deception. She was lying, not only to her parents, but to her husband, as well. It did not sit well with her.

"Now, your parents will be here in a few minutes. I never go back on my word, Psyche," he admonished her gently. "Have no fear on that score."

Startled, she looked up at him, smiling with joy and relief, even as she felt conflicted over her deception. She was grateful that he was not pursuing his line of interrogating questions any further. However, she did not like the hurt in his voice. She could at least give him as much of the truth as she could, at least on this score.

"I know that you would not go back on your word. My fears stem more from Aphrodite and her hatred of me. It would please her to cause me pain by hurting my loved ones. I fear for my parents, and for you."

Pressing a kiss to her forehead, he drew her impossibly

closer. "It pleases me more than you will ever know that you have a care for my well-being. Have no fear, I am more than capable of protecting myself, and you," he said gruffly.

"I more than care. It would kill me if anything happened to you," she confessed.

"And why is that?"

"Because."

"Because, why? Tell me, Psyche. Why would it kill you if anything happened to me?"

"Because I am falling in love with you."

CHAPTER 30

Eros felt like he had taken a blow to his chest at her soft confession. Fierce joy filled him as he tightened his hold on her. *Finally.* They were getting closer to the point when he could reveal himself to her, to stop giving her only a part of himself, and to be able to share every aspect of his life with her. His heart racing, he took a moment to bask in the knowledge that she was on the path to reuniting with him. They were so close to achieving the union they both needed, not just for themselves, but also to survive the coming war.

Lifting her up, he reverently kissed her lips. For several moments they kissed before finally pulling back slightly, both of them breathless. He murmured against her lips, "My brave, precious little butterfly. You have made me the happiest man alive. Say it again."

"I am falling in love with you," Psyche repeated, her breath caressing his lips as she whispered her growing love for him.

Eros rose to his full height. Tucking a lock of hair behind her ear that had come loose from her topknot, he took in her flushed cheeks and lips, swollen from their kiss. Desire filled him, urging him to take her to bed, to lose himself in her body, and her love.

My lord, King Andronikos and Queen Eleni have arrived. They await their daughter in the courtyard.

He reined in his need. *Later,* he promised himself. For now, her parents were waiting.

Thank you Zephyrus. We will be out there shortly.

Smiling down at her, Eros was reluctant to give up this moment between them. "Now, my love, let me take you to your parents."

Eyes bright with hopeful pleasure, Psyche's smile lit up the room. It filled him with a fierce pride that he could give her such happiness. "They are here? Truly?"

Laughing at her childlike joy, he stepped back. Tucking her hand into the crook of his arm, he led her out of their bedroom. He shook his head in amusement as she practically danced at his side, her eagerness to get to her parents evident as she urged him along.

He was reluctant to put a damper on her happiness, but he needed to remind her of what they had agreed to tell her parents about her marriage. Stopping just before the great doors that led out to the courtyard, Eros turned her to him before she could dart out. Placing his hands on her shoulders, he waited to speak until he had her full attention.

"Remember what we discussed."

Impatient to see her parents, she nodded her head as her gaze slipped to the side.

"Psyche, look at me," he said sternly.

Eyes snapping back to his at his sharp tone, she finally gave him her full attention.

Gentling his tone, Eros commanded, "Repeat what we discussed, Psyche."

"I am to say that my husband is away on a hunting trip. That you are a young man of good reputation and family.

That you are fair of hair and strong of stature. That we are happy. I am not to say or reveal anything else."

"Good. Now tell me again one more time before I let you go."

She smiled shyly. "I am falling in love with you."

Satisfied, Eros let go of her. "Have a pleasant visit, my love."

She hesitated. "Will you be here after they leave?"

"Yes. I will be waiting for you after your visit with your family is over. Go, enjoy your time with them. You have the entire evening to spend with them."

Stepping up to him, she reached up, and finding his face, pressed a quick kiss to his cheek. "Thank you."

Eros watched as she all but ran to the door. With a wave of his hand, they opened, allowing her to slip out to meet up with her parents, who waited for her in the courtyard. He watched as she ran to them, their joy as they saw her evident in their eagerness to reach her side. As they met, they became entangled in a fierce embrace, and the sounds of their tear-filled joy carried over the gentle breeze as they all spoke to each other.

Feeling the stirring of ancient power, Eros was not surprised to see Anteros standing to the right of him, while Zephyrus stood to his left. Both took in the scene before them and watched in silence as Psyche answered their many questions about her life on the island, and her husband. Pride filled him as he observed the grace she exhibited as she deftly allayed their fears, reassuring them of her happiness, all the while evading any indication that her husband was anything other than what she had told them.

He observed Psyche as she led her parents to the side entrance of the palace, intent on giving them a tour of her home. Her parents were clinging to her, arm in arm as they walked huddled together, each unwilling to let go of the other.

It made him feel better for giving them all this moment out of time. Truth be told, he owed a great debt to her parents. They clearly loved his little butterfly, and they had protected her well before he had found her. For that alone, he owed them this night.

"Is this wise, Eros?"

Not surprised that his brother should ask such a thing, Eros turned his head to look at him. "It is what needed to be done."

Seeing the troubled expression on Anteros' face, Eros sighed. His brother was the one who always took guarding their identities—and him—to the extreme. That Psyche was bringing mortals to the island did not sit well with him, and they had fought over his decision to allow this visit. His brother was vehemently opposed to the danger of discovery by any of the gods of what lay at the heart of the islands that made up their homes.

"We have been over this already. You know the danger is minimal at best. Thanks to Zephyrus' idea, no one will even know that they were here. If this works as we plan, then Psyche can still have her mortal family in her life. She loves them, and they her. Even you cannot deny that."

Anteros turned to look at him, and his expression was one Eros rarely saw from his brother. The pity in it set Eros on edge. "Their love is not in question O adelfós mou. It is the fragile nature of the mortals that I have a problem with. Her parents' life thread is close to the end, and Psyche will be separated from them whether she likes it or not with the Moirai in charge of their threads. Would it not be better to weaken the familial bond than to strengthen it? They are not even her true parents."

Before Eros could speak, Zephyrus said, "They *are* her

parents Anteros. She chose to be reborn a mortal, to mortal parents. We may never know why she made that decision, as you three never had parents. And she may never remember why she made that decision, either. I will say this, though. Since becoming a father, I now understand the bonds between a parent and a child. They are unbreakable, even by the Moirai. Khloris and I would gladly give our lives for our son. It is because Psyche's parents are mortal that they know what a precious gift time is; it is we immortals who forget. Let them have whatever time they have left in this life. Someday soon, you both will understand that which I speak of."

Anteros turned thoughtful eyes to Zephyrus. *It was obvious that Anteros was mulling over his words, though what he made of them was the question,* thought Eros to himself. It was rare for Zephyrus to offer advice in matters of the heart. It was easy to forget how much the god of the west wind had grown in the knowledge of all the various types of love since his marriage and subsequent fatherhood.

It impressed Eros, and made him wonder again how Psyche had survived, only to be reborn a mortal after their forced separation. It still plagued him that she was in harm's way, with her memory and their allies gone, and their enemies hidden, waiting to strike at them again.

This time to kill them all.

"I bow to your greater knowledge on the bonds between parents and children, old man," said Anteros, smirking.

Leveling a mock glare at the smirking twins, Zephyrus snorted. "Old man, my ass. You two are older than dirt. I am the youngest of the three of us."

"So you should respect your elders, whelp," Eros chimed in.

Zephyrus hit them with a blast of wind, sending them tumbling into the air high above the island. Launching himself after them, he followed them out over the sea, laughing as they fought a mock battle, the air carrying their laughter over the sea.

Many hours later, Eros slipped into bed. Pulling an exhausted Psyche into his arms, he pressed a soft kiss to her head, smiling as she grumbled in her sleep. It had been a good night for all of them.

CHAPTER 31

Psyche hummed softly as she worked. With the changing of the seasons, she had more time to spend indoors now that the gardens were in full bloom. She was also happy to escape the late-summer heat, as the palace was thankfully cool this time of year.

Taking a short break from working on the tapestry, she turned instead to a special gift for Phanes, and a gift for Eros. She could not make a gift for one, and not the other, she mused, for she loved them both, and she did not want one to feel left out from her affections. They had both given her so much. She had finally admitted to herself that she truly loved them, and she wanted to give them something special to show how she felt about them.

After putting in the final stitch, she sat back and carefully examined her gift to Phanes, looking for any flaws, or needed changes. Finding none, she carefully laid it out on the workbench next to the completed gift for Eros. Looking at them side by side, she was pleased with her work. She hoped that they each liked their respective gifts.

Glancing at the water clock, she realized she had a few

more hours before Phanes arrived for the evening. She quickly wrapped her two gifts, and after placing them in her basket, carried them with her to the dining hall, where she placed them on a side table that the servants had set up. After fussing with them for a few minutes, she went to the kitchen to check on the meal that she had made herself for the evening. She had prepared this special meal, wanting to show her appreciation for her man, and her beast.

She spent an hour finishing the last few items on the menu. Once everything was done, she and the nymphs set the table. Seeing that everything was prepared as she wanted, Psyche quickly made her way to the bathing chamber.

A scant hour later, after bathing and taking care to dress in her finest gown, she blew out the lights in her bedroom and waited for Phanes on the balcony attached to their bedroom. She looked out over the garden, the moonlight filtering through the clouds.

The sounds of the night creatures that made their home on the island began their nightly chorus. It was a soft song that serenaded her as she waited. In the distance, she could hear Fury as he raced around his paddock, whinnying as he passed the other horses. The sounds helped to soothe her nerves and lulled her into a dreamy state as she became lost in the moment as she waited for her husband's arrival.

A gentle breeze caressed her skin and brought her out of her thoughts. She sensed the approach of her husband. Within seconds of that instinctual knowledge, she caught the sound of giant wings as they cut through the night sky, heading her way. Excitement coursed through her veins.

Phanes was coming.

Closing her eyes and lifting her face toward the breeze, she waited with bated breath as she focused all of her senses on tracking his arrival. The breeze became stronger the closer he came, carrying with it the faint scent of musk, sandalwood, and dark spices, enveloping her in its embrace. Breathing it in, she let the scent become her guide.

Making a quick decision, she climbed onto the top of the railing. Easily standing on the foot-thick flat surface, she kept her senses focused on the scent and sounds that was her husband. She stayed very still as she felt Phanes zero in on her position, increasing his speed to get to her faster. She could almost taste his concern and confusion at her actions.

She kept her eyes closed and stayed very still, all her senses focused on him. She heard the almost impossible sound of his tightening his wings against his body. The sudden stillness of the breeze told her he was streaking towards her, wings tucked tightly against his body.

Closer. Closer. A few more seconds. *There.* At the last moment, she leapt into the sky, arms outstretched as if she were diving off one of the cliffs that ringed the island. Almost immediately, she was swept up into her husband's arms.

Laughing in delight, she pressed her lips against his, kissing him with all the joy in her heart that he was home. Snapping his wings out, he flew them up over the palace and into the night sky, never breaking their kiss. Hovering over the island, Phanes spent the next few moments returning her joy-filled kiss, slowly calming his fear and anger at her actions.

She could easily have been killed if she had fallen.

Finally breaking from their kiss, Psyche smiled up at him. Her unguarded expression conveyed so many messages, the loudest being how she felt about him. It was a punch to the gut to see her love for him so openly expressed. It doused his anger at her reckless actions. "Psyche, what were you thinking by standing on the ledge like that? You could have been killed."

"I was using my senses to track you, just like you taught

me. Are you not proud of me?" she inquired, delight in her voice.

Eros pulled her up higher in his arms and nipped her lips before replying. "Of course I am proud of you, little butterfly. I continue to be amazed by your genius. I just wish you would take pity on your poor husband. There is only so much I can handle when it comes to your health and safety."

Arching a brow, Psyche could not quite keep the smirk off her face as she gently stroked his cheek. "Delicate constitution?" she inquired solicitously. "My poor husband, you should have warned me about your sensitive and delicate nature. I will endeavor to be more careful with you, my poor sheltered flower."

Eyes wide with shock, Eros sputtered, "Delicate constitution? Sheltered flower? I'll show you delicate flower." Within seconds of his reply to her teasing, Eros tucked his wings tight against his body, sending them plummeting to the ground. Psyche let out a scream. At the last minute, he snapped his wings out and came to a gentle landing in the courtyard below their bedroom.

A giggling Psyche clung to his frame, keeping her feet off the ground. "Was that supposed to scare me?"

"I did get you to scream, didn't I?"

"What does that prove? You get me to scream from our bed play."

Roaring with laughter, Eros fell onto his back, a laughing Psyche sprawled on top of him. Leaning over him, she gave him a quick kiss before falling onto his chest as he cuddled her close, his chest still shaking. Tunneling his hand into her hair, they spent the next few moments just lying there, taking joy in just being with each other.

CHAPTER 32

Deep in the bowels of Tartarus, where the moans and screams of the souls of the damned could be heard, a small tremor rocked a forgotten corner of the prison. It was so slight that the Hekatonkheires easily overlooked it, all too used to the sights and the sounds of the misery that surrounded them.

On this night, the wardens of Tartarus were gathered at the cell of Tityos, fighting a vicious battle that took all of them as they wrestled with the rapacious giant as they tried to shackle him down on the slab of stone, leaving Tartarus dangerously unguarded.

A small fissure formed next to the door of a small cell. It easily blended with the stone wall, making it almost impossible to see. Slowly, the fissure crept along the wall, making its way to the bolt that kept the damned soul locked away.

Something struck the door from inside the cell, causing the fissure to spider web, further weakening the lock. Again and again, the heavy door was struck, the sound of a body flinging itself desperately against it echoing in the darkness. The desperate sobs muffled by the thick wood.

The next blow caused the lock to snap, and the door suddenly gave way, causing the naked prisoner to crash to the unforgiving stone floor. For several minutes, they lay prone on the ground, too weak to do anything but try to catch their breath.

"Get up. Get up. Get up. Must get up. Must get away. No time," they silently sobbed to themselves.

Trembling from unrelenting pain and cold, it took the prisoner several attempts before they were able to stagger to their feet. Leaning heavily against the door, the prisoner looked fretfully around, trying to get their bearings.

The inhuman howls of rage and agony that echoed down the corridor sent a wave of fear through the prisoner, spurring them into motion. Time was of the essence; they had to make their escape now. Slowly shutting the door to their cell behind them, they spent a few precious seconds relocking the cell door. Scooping up bits of rock and dirt, they quickly filled in the tiny fissures, masking the cracks in the wall.

Satisfied that it would be some time before anyone noticed the damage, the prisoner slowly made their way down the darkened corridor to the left of their cell, away from the sounds of the guards and their struggle with the latest prisoner.

Desperate to escape, they forced themselves to move; one stumbling step after another. It was a painfully slow journey; the eons of being locked away and tortured had taken its toll. Within minutes, their heart was pounding so hard it threatened to rip out of their chest. Out of breath from sheer exhaustion after stumbling down the darkened corridor, they came to rest against the wall.

In the distance, they could make out a faint light. Hoping it was the way out, the prisoner swept the area with a fretful gaze. No shade or guard could be found. Looking again, they came to a startling realization: there were no cell doors on this side, which meant that even in Tartarus, they had been isolated. Locked away even from the damned. They had not even been allowed the dubious camaraderie with the other damned prisoners; they had been left to suffer an eternity alone. Despair threatened to bring them to their knees in defeat. On the wings of that thought, a fire lit in their gut, burning its way through their heart and mind.

Wrath was a good motive, they thought to themselves. Feeding the hatred and rage that burned in their soul, they focused on the light. That was where they planned to go. Bracing themselves, they took a deep breath before pushing off.

Fear and determination kept them moving even when their body threatened to give up. It felt like an eternity before they reached the end of the corridor, the light getting stronger the closer they came to it.

Finally, they reached the end of the passageway and let out a soft sob at the sight that met their eyes. Tears of joy slid down their ravaged face. It was the bronze wall of Tartarus; it was the light from the torches reflecting off it that they had followed.

Several yards away, stood one of the massive gates. Hope and anticipation lent them strength. They made their way as quickly as possible towards it. After all, it would not be long before one of the Hekatonkheires returned to resume their guardianship of the gates of Tartarus. If that happened, their punishment for attempting to escape would be even worse than before.

Within seconds, they were standing in front of it. Fists clenched, they felt the chain that held back their powers loosen just enough. Using a small bit of their powers on the gate, they unlocked it and pushed it open a little to allow them to slip through. Shutting and relocking the it behind them, they hurried down the path.

Fortune was smiling on them, for this gate led directly to the surface, bypassing Hades' domain entirely. They smiled in cruel pleasure. Revenge would soon be theirs.

CHAPTER 33

It was sometime later before Psyche and Phanes were able to speak, as they were both enjoying lying on the grass under a blanket of stars. She rolled off of him and laid down on her back, looking up at the night sky, his wing providing a warm cushion between her and the ground. She loved it when she curled up on his wings. They were a warm, soft, living cushion that always gave her a feeling of safety and comfort.

For the longest time, however, she tried to avoid resting on them for too long, sure that his wings would go numb from her weight. It was not long before Phanes was able to get her to admit the real reason why she always shifted off his wings after a few minutes. He had laughingly told her that his beast—whose weight equaled two triremes at the very least—could sit on his wings for an eon and they would still not go numb, so she should not worry at all, as she was as light as a feather in comparison.

Shifting to the side, Eros rose up so that he was facing Psyche. He lifted his hand and pushed back a strand of hair that had come loose from her topknot. She turned her face towards his hand, silently begging him to continue his gentle caress. She was like the kittens in her need to be touched, and he loved to indulge her. He spent the next several minutes quietly petting her.

Sighing, Psyche turned away from him, silently conveying her need for him to cuddle her, which he readily did. He slid his arms around her, spooning her. Then he brought his other wing to cover her, creating a soft and warm cocoon to ward off the slight chill of the evening. She stretched out her hand and stroked his wing, nuzzling her face in the soft feathers that ran along the inner part of his wings.

In the bushes closest to them, they could hear rustling, and then little mewling cries. "Here comes your little army of bodyguards," he said.

Within seconds of his wry comment, the four kittens burst from the flower bed, tumbling over themselves as they rushed towards them. Psyche watched as they bumped head-first into his invisible wing, sniffing it before climbing on top, delicately making their way towards them. It always amazed her to see them seemingly walking on air when they were on her husband's wings. He never got annoyed with them, his patience endless as they pawed and played with his wings. And he always took the time to play with them, giving them attention and various toys to indulge their curious natures. It gave her a glimpse what he would be like as a father.

The kittens eventually made their way across his top wing to settle against her husband's shoulder and neck. One of them settled behind her ear, tickling her. The kittens purred and rubbed against them, headbutting them, demanding attention.

"Well, it seems that you have competition for my affections tonight. Who should I please first: my bride or her little babies?"

Looking at the three floating kittens, she replied laughingly, "Well, we *are* their parents in a sense, so I would say we should give them all the love and attention they demand as their due. They will settle down to sleep soon enough, and then we will have the entire night to ourselves."

Eros used his powers to lift the three kittens currently licking and headbutting him off his shoulder—as well as the one tickling his wife's ear—and set them down in front of Psyche. Within seconds, several small toys appeared, and the kittens' attention immediately diverted to playing with them.

"You are so good with them," she sighed, watching the kittens frolic. Seeing them always made her feel better, and their innocent antics always inspired laughter among those who watched them.

"They are quite adorable, and it is easy to be good with such creatures, as they have no malice in their hearts and are true to their predatory nature. I can appreciate that."

They watched the kittens play until one by one, they became exhausted and curled up, falling asleep, just as they were prone to do at their young age.

"Well, that did not take long," she murmured.

Then the kittens instantly disappeared. Her husband always sent them to their basket when they fell asleep on his wings, or on their bed for that matter, whenever he planned for an amorous night. Otherwise, he left them where they slept.

"Alone at last."

"My lord, do you have something in mind for this night?" she teased.

Eros leaned in and nipped her earlobe before soothing the sting with his tongue. "I am quite hungry this evening, if you must know."

"Well then, Tykhe favors you this evening as I have prepared a special meal for you. It awaits your pleasure in the dining hall." A slight shiver of pleasure gripped her body when he found that special spot below her ear with his tongue.

"I would rather have *you* for my dinner," he murmured against her neck, his breath tickling her sensitive nerve endings. It never failed to ignite her lust.

Psyche fought not to surrender to her passions as he methodically went about seducing her. Tonight was too important to be distracted by their desire. There would be plenty of time later for satisfying both of their carnal appetites, after she gave him her gift. With that thought in mind, she reluctantly pulled away from him.

"Please, Phanes. I have planned a special evening for us. I worked very hard on this meal, and I want to share it with you."

Groaning in mock misery, Eros snapped his wings—and with a move beyond what the mortal eye could see—he had her cradled in his arms and was striding toward the dining room before she could say another word.

"Fine, my dear, but I insist that I get to have you for dessert," he growled.

Entering the dining room, he gently put her down at her insistence. He could sense her growing nervousness as she fiddled with her gown. He could also tell how important this evening was to her as he took in the meal that had been laid out with care on top of the tables, all of them his favorites. Each dish carried a special memory of their time together on the island. The visible proof of her growing love for him was a pleasant punch in the gut. It filled him with a warmth that he had not felt since that cursed night so long ago.

He pushed that memory from his mind now, refusing to allow it to darken his mood and ruin this night for them. His eyes shifted restlessly throughout the room, looking to distract himself from his dark thoughts. Spying a table off in the corner, he noticed two wrapped items. They piqued his curiosity. He prowled over to the table, taking a suddenly-shy Psyche with him. Stopping in front of the presents, he turned to her, only to see how she kept twisting the ribbon of her gown. Whatever was in those packages were extremely important to her.

Gently taking hold of the hand that was twisting her ribbon to shreds, he held it against his thigh. Trying to lighten the mood, he teasingly inquired, "What do we have here?"

Eros became concerned as her gaze darted to the items and back to him, a look of apprehension in her eyes.

She took a deep breath before softly answering him. "I made a gift for both you and Eros. I thought to give them to you after dinner, but I suppose now is as good of time as any to give them to you. I hope you like them."

His heart bursting with love for her, he could not stop himself from kissing her. Breaking away, he cupped her face with both hands as he rested his forehead against hers. "Oh my little love, have no fear. I will treasure anything you have thought to give me."

Pulling back, he tucked her against his body as he turned to the two gifts on the table, each one labeled with a name. Using his free hand, he pulled on the ribbon with his name on it, quickly unwrapping his gift.

Inside he found a white chiton made of silk and linen. As he took it out and spread it across the table to get a better look at it, he noticed some unusual features. While the front was one solid piece, the back was in three pieces. The center strip was in the shape of an hourglass. It had two golden buttons at each end which fastened to the bottom of the front piece of the tunic. On closer inspection, he could see the raised crest of a pair of wings on each button. All along the edges was a rich brocade of deep blue with the Greek key design embroidered on it in gold thread.

"I made it so that it will work with your wings. The center flap goes in between them and will fasten at your waist. Will you please try it on? I want to make sure I got the measurements right."

Eros let go of her and pulled the tunic over his head. The minute it touched his skin, it disappeared from view. It fell into place, and he was stunned by the ingenuity and thoughtfulness of her gift. It was handsomely made and it fit his frame perfectly. He took a few steps back and stretched out his wings. The tunic moved with him, and did not impede his wings at all as he moved them this way and that.

"Psyche, I love this gift. It is absolute perfection. Thank you."

She blushed at his heartfelt praise. It brought her happiness that he genuinely loved her gift. He had given her so much and asked for so little in return. She smoothed her hands over his chest, testing the size and fit. "Does it truly fit? I cannot see it on you."

"It fits beautifully. I am truly blessed to have such a talented and thoughtful wife. I will wear it with pride."

Psyche smiled, relieved that the gift fit and that he loved it. It made her feel better about the gift that she had made for his beast. "Well, in that case, I hope Eros likes his gift half as much as you do."

"Of that I have no doubt. He is eager to see his gift, and I will let him rise up so that you can give him his gift, and then we will have the night to ourselves. How does that sound?"

"It sounds perfect."

Psyche felt the change in Phanes almost immediately. If someone were to ask her how she knew the difference of who was in control of her husband's body – Phanes or his drakon – she would be hard-pressed on how to answer. It was like a sixth sense, an instinctual knowing on her part.

"Psyche. Gift for me?"

"Yes, I have a gift for you, too. Do you want to open it, or would you rather I do it?"

"You open."

She moved to the table, Eros prowling right behind her, eager to see his gift. Bracing herself, she pulled the ribbon, allowing the gift to be revealed. She took a step back and let Eros get closer. She watched as he rolled out the enormous piece of fabric. It soon became evident that it was a giant sling to be worn over his body. It had the same features as the chiton that she had made for Phanes, albeit for a different purpose. She held her breath as he examined it.

"Pouch? Hold treasure? Kittens?" he asked, puzzled.

"Well, you can put treasure, food, or the kittens in the pouch to carry around, though I had something more specific in mind."

"What?"

Psyche took his hands and placed them on her stomach. "I thought you might want to carry our child around as we fly."

Eros dropped to his knees at her words, both he and Phanes stunned by her revelation. "Baby?" they said, their voices overlapping in stunned disbelief.

"Yes, I'm pregnant."

With the utmost care, they gently drew her to them, nuzzling her stomach, tears of joy sliding down their face.

CHAPTER 34

Psyche held on to her husband as he knelt before her, holding her with such tenderness it brought tears to her eyes. She could feel the tears that silently made their way down his face, and his joy at her announcement made her heart sing. She had been worried that he may not want the baby so soon after their marriage. His reaction to her news was more than she could have hoped for. How long they stayed that way was anyone's guess. It was sometime later that they were able to speak.

"Oh, Psyche. You have made me the happiest being in the world," he murmured against her stomach. His voice still held the dual tones of both him and his beast.

He pressed the tenderest of kisses against her belly, which was already beginning to show the slightest little pouch, he now noticed.

It had been one of the clues that she may have conceived that had sent her to seek the council of Pax, who had used her abilities as a goddess to confirm her suspicions. The memory of her friend's joy brought a smile to her lips. Pax had already begun planning to spoil her child, even before their birth.

"When did you know, my love?"

"I suspected a few days ago that I might be with child. I was late with my menses—which is not unusual for me—and my breasts had become rather sensitive. I was suddenly tired more often than not, and I had had the strangest cravings these past few days."

"What have you been craving?"

"Anything and everything with honey. I cannot seem to get enough of it."

"Then you will have all the honey you could ever want," he decreed.

She smiled at his command, his dominant side beginning to reassert itself. His protective nature was going to become worse, she thought ruefully. She would be fortunate if he allowed her to walk on her own two feet, let alone work the gardens.

On the wings of that thought, he stood up, and with the utmost care, Phanes led her to the nearest seat, making sure that she was comfortable on it before he protectively curved his body around hers, his hand tenderly covering their child.

"Psyche, hold still for me. I wish to use my powers to examine you, to make sure that you and the baby are alright."

"Of course."

Eros separated his conscious mind from his body and entered his wife's body. He made his way to her womb, where he gently approached the tiny little being. It was so small and delicate, barely the size of an olive. He was in awe at the life that they had created. Sending waves of love to surround their child, he was startled at the intelligence he could already discern. It was aware of his presence.

Taking a closer look, he laughed in rueful delight. A

daughter. He was going to need an arsenal of arrows to protect his little girl from the males of this world. His beast snorted in agreement, though his drakon thought it would just be easier to tear the males limb from limb if they came sniffing around their daughter. On that, they were in agreement; no one could ever possibly be good enough for their little princess.

With a last soft touch, he pulled out of Psyche's body. "My love, we are having a little girl."

Psyche's eyes widened in shock. Pax had said nothing about the sex of their child when she had examined her. "Phanes, are you sure?"

Laughing in delight, he kissed her reverently on the lips before answering. "Quite sure. She is going to be quite the handful."

"Are you pleased? I know most men want a son for their firstborn."

"Then it is a good thing that I am not most men. I am absolutely thrilled with our daughter. Now, let me feed my two little princesses. We must make sure that she grows up big and strong like her parents."

Eros spent the better part of the evening feeding her the choicest morsels of the meal that she had made for them, seeing to her every want and need. He took every opportunity to touch her stomach, his obvious pleasure in her pregnancy evident in these little caresses. He even began to talk to her stomach, playfully asking if their child had any special food requests. It made her laugh to watch his playful antics. He even talked to her belly, seemingly carrying on full conversations with the baby.

It was later in the evening as they were lying in bed, resting—at his insistence—that she broached the subject that she had been meaning to ask about since discovering that she was pregnant. Her head was resting on his chest, the echo of his heartbeat a soothing balm. "Phanes, I have a favor to ask of you."

"Anything," he murmured against her hair.

"I wish for my sisters to visit me here on the island." She could feel the sudden tension that gripped her husband. When he said nothing, neither granting nor denying her request, she pressed on. "I know your concerns, and I share them, as well. I am grateful to you for allowing my parents to visit. I want to see my sisters as well, actually. I *need* to see them, especially now."

Frowning, he asked, "But why do you feel you need to see them so urgently?"

"I need to see them because of the baby. No one on the island has had children. My sisters have been with child several times, though they have no living children to show for it. That scares me. I have so many concerns about the baby. I want to know if I am doing anything wrong, what I should expect, and if there is anything I should be doing now for the baby. I have so many questions, and no one to ask."

"You could ask me your questions," he grumbled. "I am highly intelligent, and it is my child, as well."

She lifted her head up, giving him the most incredulous expression. "My lord, do you mean to tell me that you have been pregnant?"

"Well, no," he sputtered.

"Then how could you possibly answer any of my questions, then?"

"Women have babies all the time. How hard can it be?"

She shook her head in exasperation. "Spoken like a true man. Fine then, tell me: What does it feel like when the child begins to move inside of me?"

"Well…"

"Or what should I do for the nausea that has been plaguing me these past few mornings? Why are my breasts so tender?"

"That one I can answer. It is because they are preparing to produce milk so that you can nurse our child."

"Very good my lord," she said drolly. "You could answer *one* out of my three questions, and that one that I already knew the answer to, by the way."

"Then why did you ask me that question if you already knew?" he demanded.

"To prove my point. I need to talk to someone who has been pregnant, who knows the warning signs to look out for. I need my sisters."

Eros was about to counter her argument when he glimpsed the true depths of the fear that she was trying to hide from him. It made both him and his beast sit up in alarm. "Psyche, have you been having any problems with the baby? Tell me."

"No, but I am worried. Pax said the baby was fine when she confirmed my suspicions, but that does not mean something cannot happen later in the pregnancy, or after the baby is born. Children die so easily in our world, and so do their mothers from childbirth. It scares me."

Eros pulled her tightly to him. The sudden terror that gripped him sent him into a rage wanting to destroy the threat to their wife and child. How did one fight an enemy when the enemy was childbirth?

"When I used my powers to see our child, the little one was fine. She is nestled just as she should be in your womb, but I will bring in Hera and Artemis if I need to. Eileithyia and Asclepius will attend the birth, and nothing will happen to you or our child. I swear it."

"Phanes, I know that you will do everything to protect

our child, but I still need to speak to my sisters. I want the comfort and knowledge that they can give me. Please, let them come to the island. For my own peace of mind."

Sighing in defeat, he said, "Fine. I will arrange for them to visit in a few days' time."

CHAPTER 35

Eros stepped back to run a critical eye over the project that he had started on the moment he arrived on Mt. Olympus after learning of his impending fatherhood. He stole every moment he could to work on his creation, determined to have it finished before the baby arrived. Smiling at the thought of his daughter, he lovingly ran a hand over the image he was carving into one of the panels. It was still rough, but it was beginning to take shape.

He refused to use his powers. He wanted to make this gift with his own two hands, much as Psyche and the nymphs of the island were doing by making all the clothing and blankets for the baby. His heart swelled with pride when he remembered the joy that had filled the island at their announcement. The outpouring of love and support humbled him.

He was about to start working on another section when he felt the stirring of ancient power. Shaking his head, he put aside his tools and stood up. He recognized who had entered his home unannounced. Only Anteros would dare. His brother had disappeared for a few weeks, refusing to answer his mental calls. His only communication had been a cryptic message about seeing old friends. Eros looked forward to sharing his news with his twin, and to find out what his brother had been up to.

Anteros walked into the room, sealing the door behind him. He took in the various pieces scattered all over the floor. "Picking up a new hobby? Or have you suddenly decided you want to replace Hephaistos in the pantheon?"

Laughing in delight at his sarcastic comment, Eros stepped up to his brother and pulled him into a bear hug. "Neither. I am working on a gift for your niece."

Anteros stiffened, though he returned Eros' embrace, threatening to crush his ribs before pushing away. Keeping a hold on his shoulders, Anteros locked eyes with him, joy and concern warring in his gaze. "Niece? Psyche is pregnant?"

"Yes, she is a little over two months. It is a little girl, and she is highly intelligent. She was able to communicate with both me and my beast," he boasted, his voice heavy with pride.

When Anteros said nothing, Eros' instincts screamed at him that something was wrong. His brother loved children. They were the only group —aside from animals—that Anteros genuinely liked to spend time with. "What is the matter, brother? You seemed displeased with my news."

"No, I am not displeased with the baby. I am only concerned about the timing, and with other things."

"What do you mean?"

Anteros broke away and wandered over to the panel with the rough carving. His hand absentmindedly traced the image; he was lost in thought. Eros knew better than to interrupt his brother while he gathered his thoughts. It was on rare occasions that Anteros hesitated to speak his mind, and that was only when what he had to say was of great importance.

Anteros turned to face him. "I am very pleased that Psyche is with child, but at the same time, I am very concerned. With our metamorphosis, neither one of us was certain that we could sire a child. Now we know that at least you can have children."

"Anteros, if I can father children, so can you. We are twins. Remember that brother."

A humorless smile twisted his brother's lips. "We did not start out as twins, not even the same species, for that matter. It was only as we lay wounded under the sea that we merged and changed. You gained a drakon, and I gained this shell, but at heart I am still more beast than man. My concern is what type of progeny we will father. Will our children inherit our duel nature? Will they be born with this shell, or will they be born with a drakon shell? That is if Psyche can carry the babe to term. There is no guarantee that she will not miscarry. What impact will this pregnancy have on her? She is mortal. What about the birth? Can she survive giving birth to a drakon? There are too many unanswered questions. This is uncharted territory for all of us, and I fear we are not ready to deal with this situation."

Panic and rage gripped both Eros and his beast. To have Anteros give voice to the fears and concerns that he himself had pushed to the side since learning of Psyche's pregnancy sent him into a killing rage. He wanted to destroy something, anything to release his pent-up rage and fear.

Snarling, he launched himself at the wall, punching it repeatedly. Blood dripped from his torn knuckles, leaving blood smears all along the wall and the floor. Again and again he hit the wall, only to have it repair itself after every hit. It only sent his rage further out of control, threatening to cause him to do something rash, both he and his beast mindless with rage.

"Eros, stop!"

Anteros grabbed him from behind, using his own abilities and drakon to counter his, preventing Eros from using his powers to blast the whole of Mt. Olympus to the ground, killing every immortal on the mountain.

Flashing them from Mt. Olympus, Anteros brought them to the very depths of Tartarus instead, the only place that might be able to contain their destructive powers if he was unable to get Eros back under control. Releasing his brother, Anteros blasted him, sending him tumbling to the ground on his hands and knees.

Eros turned on him, snarling.

"Get yourself under control, brother, or I will chain you down here until you see reason," Anteros warned.

Eros laughed demonically. Jumping to his feet, he charged Anteros, and the fight was on. It was a dirty, no-holds-barred fight. Both of them evenly matched. Tartarus shook from the violence of their fight, but the wardens too scared to venture anywhere near the two combatants. Their violence and rage scared even the souls of the damned trapped in everlasting torment.

It was several hours later before both Eros and Anteros slid down and rested against one of the walls, spent and out of breath from their fight. Both bore various wounds, though they quickly healed and faded away as if they never existed.

Neither spoke for some time. It was Eros who finally broke the silence. "Forgive me brother. I did not mean to lose control like that."

Snorting, Anteros glared at him. "You mean the temper tantrum, do you not? Chaos save us all if your child has your temperament. Females are so much more vicious in their anger then we males will ever be."

Eros closed his eyes, silently agreeing with his brother. A wrathful female was something to truly fear. "Thank you."

"For what?"

"For stopping me before I crossed the point of no return. I have only myself to blame. I truly did not think about trying to prevent her from getting pregnant. She is a part of me. Of us. All I want is for her to reunite our souls together, for us to love one another, and for her to be safe. Now I have become her greatest threat. I did not think this through, and she and our child may pay the price for my stupidity. I cannot lose her again."

Anteros turned to look at Eros; the misery and self-condemnation on his face was painful to see. It brought back too many bad memories for both of them. "Eros, we will let nothing harm her or the child. There are those with the skills needed to make sure that she and the babe will be fine. Now that we know what the issues are, we can prepare for them. We have come too far to fail now."

Eros looked in amazement at his brother. "Since when have you become the voice of reason?"

"Since you have been acting like me, one of us needs to be the adult, and Psyche is not here, so that leaves me."

Chuckling, Eros stood up and offered his hand to his brother. Anteros allowed him to pull him to his feet. An inhuman wail ripped through the air before he could respond to his brother's comment. It had been a long time since he had stepped foot in Tartarus. It made him wonder why his brother had chosen this location for their fight. It also reminded him of his brother's mysterious absence.

"Anteros, tell me why you disappeared these past few weeks."

Anteros' face hardened in fury. "Follow me, and I will show you."

Eros followed his brother through Tartarus, ignoring the pleas from the condemned to save them. There was no mercy for the souls who had committed such heinous crimes as those imprisoned in Tartarus. Before long, they stood in front of the door of a lone cell.

"Look and tell me what you see," commanded Anteros.

Walking up to the door, Eros placed his hand on it. Within seconds, the echo of power that still lingered in the empty cell vibrated through his body. Only one of the ancient gods could have such a power signature. Many of the primordial gods and goddesses had been locked away when Eros and Anteros had fallen. The location of their prison was still a mystery. The identity of this one was masked, though what they were was not.

Opening the door, Eros looked into the empty cell, trying to get a clue as to the identity of the prisoner. It was empty of everything; even light could not penetrate the blackness. A shudder ran through him as residual pain from the punishment that the prisoner had endured hit him hard in the gut and threatened to drive him to his knees. Chaos be damned, whoever this person was, they could not be sane after eons of enduring so much agony. Stumbling back, Eros demanded, "Who was imprisoned here?"

"That I do not know. All I know is that they are one of us, and they are free. Whose side they are on is the real question. War is coming, and a new player has been added to the field."

CHAPTER 36

Psyche stood out in the garden waiting for the arrival of her sisters. It had taken a week for the arrangements to be made for their visit. In the meantime, it had been a magical time for her and her husband. They spent every moment of the night together. He lavished her and their child with love and attention. It had brought them closer together in so many ways. Her love for him had grown until it threatened to consume her.

However, his protective nature had also intensified to new heights, which had put her on edge when he was not on the island. She could almost forget how protective he was when they were together; he had the ability to distract her. It was when he was *not* on the island that she could see how overbearing he was becoming since learning of her pregnancy. He stressed over every little thing, instructing the nymphs of the island to never leave her alone. She was under constant supervision, and it was stressful to never have a moment to herself.

She was interrupted from her musings as the wind picked up and swirled around her, signaling the arrival of Zephyrus.

Looking up at the star-filled night, she could make out the figures of her two sisters as they were carried by the wind. Within minutes, they landed in the courtyard.

Psyche rushed over to them, embracing them. Even though she was the youngest, she towered over them, having gained height after they had left home. It had been several years since they had all been together. She pulled back to see how the years had treated her sisters since she last saw them.

Aikaterini, the eldest, was the first to step out of their shared embrace, putting a slight distance between her and her sisters. Psyche felt her heart ache at how life's trials had taken their toll on her sister's appearance. Her sable hair was now threaded with silver. Her brown eyes had a sharp edge that had not been there the last time that she had seen her. She realized with a start that the last time they had all been together was at Emilia's wedding to the king of a neighboring city-state. Her olive complexion showed the passage of her life. Her mouth was slightly too small for her face, set in what looked like a perpetual frown. She carried more weight around the middle from her pregnancies, and was the shortest of the three sisters, even though she was the oldest.

Psyche turned to her middle sister. Emilia was more on the pretty side. It seemed that the years had been a little kinder to her than to their eldest sister. Her dark brown hair and grey eyes still held some of her youth. She also still retained her slender—almost boyish—frame. Psyche frowned in concern as she noted how her sister seemed thinner and more fragile than the last time she had seen her. Her skin was too pale.

She was about to inquire after her health when Zephyrus landed a few yards from them. The god of the west wind was an intimidating figure to those who did not know him. Her two sisters held on to each other, fearful of being in the presence of the ancient god.

Psyche smiled in welcome and walked confidently over to stand in front of him. Extending her hand in greeting, he clasped her hand and bowed over it, pressing a kiss to the back of it before straightening. Smiling gently down at her, Zephyrus tucked her hand in the crook of his arm and led her a little away from her sisters, not wanting them to hear their conversation. "Well met, my lady. I see that you have been successfully taming the beast you married."

"Is a husband ever really tamed, my lord?" she said wryly.

"According to my wife, it takes a strong woman to tame a beast. Or as she calls it, bullheaded males. You both have many things in common, one being having managed to tame the men in your life, though do not tell her I said that."

Laughing, Psyche murmured, "I find that I like your wife's way of thinking. I hope that someday I can make her acquaintance."

"She would like that, as well. I also wish to extend my heartfelt congratulations on the news of your child. It is a great blessing."

Psyche protectively covered her stomach with her free hand. "Thank you. I would like to ask you for some advice."

"Of course. How can I be of service?"

She sighed. "Phanes has become even more protective of me since I told him about the baby, if that is even possible. I am under constant supervision, I am never left alone, and it is slowly driving me mad. How can I get him to ease his over protectiveness?"

"I hate to admit that I can understand his need to protect you. You are carrying his child, and there is very little he can do to help you. You bear the entire burden—and all the risks—while you are pregnant, and this is a difficult thing for a man such as your husband to handle. We are warriors; it is ingrained in us to protect our families from any threat, yet we cannot fight this battle. We are helpless and unable to shoulder any of the burdens. It is not an easy thing for men such as your husband and I to deal with. I was the same way when Khloris was carrying our child."

Psyche frowned, mulling over his words before replying. "I had not thought of that in those terms, though you do make a valid point. I did not think that men thought of pregnancy in those terms."

"Some do, some do not. I would advise discussing your feelings and concerns with Phanes. Tell him that you are unhappy and he will do whatever is necessary to remedy that —though I will caution that you will never convince him to completely abandon his protective instincts. You should able at least convince him to rein in his more intrusive measures."

"Thank you. I will do as you advise."

Releasing her hand, Zephyrus took a step back and bowed before replying, "Very good. I will return in the morning to escort your sisters back home. Enjoy your visit."

Smiling, Psyche waved as he flew off into the distance. Then, turning to face her sisters, she faltered for a moment. Their hard expressions off-putting. Within a blink of the eye, their expressions smoothed, however, making Psyche doubt what she had seen.

As she reached her sisters' side, her misgivings were forgotten, though. She linked arms, leading them out of the courtyard and toward the palace, intent on showing them her home.

CHAPTER 37

"I cannot believe that you walked right up to the god of the west wind and spoke to him with such familiarity," scolded Aikaterini. "He is a god, Psyche; he could easily strike you down if he felt you were not giving him the respect that he is owed. You must be more careful."

Psyche smiled. "I appreciate your concern for my welfare, sister. Zephyrus is an imposing figure, I will grant you that. However, he has been to the island a few times since I have been here, so we have developed a rapport of sorts. "

"You have a friendship with a god?" asked Emilia.

"I would not call it a friendship, per se. More a mutual respect."

She then led her sisters into the palace, taking them on a tour. They expressed their awe and wonder at the splendor of her home. They peppered her with a variety of questions about it and her life on the island, that she was able to answer honestly—for the most part. However, she did have to deflect several questions about her husband.

Psyche was incredibly eager to reconnect with her sisters

after so many years apart. She wanted to hear how they had been faring since the last time they were all together.

"Oh, here we are. I have a surprise for both of you," she said as she led them into the treasury room, hoping to distract them from their more pointed questions.

She let go of her sisters and stepped forward, opening the door to reveal the treasures that had been placed inside. She stepped back and motioned for them to enter the room. Her sisters walked several steps before stopping in amazement at the treasures that filled a very large table set in the center of the room. Psyche stepped in and walked over to it. "I wanted to give you both gifts to take home with you, to show my love and appreciation."

Psyche motioned for her sisters to sit in the chairs that had been placed before each set of gifts that she had painstakingly chosen for them. She watched as they opened the various chests and bags filled with gold and silver, precious jewels, rare perfumes and spices, and expensive bolts of cloth. Each of them expressed shock and joy over their respective gifts.

Psyche had agonized over what to give them when Phanes had reminded her that their wealth was vast and to not hold back on her gifts to her family. It had been the same thing he had told her when her parents had visited. She still sometimes struggled to comprehend the seemingly limitless amount of wealth that her husband had at his disposal.

Then there was a knock on the door, calling out her permission to enter. Psyche saw the bell necklace that signaled that Rhea had entered the room.

"My lady, the evening meal is ready."

Aikaterini and Emilia both jumped at hearing the disembodied voice. They looked around, making the sign to ward off evil as their fearful eyes locked on the floating necklace.

"Be at ease, my sisters. This is Rhea. Forgive me, I forgot

to tell you that all the inhabitants of the island are nymphs and are invisible to mortals. Rhea, these are my sisters Aikaterini and Emilia."

Psyche silently scolded herself for causing her sisters fear; she had failed to tell them about the invisible nymphs of the island. She had become so accustomed to speaking to them that it had become normal for her.

"It is an honor to meet the sisters of my lady," said Rhea. "If it pleases you, I will arrange for your sisters' gifts to be sent to their homes while you are having dinner. They will be delivered to their homes before the dawn, when Zephyrus escorts them back."

"Thank you, Rhea. That would be most appreciated." Turning to her sisters, Psyche motioned for them to follow her out of the room. "I have prepared a meal for us out in the courtyard, where we can relax and catch up. Please follow me."

* * *

"I MUST SAY, this is a splendid meal. My compliments to your servants," said Emilia.

"Yes, it is quite good," Aikaterini agreed.

Psyche smiled as she looked over the courtyard. The nymphs of the island had outdone themselves with the meal. She made a mental note to thank each and every one who had made this night possible. Now that she was alone with her sisters, however, she hoped to get answers to her most pressing questions and concerns.

"I am so glad you are enjoying it. Now please, tell me how you both have been doing since we last saw each other? I think it was at your wedding, Emilia, that we were all together properly. How is your husband doing?" Psyche inquired.

Emilia grimaced in barely concealed disgust. "My husband's health is as best as can be expected at his old age, though he still manages to visit my bedchamber at least once a week. Thank the gods it is over in minutes and I can get away from him and his slobbering attentions."

Aikaterini turned to look at Emilia in sympathetic camaraderie. "He still has the energy to visit your bed weekly? You poor thing. At least my husband has gout at his old age, which has put a damper on his lusts. He can barely visit my bed once or twice a month, at best. I spend most of my days as a nursemaid to him. I do not know which is worse: rubbing his feet or having him paw at me every so often."

They both gave a derisive laugh and then caught sight of the shock on Psyche's face. "Oh, we did not mean to make you feel worse about your own situation. What you must suffer in your marriage bed being married to a beast,' Aikaterini said with a shudder, as she reached over and patted Psyche's hand. "You can tell us all about it, my dear sister. We understand the disgust and shock you must have felt that first time."

Emilia nodded in agreement. "I wish we could tell you it gets better, but I would be lying. It is something that must be endured, like any marriage."

Psyche looked at both of them, momentarily lost for words. It was a surprise to hear her sisters speak so disparagingly of their husbands and their marriages. The only marriage that she had as a blueprint was her parents,' and they were just as in love today as they had been in their youth. She would bet on her life that her mother had never spoken of her father as her sisters had spoken of their husbands. Or her father about her mother. Their love and respect for each other was in every word, glance, and touch between them.

Psyche remembered how excited her sisters had been to

be married to neighboring kings, to be crowned queens in their own right. It was all they could talk about at the time. They had even thought their husbands had been handsome once, so what had happened in the meantime to change their outlook?

"I do not understand. What happened? I thought you were both happy when you first married. I remember how you both said how handsome and wonderful your husbands were when you both were betrothed. You had your pick of suitors to choose from; father made sure of that. You both married the men of your choice."

Aikaterini snorted in disgust. "My dear little sister, how naïve you still are after all these years. We are the daughters of a king, so we had little choice in the matter. Royalty marries royalty, alliances are made through marriage, and ours were no different. We have just made the best of the situation. We have status, servants, and prestige as queens, but at the end of the day, we are married to men—and must bed those men—not the crown."

Emilia nodded in agreement. "It is our duty to perform our wifely obligations. There is little to no pleasure in it for us. We must find our own pleasures elsewhere. Our husbands only visit us to beget a legitimate heir; that is the price we pay for our privileged life. Believe me, I am very happy when my husband spends his nights with his hetaerae, or one of the servants."

Psyche watched in horrid fascination as Aikaterini agreed. She was distressed that her sisters had not found the happiness and joy in their marriages as she had found in hers. It made her reluctant to discuss her relationship with Phanes, not wanting to rub salt in an obviously open wound.

She thought about all the attempts her parents had made to marry her off over the years. Her mind drifted to Alexander and her other suitors. Would a marriage to any of them have resulted in the same bitterness and disappointment she saw in her sisters? She was afraid the answer might be yes. If not for her beauty, she may well be experiencing the same bitter disappointment as her sisters. For the first time in her life, Psyche realized that her beauty may well have been a saving grace—not a curse.

"You both wish your husbands bed other women?"

"Gods yes, don't you?" asked Emilia.

Images of the nights she and her husband spent making love flowed through Psyche's mind. Each memory was filled with passion and pleasure. Even she—with no experience to speak of —knew that her husband was extremely knowledgeable and skilled in lovemaking. His carnal desires were strong. To think of her husband sharing himself with other women was a punch to the gut. It was a vicious pain that robbed her of breath. His promise to stay faithful on their wedding night flirted through her mind. Phanes stood by his word. *He would never break a vow,* she told herself.

"Psyche? Psyche!"

Snapping back to the present, she looked at the concern on her sisters' faces. "I'm sorry. What did you say?"

"My poor sister, it is a wonder you have not lost your mind trapped on this island. This gilded cage must be suffocating. Please, tell us the truth about your husband and where he is," Aikaterini implored.

"And *what* he is," added Emilia.

Shifting restlessly in her seat, Psyche took a sip of her pomegranate juice, delaying answering their questions for a few precious seconds as she thought of what response to give them. "My husband is a young man of good reputation and family. He is away on a hunting trip at the moment."

Even to her own ears, her words sounded rehearsed. When she said no more, an indecipherable look passed between her sisters. After silently communicating for a moment, they turned expectantly to Psyche. "And?"

"He is fair of hair and strong of stature. He is kind and generous. He makes me happy."

Aikaterini snorted. "They all start out that way. They trick you into believing that they will always treat you as they did before the marriage. The thrill of the hunt. Once they have you, when they no longer have to work for your affections, their true colors are always revealed."

Emilia nodded. "Men have been using that tactic for eons. My husband showered me with attention and gifts before we married. He made promises to be faithful, to treat me with care and affection. However, once I confessed my love for him, he changed. He became less concerned about my feelings. The thrill of the hunt was gone. You will see."

Psyche looked at the both of them, barely able to stand listening to their words. It sent a secret fear racing through her body. Would Phanes treat her differently now that she had confessed that she was falling in love with him? Was it the thrill of the hunt that drove him?

No, she scolded herself. Their relationship was nothing like her sisters' with their husbands.

"I can see you telling yourself that your marriage is different," Aikaterini said.

"How—"

"Please, even after all these years, you still cannot hide your thoughts from me. I helped take care of you, remember? It is not that hard to see the thoughts spinning in your head. We are not trying to hurt you, sister, just prepare you for the inevitable. Men of power are all the same."

"My husband is not a king," she protested.

"No,' Emilia agreed, "but he *is* a man of money and power. One only has to see this island home to know that. He is powerful, and powerful men only want certain things from their wives."

"And what would those certain things be?" demanded Psyche.

"A caretaker and heirs," replied Emilia.

Aikaterini nodded in agreement. "The wife manages the household and provides the legitimate children. We are essentially servants and broodmares," she said, reaching over to grasp Emilia's hand, "though we both seem to be failures when it comes to providing living heirs."

A chill ran down Psyche's spine at her sister's words. Without conscious thought, her hands covered her stomach, the telltale gesture causing her sisters to gasp in surprise.

"Psyche, are you with child?"

She nodded her head, unable to speak without betraying how upset her sisters had made her feel.

Tears filled her eyes, and she found herself enveloped in their embrace. Her fears and emotions were at the forefront of her mind. She tried to maintain her composure, but it crumbled when Emilia asked her in a tear-filled whisper, "Is this your first pregnancy?"

"Yes," she whispered. "I am so afraid for the baby. Please tell me what to do to protect her. I don't want to lose my baby."

Psyche felt Emilia stiffen at her plea before she pulled herself away. "I just lost my fourth baby several weeks ago. I was seven months along."

Psyche gasped in horror at Emilia's revelation. She looked at Aikaterini, who nodded as well. "I miscarried my last child about eight months ago. That was the third baby for me. I was about three months along this last time."

"By the gods, I am so sorry," Psyche said passionately. "I did not know you both had lost so much. Why have you not said anything in your letters? I would have come to both of you."

"And what could you have done? Be the center of attention, as you always are? It would have caused more problems and stress for me than I needed at the time," Aikaterini said, her voice thinly laced with contempt.

The slap of her sister's comment sent Psyche reeling back, stunned by the underlining jealousy she heard. In that instant, she hated her looks all over again. The fact that her own family felt they could not deal with the problems her physical appearance caused made her want to crawl into herself. "Is that what you think?"

"Aikaterini!" scolded Emilia. "You know that Psyche is not at fault for how people react to her looks." Sighing, she shook her head as she took hold of Psyche's hand, drawing her attention. "We know that you never wanted all the attention and problems that your beauty has caused you and the family. It was not that we did not want to reach out, it is just that it was—and still is—a painful subject for us both. Every baby that we lose is one more dagger in our hearts. To hope that this time will be different, only to see our babies die over and over again. It has gotten to the point that I now dread the possibility of conceiving, for I wish never to become pregnant again."

Aikaterini nodded in agreement. "Forgive me Psyche, I did not mean to lash out at you. Seeing you pregnant…" she broke off, unable to finish.

"I understand."

"Now, do you have any questions for us about your pregnancy?" Emilia asked.

"Yes, I have so many concerns."

"Well then, let us help you."

* * *

AIKATERINI AND EMILIA watched as Zephyrus disappeared into the night sky. Their servants with their gift-laden carriages were waiting for them down the hill from where they had been left, thankfully out of earshot.

"I cannot believe it. Psyche is married, and happily so, to a rich young man while we are married to old fools. Where is the justice in that? Did you see the amount of power and wealth she has at her command? It is disgusting. Her husband lets her be free with his wealth, while we have to beg our miserly husbands for a few coins. I am sick and tired of her always being the favored one, while we live in the shadows of her beauty and fame," Aikaterini bitterly complained.

Emilia snorted in disgust. "I know how you feel. I had hoped that she would finally get what she deserves when I heard what the Pythia had prophesied for her. Imagine her married to a beast! It warmed my heart when I thought of what she would suffer at his hands, but it seems fate has smiled on her yet again, and given her *more* than she deserves. What I would give to trade places with her: wealth, power, and a virile lover for bed sport."

"I, as well, sister."

"Then perhaps I can be of some assistance."

Aikaterini and Emilia whirled around. At first, they could not see the person who had spoken in the dead of night. As the moonlight peered through the evening clouds, they could barely make out a cloaked figure off in the distance.

"Who are you? Show yourself!" Aikaterini demanded.

"Who I am is of no concern. What is more important is what I can do for the two of you. Your sister is married to an immortal, and is living the life you both should have been living in her stead. She has stolen so much from you with her unnatural beauty: your parents' love and affection, friends, even potential lovers. Your own husbands lust after her. How many times have they whispered her name while they rutted upon you? Always being compared to her, and always falling short. Now she will give birth to a healthy child, while you two have buried yours. I can help you with your heart's desire: to see Psyche punished, and for you to take her place. Is that not what you truly want?"

Aikaterini and Emilia shared a long look before Aikaterini asked the mysterious figure, "How do you know all this?"

"I know many things. I know the pain of watching someone take what belongs to you. To be helpless to stop them. It is a burning wound that festers; the only way to cure it is to cut out the infection."

"Why would you help us?" demanded Emilia.

A chill went up their spines at the evil laughter that emanated from the cloaked figure before it answered the question. "Your sister and her husband have much to answer for. They have taken much from me and I owe them a debt, and I always pay my debts. Now do you want my help or not?"

Smiling in malicious glee, the two women nodded their heads, eager to see Psyche brought down.

"Good. Now listen closely. Here is what you need to do."

CHAPTER 38

With the final stitch, Psyche sat back to look at the scene she had just finished. She stared at it in shock, unable to comprehend what she was seeing before her. She had no real memory of working on it, no conscious thought of what the next chapter of the story she was weaving in the threads of her tapestry was going to tell. It was as if she had been in a trance, her hands and mind disconnected from each other.

It was violent. Vicious in its brutality.

Turning her head away, she took a moment to just breathe, desperately trying to get the shudders of fear that wrecked her body under control. It was some time before she was able to muster the courage to face the tapestry before her again.

She forced herself to look at the scene. At first it was difficult to make out the details. The various threads she had used were dark: deep blues, several shades of grey, black, and charcoals. The sudden flashes of white, gold, and red brought the violence to the forefront.

It was a view of a cloud-filled night over a raging sea. In

the background, she could make out a cliff. Several men and women were floating in the red-stained sea, their lifeless bodies battered against the rocks that dotted the turbulent water. Many of them sported the wounds of battle. Bodies ripped to shreds, large gaping wounds, faces twisted in the last throes of fear and agony.

A golden-winged being stood on the cliff, looking dispassionately down at the dead. His windblown blond locks barely brushed his board shoulders. He was a warrior, and he was beautiful. It was almost too painful to look at such beauty against the ugliness of the dead and dying night. A dark-skinned serpent wrapped around him as if in an embrace. In his hand was a blood-soaked dagger.

A sense of familiarity struck her. She *knew* him. As she moved closer to get a better look, the sound of heavy footsteps approaching the room broke the silence.

Psyche quickly covered the tapestry; the scene that she had just finished was too disturbing to look at a moment longer—let alone allow her husband or any of the nymphs to see it. She had no answers for the inevitable questions her tapestry would incite.

By the time the door opened, it was safely covered, the decoy tapestry in its place. The subtle scent of musk, sandalwood, and dark spices filled the room. Turning, Psyche smiled with open joy. "Phanes."

Opening her arms, she felt the strong arms of her husband wrap themselves around her. Her feet left the ground as he brought her up, capturing her lips in a kiss. Gods, she loved the way he kissed. Several minutes later, he set her gently on her feet before sliding down to his knees before her.

He kept her safe in the circle of his arms and wings as he nuzzled her stomach, giving their child her nightly kisses and sweet greetings from her father. It never failed to set her heart aflutter with love as he showered their daughter with his love and affections.

"And how is my little princess tonight?" he murmured against her stomach.

"Your little princess has been very active today. I do believe she may have inherited your wings with all the fluttering about she has done."

"Really? Well, young lady, no flying about until you are of age," he said in a mock-stern voice.

Laughing, Psyche stroked his hair, the soft strands gliding through her fingers. It did much to calm her nerves after seeing the new scene in the tapestry.

"Are you done for the evening?"

"Yes, I am done working on the tapestry for now."

"Good, then I have something to show you before dinner."

He stood up and swept her up into his arms before heading out of the room. The torchlights in the corridor all went out all at once, leaving them in darkness. "You do know that I can walk? Being with child has not made me an invalid."

"Have pity on me. I will soon be outnumbered. I like holding you and our child. It gives me pleasure and peace. You would not deny me that, would you? Especially when our child is still safely contained in your womb. Heaven help us both if she has your sense of adventure and my wings. I will be sporting grey hair in no time, trying to keep up with the two of you."

"And what color would your hair be now, my lord? I would like to know before you turn old and grey," Psyche asked, laughing, not expecting a direct answer since he was always coy when she had inquired in the past.

"Blond."

"Blond?" she asked. A chill went down her spine. She was shocked at his direct answer.

"Yes."

"And what color are your wings? Were you born with them, or did they appear later?"

"They are white and gold, though the gold has become more prominent of late. I was born with them. Why the sudden interest?"

Psyche felt faint. He was describing the very being she had woven this evening.

When she stayed silent, Eros stopped to look down at her. She was pale as a ghost. "Psyche. What is wrong? Are you in pain? Is it the baby?"

Snapping out of her fear-laden thoughts, she looked up at the faint outline that was her husband. *It had to be a coincidence,* she told herself. Nothing more. "Forgive me, I did not mean to concern you. I just felt a little faint, is all. I'm sure it is nothing."

"It is not nothing," he bit out. "If you are unwell, you must tell me immediately. I will get the healers here at once."

"No! There is no need for healers. I am sure it is just hunger pangs. With my morning sickness, I have not eaten as much as I normally do. I will feel better once I eat, I am sure of it. If I don't, then you can send for the healers."

"Psyche, why have you not told me you were having problems?" he demanded.

She sighed. "Because I am *not* having problems. Morning sickness throughout the day is perfectly normal. Both my sisters and the healers have assured me of this. I feel better after having some toast and the chamomile tea that the nymphs make for me. I forgot to eat lunch today because I was not hungry, but now I am, so please do not make this more than it is," she pleaded, with tears in her voice.

Phanes drew her in closer, as if he could shield her from any harm. "Fine. However, if you are not feeling better after dinner, I will confine you to our bed and I will bring every healer in the known lands and have you tended to round the clock."

"Fine. Now can I please see what you wanted to show me?"

"Food first."

"Phanes, please. I won't be able to eat until I see my surprise," she begged, needing the distraction from her disturbing thoughts.

Grunting in mock annoyance, a plate of toast drizzled with butter and honey appeared floating in front of her. A flask—filled with her chamomile tea, she was sure—landed gently in her lap. "We will compromise. Eat this small snack and I will show you my surprise, and after, you will eat a proper meal. Deal?"

"Deal."

Eros watched her eat the slices of toasted bread. He took a bite when she offered him a piece, licking her finger clean of the honey that clung to her skin.

She gasped as desire hit her core, sending pleasurable waves throughout her body.

After she finished the last piece, she licked her lips to get the last of the honey, tempting him to head to their bedroom instead. The little minx knew exactly what she was doing, trying to get him to forget about her feeling faint.

"Now then, let me show you your surprise."

He headed down the corridor leading to their private wing. Instead of turning left, he turned to the right and went to stand in front of the door leading to the nursery.

Eros gently put her down until she was standing in front of the door. Placing his hands over her eyes, he said, "Now keep your eyes closed until I tell you to open them. No peeking."

"I promise, no peeking."

Once he was sure her eyes were closed, he dropped his hand. Within seconds all the torchlights flared, bathing the corridor and the nursery with vibrant light.

Opening the door, Eros took Psyche's hand and led her in the room. After several steps, he stopped and turned around, pleased to see that she still kept her eyes tightly closed.

"Alright, you can open your eyes now."

Psyche blinked as her eyes became adjusted to the bright light. Then she gasped as she saw what sat in the center of the nursery.

CHAPTER 39

Psyche looked in amazement at the giant wooden cradle that sat in the center of the room. Even from a distance, she could see that it was beautiful, a true work of art. Tears filled her eyes at the loveliness of it as she walked over to the cradle to get a better look, her husband keeping pace behind her. The closer she got to it, the more elaborate it became.

She ran her hand lovingly over its carved surface; it was so smooth it felt like silk beneath her fingers. There were no rough edges anywhere; the artisan who had created it had been meticulous in sanding it down to a polished gleam.

She slowly circled the cradle, caressing it with her hand as she took in all the details. Two kneeling winged beings—one male and one female—were on either end looking down to where their child would sleep, their arms and wings forming the main body of the cradle. Butterflies - some in flight and others in repose—were carved into the piece, with one sitting on the shoulder of the female figure.

Holding up the cradle on its back was a large drakon, its head peaking over the wings of the two figures. She recognized it was Eros. The love she felt radiating from the piece pierced her heart like an arrow, and she felt an answering surge of love.

When she remained silent, Eros felt a growing sense of unease. He feared that she did not care for the gift. Before he could say anything, however, she suddenly threw herself into his arms, letting out a sob, holding him tightly. Her tears on his bare chest sent him into a slight panic. *She hated it.* "Psyche, I will get rid of it. I will make another cradle, whatever you desire, just tell me what I did wrong."

She pulled back in surprise. "*You* made it?"

"Yes," he replied, somewhat defensively. His pride stung by her incredulous expression. "I made it with my own hands."

"Where did you find the time to make it?"

"I made it during the day. What do you think I do when I am not with you? It made our time apart more bearable."

A wistful expression graced her face. "I have no idea what you do or where you go during the day; you never tell me anything."

Guilt ate at him. The resigned tone of her voice told him she was not pushing him for information, just voicing her thoughts. Hiding who and what he was from her was becoming more unbearable every day, more so since the pregnancy. He wanted to spend his days *and* nights with her, but he was determined to follow through with his plan. *Just a little while longer,* he silently promised himself.

"You know I would tell you if I could," he said. "I *can* tell you that the time when I can reveal all to you is closer at hand."

He watched as hope filled her eyes.

"How much longer must I wait?"

He pushed back a lock of her hair before pulling her back into his embrace, tucking her head under his chin before answering. "Perhaps before the baby arrives, or shortly thereafter. I promise it won't be long now."

"Alright," she murmured.

They stood there, neither wanting to break the silence between them. It was the sudden and powerful surge of love and pleasure emanating from their daughter that broke them out of their reverie. Eros was startled by the sheer strength of the surge of power. He looked down at Psyche, about to question if she felt what he had, when he noticed the faint glow emanating from her stomach. She gasped at the sight and covered it with her hands, a small smile curving her lips. Within a few seconds, the glow slowly went out.

Psyche looked up. "Did you feel that?"

"Yes, it would seem that our daughter has inherited some of my powers. Does it concern you?"

She shook her head. "No. All I felt was pleasure and love. Our daughter having some of your powers gives me some comfort that she will be strong and healthy. I am more concerned when I think about her birth than anything else."

Eros frowned, not liking the idea that she was still afraid of childbirth. "What is worrying you?"

"Well, when I think about what our child will inherit from us, I keep thinking of how I could possibly give birth to a child with wings, or a child with an inner beast. It is difficult enough for a woman, without that consideration."

The concerns that Anteros had voiced when he first learned of Psyche's pregnancy rushed back to him, and he felt the same fear and rage that consumed him. In that moment, he hated himself all over again for the danger he had placed his wife and daughter in by not thinking this through. He should have prevented her from getting pregnant until she was an immortal again. The fact that she had thought of such possibilities on her own was a stab in the chest. She should not have to deal with such fears. He had only himself to blame.

"Psyche, I give you my word. I will be by your side when you give birth, along with the healers. You have nothing to fear. I will make sure that you feel no pain and have an easy birth."

She smiled indulgently at him before murmuring a soft, "Thank you."

He wanted to address the issue further, but Psyche had other plans.

"Now, about the cradle."

"Yes, what about it? I will make another if you desire."

"It's beautiful and absolutely perfect. I love it; don't you dare get rid of it," she commanded.

"Then why were you crying when you saw it?"

"Those were tears of joy; I am pregnant, and have been rather emotional lately. You will just have to suffer through it. This is the most wonderful gift I could ever ask for, and it is the most perfect cradle for our daughter."

She held out her arms in expectation. Shaking his head, he lifted her into his arms.

"Now then, let us go have dinner, and then, my dear, I plan to show you just how much I love your gift in our bedchamber."

Laughing, Eros carried her out of the nursery. "As you wish."

CHAPTER 40

Psyche hurried down the corridor leading to the outer courtyard. Her sisters were arriving at any minute, and she was running late this evening. She had been working on the tapestry and had lost track of time again. It was a time-consuming obsession to work on it as her pregnancy progressed. It helped keep her mind off other things.

She suspected that her husband was the winged creature in the new scenes that she had created—or at least was somehow related to the mysterious figure. After his startling direct answer about the color of his hair and wings, he had been more open of late in letting more details about his physical appearance slip out. She now knew his eyes were blue—though she was not sure what shade—and his skin was lightly tanned from the sun.

So she was married to a tall winged being with an inner beast, who had blond hair, wings of gold and white, blue eyes, tanned skin, and a physique that even Adonis could not rival. He did not fear the gods—though they feared him, according to the Pythia—and he was most likely immortal and one of the pantheon, if her suspicions were true—though he would never admit to such a membership.

He had an anger and contempt for many of the Greek gods that he tried to hide—though not well enough when he was around her. It came out in subtle waves whenever he thought no one was paying attention. It showed how comfortable he had become of late in her presence, and that sent a warm glow through her, as strange as that was.

Phanes was loving and kind, loyal to a fault to those he considered his, and he had a wicked sense of humor. He treated those on the island with a great deal of respect and courtesy, and in turn, he was given the same. However, he could also be cruel and cutting to those he held in contempt. He *was* prone to a mercurial temperament.

Yet all that could be a ruse, Psyche mused. The gods were known to play tricks on mortals. Though her husband had never lied to her that she knew of, he had never given her the complete truth, either. She knew he held back many things from her: who he truly was, why all the secrecy behind his identity, his powers, and how he protected her from Aphrodite were just a few of his secrets.

A shudder of fear traveled down her spine. Of late, on several occasions she had had the feeling that someone unknown to her and the residents of the island was watching her, stalking her. A sixth sense warned her that she was being hunted. At times it felt like a malevolent being was crouching in the shadows, waiting for a chance to get her. At other times it felt like a predatory animal similar to her husband's beast was watching her every move, keeping her in its line of sight.

Her sense of impending doom had become stronger with each thread that she weaved that brought her closer to finishing the tapestry. The countdown was almost finished, though to what, she could not say.

It was at that moment that she was suddenly brought out of her dark thoughts by her daughter's hard kicking.

She stopped to rest and catch her breath at the foot of the stairs. Looking down at her stomach, she smiled ruefully at the acrobatics of her baby. "Now, now, little one," she murmured softly as she stroked her belly, "you need to settle down for the evening while I spend some time with your aunts."

Psyche felt an answering flutter, and it took a moment before the baby settled down. Taking a deep breath, she walked out the door to see her sisters landing in the courtyard on Zephyrus' wind.

Psyche hurried over to him to give him her thanks for bringing her sisters to visit again. Smiling, he gently brushed aside her gratitude and flew away after informing her that he would be available whenever her sisters were ready to depart.

Turning, she smiled at Aikaterini and Emilia and hurried over to kiss their cheeks. Linking arms with them, she led the way into the palace for the evening meal.

"How are you both faring this evening?" Psyche inquired. "I hope your journey was not a taxing one."

Aikaterini patted her hand. "Well, my dear. Very well. I am just grateful to have my feet firmly on the ground again."

"Yes," Emilia agreed. "Though I will confess it is quite scary to be flown on the wind for such a distance. Let alone be in the presence of one of the gods."

"Oh, I love being flown about. I find it quite exhilarating." Psyche cursed herself as soon as the words left her mouth. She had not meant to let slip such a damning detail about her life on the island. Her husband's warning was still ringing in her ears from the previous night.

Phanes was not happy with this second visit by her sisters. If truth be told, he had not been happy with the first, either. He seemed to have major misgivings when it came to her sisters, yet he had no such issues with her parents. He had been insistent that they did not have her best interests at heart, that they were a threat to her—and the baby.

Psyche bit her lip in consternation as both Aikaterini and Emilia sent her probing looks.

"Really, my dear? Do you mean to tell me that Zephyrus takes you out on the wind whenever you wish?" Aikaterini inquired.

"Why, Psyche," Emilia chimed in, "what a little adventuress you are. Is that what they are calling it now? Flying, indeed," she said, chuckling with a knowing grin. "However do you keep such a delicious treat all to yourself without your husband discovering your little indiscretion?"

"Yes, do tell, my dear."

Psyche felt her cheeks flush with the rise of her temper. "I meant…that is to say…"

Aikaterini gave her a hard stare. "Sister, you must be more careful. Taking a lover as a married woman is a serious issue. What if the child is born with a set of wings? How will you explain such a thing to your husband? He could well kill you for such an offence."

"Phanes would never hurt me, or any child, for that matter."

Emilia shook her head. "Sister, men want children from their own loins to inherit their name and possessions. A bastard child is worse than no child at all to many, especially a man as powerful as your husband must be to have such wealth. This is no small matter. Please tell us you have not been so foolish as to take a god for a lover. You know as well as we do that the women and children of such affairs are the ones to suffer punishment, while the gods go on their merry way to the next conquest, with no thought to the carnage they leave in their wake."

A frown flittered across Psyche's face; her sisters' misunderstanding of her life on the island gave her pause. Or was it a misunderstanding? Her husband was an immortal being—a god, if she were being honest with herself—while she was a mortal. How long would this half-life of a relationship between them last? She would grow old and eventually die, while her husband lived on, perhaps moving on to his next conquest. And what of her child? The lives of the demigod children rarely ever ended well for them. Was she damning her daughter to an uncertain future?

It would do no good to admit her suspicions that her husband could well be one of the gods, or that Zephyrus was not her secret lover. A shiver ran down her spine at the thought of what her husband would do if she ever took one. His threat to destroy any who dared to try to take her from him still resonated all these months later.

Psyche was pulled out of her thoughts when Aikaterini nodded her head in agreement. The concern her sisters had for her well-being—albeit without any merit—did much to assuage her feeling of upset over their misunderstanding of her life on the island.

"I am not having an affair with Zephyrus," she finally replied, hoping that her sisters would leave her slip-up well enough alone.

Before they could question her further, they entered the dining room, where Rhea and several of the nymphs were waiting for them. All three women settled down in the dining hall and spent the next hour catching up on each other's lives since their last meeting.

After the last of the dishes had been cleared away, the three sisters relaxed, sipping goblets of pomegranate juice, chatting about various bits of gossip. Their conversation ebbed and flowed until they fell into a relative quiet, exhausting all the small talk the three could summon among them.

Aikaterini turned to look at Emilia, and seeing her give a small nod, they both turned to Psyche, a concerned look on their faces. "Little sister, we have a confession to make. After our last visit, we went to the temples of Eileithyia and Hera to make offerings. We were concerned about your baby, and we wanted to get advice from the priestesses about how to best help you."

Eyes glistening with tears, Psyche was overwhelmed with love for them. "My dear sisters, I don't know what to say but thank you."

Emilia smiled. "We are family, bound by blood. How can we not try to help you, especially with how isolated you are on this island?"

Aikaterini nodded. "Yes, the priestesses were most helpful. They have given permission for you to stay at either temple when you are close to your term, and be there, so that they can give you all the assistance you could ever need."

"Yes," added Emilia. "And of course we will be there, as well. Isn't that wonderful?" Then she frowned. "Although will your husband be willing to allow you to journey off the island?"

Aikaterini piped up. "Yes, Psyche. Will he allow Zephyrus to fly you to one of the temples when you are close to your time?"

Psyche struggled to come up with an appropriate response to her sisters' questions. She did not want to appear ungrateful, but she could not reveal any details about her husband, or the fact that he had already planned to have the best healers attend her. "Oh, well. He has already made arrangements for when my time is near."

"What arrangements has he made? Babies have a schedule all their own, and can be quite unpredictable when they are ready to emerge—not to mention all the complications that can happen during the birth. I cannot tell you how many times we were caught unprepared because the babies chose to come too soon—or late."

Emilia nodded. "Yes, men have no clue to the battle we women fight to bring our babies into this world."

Psyche restlessly got up without a word and went over to the side table to pick up the small oinochoe of pomegranate juice, trying to hide the fear and panic her sisters' comments had caused her.

While Psyche had her back to her sisters, Emilia quickly poured liquid from a vial hidden in her necklace into Psyche's drink. The two sisters shared a smirk. Then Emilia hid the vial, while Aikaterini gently shook the goblet to mix the liquid into the remains of Psyche's drink. By the time Psyche turned back to fill all their drinks, there was no evidence that the two women had tampered with hers.

"Here, Psyche, let me take that," said Emilia, as she stood and took the oinochoe from her, filling all their goblets. "Relax and enjoy your drink. I'm sorry if we upset you with our concerns; it is just that we worry for you."

Psyche gratefully took a few sips as her sisters looked on. Almost instantly, she started to feel lightheaded. Unable to keep her eyes open, she began to sink back as Emilia grabbed the goblet from her hand and put it on the table. Aikaterini stood up and made sure the room was completely secured before returning to Psyche's side. After checking that the potion had taken hold of her, both sisters took a seat on either side of her.

"Now Psyche, tell us the truth about your husband."

CHAPTER 41

Psyche drifted in languid bliss between wakefulness and sleep. Her dreaming mind had her floating out among the stars, cradled in the center of a swirling mass of multicolored clouds. All around her, the stars danced like candlelight caught in a gentle breeze, swaying to and fro to music only the heavens could hear.

Sighing with pleasure, her attention was drawn back down to her bed of clouds, her hand disappearing the further it went in, yet it held her as securely as any bed. Turning over onto her hands and knees, she arched her back in a stretch, much like her kittens did after a nap. It felt so good to get the kinks out of her back, especially as her body changed with her pregnancy. A sudden urge to play gripped her, and the bed of clouds responded to her wish.

Out of the corner of her eye, her attention was caught by a curling wisp of smoke that reminded her of the cords that the kittens loved to attack. Turning to face it, she wished that it was distinct and a different color so that she could catch it. As soon as the thought entered her mind, the ribbon of smoke changed color to a lovely shade of pink and began to tease her, moving closer and then darting away as soon as she tried to snatch it.

Giggling, she crouched down, shook her bum, and then pounced on the ribbon of smoke. The bed of clouds easily held her. She pounced again and again as she chased the ribbon. It kept being pulled away from her at the last moment, however, reforming a few feet away.

On her last try, she finally caught it. Laughing in triumph, she used it to tie her hair back off her neck before falling back onto the bed, flinging her arms and legs out just like a starfish. Then she closed her eyes, letting her rapidly beating heart settle back down.

It was while she lay there that she became aware of a voice disturbing her rest. At first it was a low murmur, but it kept increasing in volume until it became too loud to ignore, pulling her out of her nap. She frowned in annoyance at the persistent calling of her name.

"Psyche."

She opened her eyes and watched in muted fascination as multiple stars above her moved to create the outline of two shadow women. The two star maidens looked vaguely familiar to her. She reached out a hand to touch them, but they were too far away.

"Psyche."

"Psyche, can you hear me?" said a familiar raspy voice from one of the star maidens.

She knew that voice belonged to someone she loved and trusted, but she could not remember who. The more she tried to identify the speaker, the more elusive the knowledge became as pressure built in her head. It only eased when she let go of her pursuit of the identity of the speaker.

It did not matter, her mind whispered.

"Yes," she murmured.

"Now Psyche, tell us the truth about your husband."

"My husband?"

"Yes, tell us about him," echoed a second familiar voice, though this one had a higher pitch.

Thoughts of Phanes filled her mind. Image after image danced through her subconscious until it stopped at her most recent memory. Phanes had surprised her in the kitchen while she was preparing the evening meal. One minute she was laughing at the story Rhea was telling of how she had found the kittens sound asleep in a bowl that had been filled with bits of various meats. Bits of fat and meat clinging to their little whiskers, the kittens had snuck past the cook and gotten into mischief when she had stepped out of the room for a moment. Not one scrap of meat was left for the meat pies the cook had been preparing for the evening meal.

Tears were streaming down her face as Rhea imitated the strident yelling of the cook when she discovered the little thieves in her meat bowl, blissfully sleeping as she cursed them to Tartarus and back. It was the reason why Psyche was in the kitchen preparing an alternate evening meal, to help soothe the cantankerous nymph who ruled the kitchen.

One minute Psyche and Rhea were laughing over the antics of the little thieves and the next the room was plunged into darkness, Rhea gone, and her husband slipping up behind her to wrap her up in a loving embrace, pressing a kiss against her throat. When he inquired what had made her laugh so hard she was in tears, he soon joined her when she recounted the story of the four kitchen bandits.

Phanes had laughingly promised to pardon the little thieves for their crimes against his dinner if he could have her instead for his meal. She had playfully agreed to sacrifice herself to save their poor little souls, whereby he promptly lifted her unto the table and proceeded to make good on his promise, much to her delight.

Her lips curved into a sensual smile. "He is wonderful, kind, and a very inventive lover."

"No," said the raspy-voiced star maiden, sharply. *"Tell us* who *and* what *he is."*

"No, I cannot tell you." Psyche resisted the urge to answer; her desire to protect her husband and to keep her promise to him warring with the desire to tell the star maidens what they wanted to know. A dull throbbing pain began in her head when she remained silent.

Above her, the stars began to blur and fade, and her vision dimmed. Her bed of clouds began to fade away, to be replaced by an increasingly harder surface. A chill ran down her spine.

For what seemed like hours, the two voices alternated between commanding and pleading for her compliance with their questions. Time passed, Psyche holding strong to keep her vow to her husband, despite the ever-increasing pressure and pain her resistance caused her. The voices grew more exacerbated at her resistance, and she pleaded for the star maidens to stop hurting her. She curled up into the fetal position, holding her pounding head while the star maidens argued.

"Psyche, you leave us no choice. If you do not give us the information we seek, we will have to punish you, and you do not want that."

"Please stop,' she begged. "I promised him. I cannot tell you anything."

The star maiden with the raspy voice sighed. *"It is a shame, really, but you are still young. You may be able to have more children after this, if you survive."*

Panic raced through Psyche at those words. They could not mean what she was thinking.

She watched in helpless horror as the star maidens above her changed shape, their forms solidifying. Snakes sprouted from their heads and their eyes turned a viperous yellow, while their legs melted into each other. Scales covered every inch of their exposed skin, claws and fangs replacing teeth and nails.

Gorgons.

Dear gods above, help me! Psyche screamed in her mind. She was surrounded by them. She desperately tried to move, to get away, but her body was sluggish and refused to cooperate. Sweat dripped down her face as she continued to struggle before she finally ran out of strength. She was frozen in place, her body no longer under her control.

Psyche tried to fight them as they wrestled her to her back. They ripped open her dress with their claws, exposing her belly. One gorgon moved to lean over her face while it held her hands above her head. The snakes in her hair began to slither and hiss before one sank its fangs deep into her forehead, injecting her with poison.

Immediately, pain sliced threw her head, as if a knife was slicing through her brain, peeling layer after layer off as she silently screamed. She was sure blood was pouring down her face, getting in her eyes, blinding her. "Why are you doing this? Stop! Please don't hurt my baby!"

"You have only yourself to blame. Tell us what we want to know."

Then a sharp pain stabbed across her belly when one of the snakes from the other gorgon's head bit into her stomach, causing her to cry out. She tried to fight them off, desperate to protect her child. The harder she fought, however, the worse the pain became, until she was begging them to show mercy.

"Psyche, stop fighting and tell us what you know about your husband."

"I cannot," she gasped in pain.

"If you tell us what we want to hear, the pain will stop and we

will give you the antidote to the poison. Choose Psyche: your unborn child or your husband's secrets."

Painful contractions ripped through her. She looked down at her naked belly in horror as it swelled. Black streaks were forming across her skin. She felt her baby violently twisting and turning. She could hear her child screaming in agony as two little hands appeared under her skin pushing upwards, her child trying to claw her way out to escape her poisoned womb.

She had to save her baby before it was too late.

Terror gripped her, the threat to her child chilled her blood, and she finally did what no amount of pain could force her to do. She broke her promise to her husband. Shattered, Psyche gasped, "I do not know for sure what he is, for I have never seen him."

"What? You lie."

"No, I swear. He only comes to me under the cover of night. He can make himself invisible to human eyes, just like the nymphs. Please give me the antidote."

"Not yet. Do you feel that pain in your belly? Your body is getting ready to rid itself of your child. She will die. Tell us everything you know. You must know something more about him."

Unimaginable pain ripped through her, causing painful convulsions that left her breathless, yet she fought to tell them what they wanted to know. "He has wings…white with…golden edges. He is powerful. I think…he is one of the…gods…of Olympus. He told me…..he has…blond hair and blue…eyes. He is tall and muscular…a rival to…Adonis. Please give me the antidote. That is all I know. I swear."

"Good, Psyche. Tell us one more thing before it is too late to save your child. Does he take on another form?"

"Yes…he has…an inner beast…a drakon…named Eros."

* * *

AIKATERINI AND EMILIA exchanged startled looks at what Psyche revealed. It was just like the mysterious figure had said; their sister was married to an immortal, and not just *any* immortal, but the god of love himself, just like their ally had hinted at. It explained so much of the secrecy behind their marriage, why Psyche had no clue as to the true identity of her husband. A beast, indeed. It was probably just another trick of the gods. If Aphrodite found out that Psyche had not been punished, but had in fact been rewarded, the heavens themselves would shudder under her fury.

The sisters shared a calculating look. It would seem that they would have to make a special stop at one of their temples; such blasphemy could not be allowed to continue. Aikaterini nodded at the mantle. Looking at the candle that had burned low, the sisters knew that their time would soon run out, but they still had the last part of the plan to complete before they left the island.

Emilia watched while Aikaterini leaned down over Psyche, blocking her view of the glowing amulet that they had placed on her forehead after slipping the sleeping potion into her drink. "Be careful," she warned. "Remember not to let it touch your skin, or you, too, will be trapped in a nightmare, just like our dear little sister."

Aikaterini loathed being anywhere near the cursed object. Just being in its presence caused anyone within a few feet of it to have vicious nightmares. She had learned that the hard way when she had hidden it beneath her bed before coming to the island. She still had not fully recovered from the horrific daemons that had plagued her sleep.

Careful to keep from touching the amulet, Aikaterini carefully whispered the spell above it, making sure to say it right. She quickly pulled away when the amulet's center stone started shooting small sparks into the air. The sisters watched in horrid fascination as the sparks landed on

Psyche's forehead, sitting there for a full moment before slowly worming their way under her skin.

When the stone's sickly yellow light died out, Emilia gingerly covered it with a thick cloth before quickly shoving it into a leather pouch, its power gone. The two sisters then swiftly set about getting the room back to order, and only when they were assured that no one would be the wiser did they give the command for Psyche to wake up.

Psyche stretched languidly before opening her eyes to see her two sisters sitting around her quietly discussing the latest gossip from back home. Puzzled, she looked around, not sure how much time had passed. The last she remembered, they were discussing… She frowned. She could not remember exactly what they had been discussing. She felt out of sorts, her body had a slight achy feel to it, and she felt slightly nauseous.

"Ah, sleepyhead has finally rejoined the living. Welcome back Psyche. How was your nap?" Emilia inquired with a knowing grin.

Embarrassed at having neglected her guests by falling asleep, Psyche sat up and pushed her hair out of her face, grimacing as her body protested. "Forgive me. I do not know what has come over me. How long was I asleep?"

"Think nothing of it, my dear. It is quite natural to fall asleep at any given moment at this stage of your pregnancy. It is best just to get as much rest now as you need. The gods know that you will get precious little once the baby arrives."

"Yes, it was only for a half hour at most, nothing to worry about. Though I am afraid that we do have a dreadful confession to make."

Psyche looked at the guilty looks on her sisters' faces, having no clue to what they could possibly be guilty of.

"What is it?"

Sharing a look, her sisters both turned to give her a

pitying glance as Emilia answered, "I am afraid that Aikaterini and I ate the last of the sweets."

* * *

LATER IN THE EVENING, after Zephyrus had dropped them off on the cliff's edge, the sisters hurried to the rendezvous site to meet with their mysterious ally. They could barely contain their excitement over how successful their mission to destroy Psyche had been. And no one was the wiser as to what had transpired that evening.

"I wish we could be a fly on the wall when the amulet's power takes control of Psyche's mind," Emilia gleefully said.

Aikaterini nodded in agreement. "Yes, it was nice to see our dear sister finally get a taste of the pain we have endured all these years. She has been blessed with a charmed life, worshipped and feted over all because of her unnatural beauty. She does not deserve any of it."

They stopped at the fork in the road, one leading to where their carriages were to take them home, and the other leading to where the cloaked figure awaited them. They carefully picked their way to their mysterious ally, eager to report the night's success.

The two stopped abruptly when they saw the cloaked figure emerge from thin air a few yards in front of them. The smiles slipped from their faces to be replaced with barely disguised fear. The hairs on the back of their necks rose in warning; the air heavy with malevolent power. They clutched each other's hands, fighting the desire to turn tail and run for their lives.

"I see you two are still in one piece. You must have been successful. Tell me what you have learned."

Aikaterini quickly recounted the night's events, telling all that they had discovered. The cloaked figure remained silent, only interrupting to make sure that the two had followed their instructions to the letter concerning the amulet and the spells that they were to whisper in Psyche's ear before waking her.

"Yes, we did exactly as you said. You have nothing to fear," Emilia said.

Laughter met her statement. "Oh my dear, it is not *I* who should be afraid, but the two of you if you failed in your task. Now give me the amulet."

Aikaterini tossed the pouch, and watched as it disappeared in midair. "What do you want us to do now?"

"We wait. Go home and say nothing. We will know soon enough if this night was a true success."

The cloaked figure disappeared, leaving the sisters to make their way home in scared silence.

CHAPTER 42

Eros flew across the sea, desperate to get home. Thoughts of Psyche and his unborn child filled his mind, pushing him ever faster. He hoped to reach them before sunset, wanting to steal even more time with her.

He resented the time he had given up the previous night to her sisters, as well as searching for more information about the mysterious immortal who had escaped their prison in Tartarus. For the first time since bringing Psyche to their island, he had not spent the night with her, having been stuck on Mt. Olympus dealing with Aphrodite's petty machinations and his brother's hunt.

Eros had been in a foul mood by morning's light, so in revenge, he had dropped a hint to Hephaestus on how to catch Aphrodite cheating on him with Ares. His revenge—for he had grievances with both Aphrodite and Ares—had come quickly as the cheating lovers had been caught in an unbreakable net during an afternoon liaison. He smirked; he could still hear her screeches ringing in his ears after being caught with Ares, the gods surrounding the bed, all bearing witness to her cheating and humiliation.

Suddenly, Anteros appeared at his side. "Well O adelfós mou, should I be worried that you wish to take my place as the god of requited love and the avenger of the unrequited?"

Eros chuckled. "We have been doing that lately, haven't we? Trading places and personality traits. Reminds me of our youth."

Anteros snorted. "Chaos help the world if we ever revert back to our youthful selves."

Eros nodded, his brother's comment throwing open the door on memories best left forgotten. They had been rabid beasts—both literally and figuratively—after rising from the sea. Wild with grief and anger without their soul mates to anchor their baser instincts, they had lashed out at a world that had betrayed them. Both had committed acts that to this day shamed them, and they still had not made amends for, which brought to mind just why Anteros had chosen to become the god that punished those who rejected love.

What would he do should his soul mate ever return?

"Do you ever think of her?" asked Eros.

Anteros stopped in midflight. Eros did, as well, regretting his question when he saw the impact it had on his brother, though needing to know the answer. Eros desperately wanted to save him from the destructive path he had chosen. Anteros had been pulling away from him since he found Psyche. He knew his brother. Anteros was preparing to sacrifice himself in the coming war, of that he had no doubt. His brother thought he was expendable, having lost all hope after their betrayal. Eros needed to save his brother, however. He could not lose him now, when they were so close to achieving their goals. To finally find happiness after all they had suffered. He would not lose his brother, and Anteros be damned if he thought otherwise.

Eros needed him just as much as he needed Psyche.

He stared at Anteros' profile, his brother refusing to look

at him. He knew the gut-wrenching pain his question had caused him.

They hovered in silence, the only sound the gentle flapping of their wings, before Anteros finally answered softly. "Not a day goes by that I do not think of her."

Eros nodded hopefully. "Do you—"

Anteros turned dead eyes on him, sending a shudder of involuntary fear down his spine at the monster staring back at him. Anteros growled, hatred dripping from every syllable. "I think of how I will hold her gaze while I strangle the life out of her. She *will* pay. They will *all* pay, and no one—not even you—will be able to stop me. This I swear on my life. "

With that vow, Anteros flew away, heading to his island home on Antipaxos.

CHAPTER 43

Eros landed in the courtyard just after sunset. Seeing a bench, he slowly walked over to it, exhaustion causing his wings to drag. He sat down, hunched over as grief settled into his bones, making even the smallest movement painful. Even after all these years, the bitter taste of their betrayal at the hands of Anteros' soul mate made him want to retch. Memories best left forgotten tortured his mind. The happy ones were the worst. It made her treachery all the more inconceivable. Her betrayal had blindsided all of them.

Why had she betrayed them? It was because of her that they had lost the war, the primordial gods sealed away, only to return when he and Psyche reunited in love and trust in their new forms and identities. The scar that cut across his chest—the one that permanently severed him into two beings—throbbed painfully. That unanswered question haunted both brothers. Perhaps even subconsciously, Psyche, as well. It could explain why she had chosen to be reborn a mortal, too traumatized from such a vicious betrayal to live amongst the gods again.

His brother's distrust of women—and soul mates in particular—made the hope that he could ever fall in love again with someone other than his soul mate an impossible dream. That Anteros could even function was a miracle, though it was more likely a testament to his burning desire for revenge. There was no punishment that could ever fit the crime that she had committed against them, especially to Anteros.

She had almost completely destroyed the heart and soul of Ophioneus before their fall. Anteros was the result of that brutal metamorphosis, rising from the depths, reborn into the vengeful god of unrequited love that he was today. And every person he punished was a whetstone in anticipation of the torture he planned for her to suffer.

Eros shuddered at the thought of what Anteros would do if he ever found her. It was possible—even probable—that she would return with the others once he and Psyche sealed their soul back together. Tartarus would weep tears of blood from the brutal torture his brother would mete out before he finally killed her.

Eros was sick over the pain he caused Anteros with his question. He was tired from the heavy burdens he carried, the weight threatening to tear him down. If he failed, the universe would unravel. The primordial gods, in their madness after being locked away for so long—should they somehow be released before Eros and Psyche reunited—would destroy all that they created in their wrath.

Even if Anteros survived the war, he would go insane from killing his soul mate. What few shreds that were left of the loving and compassionate nature that was Ophioneus would die should Anteros follow through on his plan to kill her. She was his anchor, even with her betrayal. He would be a rabid beast, killing anyone and everyone in his path.

Eros would have no choice. His brother was too

dangerous unfettered; the only way to stop him would be to imprison him. Was he to find his soul mate only to lose his brother to his? How could he save the world if he could not even save Anteros?

A single tear slid down his face before dropping onto his hand. For a time he sat there, lost in thought before his attention was caught by the glow reflected by his tear.

Looking up at his home, he noted the soft glow coming from the balcony outside his bedroom. It was the lone light coming from their home on this moonless night. Then Psyche stepped out on the balcony. Eros caught his breath while she looked up at the sky, waiting for him, as she was wont to do of late. Seeing her made his heart race with need. She was their hope—his and even Anteros'— and perhaps their salvation, as well. When she reunited their soul, she would hopefully come into her full power. Who knew what powers she had locked inside of her?

Surely, between the two of them, they could find a way to save Anteros, and the world.

He stood up, and snapping out his wings—the burdens and grief he carried lighter than before—he flew up, landing behind his wife. On silent feet he made his way to her, watching in fascination as she tilted her head to the side, sniffing the air. A soft smile curved her lips before she said, "Good evening, husband."

CHAPTER 44

"Good evening my little butterfly," he greeted as he wrapped his arms tightly around her. He pressed a kiss to her neck before resting his chin on the top of her head. "How did you know I was here?"

She laughed softly. "I scented you."

"What?"

She rested her arms over his, both of them cradling her baby bump. "You always smell of musk, sandalwood, and dark spices. You do remember our game of copycat? Well, I have taken your advice. I have been developing my other senses, and you were right."

Eros chuckled. "I loved playing that game with you."

Psyche smiled. "So did I."

They stood there silently for a while, content being in each other's arms. Psyche felt the tension gradually fade from her husband's body. Whatever was bothering him, she was loathe to bring it up, not wanting to add to the stress she had observed in him of late. Part of it was due to her pregnancy, of that she was sure of. She knew he feared for her and the baby, but something else was bothering him. She would ask him tomorrow; tonight she had other plans for them.

Stepping out of his embrace, she felt him take her hand and lead her into the bedroom. At the foot of the bed, she stepped back and pushed him down until he was sitting on it. She brought her hands slowly up his body until she reached his face. Cupping it, she brought her lips within a hair's breath of his before whispering, "I plan on claiming my long overdue prize."

"Do you now?' he murmured. "What carnal pleasure does my lady desire as her prize?"

She quickly pulled back and stood up when he leaned in to kiss her. "Tonight *I* am in control. You must follow my every command. That is my desire. Understand?"

Even though she could not see his expression, she felt his surprise at her request. Her husband was a dominant man who loved to be in control of their lovemaking. At first, with her lack of knowledge and experience, she had been fine with him being in control, and had even welcomed it. With the passage of time, however, her confidence in her sexuality had grown. Now when she tried to assert herself during their lovemaking, she ended up getting lost in the pleasure and giving up control to her husband.

She wanted to explore, to see where *her* desires would lead them.

"Are you going to submit to my desire?"

A rough growl met her question in the darkness, and a shiver of excitement raced through her body at the sound of his lust. "Your wish is my command. What is your first order?"

Psyche took a further step back, just out of his reach. "Do not touch me unless I give you leave to do so. For now, just watch and feel."

She untied the *anamaschalister* that crisscrossed the top of her gown. Holding the ribbon in her hand, she was about to drop it when a wicked idea came to her. "Give me your hands."

He stretched them out, making sure that she could find them in the darkness. Quickly wrapping the ribbon around his wrists, she loosely bound them.

"I hate to point this out, my love, but this strap is rather pitiful. If you truly wish to restrain me, you will need something much stronger than that little ribbon."

"I know that you could easily free yourself. This is simply a symbol. As long as you are bound, you are to obey my every command. Once I free you, consider the prize paid in full." Giving the ribbon an experimental tug, she was satisfied that it would stay in place.

Phanes slid his fingers over her wrist, stealing a caress. She lightly tapped his hand in reproof. "Naughty one, did I not just say that you could not touch me without my express command?"

A rough chuckle met her question. "Yes you did, but I cannot help myself. You are temptation itself."

Psyche fought to keep a stern expression on her face, not wanting to give in to laughter. "Well then, since you lack control, I must make sure that you follow my commands. Lie down in the center of the bed, wings spread. Now put your hands behind your head and keep them there. Understand?"

"As I said, your wish is my command."

She focused her attention on listening to her husband's movements. The bed made a soft groan as he moved to the center of it. She heard the whisper of his wings when he stretched them out as they glided over the bed coverings. A few more rustling sounds, then all was quiet. "I'm in position, as ordered, my lady."

"Good. Now watch me." She reached up and unclasped the pins holding up her peplos. The gown pooled at her feet, leaving her naked. Stepping out of it, she crawled onto the bed, settling next to his hips. Reaching out, she laid one hand over his heart and one over his hip. "Use your powers to undress. I want you bare to my touch."

Almost immediately, hot bare skin met her hand. She felt his heartbeat pick up speed and reached over to the side table, where she had placed some items in preparation for the evening. Taking the container holding the warmed honey, she dipped her finger in it, testing it. Satisfied, she tilted it over his chest, drizzling a small amount on it. She knew when it landed on him by the quick inhale he made. "Is it too hot?"

"No, though I wonder if I should be concerned with your intentions towards me this evening," he said, his voice tinged with mock trepidation.

"What do you mean?"

"Well, considering your obsession of late in drowning everything edible in honey, I fear you plan on devouring me."

Psyche couldn't contain her laughter at his concern. "Ah, you have discovered my dastardly plans. I *do* plan on bathing you in honey and eating you up," she said in mock sympathy.

She leaned over and followed the trail of honey up his chest, then took a quick nip of his pectoral. Licking her lips, she looked up at him with lust in her eyes. "You are delicious, and I plan on savoring you tonight." Crawling up his body, she came within a hair's breath of his lips before murmuring, "I promise to devour you slowly."

She closed the distance between them, meeting his lips in a kiss so intense that it threatened to make her forgo her plans for the evening. Fire raced through her body, igniting a hunger in her. Pulling back before it consumed her, she sat back up, noting that her husband was as affected as she was by their kiss.

"Come back here," he commanded, his voice rough with desire.

Psyche shook her head, a taunting smile gracing her face as she threw his words back at him. "Patience, my love. Pleasure should always be savored, never rushed. All the better to enjoy the experience. Is that not what you always tell me during our lovemaking when you have me begging?"

An involuntary shudder racked his body, tense from his struggle to keep his word and follow her commands. Low growls filled the darkness.

Chains suddenly appeared, shackling him down to the bed. She felt them against her body. Using her hands in the darkness, she followed the trail of them. His wrists were shackled behind his head, the chains running over and under the bed. His legs were spread apart and shackled to the far corners.

Psyche felt a weight around her neck with an object nestled between her breasts. Lifting her hand, she traced its shape, identifying a necklace with a key. She instinctively knew it was the key to unlocking his chains. "Why are you chaining yourself?"

"I don't know if I can keep my word to you. My self-control is weak tonight. Better that I be chained down then to disappoint you. They can hold me. You have the key to release me when you wish."

"You mean you are trapped until I release you?" she asked, stunned.

"Yes, once these chains are locked, only the key will unlock them. My powers are practically useless against them."

Psyche was speechless. She knew her husband spoke the truth about being trapped. He had no reason to lie. The level of trust he had in her brought her to tears. She could do anything to him. His life was in her hands. She was determined to be worthy of his faith in her.

"So, you are at my tender mercies, my love. Then I will have to see just how much pleasure you can handle. Be strong, and you will be rewarded."

"Lucky me," he said, deadpan.

Psyche couldn't hold back her laughter. He joined her, their shared amusement lightening the mood. Picking up the honey, she drizzled some more over his chest. She used it to paint; his smooth chest was her canvas. The only sound that broke the silence was his ragged breathing as she took her time drawing a detailed picture. "Can you guess what picture is on your chest?"

He was silent for a minute. "You drew my drakon."

"Eros."

"Yes," he replied, a slight hesitation before he said, "Eros."

She pushed herself down his body. Rising up on her knees and turning, she straddled his upper thighs. Dipping her finger in the honey, she brought it to her lips, licking it. Phanes let out a soft growl.

She dipped her finger again, heavily coating it in honey, and brought it to rest just under her ear. Trailing her finger down her neck, she stroked a path first to one nipple, then the other, coating them in honey. Aching desire raced through her.

She leaned over him, her nipples creating a trail of pleasure as they barely grazed his chest as she crawled her way up his body. By the time she reached his lips, they were both shuddering in pleasure. Leaning up, she teased him with her breasts, keeping them just out of reach of his mouth. He strained against the chains as he tried to capture one of them, all the while growling and bucking under her, trying to force her closer, desperate to reach her, touch her, taste her.

Taking pity on him, she moved the scant inch separating

them, allowing him to latch on to her nipple. Then it was her turn to gasp as intense pleasure/pain pierced her, causing her sex to clench in painful need. She was torn between wanting to pull him closer or push him away.

When the pleasure threatened to take her over, she pulled back out of his reach. A rough growl escaped his lips at her retreat. "Come back here," he commanded again.

She shook her head. "No, my love. I will not be denied my treat."

"Treat? What treat?" he asked, confused.

Instead of answering his question, she swiftly moved off his body and got into a semi-reclined position next to him. She leaned forward and took him into her mouth, wringing a started grunt of surprise from him. She had wanted to do this for so long, but never got the chance. Releasing him from her mouth, she took him firmly in hand as she slowly licked up his shaft. Reaching the top, she placed a soft kiss on the crown before reversing direction.

Psyche spent several minutes exploring and worshipping his manhood: licking, sucking, stroking him to madness. She worked him up several times, stopping right before he could find his release, before beginning all over again. She smirked at him as he tried to convince her to let him orgasm. He alternated between pleading, commanding, and bargaining with her.

Finally taking pity on him, she said, "I will grant you one boon, my love. How do you wish to find your pleasure?"

"Ride me," he panted. He sounded truly desperate.

"You wish to be my mount, then. Will you be good and let me set the pace?"

"Yes, and you don't even have to feed me apples, just your sweet body."

She gave a rueful laugh at his smart remark. She loved it whenever his playful side came out.

"Hold absolutely still." Climbing on top, she guided him into her. She slowly sank down until she was fully seated. She shimmied her hips slightly, making them both groan in pleasurable pain. Rising, she set a steady pace, slowly building up the pleasure.

Before long, she was picking up the pace, riding him hard, both of them desperate to reach their pleasure. All of a sudden, she threw back her head and screamed as her orgasm ripped through her. Phanes gave an answering roar as he followed closely behind, both of their bodies taut as wave after wave of pleasure tore through them.

Psyche slumped over his body in exhaustion. They lay there, too tired to move. After several long minutes, she reached up to the key hanging around her neck, pulling it over her head. She unlocked the chains holding her husband down. After opening the last lock, the chains disappeared, along with the key. She settled her body on top of him, cuddling him as she slowly drifted in and out of sleep.

"Psyche?" he whispered.

"Hmm?" She wrinkled her nose in annoyance. "Why aren't you holding me?"

"Well, my hands are still tied. Have I fulfilled my end of the bargain?"

It took a minute for her to remember the terms of her prize, and when she did, she patted up his body until she reached the ribbon. Giving it a tug, it quickly came undone, signaling the fulfillment of their bargain.

He wrapped his arms around her as the two of them drifted off to sleep.

* * *

Psyche woke up, shivering from the cold. Looking around, she realized she was alone, no longer in her bedroom. Fear gripped her.

The field. She was back in that nightmare world, surrounded by the mist. It was heavier than ever, twisting and swirling, creating ominous shapes.

The hair on the back of her neck rose in warning. The shadow figures were back. Only this time, they were more distinct. More aggressive when they moved toward her.

"Enough of this. What do you want from me? Tell me!" she pleaded with them.

All of a sudden, the figures stopped. They moved back, separating to create two rows of shadow-people facing one another. Then a narrow pathway formed between them that went on for what seemed like for miles. As quickly as they moved into position, they stilled. A phalanx. That is what they reminded her of. Not a sound could be heard. She waited in fearful anticipation.

She did not have long to wait.

Movement along the path caught her eyes. One lone figure walked slowly toward her. With each step its form became more solid, its features more distinct. Psyche stood frozen. By the time the figure reached her, she let out a shocked gasp. It was her. *It was like looking into a mirror. "What in all that is holy is this? Who are you?* What *are you?"*

Her doppelganger smiled sadly. "I am you, Psyche."

She took a stumbling step back. "No, this isn't happening. You can't be me. This is a trick."

"No trick. I am made up of all of you: past, present, and future."

Psyche shook her head. "You sound like the Fates. What do you want? What is this place? Why do you haunt me?"

Her doppelganger sighed. "To warn you. You and the child are in terrible danger, and time has run out."

Psyche's face paled as her blood ran cold, and she protectively covered her baby bump. She would do anything to protect her unborn child. "What threat?"

"I will show you. Follow me."

Psyche hesitated for a few seconds, not sure what—or who—to trust. However, the threat to her baby made her move forward. Knowledge was power, and she refused to be ignorant—and therefore powerless—due to fear.

As she followed her mirror, the shadow figures remained motionless. Not a sound could be heard. Not even her own footsteps. She gathered up her courage, and for the first time took a good look at them, coming to a stumbling halt when she finally recognized several faces from her past among them.

Gods above, they were shades. The souls of the dead. The shadow figures were the souls of people she had known throughout her life. She was in the Underworld.

Miltiades. Her father's general, who died when she was a young girl.

Cleomenes. Her mother's brother. He had died when his ship had sunk in a storm a few years ago.

Clio. Her nursemaid. She had died after a short illness.

Psyche was unable to hold back a sob when she recognized one particular shade. Stefania. Her dear, sweet Stefania. Old age had finally claimed her in her sleep. Stepping up to her, Psyche reached out, trying to touch her. She let out a painful moan when her hand went through her. She quickly pulled her hand back. "Stefania? It's me. Psyche."

When no response came, Psyche turned her head toward her mirror. "Why won't she answer me? The shades can speak. I know they can. They tried to speak to me before. Why are they frozen? Tell me!" she demanded, her voice heavy with anger and tears.

Her doppelganger stilled, turning around. She kept her voice low as she answered, as if she feared being overheard. "They are frozen because the monster knows that they have been trying to warn you of the danger. Both the ones who knew you in life, and his many victims over the centuries. Come, we don't have much time. If you wish to free them and to save yourself, then follow me."

Psyche turned in a circle to take a closer look at the shades of people she did not know. She was horrified when she realized that women and children made up the bulk of the dead souls. Almost all of them holding infants in their arms. All bore evidence of varying levels of violence. Psyche pressed a trembling hand to her mouth, trying to hold in her screams. These women and children had died hard.

Taking a step forward, she abruptly stopped. She took one last longing look at Stefania. The woman she thought of as a surrogate grandmother to her. "I will find a way to free you. I promise."

Turning away from her was heart-wrenching. Psyche hurried down the path, desperate to escape the silent wraths. By the time she caught up to her double, they were at the end of the line. There, in the center, was a familiar sight. It was her bedroom.

"What are we doing here?"

"You have been lied to by your husband. All those poor women were lied to, as well, and they and their babies paid the ultimate price. The Pythia tried to warn you. We tried to warn you. Your husband is a monster, a gorgon. That is why he never wanted you to look upon his face. You would have turned to stone. He can hide his true form under the cover of night, but never in the daylight. You are not his first wife. All those women and children you passed by? They were his brides, as well. He enjoys tricking them. Once he earns your love and trust, then impregnates you, the countdown begins. He will wait until your labor begins before striking, then he will rip the child from your womb and devour it as you bleed out. Killing you both. If you are lucky, you die quickly. If not..."

Psyche trembled in terror. It could not be. It had to be a trick. "You lie. Why would he devour his own children? It makes no sense."

"It makes perfect sense. He is an immortal. He is one of the monsters who fought Zeus in the Gigantomachy. He was cursed by Zeus. As punishment for his crime, he is driven to breed, but should a child of his ever be allowed to live, it is destined to kill his father. He can never let that happen, so he kills both the child and mother

at the moment just before birth. If you don't believe me, watch for yourself."

Before her eyes, Psyche was forced to watch as woman after woman lived the last year of their lives in her bed. The sounds of fear, then pleasure, then love, and finally, screams of agony and horror played over and over again. The pitiful mewling of the babies brought her to her knees. The last image was of her, and her baby. "Stop, please. Enough. I can't...no more..."

The images stopped. Falling forward, Psyche barely caught herself before completely collapsing to the ground. It was true. It had to be true. Dear Hestia, please, not my baby, she prayed.

A soft hand smoothed the sweat-soaked hair from her brow. Her mirror gently cupped her face. Psyche looked up at her, barely making her out through her haze of tears.

"Now you know. You are our only hope. You must break the curse. Only then will all the shades be free, and only then you and the baby will be safe."

Psyche nodded, slowly getting to her feet. "Tell me what to do."

Her doppelganger handed her a dagger. "Take this, plunge the blade into his heart, and kill the beast now that he is asleep. Quickly, before he wakens. It is the only way. Go!"

Psyche looked down at the dagger, then turned toward the bed. She could see the outline of her husband under the covers. Slowly, she crept toward him, trying not to make a sound. The light from the lone oil lamp cast ominous shadows across his body. She drew next to him. His arm was thrown over his face, hiding it from her view. She took a fortifying breath before raising the dagger over her head. Acting quickly, she swung it down, slicing through her husband's flesh.

CHAPTER 45

"PSYCHE!"

The agonizing shout of her name broke her out of the trance she had been caught in. Her eyes snapped open, and at first she was disoriented, the bright light in the room blinding her as her eyes fought to adjust. Blinking, she looked down, and an eternity seemed to pass as she sat frozen, trying to process the scene before her.

Phanes. Her husband. She was finally seeing him. Her eyes feasted hungrily on him. Her heart wept with joy. He finally trusted her enough to reveal himself. He was so achingly handsome. Blond and blue-eyed, he had said. What a typical male answer when describing his coloring. It didn't even remotely come close to describing his beauty.

She recognized him. Eros. Her husband was the god of love. An immortal. How could she not have guessed? All the clues were there. She *should* have recognized him, especially when his drakon told her their true name. Then it came to her. Aphrodite and her vendetta against her. Of course. No wonder he kept his identity secret.

His tousled blond hair was threaded with multiple shades

of gold, sunlight, and silver. His eyes were so many shades of blue, and they were so vivid, they glowed. Even as the thought crossed her mind, his eyes quickly dimmed, the light flickering like a candle that had reached its end.

Pain. He was in pain.

"Psyche. Why?" he whispered brokenly.

Confused, she dragged her gaze from his face and looked down. A startled cry burst from her as she stared uncomprehendingly at his chest. Blood. So much blood. His chest was covered in it. A knife wound clearly visible in his upper shoulder. She went to grab the blanket, to press it against the wound and hopefully staunch the flow.

She froze, staring in disbelief at what she was clutching in her hand, the sheet temporarily forgotten. A dagger. Her hand trembled. It couldn't be. Dear gods, no. A bloody dagger was in her hand. Both were covered in her husband's blood, marking her with the evidence of her crime.

No! her soul screamed in agony. She couldn't have done such an evil deed. She couldn't have stabbed him. Not her beloved husband. The man she loved with all her heart and soul. But the damning evidence was right in front of her. Her guilt undeniable.

He let out a soft moan, snapping her out of her frozen state.

Dropping the dagger, she frantically ripped the sheets and pressed them against his wound. It had to stop bleeding. *He would heal,* she desperately thought to herself. He could heal himself. He had to be alright. He was powerful. A god. There was no way he could die from an ordinary stab wound. He would be alright. He *had* to be alright. Even as her jumbled thoughts raced through her mind, the wound continued to bleed. It wasn't stopping. The sheet quickly became soaked with his blood.

Why wasn't it stopping? He just lay there, not moving.

Not fighting. Silent. He wasn't raging at her, condemning her for trying to kill him. He just lay there. A soul-shattering expression of defeat in his eyes. Death. He looked like he wished to die from her betrayal. She pressed harder. She had to save him. He groaned weakly in pain.

"Help! Please, somebody help us!" she screamed, frantic.

A sudden animalistic roar rent the air outside their bedroom. The strength of its inhuman rage and agony tore through the palace, shaking it to its very foundation.

Eros curled his fingers around her wrist. For a brief moment, the world came to a standstill as they gazed into each other's eyes. In that one moment, they shared a lifetime of what could have been. The life they could have shared. A dozen thoughts reflected in their depths. Regret. Love. But the most heartbreaking was the bitter defeat in his eyes before he looked away, pushing her hand off him. She suddenly found herself pushed off to the side of the bed, Eros staggering to his feet. He stumbled, weak. "Pax!" he shouted.

Pax appeared, her normally rosy complexion pale at the sight of a blood-stained Eros. "What happened?"

He shook his head in despair. Psyche wept silently. He could barely bring himself to look at her. When he finally did, she crumbled in shame on the bed. She couldn't bear the shattered look of betrayal on his face.

"It doesn't matter. Just protect Psyche. No matter what happens."

Then he turned his back on them and flew out the window, transforming into his drakon form. In the distance, she could make out another drakon winging its way to the palace. It was a mirror image of her husband's beast, though this one was all black with silver-tipped spikes. They met in midair, a clash of claws and teeth as they grappled with each other, both fighting for supremacy.

"Phanes!" Leaping off the bed, Psyche ran to the terrace,

desperate to get to her husband. Pax ran after her and grabbed her before she could climb onto the rail.

"Stop, Psyche! What do you think you are doing?"

"You have to help him! Please! He's injured. I did that! Why did I stab him? Why? I don't know what happened. It wouldn't stop bleeding. He could be dying. Please!"

She rambled as she fought Pax, hysterical in her fear and confusion. She fought to get free, but Pax stubbornly held on to her, preventing her from foolishly trying to go to her husband while he battled the other drakon. Finally wearing herself out, she collapsed in Pax's arms, crying uncontrollably, watching in hopeless grief as her husband fought.

Pax questioned her in disbelief as to her confession. "You stabbed Eros? With what? Why would you do that?"

"I don't know. I don't remember doing it," she answered brokenly, collapsing to the floor, unable to tear her eyes away from the fighting drakons. The two beasts were engaged in a vicious battle. It was her fault. All of this was her fault.

"Where is the knife? Tell me now, Psyche!"

"I think it's still on the bed."

Pax left her on the floor of the terrace, and sprinting to the bed, she tore it apart until she found the dagger. Racing back to Psyche, she knelt down next to her. "Psyche, look at me. We don't have much time. We need to know what happened, and why. I need to search your mind."

Before Psyche could answer, Pax laid her hand on her forehead. She felt a ghostly touch going through the many layers of her mind. It went deeper and deeper until it stopped. It had found what it was looking for. Psyche felt the pressure build as it focused on the hidden memory of the past few hours. A sudden sharp pain caused her to cry out, drawing the attention of Eros. He turned, his focus shifting to her for a split second, leaving him exposed and vulnerable.

It gave the other drakon the opening it was looking for.

The black drakon slammed into Eros from behind, sending him crashing far out into the sea. The water rose up and captured him, imprisoning him within a whirling mass of churning waves. With Eros temporarily out of the way, it turned its attention to the two women on the terrace. Spying Psyche, it let out a vicious roar, locking onto her as it flew directly at them at incredible speed. It was coming for her. She watched it, making no move to save herself, too distraught with guilt to care for her own wellbeing. She wished she was dead. She deserved death for what she had done.

Pax moved protectively in front of her. Right before the drakon could reach them, a wall of earth shot up, creating a barrier. The drakon crashed into it, unable to stop itself in time. It clawed at the earthen wall in rage, but the wall grew in size every time the drakon tried to go over it. The beast began to throw its massive body against it, battering it in a violent frenzy. It let out a scream of rage at being thwarted from its target. The wall shuddered under the heavy blows. It wouldn't hold for long.

Pax grabbed Psyche, pulling her to her feet. "Hurry! We have to run—"

The earthen wall suddenly exploded, sending dirt and debris everywhere, knocking the women into the air. It sent the two women in opposite directions from the sheer force of the explosion. Pax crash-landed into a field, knocking her out cold. The force of the blast sent Psyche high up into the air, but before she could crash-land to her certain death, she was caught in the grip of the black drakon. It flew with her to the other side of the island before dropping her onto a rocky outcrop overlooking the sea.

Psyche was disoriented from the blast. She struggled to catch her breath. When she tried to sit up, the black drakon leapt forward, crouching over her, caging her in, its malevolent, blood-red gaze locked on her prone body. It lowered its head to within a few feet of her.

Psyche could see the hatred in its eyes.

You treacherous bitch! You betrayed my brother. You rejected his love. You tried to kill him. You are just like her!

"I'm sorry. I didn't mean it. Please, you have to help him," she begged. He was going to kill her. She deserved to die, but her baby did not. She wrapped her arms around her waist. "Please, do what you must, punish me, I deserve it, but please don't hurt my baby, I beg you."

I would never harm by brother's child. I am not the monster here. You are! You are a threat to Eros, to the child you carry, to Pax, to everyone. Eros may die from your treachery. I only punish betrayers such as yourself. I condemn you to the depths of Tartarus. I will take your child into my safekeeping. It is innocent and will not suffer because of your betrayal. She will grow up safe from treacherous bitches like you, and her.

The drakon pried apart her arms, pinning them to the ground. He eyed her belly, his mouth opening wide. She closed her eyes in defeat. He was going to rip her apart. Before he could take her child from her womb, he was knocked off of her.

Psyche opened her eyes, shocked to see her husband standing over her in his human form. He had saved her. He must still love her. Maybe he could find it in his heart to forgive her? "Phanes?"

"My name is Eros. You betrayed my love, my trust. You betrayed us. We could have had it all. Now we have nothing but ashes."

He turned his back on her, spreading his wings to leave. She pushed herself to her knees, wrapping her arms around his legs. "Please,' she begged, sobbing uncontrollably, "don't leave me. I'm sorry. I don't know why I did it. I will do anything. Punish me, lock me up, but please don't leave me."

Eros stood still. He refused to look at her, to touch her. "You are free to go. We are done. Live your life among the mortals, Psyche. Thanks to your actions today, our daughter will be born a mortal, instead of a goddess. That is punishment enough."

Psyche fell forward when Eros suddenly disappeared. Then she pushed herself up onto her knees. Everything was gone. Eros, the black drakon, the palace, everything. Gone. She found herself alone and abandoned on a desolate shore. Frantically, she looked around. Faint lights flickered in the distance. Her fractured mind recognized the landscape. No, it couldn't be.

Pylos. She was back at her parents' city-state.

"EROS! COME BACK! PLEASE COME BACK!"

Silence. She waited, and waited, but no answer came. He was gone. It was over. Heartbroken, she collapsed to the ground, and her tears soaked into the earth as she brokenly whispered, over and over again, "I'm sorry."

CHAPTER 46

Eros opened his eyes. He was nearly sightless. His vision blurred from unshed tears, and he was unable to move away from the agony shredding his soul. He could barely breathe it hurt so much. He feared if he moved, he would shatter into a million pieces. The silence was damning in its stillness. In that silence, his beast cried out in hopeless agony.

Psyche was gone.

His mind flash backed to last night. He had planned on revealing himself to her, but she had surprised him with her request. Her wanting to finally claim her prize from their game of copycat all those months ago had changed his plans. He had decided he would reveal his true identity to her the following morning, instead.

He imagined her surprise when she woke up the next day with him still by her side. His excitement at finally being able to reveal all to her had strained his control to the breaking point. He had shackled himself, literally leashing his dominant nature so that he could fulfill her request for control of their lovemaking. He had trusted her. It had been perfection, both of them falling into sated slumber afterwards.

He remembered slowly waking up the next morning. Psyche stirring next to him, feeling her pulling away from him. Eyes still closed, he had reached out to her, intending to draw her back down so they could embrace, only to feel the pain of a dagger slicing into him. He thought their ancient enemy had found them, attacked them. He was prepared to defend his wife and child with his life if necessary. Then he had opened his eyes. He couldn't defend himself from the reality of who had attacked him.

Psyche had stabbed him. His precious wife had tried to kill him. His other half. No. That wasn't right. It wasn't the dagger that dug into his flesh that had doomed him; it was her actions and words. Her words of absolute rejection that dripped poison from her lips into his soul as she stabbed him. She had killed his heart and soul. His body just hadn't caught on to it yet.

He looked down dispassionately at the weeping wound in his chest. She had missed his heart by a few inches, yet it was wrecked just the same. Even if he had been stabbed in the heart, he would have lived. A stab wound itself was not lethal to him, but Psyche's betrayal was. Once again, a soul mate was the cause of their death, only this time, there was no coming back from it. He shook his head. Perhaps Anteros had been right after all. Take back what belonged to them, never trust them. Even as the thought passed through his mind, what was left of his heart and soul rejected it.

His knees suddenly gave out. His strength finally depleted, he collapsed forward, uncaring to even try to break his fall. He lay on the ground, a broken marionette. Lying there, he slowly became aware of the shaking of his body. Cold. He was shivering uncontrollably. It spread sluggishly through his veins, starting from the tips of his limbs and wings, making its way towards his heart. He was intimately aware of this unique cold. He had felt it once before. It was death's calling card, and yet, he could not die. He would live, more's the pity, to suffer this heartache for eternity.

He lay on the ground, his will shattered, just like his hopes and dreams of a future with Psyche. He wanted Thanatos to come and claim him, the sweet promise of death a welcomed one, but it was a vain hope. He wished to return to the void, to go *beyond* death. He wished for oblivion. His one regret was that his beast would suffer with him. He couldn't save him this pain and agony any more than he could himself.

"EROS!"

He heard the anguished cry from a distance, the sound of people running from all directions towards him. Anteros reached him first, dropping down on the ground beside him. His brother gently turned him over, gathering him up into his arms. He held him propped up against his body. Anteros' body gave off such heat, it felt like he was sitting against a campfire. It partially roused him from the cold grip of his emotions.

Eros looked up, blinking until his vision cleared. When he could finally focus, he was shocked to see the tears streaming down his brother's face. Anteros was crying. His brother had not shed a tear in eons. Eros could only remember one other time that he could remember seeing his brother cry.

The Betrayal. Anteros hadn't shed a tear since the treachery of his soul mate. The ability to cry beaten out of him when his love for her had been driven out of him by bitter hatred. The irony that it was Eros' own soul mate who brought back his brother's tears was not lost on him. Their lives were a mirror in so many ways, including the ultimate betrayal by the women they trusted above all others, and loved.

"I'm sorry brother…I failed…"

"Stop talking. Save your breath," Anteros angrily commanded. He placed his hand over the gash.

Eros felt his brother's healing powers flood his body as he tried to close the wound, trying to repair the damage to his torn flesh. It was a waste of time. The wound was not mortal, his wife's rejection was.

"No use…brother…powers dying…"

"Shut up! You. Are. Not. Done!" Anteros bit out savagely, his voice heavy with helpless rage and grief. "Fight! Damn you! Fight!"

Eros shuddered, his heart battered even more, his brother's pain overwhelming their shared bond. He didn't think there was any piece of his heart left to break, but he was wrong. What was left of it shattered completely. He had failed. It was a viciously bitter poison.

Poison. His mind flashed back to that cursed night so many eons ago when he and Anteros had lost everything. The war, their mates, even themselves. He suddenly cried out when white-hot pain tore through him, the scar on his chest suddenly tearing open, blazing hot with renewed agonizing pain. The wound that had never truly healed. The scar a physical manifestation of the missing piece of his other half, of his past life, and his soul. The damage only reuniting with his soul mate could finally truly heal. He was being torn into shreds once again.

His mind raced again to another memory. He remembered when he had received that terrible wound. He should have died that night. In truth, both he and Anteros should be dead. Yet they *could* never die, being one of the deathless gods. The sweet release from their pain and suffering was forever denied to them. It had been Thesis who had helped save them. Their ironclad will and determination to utterly transform their very beings had also saved them. Or condemned them. No one could have predicted what their metamorphosis would mean to their world.

Sweating, panting, and withering from the pain, Eros squeezed his eyes shut, but even closed, it couldn't stop the memories breaking free from their long-held prison in his mind. It was on this very cliff where they had first "died" at the hands of their ancient enemy. Lured to the island by the screams of the androgyny—conjoined humans made up of both sexes—who had taken refuge there, he and Ophioneus—Anteros in his original serpent form—had been horrified by what they had found. The androgyny had been cut in half, torn physically from their soul mate, slaughtered, their lifeless bodies thrown into the storm-swept sea like so much refuse. Their bodies bobbing obscenely in the blood-red water.

The echoes of the fear and agony of the deaths of their chosen children among the mortals had bled into their very souls, momentarily shackling them to the spot, their empathic abilities on overload from such depraved cruelty. It was in that one vulnerable moment that their rival had struck with such devastating accuracy. The swing of the scythe slicing into them, forever dividing them into three. Phanes' hermaphroditic body cleaved in half, forever separating him into two distinct bodies, one male and one female, suffering the same fate as his children. Ophioneus-Anteros in his original serpent form, was cut down as well.

Eros remembered falling into the sea, Ophioneus and his male half crashing into the water, joining their children in their watery grave. They had been surrounded by the dead. It had seem a fitting end. At least they would all be together for eternity.

Eros frowned as a long-suppressed memory finally broke free. *No,* his mind taunted him. They hadn't all been together in the sea. Only he and Ophioneus. Thesis had fallen backwards, not forwards. She had been left behind on this very cliff. Alone. *No!* his mind screamed. Not alone. She had been left behind to face their ancient enemy by herself.

Another memory came, this one more horrific then the last. Eros remembered now. After hitting the water, he had been sucked down. He had been crazed, desperate to find his other half. He had searched for her under the waves, but she was nowhere to be found. It had been Ophioneus who had finally pulled him back to the surface. He remembered franticly grabbing the bodies floating face down around him, turning them over, only to push them away when he realized it wasn't her. Ophioneus helped. Again and again they did this, never finding her. Eros screamed for her. Over and over again he called out, becoming hoarse, but no answering cry met his screams. Then the horrific realization had hit him: She wasn't in the water. Finally, he had looked up.

The scythe. It was the first thing that caught his eye, how it glowed and gleamed in the moonlight. Even the blood on it glowed as it slowly dripped to the ground. Their enemy was facing slightly away from them, their focus inland, on what lay on the ground. He saw the movement of their lips. He couldn't make out what was said, but he knew it was Thesis they spoke to.

He tried using his vast powers to attack their enemy. Nothing. His shattered powers were stretched to the breaking point trying to keep him alive. No matter, then. He was a weapon. He just had to get to them. His wings were damaged from the crash into the sea, and more, they were weighted down with water. It did not matter, though. He somehow had found the strength to swim to an outcrop of rocks, and after hauling his broken body onto it, he had been able to snap out his wings and take off, Ophioneus lending him strength as they rose together into the night.

The pain was crippling, but the terror for his other half

fueled his determination to reach her. His vision tunneled. Time slowed to almost a standstill. He had been unable to hold back the roar of anguished rage when he saw the mangled body of his other half. She lay broken, but even though her body was wrecked, she was defiant to the very end. The scythe pressed against her heart, but his soul mate had turned to lock eyes with him, determination radiating out from them. In that split second, she sent him one last message.

Forgive me, my love. Live. Do what you must to survive. We will be reunited again in the next life. I promise.

Before he could even guess at her intentions, she murmured something before she found the strength to launch herself forward, the scythe slicing through her heart as she slammed a dagger into the neck of their enemy. The tearing of her heart by the scythe released her powers in a devastating cataclysmic eruption that threatened to tear apart the very fabric of the universe. It destroyed her body, and it set the world ablaze in a blinding light.

It was only the combined forces of Eros and Ophioneus that prevented the destruction of the universe. Their bodies became a powerful magnet, drawing the power back into their bodies. It slammed into them, tearing them apart, scattering their very cells across the sky, only to have them combine in new and devastating ways before falling back down and being swallowed up into the sea.

There they had lain, broken, transformed, bonded. They had become twins in the truest sense, both becoming a hybrid of each other. Never to be what they once were, especially Ophioneus. He had become Anteros, the god of unrequited love. Their transformation into the first chimera, primordial god and primordial serpent. Whole and yet lacking, each needing their soul mate to complete them.

Did she blame him for leaving her to face their enemy on

her own? Could she not handle what he had become, what he had done to survive all these years? Had she finally remembered, only to be disgusted by his transformation? These unanswered questions taunted him.

All his plans, all his efforts to find her, to reunite with her, it had all been for nothing. The soul-destroying loneliness of their forced separation, the countless years looking for his other half, the loss of the war, the intricate machinations to create a world safe for his soul mate to return to…all for nothing. It blackened his soul. He had failed: himself, his child, his brother, the primordial gods, his beast, and the people who depended on him.

He had even failed Psyche.

"Eros! Come back!" He was brought back to the present by his brother's cries. He looked up to Anteros' ravaged face. "Powers fading…you have…to carry…on the fight…break… the seal…holding the primordial gods…dormant…"

Anteros threw back his head and roared, the sound a combination of him and his inner drakon. It shook the island. Eros' own beast whimpered in sorrow at its twin's pain. When he turned back to Eros, Anteros' eyes glowed with red-hot embers. "You damn fool. We are all lost without you. I am the opposite of you. I can't *be* you. Without love, the world is doomed. Love is what saved us, and without love, we are dead. As long as there is life and love, there is hope. Remember? That is what you told me when we were betrayed. You are needed, I am not. We joined our life force that day to save the world, and now it's my turn to save you."

The bond between them suddenly lit up in painful flames as Anteros did the unthinkable. He began to drain his life force into his body.

Eros struggled to stop him. He would not trade his life for his brother's. He couldn't allow his brother to forever weaken himself, to become a husk of his former self. "Stop! Please…stop…"

With every passing second, Eros felt his life force's strength return, even as his brother weakened. Eros and his beast fought, neither wanting their brothers to sicken. But neither of them could win against the combined power of Anteros and his beast's will—not in their weakened condition.

It was the arrival of Pax that saved them. "Eros! Anteros! Stop!"

Anteros ignored her. Instead of stopping, he increased the flow, determined to save Eros before she could try to stop them.

"Pax. Stop him. He is destroying himself," Eros pleaded.

She didn't even hesitate. Pax blasted Anteros with her power, momentarily stopping Anteros' sacrifice as both he and his drakon turned to confront the new threat. It was that split second that Eros needed to shut down his end of their connection. He used his newfound strength to put a stranglehold on their bond, preventing his brother from trading his life for theirs.

Pax lent her strength to him. In the distance, he felt Antipaxos—Paxos' twin sister—join her power to them, as well. Between them, they prevented Anteros from draining any more of his life force. His twin snarled in frustrated rage, and his body tensing, he prepared to attack Pax.

"Don't even think of it. You already used up your one pass when you attacked me and Psyche. Try it again, and I'll roast your scaly ass and serve your carcass to the sharks. Stand down."

At the mention of Psyche, Anteros scowled. "Where is that treacherous bitch? You can't protect her from me. She will die for this."

"No, she won't. She is innocent," Pax countered, her voice

ringing with such conviction that it grabbed Eros' attention. Hope was a fickle mistress. "What...do you mean.....she is innocent?"

Instead of answering, Pax laid her hands on each of their foreheads, showing them the memories that she had gleaned from Psyche's mind. As well as her memories, they saw her dreams, and her nightmares. It was her nightmare from last night that set both Eros and Anteros into a rage.

They had been played. All of them.

The twins instantly recognized the malevolent power that had taken hold and twisted her mind. It was their ancient enemy. They had finally found them. How? They had taken such great pains to hide their true identity. Yet they had been found out. Eros targeted again. How did they get past their many defenses? There was no way that they could have gotten anywhere near their island homes, let alone Psyche. There had to be a spy, a—

"Her sisters," Anteros snarled.

Pax nodded. "Yes. Her sisters were here two nights ago. The nightmare was last night. They were left alone with Psyche for over an hour, and I detected traces of a sleeping potion in her body. They have to be working with the betrayer."

"Be that as it may, Psyche still rejected him. She tore open the wound, leaving him to bleed his powers, his life force away. The damage is ultimately hers, and it is she who must undo it." Anteros locked eyes with Eros. "Release your hold on our bond. I swear I will only use it to buffer your strength until we can figure out a way to fix this."

Eros sighed; a seed of hope taking root in his soul. It was enough to make him fight. Perhaps all was not lost. He did as his brother asked. Almost immediately, he felt the draining of his life force slow down, though it did not stop. It would buy them some time before he was completely powerless; his were draining out of him from the wound. Though how much time they had was anyone's guess.

Anteros picked him up and flew him back to his island of Antipaxos. He made his way to the hidden cavern where he made his underground home. Landing in his bedroom, he was not surprised to see Pax's twin sister Anna waiting for them. She pulled back the covers of the bed and stepped back, making room for them. Anteros carefully laid Eros down, covering him with the blankets. Gently cupping his face, Anteros commanded, "Sleep. Save your strength. Have no fear. I will not hurt Psyche. Sleep."

He waited until Eros fell into an exhausted sleep. Motioning for Antipaxos and Pax—who had followed close behind—they went out into the hall.

The sisters shuddered in fear at the dead look in Anteros' eyes. The beast was staring at them. His drakon was crazed; it wanted vengeance, and it would not be appeased easily. The gods would have to have mercy, for he would have none.

"Stay with him. Watch him. I will be back shortly."

"Where are you going?" Antipaxos demanded.

"To see Psyche's sisters.

CHAPTER 47

Aikaterini hurried down the hall, tugging at the loose ends of her chiton that she had haphazardly thrown on when she had been roused from her bed. At first she had been angry at the disturbance, thinking her husband had returned early from his hunting trip and wanted her to tend to his aches and pains. Or worse, to entertain his lusts.

She shuddered in disgust. Sex with her husband was a tortuous affair. She hated his slobbering attentions. His pawing of her body, the lack of any pleasure, and worst of all, the unwanted pregnancies. Well, at least she had found a temporary solution to that last problem.

Desperate to avoid his bed as much as possible, Aikaterini had traded a few precious pieces of the gifts that Psyche had given her to pay a *pornai* to be his personal pleasure servant. She had converted nearly all the rest of it to drachmas.

Her husband had no clue to the fortune she now had hidden in her possession. That fortune—combined with the precious few coins she had managed to skim over the years from the household budget—would enable her to finally run away, taking her secret lover with her. Or not. Variety was the spice of life, after all. It had worked for the most part, but he still called her to his bed every now and then to try to impregnate her, to get his longed-for heir.

Aikaterini snorted in amusement. He would get no legitimate heir from her. Not now, not ever. Little did the old fool know that she had been drinking a special tea for several months now to ensure that no seed of his ever took root in her womb ever again. She was done. Let his bastards fight over the throne when he died. She would be long gone.

The gods must be favoring her this night, she thought to herself. Her husband was still hunting. When the servants told her that her sister needed to see her urgently, she was alarmed. The journey between their two neighboring city-states was difficult because of the mountains separating them, and for Emilia to make the trip at this time of night meant something momentous had occurred. Perhaps their mysterious partner had brought news. Her lips twisted in an ugly smirk. Hopefully Psyche had finally received her just rewards.

Aikaterini congratulated herself on a scheme well played. Not only had she played Psyche, but her parents, as well. How she had tried to find her sister. She had cried and lamented poor Psyche's fate. Her parents had bought her story. That she was gone, a victim of the beast the Pythia had foretold in her prophesy to her father. It served them right for loving her more, their precious favorite.

Reaching the door to the receiving room, she pushed opened the door. "Well Emilia, what news—"

Aikaterini came to an abrupt halt, robbed of speech as the woman turned to face her. It wasn't Emilia, it was Psyche. Before she could gather her wits, Psyche threw herself into her arms with a sob. "Oh sister, thank the gods."

Her mind scrambling, Aikaterini held Psyche in a limp embrace. A sudden blinding pain ripped through her head, causing her to cry out. Before she could fully process it, the pain was gone. She found herself sitting down, Psyche sitting huddled across from her.

Slightly disoriented and desperate to get a handle on the situation, she asked, "Psyche, what are you doing here? Are you well? How did you get off the island?"

Psyche looked up, her eyes resembling bruised flowers, tears dripping down her face. "Aikaterini, I did a horrible thing. I broke my husband's trust, and now he has forsaken me."

Bowing her head in shame, Psyche allowed the curtain of her hair to cover her face before continuing. "I had a horrible nightmare that my husband was a monster. I woke up in a terror. I had a dagger hidden under the bed. I grabbed it and..."

"And what?" Aikaterini demanded when she trailed off. "What did you do, Psyche?"

She watched as Psyche wrung her hands in distress, her body hunched even more in shame. Aikaterini couldn't contain an evil grin, pleased beyond measure that their plan had brought her so low. Finally, Psyche was paying the price for her unnatural beauty and the undeserved easy life she had lived, so unlike her two older sisters. But she had to force the glee out of her voice and expression. Soon. Soon she could celebrate her triumph, just not yet. She still needed to know just how successful their plan had been.

In a small voice barely above a whisper, Psyche finally answered her. "I stabbed him."

Aikaterini drew back in shock. "You did *what?*"

Looking up, Psyche suddenly jerked forward, getting on her knees in a supplicant's pose and grabbing painfully tight hold of her hands. Aikaterini was shocked by the strength of her grip, and was about to pry her hands free, but she was caught by the intensity of Psyche's gaze.

"I stabbed him. Oh sister, it was horrible. There was blood everywhere. I thought I had killed him, but thank the gods, it is impossible for me to harm him. He is not human, but one of the gods. Eros. I was the wife of the god of love. But no more, thanks to my betrayal."

Aikaterini struggled to keep her emotions in check. Close. They were so close. *Just a few more machinations and Psyche would be completely ruined,* she reminded herself. This was the moment she had waited for since the cursed day her mother had birthed her youngest sister. "What do you mean, wife no more?"

Aikaterini hadn't thought that Psyche could look any more miserable, but she was wrong. She watched in silent glee as her sister's misery became more intense. She could swear that her body seemed to cave in on itself as her grief increased. It was a delicious sight to behold.

"He has forsaken me. He said that I was no longer his wife. That my actions had proved how unworthy I was to be the wife of a god. He said that our child will be a bastard. But that is not the worst of it."

"Oh Psyche, my poor little sister," Aikaterini murmured, gathering her up into an embrace. Psyche's body trembling, her pain too great to contain. "What could possibly be worse than what you have already suffered?"

A low moan of pain escaped Psyche's lips before she answered. "Eros said that he chose the wrong sister, but that he would rectify that mistake. He said that he has decided to take *you* for his bride. That *you* have proven to be the dutiful wife that he desires, and that it would serve me right to see my sister take my place by his side—and bear his heirs. That is why he sent me here. So that I could give you his message. If you agree to his proposal, Zephyrus waits for you by the cliff. You must jump off it. By doing so, you will show your faith and trust in Eros, something that I lacked. Zephyrus will catch you and bring you to our....I mean...the island, where you will be made into an immortal and rule by his side for all eternity."

Speechless, Aikaterini had to take a minute to get control of her exultation. She had done it. She had won. Psyche had been cast out and forsaken. Her sister was utterly cowed and humiliated.

The best part was that Aikaterini was being rewarded for her machinations. Finally she would receive what she was her due after all these years of living in the shadow of her younger sister.

And what a reward it was. To be made a goddess and have the god of love as her husband. She would never suffer the loss of her beauty, an illness, or the ravages of time. She would know the pleasure of having a virile lover in the bed sheets, for the god of love was legendary for his skills in the bedroom. If the cost for such a gift was that she had to bear a few children, so be it. She could always pawn them off to the nymphs of the island to care for them.

While she enjoyed the life of a goddess, Psyche would spend the rest of her short mortal life suffering in the knowledge of all that she had lost. Now that she thought about it, Aikaterini was impressed by the ruthless nature of Psyche's punishment. The gods were famous for their cruel and ingenious punishments to the mortals who had crossed them, and Eros had devised a truly vicious and soul-crushing punishment. By forcing Psyche to deliver such a message to Aikaterini, Eros had driven the knife deeper into her tender heart, breaking her spirit.

"You cannot be serious," Aikaterini said, trying to keep the glee from her tone.

"I am serious, but the choice is yours alone. If you accept his terms, you must make the leap before midnight tonight. If you reject his offer, I must go to make this same offer to Emilia—who is his second choice—though he made his preference known when he spoke of you," she said, tears dripping down her face.

"Psyche—"

"Take the offer, Aikaterini. Please. I know the fault lies with me, but my baby is innocent of any crime. She should not be cast out because of my lack of trust and faith. Please, take Eros' offer. You have always been a kind and loving sister. I know you can convince Eros to take our child back. I accept my punishment, but I will at least be at peace as a mother if I know that my child is safe with her father, and you—her aunt—loving and protecting her. Please Aikaterini, it is all I ask."

"Of course Psyche. I will do as you ask. I will accept Eros' offer for your sake, and the sake of your poor child. Have no fear, I will gladly do everything in my power to see that you and your child receive your just rewards," Aikaterini replied, barely able to keep the lie of her promise out of her voice.

Psyche kissed her hands. "Thank you, dear sister. I knew I could count on you."

Stupid girl, Aikaterini sneered to herself. She had no intentions of helping Psyche and her unborn child. If anything, she would relish watching her and her bastard daughter suffer. It would be a delight to see.

Psyche abruptly stood up. "You must hurry. Time is running out."

Within minutes, Aikaterini was dressed and on the road leading to the gates of the city-state, Psyche leading the way through the pitch-black night, lit only by a small flame of an oil lamp. Once the two women had slipped passed the guards on duty, they made their way to the old shepherd's path. It was at the fork when Psyche called a stop to their flight. "I can go no further. The rest is up to you," she said, before handing over the oil lamp. "Go, take the left path, that one leads to the cliff, where Zephyrus awaits you."

Aikaterini nodded. "Goodbye, sister."

Before she could respond, Aikaterini turned away from Psyche and briskly made the trek to the cliffs. Had she but turned around once, she would have caught the image of Psyche transforming into that of a winged god before disappearing, but she did not look back, too eager to meet her fate. The closer she got, the louder the sounds of the sea crashing against the rocks broke the silence of the night. The wind was steadily getting stronger. Zephyrus must be near.

Her heart racing from excitement, a wild frenzy suddenly seized Aikaterini. Tossing the oil lamp to the ground, it shattered against the rocks. The oil splattered far and wide, creating a straight path of fire leading directly to the edge of the cliff. The unnatural pattern was further proof of the god of the west wind's presence. Picking up the hem of her dress, she ran along the lit path, heedless of anything else.

Reaching the edge of the cliff, Aikaterini cried out, "I accept Eros' offer! Catch me, Zephyrus ,and bring me to him!" Flinging herself over the edge, she was quickly caught up in strong arms. She let out a laugh of delight, finally sure she was going to be rewarded for her intelligence and cunning.

"Yes, Aikaterini, you are going to receive your just reward," a vicious snarl answered her silent thought before her head was yanked violently back by her hair.

Aikaterini could only make out two glowing red eyes staring down at her in the pitch blackness of the night. The hair on the back of her neck rose as terror gripped her.

This was not Zephyrus. It was a predator.

A sudden flash of lightning illuminated the night sky, briefly revealing the creature that had her in its grip. It was the stuff of nightmares. A hideous gorgon with batlike wings of blackest night held her in its talon-tipped fingers. It was covered in silver-tipped black scales that gleamed in the light. Razor-sharp spikes crowned his head. Large serpent fangs protruded from its mouth.

Fangs that were suddenly buried deep in her mouth, injecting poison in its macabre kiss. It raced down her body, and no part of her was safe from its reach. Everywhere the poison traveled, it left behind a trail of such ice-cold tendrils that it burned. Shudders wracked her body.

She let out a muffled scream in pain and terror, but as quickly as she screamed, it was cut off abruptly by an unnatural force. The only sound she could hear was her wildly beating heart.

After what seemed like an eternity, the creature lifted its head and grinned, her blood staining its lips and fangs. "What is the matter? Didn't you enjoy your first kiss from a god?" he scorned.

A low keening sound was all the answer he received, blood choking her as it overflowed from her mouth. Her eyes were wild, begging for mercy.

The creature shook his head in mock sympathy. "Poor Aikaterini. You truly believed you were so clever, so much more worthy than any other female. You really are a stupid, pathetic, little mortal. You could have had it all, had you just been a loyal, loving sister to Psyche. Did you know that she was planning on petitioning Eros on your behalf? To free you from your miserable marriage? No? I thought not. You would have been given a life of pleasure and ease, but instead you betrayed her love and generosity in the cruelest of ways."

Aikaterini tried to deny the accusation, but she was too

weak. She could barely shake her head before what little strength she had deserted her. Her feeble attempt backfired, and rage lit up the creature's eyes.

"Do not lie to me," he hissed. "I read your thoughts. It was you who came up with the seeds of the nightmare. The pendent merely magnified Psyche's fears, but you stoked the flames. You and our immortal enemy joined forces to harm my brother and his soul mate. For that, you will suffer unlike any other. Your punishment will be whispered about even among the immortals as a warning as to what they can expect for daring to harm us."

Suddenly out of the night sky, several other winged monsters joined them. Aikaterini recognized them immediately. The Erinys. The three goddesses of vengeance and retribution circled them. Behind them, lurking in the shadows, was Thanatos.

Death had come for her.

The gorgon holding her in its grasp nodded to the others before turning its attention back to her. Running its forked tongue along her cheek, tasting her tears, he laughed at her shudder of revulsion before pulling back.

"Since you so relished the idea of Psyche's suffering by being wedded and bedded by a monster every night, only to be slaughtered by having her child ripped from her womb, I thought you would enjoy the same treatment. Rejoice, Aikaterini, for tonight is your wedding night. You will live out your afterlife as the wife and bed partner of a monster. And as a mother, whose monstrous children are ripped from her womb."

With that, he dropped her to the churning sea below. The Erinyes let out a bone-chilling chorus of screams as they flew down with her. Thanatos bowed before joining the Erinyes. Aikaterini was dead from the poison long before her body crashed into the rocks below. Thanatos ripped her soul from her body, dragging it down to the depths of Tartarus.

The gorgon landed on the cliff, its monstrous features melting away. In its place stood Anteros, who looked down dispassionately at the broken body of Aikaterini. "One down, one to go."

CHAPTER 48

"My lady, you have a visitor."

Emilia opened her eyes, sending a harsh glare at the servant who dared disturb her. By the gods, she could not get even a moment's peace to enjoy her bath. "Tell them I am indisposed," she snapped.

"My lady," the servant persisted, a slight tremble in her voice, "it is your sister. She said it was urgent."

"My sister? At this hour? Very well, have her wait for me in the receiving room. Provide her with refreshments and let her know that I will attend her shortly."

"Yes, my lady," the servant said, hastily beating a retreat to do her mistress' bidding.

A half hour later, Emilia made her way to the receiving room. *What on earth could have possessed Aikaterini to make such a journey at this time of night?* she thought to herself. Perhaps she had received a message from their mysterious ally. Oh, what delicious news that would be. It would be wonderful to know that their plan to destroy Psyche had come to fruition. How she loathed her baby sister. So perfect, so well loved by all, while Emilia had ever only received the crumbs.

At least her sister had picked a good time to make the journey to her home. Her husband was finally out cold from the sleeping potion that she had slipped into his drink. Unfortunately, it had taken much longer than usual to take effect for some reason. Her husband had found the time to use her body for his own pleasure before passing out on top of her. She shuddered in disgust. No matter how hard she scrubbed her body, she could still feel him on her skin.

May the gods be merciful and not let his seed take root in her womb again. She would hate to have to stage another "accident" to rid herself of it. Their mysterious ally had promised to help both her and Aikaterini escape their respective marriages. Emilia could not afford to get pregnant again.

Thinking of the babies she had lost made her hate Psyche even more. Emilia had made the decision to put an end to all her later pregnancies after suffering one miscarriage after another. Every pregnancy had brought her nothing but sickness and misery. She hated what it did to her body and her health, but all her husband cared about was getting his heir. That was all *anyone* cared about. If she died, her husband would replace her with a new wife before her body was even cold. On that, she had no doubt. She valued her life far more than any brat, and truth be told, she loathed children. She had no maternal instincts whatsoever.

She couldn't wait for her escape from this miserable existence. She had been planning it for years. Everyone always forgot about her. It was always Aikaterini and Psyche. She was an afterthought at best. Well, she would show them who was the most clever of them all. Emilia was done being in the shadows of her two sisters. She had planned her escape well.

Reaching her destination, she pushed opened the door. Then she stopped in her tracks. It was not Aikaterini standing before her, but Psyche.

"Psyche? Is that you?" she asked, her mind scrambling.

"Oh Emilia, thank the gods. I need your help."

Psyche threw herself into her arms, sobbing wildly. A brief pain pierced her skull. It almost felt like something had torn her mind apart, trying to find something important. As soon as the pain registered, it faded into nothing. It left her slightly disoriented.

Trying to buy some time to think, Emilia led Psyche to the seating in front of the hearth. The fire provided warmth and light. Emilia was disgusted to see that even crying and upset, Psyche was still beautiful. If anything, her allure grew even more as her grief brought into focus her unnatural beauty.

"What has happened? How are you here, Psyche?"

"Sister, I have done a terrible thing."

Emilia listened to the details of the events that led to Psyche arriving on her doorstep in stunned silence. Jubilation filled her. Their plan had worked better than even she had thought possible. They had managed to destroy her life. It was a delicious sight to behold—her sister, who had been the bane of her existence since her birth—finally brought down, defeated and rejected. Emilia had to fight to keep her composure; it would not do for her sister to see her delight at her misery.

"Oh, you poor dear. What will you ever do? Pregnant and forsaken by your husband."

Psyche hung her head in shame, "It is much worse than that, sister. Before my husband banished me from the island, he bade me to give you a message."

Emilia froze. Was it possible that Eros knew that it was she and Aikaterini who were in league with his enemy to destroy their happiness? No, that was impossible. Wasn't it? She had to tread carefully. "What message?"

"Eros said that he picked the wrong sister for his bride,

but that he would rectify that mistake. He has decided to take you instead. You have proven to be a faithful wife, and he thought that it would serve me right to see my sister take my place by his side, and bear his children. That is why he sent me here. So that I could give you his message. If you agree to his proposal, Zephyrus waits for you by the cliff. You must jump off it. By making that leap of faith, you will prove your trust in him, something that I lacked. Zephyrus will catch you and bring you to the island, where you will be made into an immortal and rule by Eros' side for all eternity. If you do not wish to be his, I am to make the same offer to Aikaterini, though you are his first choice."

Emilia was silent, stunned speechless by Psyche's message. A goddess. She would be elevated from a mere mortal to the Greek pantheon. She could hardly contain her emotions. She would finally receive what she was due. There was no way in Tartarus that Emilia would allow such a prize to slip threw her fingers. Aikaterini would not steal this prize from her any more than she would allow Psyche to reunite with her husband. She just had to play the part of a sympathetic sister for just a little longer.

"Psyche, you must be joking. How can this be? What about your baby?"

Emilia watched as the fire from the hearth cast shadows across Psyche's features. For a second, she could have sworn that her eyes glowed red with hatred. It sent a shiver of fear down her spine. Before she could even blink, Psyche's eyes were back to their normal hazel, making Emilia believe it was the play of the hearth's flames that had made them appear like the malevolent gaze of a serpent's. It must have been the sheen of tears that filled her eyes that had caused the strange illusion, Emilia told herself.

"My child has been forsaken by her father. I have no

choice but to give her to the temple of Artemis so that she may have a chance at a decent life. I will not visit my shame and curse on her," Psyche said, her voice drenched in tears.

Emilia took hold of her sister's ice-cold hands, "I know it must pain you, but that really is for the best. You would not want to visit on your daughter the curse that your beauty has brought to you and the family. What will you do?"

"I do not know, but that is neither here nor there. Will you accept Eros' proposal? Time is running out for you to make a decision. You must be at the cliff before the stroke of midnight. If not, than you will have lost your one opportunity to be his immortal bride."

Emilia gave what she hoped was an innocent look. "But Psyche, how would you feel if I accepted his offer? I would be replacing you. How can you even bring yourself to offering me such a position?"

"I have no choice but to deliver his message. In any case, I want you to accept his offer, if for no other reason than you can advocate for my child's safety. I know that you can convince Eros to acknowledge my child and to bring her back to the island. I will have at least that comfort."

"Of course, Psyche, you can rest assured that I will do what is necessary to see that you and your child receive what you are owed."

Psyche sent her a small smile. "As I will pray that you do as well, dear sister. Now what is your answer?"

Emilia made a show of considering her response. She did not want to show her hand just yet. "You know the state of my marriage. I will accept his offer, but I will do this only for you, my dear."

With that, Psyche quickly stood up and urged Emilia to quickly follow her out of the palace. The two made their way to the road leading out of the city-state; the gods seemed to be guiding them, since they were able to leave without being stopped by any of the sentries guarding the defensive walls.

Psyche lit an oil lamp once they were a safe distance, and then began to lead the way to the cliffs. Once they were on the path for a while, she called a stop to their flight. "I must leave you here. Zephyrus is waiting for you. Safe travels, Emilia."

Emilia nodded. "Thank you, and to you, as well."

Psyche watched as she hurried down the path. When Emilia was out of earshot, she let out an evil chuckle, her body morphing into the masculine winged form of Anteros. "Don't worry, Emilia. I will make sure you safely arrive in Tartarus."

Emilia hurried toward the cliffs, anxious to meet up with Zephyrus. She would be damned if she allowed Aikaterini to snatch this prize from her. Of the two, she was the most deserving to be a goddess. Mortality was a curse. She would escape that fate; her two sisters could suffer the indignities of growing old and dying.

Aikaterini thought she was the clever one in the family, when in reality, it was Emilia who was the brains between the two of them. She knew how to manipulate people and situations to her benefit, making it look like she was just a bystander. Better to be the one pulling the strings behind the scenes than to be out in front. Aikaterini craved attention and praise, and she refused to learn that it only made one a target to your enemies. It was far easier to defeat your rivals when they had no clue to your identity. That was Psyche's downfall: the fool thought that her sisters loved her, when in reality, they resented and hated her, just like Emilia resented Aikaterini.

She laughed. *Now look at them,* she thought to herself. She would be worshipped and her name remembered for all times, while her family would be forgotten.

Seeing the cliff's edge in front of her, Emilia tossed the oil lamp aside, gathered her dress up, and made a mad dash to the edge. Gathering her courage, she called out as she leaped over the edge, "Zephyrus, take me to Eros! I accept his offer!"

For a second, she felt nothing but air, and a brief panic hit her. Where was he? Before she could cry out in fear, strong arms caught her up in a tight embrace. She laughed in triumph. At last, she had won. She wrapped her arms around Zephyrus' neck and shamelessly pressed up against him. It had been too long since she had a virile male in her arms—or her bed, for that matter.

It took her a moment to realize that they were hovering, not heading toward the island. "Well, what are you waiting for? Take me to Eros," she demanded.

Emilia cursed when a hand tunneled roughly into her hair and violently yanked back her head. Her tirade was cut off abruptly. It wasn't Zephyrus who held her, but a monster. A hideous gorgon with batlike wings of blackest night held her in its talon-tipped fingers. It was covered in silver-tipped black scales that gleamed in the light. Razor-sharp spikes crowned his head. Large serpent fangs protruded from its mouth.

"Who are you?" she cried out. "Let me go!"

The monster laughed. "As you wish."

Emilia dropped like a stone. She fell toward the rocks that jutted out of the sea along the cliffs. Too terrified to scream, she could only watch in paralyzing fear at her imminent death. Before she hit the rocks, she was snatched up at the last minute and tossed back up the cliff side. For the next several agonizing minutes, the creature kept up its cruel torment. It would catch her at various points as she fell, grabbing her before she crashed onto the rocks below. Then it would throw her back up the face of the cliff. The monster kept pace with her the entire way before catching her in its grip at the top of the cliff face, only to drop her back down.

Again, and again. Each time, she begged it to stop.

Finally, the creature lost interest in its game of cat and mouse and tossed her onto the ledge of the cliff. She curled up into the fetal position. A quivering mass of hysteria, she rocked herself, muttering nonsense. Her mind was broken.

Anteros—still in gorgon form—landed next to her. He looked down at her dispassionately, his lips curled in disgust. "Weak."

Summoning the Erinyes, he did not have long to wait for the three sisters. They appeared before him. "My lord Anteros, is this the other mortal you wish us to punish?"

"Yes, this is the traitor. Give me a moment, and then you can have your fun."

Alekto, Megaera, and Tisiphone formed a loose circle around Emilia. Anteros knelt down, and gently cradled Emilia's face. Using his powers, he made sure that even in her crazed state, the small part of her rational brain heard and comprehended his words.

"You have been found guilty of familial betrayal, of blasphemy against the gods, Emilia. For what you have done, I condemn you to the pits of Tartarus. But don't worry, your sister Aikaterini is already there waiting for you. You will have the pleasure of sharing her punishment. Since you both coveted Psyche's husband, you can share your sister Aikaterini's new lover. I'm sure you will enjoy spending all of eternity with your co-conspirator."

Smiling in satisfaction, Anteros stepped back. With a wave of his hand, he sent Emilia tumbling over the edge of the cliff. No scream slipped from her lips. The only sound that pierced the night was her body when it smashed against the rocks. The Erinys flew into the night, Thanatos rising up to join them. In his grip was the spirit of Emilia. Together they flew off, disappearing into the night.

"Two sisters dealt with, one more to punish. You can run, but you cannot hide from me forever, Psyche. That, I promise you."

CHAPTER 49

Paxos and her twin sister Antipaxos tended to Eros, but the wound on his shoulder refusing to heal. They repeatedly had to use their combined powers to get his blood to clot. His powers were slowly draining out of him. He was delirious with a high fever, and both of them were closely watching for signs of his drakon trying to break free of his control. Should that happen, they feared what he would do to the world in his current state.

"This makes no sense. He is one of the deathless gods. He cannot die! Even after the fall, when he and Ophioneus were torn apart and transformed, they still lived," said Pax.

Antipaxos—Anna to her loved ones —shook her head. "Metamorphism is both death and life. One cannot happen without the other. It is not a true death, but it is a form of it. They will never be what they once were, and who knows what being rejected by his other half will do to him now? This may yet be another metamorphosis; a death and a rebirth."

"But reborn as what?"

Anna shrugged. "Who knows?"

It was a sobering thought. The two primordial goddesses remembered well that fateful night when both Eros and Ophioneus had been cut down by their enemy and had fallen into the sea. The abattoir that had met them had been horrific. Even then, both had been unable to die, withering in pain so intense the sea wept blood-red tears. The two sisters had raced against time, desperate to get to them before their mortal enemy could find them and cause them more harm. While they had been able to spirit them away to protect them to their respective islands in order to heal, they had been too late to prevent what was to become of them.

Their transformation had already begun with the mixing of their blood.

Pax and Anna had watched as the two had transformed into their current forms. Ophioneus had changed the most; his beast hidden within the shell that was the mirror image of Eros. His adoption of a new name and becoming the god who punished those who rejected love was the biggest transformation between the two. He had literally transformed into the opposite of Eros; a vengeful god whose sole loyalty was to those who he considered his. Those who rejected any form of love were ruthlessly punished.

Eros' transformation had been no less striking. He was no longer androgynous or in possession of his entire soul, his female half forever physically torn from him and hidden away, the poor humans suffering the same fate. All of them searching for their other half.

Eros had also gained a beast, a twin to Ophioneus. They had become twin brothers in the most literal sense. What should have weakened them had in actuality made them stronger. They were primordial gods whose strength and powers had grown exponentially since the fall, the mingling of their ancient blood creating something new, something feral, a feat that should have been all but impossible.

Currently the two brothers were almost equal in power to all the other primordial gods combined. Should their lost soul mates follow suit, then the four of them would have the power to conquer all the other gods—primordial, Titan, and Olympian combined—and reshape the universe. That is, if Anteros did not kill his soul mate first for her part in the betrayal. It was one of the main reasons for the schism between them all today.

"Could the blade have been laced with poison?" Anna asked.

Pax shook her head, "No. I inspected it immediately. It is a common bronze dagger, not an adamantine blade, like the one Kronos used on his father, Ouranos. Even if it had been, I doubt it would have any real effect on him. It is Psyche's blade, the one she brought to the island. It was clean, no trace of any poison. Anteros inspected it, as well. No, it is Psyche's rejection of him that is the true cause of this wound."

A gentle rose-scented breeze filled the room, announcing the arrival of Khloris and Zephyrus. The couple were one of the few trusted with the primordial's secret of the true nature and identity of Eros and Anteros.

"How is he?" Khloris asked as she unpacked the items from her basket.

Anna shook her head. "There is no change. His wound will not heal, yet he cannot die, so he suffers with no hope of relief. Though the true wound is to his heart and soul."

"How could she betray him?"

"Because she is weak," Anteros answered Khloris, suddenly appearing in the room.

A shiver of fear ran down the spines of all of them at the sight of Anteros. His eyes were the swirling red of his raging beast, which meant that his control was razor thin. His need to punish those who had harmed his family was barely contained.

Zephyrus subtly placed himself between Anteros and the women, making sure that he did not block Anteros' sight or path to his brother. Any perceived threat would set off his predatory instincts, causing him to attack. Without Eros to keep him in check, Anteros was a monster about to break its bonds. No one would be spared should that happen.

"I have brought nectar and ambrosia, Anteros. I want to try and use it to see if it will help heal his wound," Khloris said, bringing his attention to the items she had laid out. He prowled over, inspecting them. Once he was satisfied, he gave a curt nod of approval.

Khloris made sure to keep what she was doing in plain sight, not wanting to set off a fight that would potentially end in the slaughter of many in the room. The others watched while she applied the salve to Eros' wound. Time passed, nothing happened. New formulas were suggested and tried, always ending in failure. Khloris and the others tried multiple variations of the mixture, but still nothing worked.

Anteros finally called a stop. "It is no use. Eros and I are not bound to the need for nectar and ambrosia for our health and powers, like the Olympian gods. Primordial gods and the Titans have no need for it; only the Olympians suffer that curse."

Zephyrus cast a worried glance at his wife. The knowledge that the Olympian gods were cursed was a closely guarded secret by them. Their lives, health, and powers were forever tied to their need for ambrosia and nectar after the war with the giants. Without it, they would weaken and die. If they ever discovered that others outside the Olympian gods shared this knowledge, they would stop at nothing to silence them—and their enemies would stop at nothing to gain it.

If anyone found out that Khloris was now the key to the

Olympians' survival, she would be hunted by all: the Olympians *and* their enemies. The Olympians would cage her and hide her away from everyone, while their enemies would hunt her down and torture her. Both fates would be worse than death. Zephyrus would slaughter anyone who dared lay a hand on his wife, or tried to take her away from him. He had already killed to protect his family; he would gladly do so again.

"Then what do you think will work? We have to do *something*. Already the world is being affected by his illness," Khloris stated, casting a troubled glance to Anteros.

"What do you mean? What is happening?"

Anteros answered. "What she means, Anna, is that love is slowly leaching from the living. The weaker Eros becomes, the more love retreats from the world. Without love in any of its forms, the living will become apathetic to life, and we will soon see the world start to wither and die from it."

"What about Aphrodite? Won't she—" Zephyrus broke off at the quelling glare from Anteros.

"She is the goddess of *vanity and beauty*. The only true love in her is the love she has for herself. She is just the pawn that Eros and I used to mask our powers. She—and all the others—will soon realize that she was never the true source of love in our world. Without Eros, love in all its forms will die."

"How long do we have?" Pax asked.

"I don't know, but once it gains momentum, it will be hard to keep this secret from the Olympians. We need to find Psyche. She is the only one who can possibly heal Eros."

Pax met Anteros' challenging stare with her own. "You *know* she was placed under a spell. She acted under a mother's instinct to protect her child. How can she heal Eros when her memories and powers are still locked away somewhere even she cannot find? What do you plan on doing to her?"

Anna moved slightly to put herself in a better position to defend her twin sister. Khloris shifted, throwing her support behind the women. Zephyrus stood ready, as well. Everyone held their breath as the two engaged in a battle of wills.

"You think to challenge me, Paxos?" Antèros snarled. "It did not go too well for you the last time."

Pax smirked. "My attention was divided before. It won't be this time. Harm me or mine, and I will turn your hide into a new pair of sandals. Now tell me, how do you plan on having Psyche save Eros?"

"Since it was her distrust that harmed him, it will be through a series of trials to prove her love and trust in him."

"And if she fails?"

"Then I will have no choice but to rip her soul from her and forcefully reunite it with Eros' soul. The choice is hers."

* * *

PSYCHE LAY STILL under the hot blazing sun and to the sound of the waves crashing against the shore. She tried opening her eyes, only to shut them again quickly. They were gritty and swollen from crying. When she tried again, her vision was blurry and it took some time before she could finally see with any clarity.

Her head pounded and she felt sick. She slowly pushed herself into a sitting position, groaning in pain, her body stiff and aching. It made moving a small torture, but she could no longer stay crumpled on the rocky shore any longer. She had to think of her child. Stumbling to her feet, she took in her surroundings. In the far distance was Pylos.

A part of her longed to go to her parents. To be the little girl whose parents shielded her. She knew she would find refuge there, with them. But she was no longer the girl she was before her marriage, and she could not bring the wrath of the gods upon her parents—or their kingdom— on their heads. She was a hunted woman, if not by Aphrodite, then by the drakon that had attacked her. If she went to Pylos, she would be putting a target on their backs, and it would be the first place anyone looked for her.

She was also a married woman, with a child in her womb to guard and protect. Pylos was no longer safe, or her home. She had to find a way back to the island, back to her husband, back to make amends. Phanes. No, that wasn't right. Eros. She was married to Eros, the god of love. And she had betrayed him in the worst possible way.

Grief hit her hard, bringing tears to her eyes and threatening to sap what little strength she had left. What had happened? She still couldn't wrap her mind around what she had done. None of it made any sense, and until she could figure that out, she was a danger to everyone she came into contact with. Plus, she had no way of knowing who to trust.

No, she had to find a safe place to rest, to think, and to plan her next move.

Turning her back on her childhood home, Psyche slowly made her way further inland, following the well-worn path leading to higher ground. She walked for hours, stopping periodically to rest, before pushing on, a vague idea of where she was going in her mind.

It was late afternoon, when she was exhausted and soul weary, when she failed to pay attention to where she was going. She did not see where the ground gave way by a river's edge, the water wild and churning. Letting out a startled scream, she plunged into the deep water. It swept her under, threatening to drown her.

Yet just as suddenly, the river gently brought her to the

surface, and carried her over to the riverbank, whereby it set her safely down.

"Eros? Is that you? Please, answer me!" she cried out.

"No, little mortal, bride of Eros. I am afraid he is not here."

Psyche looked around, trying to find the source of the voice. Seeing no one, she became terrified that her enemies had found her. Preparing to make a run for it, she froze when the voice came to her again.

"Do not be afraid. I mean no harm to the bride of Eros. He is an enemy unlike any other, and I have no wish to anger him by harming his bride. Please be at ease."

"Who are you?"

"A better question would be *what* am I," said a voice from behind her.

Psyche turned to see a figure lurking among the trees, the shadows obscuring who—or what—it was. "Show yourself, please."

"Of course, my lady. But please, do not be frightened. No one here means you any harm. I am a friend of your husband, and to you." The mysterious figure moved into the waning sunlight. A tall, muscular male stepped out of the shadows. He was naked save for a loin cloth that hung low from his waist. But it was not his near-nudity that caught her by surprise. No, it was the horns that peaked out of a wild mane of hair that grew out of the sides of his head that gave her the first clue to his identity. He had eyes that were almost black, a full beard, and a snub nose. She dared to look down. The male was covered in a thick pelt of brown fur, starting from his hips to legs, that was goat-like in form, to the tips of his hooves.

Psyche gasped. "My lord Pan. Thank you for saving me."

Pan chuckled. "I fear you are thanking the wrong person.

The nymph who lives in the river is the one you should thank. I am here to help a fellow goddess in need."

"And who would that be?"

"You."

Psyche looked at him in disbelief, trying to figure out what game he was playing. "I am no goddess. My husband is a god, and therefore, my child would be a demigoddess, but I am a mere mortal."

Pan chuckled. "Well then, I stand corrected. The sun will be setting in a few hours, and the nights can get quite cold around here. Please, my lady, for the sake of your health—and that of your child—allow me to offer you food and shelter for the evening. I swear on the river Styx that you will be safe with me, and from those who are hunting you."

Psyche shook her head. "But will you be safe from them?"

Pan looked at her in awe and admiration. "My lady, you honor me with your concern for my wellbeing. Have no fear, I will come to no harm for offering you food and shelter. Please, we must hurry if we are to get to my home."

Pan offered his hand. Psyche took it and allowed him to help her to her feet.

"Then I will take you up on your kind offer."

Together they walked into the forest, and were quickly swallowed up by the trees, right as a massive shadow of a winged beast darkened the sky.

CHAPTER 50

Psyche sat by the crackling campfire, wrapped in a heavy blanket. She felt much better after eating and bathing. Her clothes were washed and drying on the rocks next to her. Now that her mind was unencumbered with trying to find food and shelter, it had turned to the events of the past few days. Grief and despair threatened to drown her under their weight.

Turning her attention to the figure sitting across from her, she watched while Pan made repairs to his flute. He had been a most agreeable and respectful host, a far cry from the many stories about his lecherous nature. Pan had kept his word, making sure that she was safe and comfortable in the cave that he called his own. It gave her the respite that she needed from the stress of the last couple of days.

"How are you feeling?"

She managed a small smile. "I feel better, thanks to you."

"Good. Good. Now, if I may be so bold, what are your plans for the future? You are welcome to stay here for as long as you wish, though somehow I do not think that it would be in your best interests to do so. You have a husband to find and reconcile with."

Psyche's heart clenched at the mention of Eros, and she clutched the goblet of pomegranate juice that threatened to spill as she trembled in shame. "I don't know if he will ever forgive me for what I have done to him."

"Hmm, it is a pickle you find yourself in. I must confess, I was quite shocked at your confession. A gentle girl like you, stabbing your husband in his sleep? You don't seem the type, especially since I can see the love you have for him. I would guess that you were under a spell. The gods do so like to play their little games. And mortals do make the best pawns."

"A spell? But how? I thought I was safe from the gods on the island?"

Pan looked up at her. "From immortals, yes. But when you invite the traitors into your home and to your bosom, it is easy to be led astray."

Psyche frowned. "You are speaking of my sisters. But they—"

"Hated you, were jealous of you," he interrupted her. "You know, in your heart of hearts, that what I say is true. You loved them, but they did not love you. It is a pain unlike any other, when your family—the ones who should love you, want the best for you—are the very ones who harm you the most. I know this pain; it cuts deep and leaves scars on your heart and soul. You blind yourself to it, wanting it to not be true. You would do anything for them; suffer slights and heartache for them, to be worthy of the love your family should have for you. It makes you question your own self-worth, for if they cannot love you, how can anyone else? Isn't that right?"

Pressing her hand to her mouth, Psyche was unable to muffle the sob that broke from her lips. She thought she had no more tears to shed, but she was wrong. Strong arms held her as she cried, her heart breaking all over again. It was true; everything he said was the truth. She had not listened to her husband's concerns about them. She had brought about this tragedy by inviting her sisters into her home.

"How?"

Pan sighed. "Your sisters made a pact with an ancient enemy of your husband. They traded you for personal gain, and now they are paying the price for that betrayal."

"What do you mean? What price are they paying? Did Eros punish them, too?"

"Not Eros. Anteros, his twin brother. The one who attacked you on the island. He is the one who punishes those who reject love. He is an enemy who you do not wish to have. And now you must add him to the list of gods who want to punish you."

A fission of terror ran down Psyche's spine. She remembered the hatred in his eyes when he had pinned her down. She did not want to face that monster again. "So what do you suggest I do, then?"

"Go to the goddesses Demeter and Hera. See if one of them will give you sanctuary until you have safely delivered your child. You cannot keep running from those who mean you harm without endangering the little one. I would offer you sanctuary, but I fear for you, for when you deliver." He chuckled ruefully. "I am the god of fertility, not of childbirth. I am afraid my skills are rather limited in that regard. I plow and seed the fields; I do not bring in the harvest."

Psyche gave a watery chuckle at his pun. Plow and seed the fields, indeed. "What about Eros? How do I make amends?"

"Pray to him when you have found sanctuary. He will hear you. With a love like the one you two share, I doubt he will be able to resist you for long."

Psyche sat back and nodded. "Your council is sound. I will do as you say. I will leave in the morning."

Pan smiled at her. "Good. Now get some rest. I will bring you to Demeter's temple in the morning."

Pan watched as exhaustion took hold of the poor girl. When he was sure that she was sound asleep, he made his way to the entrance of the cave. Stepping out into the moonlight, he saw a figure lurking in the shadows.

"Is it done?"

"Yes, Anteros. It is done."

* * *

APHRODITE SANK DEEPER into the swirling waters of the hot springs. Closing her eyes, she let out a sigh of pleasure. It had been a rough few months, and she desperately needed to relax. She could not let stress mar her beauty in any way. After being caught by her husband, Hephaestus, in bed with her lover, Ares, it had been a trying time. Hephaestus had humiliated her by calling all the gods to bear witness against her and Ares, trapped in the net he had devised, and then he had the nerve to demand his bride price back from Zeus, thus ending their marriage. Hephaestus? The ugly, lame god? Rejecting *her*? How dare he? He should be grateful that she allowed him to bed her occasionally. He left her just because she wanted to keep having lovers on the side.

It was unthinkable.

At least her temples were back to normal now that Psyche was out of the way, the people worshipping her—not that pathetic mortal—as they should.

Psyche. Even her name still brought a spurt of jealous rage to Aphrodite's heart. The little upstart had up and disappeared. None of her spies could find the girl, let alone reveal the name of her husband. She had tried to find out her fate.

She had stationed nymphs loyal to her to watch her parents, which had been a waste of time. All they did was mourn her. They never received any word about the fate of their youngest daughter. No one in Pylos had any clue where Psyche had gone to after being left on Sfaktiria. She was presumed dead, or worse. Had any of them known her whereabouts, she would have tortured the information out of them.

Aphrodite had tried to seduce the information out of Eros, but he had been almost violent in his rejection of her advances. It had sent a delicious fission of desire through her. She loved it when bed play became almost violent. It was why Ares was her favorite lover.

Eros refused to tell her who Psyche was married to, however; only that she had gotten her wish. Psyche was married to a beast. Oh, but the fire in his eyes every time she mentioned the wretched girl's name made her suspicious. Something was afoot there; she just could not figure out what it was.

Her mind drifted over the events of the last few months. Eros had been scarce of late, not up to his usual antics. He still caused problems for the pantheon, but he seemed more distracted of late. Always disappearing.

"My lady!"

Startled out of her reverie, Aphrodite snapped her attention to Astera, the nymph daughter of Helios, standing in front of her. "What is it?"

"My lady. You must come back to Mt. Olympus. Eros is wounded. Love is disappearing from the world. It is terrible—"

"Stop! Slow down. What do you mean, Eros is wounded?"

Astera dropped to her knees, scared and winded. "Eros secretly married Psyche. She betrayed him, and now he lays wounded. She is missing, and love is leaching from the world. The pantheon is demanding that you return and deal with the situation."

Astera winced at the high-pitched shriek that pierced the air. The string of curses that followed would have made an Athenian sailor blush. Astera counted herself lucky when Aphrodite disappeared, heading to Mt. Olympus. "I hope you know what you are doing, Anteros," she muttered under her breath.

* * *

APHRODITE STORMED through Mt. Olympus after confirming the story that Astera had told her. The damn traitor. He lied to her. He had married the little wench, hiding her away on his island home, where no one could find her. No wonder she couldn't find out what had happened to her. He would pay for betraying her. Married to a beast, indeed. He *was* a beast. A lying, rotten beast, she fumed.

"Aphrodite, are you alright? What are you muttering about? What lying beast?"

Not realizing that she had been speaking her thoughts out loud, she let out another curse under her breath. She saw Demeter and Hera standing together off to the side, looking at her with barely concealed amusement. Of all the goddesses to run into, it would have to be these two.

Her day just kept getting worse and worse.

"Eros is the beast. He married that little mortal Psyche behind my back, and is now lying wounded by her hand. She is missing, and now I have to fix the problems he has created with his stupidity. It is quite taxing."

Demeter and Hera exchanged a look. "Well, if Eros married her, then that is that. Perhaps it is a blessing in disguise. Marriage has a way of changing a person. Maybe this is exactly what he needed. You will have to accept this union. It is done."

"Besides," added Demeter, "You need to take care of yourself. It would not do for you to wear yourself out. Forget about the girl. She is a married woman now. Mortals only live for so long. They are like fireflies, their light quickly extinguished."

Aphrodite gave them a mock smile. "Be that as it may, I will hunt this girl down for the insult she has leveled against me, and to poor Eros. I must now undo the damage she has caused. When I do find her, I will make an example of her, and all those who give her asylum, be they gods or mortals, my wrath will know no bounds. That I can promise you."

With that threat, she stalked off, leaving the goddesses to stare after her.

CHAPTER 51

Pan was as good as his word. He refused to allow Psyche to continue her travels until she had fully rested, had a decent meal, and a thick warm cloak to wear. He then led her through the forest, making sure that they took frequent stops. The goat god was quite protective of her and the health of her baby.

It was at the edge of the forest that she first caught sight of a temple in the distance.

"This is as far as I can take you," Pan said, pointing out the path. "That is Demeter's temple. If you do not find what you seek there, continue on this same path for half a day's journey and you will reach the temple of Hera."

Pan handed her a small knapsack filled with provisions. "I am sorry that I cannot accompany you further, but the forest is the end of my domain, and the goddesses do not like it when I venture too far into their lands uninvited."

Psyche took the knapsack and looped the strap across her chest. It was heavy, but not unbearably so. Pan had made sure that she had plenty of food and drink to continue on her journey. She was grateful for his kindness. She had nothing but the clothes on her back to call her own, with no way to pay for anything. She was at the mercy of those she encountered until she could find refuge—or be reunited with her husband. It was a humbling experience.

She managed to surprise Pan when she turned and hugged him. "Thank you for everything. I will never forget your kindness. I will sing your praises and honor you always," she murmured, grateful beyond words.

"Be careful, my dear. Remember, the gods are hunting you. They offer rewards for your capture, and many will betray you. Stay away from the homes of man. Stick to the forests, for you have an affinity with the natural world, and its creatures will guide and protect you always. All you have to do is ask." Pan patted her on the back before setting her firmly on the path. Giving her a little push, he watched as she walked toward the temple.

He stayed even when she was no more than a speck in the distance. "Stay strong, little goddess."

* * *

PSYCHE ENTERED the temple of Demeter. "Hello? Is anyone here?"

Silence met her.

She stepped further into the temple, exploring the building, searching for any sign of life. Looking around, it became quickly apparent that it was not abandoned, for it was filled with tools, various grain harvests, and other offerings. She also saw that it was in a state of disarray. It was quite obvious that the field workers and the priestesses had spent a hard day's work bringing in the harvest before quickly heading back home for the night, most likely exhausted.

Shaking her head at the mess, Psyche knew that if the goddess saw the state of her temple, she would find it disrespectful. So Psyche took off the knapsack and her cloak, putting them off to the side. Using the fire from the central hearth, she lit all the torches, flooding the temple with light.

She then set to work.

Psyche spent much of the night tidying and organizing the temple. She carefully cleaned the sickles, mindful of the sharp edges, before hanging them on the hooks on the wall. She did the same with the other farming tools, as well. She organized the grain into various sorting bins, dusted the furniture, and swept the floor of any debris.

Psyche had just finished putting away the last of the offerings in front of the statue of the goddess when she felt an unearthly presence behind her. Looking over her shoulder, Psyche saw a woman with hair a rich dark brown, crowned by a wreath of various plants. Her eyes glowed green, and light emanated from her lush form. Psyche was shocked to see that the woman was the goddess Demeter. She quickly dropped to her knees, bowing her head. "My lady Demeter, you honor me with your presence."

"My child, you honor me with your piety. I can see you have a true and loving heart. It is a shame that the goddess Aphrodite has declared you an affront to the gods. She is determined to see you punished. I am afraid that it is only a matter of time before she finds you."

Psyche trembled. "Please, my lady, as a mother yourself, will you not give me refuge at least until I have given birth to my daughter? I have done nothing to the goddess Aphrodite. My beauty is not of my doing, and I cannot be held accountable for the actions of others. If I stay hidden, perhaps she will forget about me. Have not her worshippers returned while I was away? Time will soon erase my beauty. Mortal years are but a moment for the gods. Can you please give me refuge? Aphrodite may well forget about me in the meantime."

Demeter shook her head sadly. "I cannot go against a member of my family. She has declared her intentions to punish you, and I cannot go against a fellow goddess. The most I can offer you is not to turn you in for the piety you have shown me. Now, you must leave my temple. Take an oil lamp to guide you. It may be best if you turn yourself in and beg Aphrodite for her forgiveness. Now go."

Demeter disappeared as quickly as she had appeared, leaving a heartbroken Psyche weeping on the floor of her temple. Wiping the tears from her face, she eventually gathered her meager belongings, and taking the oil lamp, made her way back outside.

It was just after midnight, and not even the moon was out. Psyche carefully picked her way over the uneven terrain. She had to find shelter for the night. She could not afford for Demeter to change her mind, or for anyone else to find her. Remembering Pan's words, she traveled down the path for over a mile until she came to the edge of a forested patch of land. She was exhausted from the events of the day, but she couldn't afford to stop until she had shelter for the evening. The nights could get quite cold.

She entered the woods, going as far as she could, gathering fallen branches and dried grass. Finding an outcrop of rocks that formed a natural shelter, Psyche quickly picked up loose stones, and using the branches and dried grass, made a campfire.

Once she had a roaring fire going, she settled down against the rock wall. The fire should keep her warm, and safe from wild animals. Pulling open the knapsack, she was grateful for the provisions that Pan had provided for her. Inside she found bread, cheese, olives, figs, and two flasks of pomegranate juice, but it was what she found hidden that made her cry all over again. There was a smaller pouch filled with several gold coins. It was enough to provide her with a good start should she ever find safe refuge. She offered up a quick prayer of thanks to the god.

After eating and repacking the food and coins, she sat back. She was startled out of her light doze by the sudden kicking of her daughter. Overwhelming grief and fear gripped her. She had to protect her innocent child. "I know, little one. Mama made a huge mistake and I am so sorry for putting you in danger. I swear, I will protect you. Even if I must give my life to do so."

Psyche looked up at the stars in the sky. "Phanes...Eros. If you can hear my prayer, please know I am so sorry. I don't know what made me do what I did. I want to make amends, and I will do whatever is necessary to prove my love and trust in you. Please forgive me."

Closing her eyes, she then fell into a fitful sleep.

* * *

THE NEXT MORNING, Psyche traveled further down the winding road. She covered her head with her cloak, trying to keep prying eyes from identifying her. Other than a lone shepherd tending his flock of sheep, she was alone for the most part. Well, except for the inordinate amount of animals that seemed to be out and about. It almost seemed as if they were following her.

She brushed off that idea as a wild fancy on her part.

She stopped midday by a waterfall to rest and eat a light lunch. She had to be careful and conserve her rations. She didn't know how long it would take to find shelter, and she dare not go into any town or small village in case she was recognized—or worse—thought to be Aphrodite herself again by the people. Standing up, she stretched and headed to wade in the shallow pool. The water was cold, but it was refreshing on her tired feet.

She turned toward the shore, carefully stepping onto the rocks, when she came to an abrupt halt. On the banks of the wading pool, mere inches from her foot, was a sand viper. Its distinctive v mark on the back of its head that continued as a zigzag pattern down its body was evident in the bright sunlight. She froze in fear. The snake bared its fangs, ready to strike. It lunged at her ankle. Screaming "stop," she closed her eyes and braced herself for the pain of the bite.

Heart racing in panic, Psyche stood frozen. It took a few minutes before she realized she had not been bitten. Opening her eyes, she was shocked by what she saw. The viper was frozen in mid-strike. Its mouth was wide open, fangs ready to pierce her flesh. One could easily mistake it for a statue but for the manic movement of its eyes.

Taking several deep breaths, desperate to get her racing heart and mind under control, Psyche stayed in place. A fragment of a memory came to her. Fury. This was much like the first meeting she had with the stallion. Each time she had been scared, something like this had happened, but looking at her memories, she now remembered something else. A surge of power that had filled her body right before she had spoken, both animals frozen in place, only their eyes giving evidence that they were being held against their will by an invisible force.

Examining her memories closer, Psyche remembered other times when something similar had happened. The agora. The time she had almost been mobbed by a crowd of people wanting to touch a living goddess. They had scared her and her potential suitor Alexander with their fervor. She remembered yelling a command, and the crowd stopping. The sudden stillness of every living thing in the agora, all of them looking like statues. The palace guards rushing to get her and Alexander to safety.

She later learned that it was only after she had left the

market that the people began to move again. It was one of the damning events that had led her father to go to see the oracle after Alexander had renounced her. She had brushed it off, wanting to forget about that terrible day. Now she closely examined it, and other memories of similar events.

An idea came to her. Her husband had once said she had untold power in her, that she needed to use her other senses beyond her sight. That she would be all the more powerful once she learned to harness it. He had been trying to tell her something beyond how to play their game of copycat, something far more important.

Psyche focused inward, searched for the trigger in her mind. Once she felt she had found it, she turned her focus on the snake. Gathering her strength, she gave a command. "Close your mouth."

She felt a small spark of power. The snake followed her order. Giddy with disbelief, still keeping her focus, she gave another directive. "Move to the left until you reach the flowers. Then stop."

Again, she felt a small rush of power before the snake followed her command. The flow of power felt much like the rush when she was scared. It was easy to confuse the two. "Go away and never bite anyone unless they attack you," she commanded.

The snake quickly left the area. Psyche collapsed next to the pool, stunned. If she had the ability to control people and animals, it gave her the power to protect herself and her child, at least from mortal threats. She would have to practice as she traveled.

She got up, and picking up her meager belongings, she got back on the road. All the while she tried her newfound abilities out on the animals that she came into contact with. With each use, her powers became easier to control.

By late afternoon, she came across a lone merchant and

was able to get a ride in his cart, making him believe that she was a young man, and later she used her abilities to make him forget he ever met her. It was exhilarating, but she had to caution herself. She could never use this newfound ability for anything other than good—or for protection.

The merchant dropped her off near the temple of Hera. Waving him off, she entered it, finding it empty. She knelt in front of the altar. "Hera, please hear my prayers. As the goddess of marriage and motherhood, I beseech you. Please give me shelter and protection in my time of need."

A flash of light lit suddenly the interior of the temple, its intensity blinding. Opening her eyes, Psyche saw standing before her the raven-haired queen of the gods. Hera stared down at her, her sky-blue eyes sympathetic, giving Psyche hope that she had at last found refuge.

"My lady, you honor me with your presence."

Hera shook her head. "My dear child, I wish I could help you, but Aphrodite is my own daughter-in-law. I cannot go against my own family to help you. It is not done. Even now, Aphrodite's nets are closing in. It is just a matter of days before she captures you."

Psyche cried out in despair. "If you won't help me, the goddess who is charged to offer protection to wives and mothers, what hope is there for me and my child? My babe is the daughter of Eros. Surely she at least merits protection by the pantheon, by the protector of children?"

Hera smiled sadly down at her. "Your child's fate is tied to your own. Eros is the father, but your marriage is not recognized by the pantheon; therefore, she does not have any more rights than any other demigoddess. He has not claimed you, or the child, publicly. He lays wounded even now. You caused great harm to Eros. Your best chance is to turn yourself in to Aphrodite. Beg her for mercy and you may yet be able to provide a decent life for your baby. Now, you must leave my temple, Psyche. Do not go to the temples of any of the other gods, for you will find no refuge among them. All have sided with Aphrodite."

With that warning, Hera left her crumpled on the floor. Psyche was stunned. Hera had been her last hope among the gods for help. She had no one else. She was truly all alone in the world. Even her husband would not answer her prayers.

Guilt and grief choked her. She had tried to kill her husband. He was hurting and she was the cause. The gods would show her no mercy for that. Eros must truly hate her. She couldn't blame him; she hated herself as well for what she had done.

Crying, Psyche left the temple. She knew she had no choice. She was a hunted woman. Time had run out on her. Gods, mortals—all would hunt her down. She had only one option left. She traveled further down the road. It took hours, but by the time the sun was setting, she finally came to another temple.

Going inside, she slowly approached the dais. Kneeling down, Psyche bowed her head. "Aphrodite. I have come to surrender and to beg you for mercy."

Her prayer was met by a delighted laugh behind her. "Finally, you are in my clutches."

CHAPTER 52

A shiver of fear raced down Psyche's spine. Aphrodite stood behind her. Not wanting to have her enemy at her back, Psyche shifted slightly on her knees so that she could have the goddess in her sight. A part of her wished she hadn't done that when she caught sight of the malicious glee on the goddess' face. Hatred twisted the beautiful face of Aphrodite. Psyche swore she could feel the hatred pouring off of her.

Before she could respond, Aphrodite leapt forward, grabbing Psyche by her hair. She pulled her head so far back that Psyche feared she meant to snap her neck. Crying out in pain, she was unable to get her footing under her as Aphrodite used her superior strength to practically lift her off the ground by her hair. The pain was agonizing, and Psyche clawed at Aphrodite's hand, desperate to break her hold.

Aphrodite laughed at her before delivering a hard slap across her face. Pain exploded in Psyche's head as Aphrodite rained blow after blow on her. Her vision blurred, Psyche tried to protect herself, but Aphrodite was too strong. She feared that she would soon lose consciousness, and she thought that she might never wake up if that happened.

Getting tired of hitting Psyche, Aphrodite finally dragged her by her hair to the dais. Crying out in pain, Psyche struggled to keep up, but she was unable to. It felt like her hair was being pulled out of her head by the roots.

Aphrodite flung Psyche down on her back at the foot of the throne that appeared in the middle of the raised platform. Taking a seat, Aphrodite kept Psyche in place by placing her foot on Psyche's belly, the threat very clear.

"Look what you made me do, you little harlot. You made me break out into a sweat."

Two servants instantly appeared on either side of Aphrodite. One blotted her forehead while the other gently fanned her. Then the goddess waved them off, turning her attention back to Psyche. "Do you know why I hate you so much?"

When Psyche failed to answer right away, Aphrodite pressed down hard on her belly, her child protesting the rough treatment.

"Because people believed I was you, and worshipped me in your place," Psyche said quickly, hoping that her answer would appease the goddess. She had to protect her baby, and Aphrodite made it very clear that she had no regard for the welfare of her daughter.

The goddess laughed, the sound ugly in its demented rage. "Oh, you stupid little mortal. I hate you for that, and so much more! You stole my worshippers. You tried to replace me. I am a goddess! All bow down to me. But then you came along. A pathetic mortal. You are nothing. Do you hear me? Nothing!"

Psyche watched silently, praying that Eros, Pax, or anyone would hear her prayers and save her from Aphrodite. The goddess seemed almost unhinged in her rage. It was truly frightening.

Then just as suddenly, Aphrodite calmed down. She turned a contemplative eye to Psyche's belly, at the protruding mound that she was unable to hide—or protect. Her child chose that moment to kick where Aphrodite's bare foot pressed against her stomach, making her displeasure known.

"No, Psyche. I despised you for your beauty, that fooled mortals into thinking you were me. If that had been your only crime, your punishment would not have been as severe. But then you had to take the one thing I desired more than anything else. I hate you more for seducing the one god who has never shared my bed. For being the one he loved so much that he brought you to his island. For being the woman he chose to keep and be loyal to. For deciding that *you* were be the mother of his only child. For that Psyche, I will destroy you."

Psyche's relief was short lived when Aphrodite took her foot off of her to stand up. With a snap of the goddess' fingers, the two servants appeared on either side of Psyche, each grabbing one of her arms, pulling her up to her knees between them.

"Take her to the dungeon. You know what to do."

The two servants dragged Psyche away. Too weak to offer much resistance, she was brought to an underground chamber, deep in the bowels of the temple. Inside, the two servants ripped her clothes and the knapsack from her body, uncaring of any damage they did to her. Both refused to speak to her, let alone listen to any of her pleas to not hurt her child. Then they chained her up between two strong columns.

Psyche watched in horror as the two servants took out what looked like oiled bull whips. She had once seen the damage such whips could do. They would tear her flesh to shreds with each strike. The goddess was going to have her whipped. If she was lucky, she would only be badly scarred for life. If not, she could easily die from the pain and trauma.

The servants took their positions, one in front of her, the other behind her. The one in front finally spoke. "You will receive one hundred lashes between the two of us. There will be no part of your body untouched by our whips. We will not stop, no matter how much you scream and beg. If you pass out, we will wake you before continuing with your punishment. But know this, harlot: This is only the beginning of your torment. The mistress has many plans for you, and you will not deprive her of her revenge. The mercy of death has been denied to you."

Psyche squeezed her eyes shut and hunched her body in as far as her shackles would allow in a vain attempt to shield her baby. She braced herself when she heard the duel sounds of the whips cracking through the air. She waited for the pain to hit her.

Nothing happened.

Straining to hear anything over her wildly beating heart and ragged breaths, she tried to hear where the servants had gone. Nothing but silence met her. Cautiously, she opened her eyes. The servant in front of her was missing. She dared to sneak a peek behind her. She was alone.

Then the room dropped away, and Psyche found herself standing in the middle of a field. Out of the darkness, a figure separated itself from the shadows, approaching her on silent feet. The closer it got, the more defined its features became. It was a large, winged male. The way it moved was both beautiful and terrifying. It did not walk; it prowled like a predator.

Something about it tugged at her memories.

Her heart leapt in sudden joy. "Eros?"

The mysterious figure stopped a short distance away from her, and all of a sudden, lightning rent the sky above. The sound was like the crack of a whip, causing her to cry out in fright. The lightning thundered again, only this time it struck the ground all around her, setting a ring of fire around her and the silent winged male. The blaze from the fire lit the night, and she was able to clearly see who stood in front of her. It was not her husband, but he could have been a twin to Eros, except for his coloring. Where Eros had blond hair, blue eyes, and white wings, this male had black hair, brown eyes, and black wings.

"Who are you?"

The male smirked. "I forgot we have not been formally introduced, though we have met before. My name is Anteros. Eros is my twin brother. Perhaps this will jog your memory?"

In the blink of an eye, the black-and-silver tipped drakon that had attacked her stood in his place. It looked down at her with malevolent red eyes before quickly changing back.

Psyche stumbled backwards. "How is Eros? Is he alright? Where—"

"He is gravely wounded, no thanks to you," Anteros snarled, cutting her off. "Even now, in his delirium, he cries out your name. The stab wound refuses to heal. He suffers because he thought you loved him, that you trusted him."

"I do love him! I—"

"Stabbed him when he slept. Is that what you call love?"

Psyche hung her head in shame, tears sliding down her face. It was true, all of it. She had no excuse for what she had done.

"Well? Have you nothing to say in your defense? I can assure you, Aphrodite's punishment is far more merciful than what I can do to you. Don't you want to plead your case before I sentence you for your crimes?"

Psyche shook her head in hopeless despair. Dropping

down to her knees, she looked up and locked eyes with him. "All I ask is that my daughter lives a good life with her father. If there is a way that I can heal him or undo what I have done, I would give anything in my power to do so. To give my life for his. But if not, I beg you. Just heal him and protect his child."

Dropping her head down, she waited for the death blow she was sure he intended to deliver to her. She remembered how he had threatened to rip her child from her womb, but that he would never harm his niece, so she simply waited.

She was startled when she felt his hand gently cup the side of her face, so at odds with his earlier treatment of her. He knelt down in front of her, tipping her head back so that he could look deeply into her eyes. Neither of them said a word, but she felt him moving in her mind, gently probing, testing the veracity of her commitment, all the while trying to ferret out her secrets. A brief pain lit her brain before fading away.

Whatever Anteros found in her mind seemed to satisfy him. "So be it."

Placing his other hand over her heart, he sent a massive blast of energy into her. It felt like he was ripping her to shreds and putting her back together again at the same time. Silent screams filled her heart, mind, and soul with unimaginable agony, paralyzing her as the pain ripped through her. The agony was coming from within her, but also from outside her.

Eros. She was feeling both his and her pain at the same time. She felt Eros suffering the same when she heard the echo of him screaming her name in her head. It proved too much, and Psyche lost consciousness, with Eros' name on her lips.

Anteros caught Psyche before she hit the ground. Gathering her up in his arms, he took off with her. He had very little time to get his plan into place before Aphrodite made an appearance to see how Psyche's punishment was progressing. His lips curled in disgust. That spiteful goddess had not cared at all for the harm she would have done to the little one.

Glancing down at Psyche's stomach, he was pleased to see the little ripples of movement that the baby was making. He had shielded the baby from what he had had to do in order give Psyche a chance at redemption. If she succeeded, Eros would fully recover and be reunited with his soul mate in her current manifestation, together forever in two bodies. If not, Anteros would be forced to rip her to shreds in order to get at her soul, and use it to heal Eros.

Landing outside Aphrodite's temple, Anteros headed toward the dungeon, unseen by prying eyes. He entered the room and placed Psyche on a pallet of blankets in the corner. After covering her with a blanket, he sat in front of the hearth, waiting for her to wake up. He didn't have long to wait.

Psyche opened her eyes, only to close them again quickly when pain shot through her. She felt awful; a dull, persistent ache radiated throughout her body, coming in waves of intensity. She stayed very still and breathed through it. It took several minutes before she felt that she could even move.

She opened her eyes again a while later to get her bearings, only to find herself back in the dungeon. Startled, she sat up, looking around to see who was in the room with her. She spotted Anteros sitting in front of the fire, watching her.

He stood up and prowled over to her, silently handing her a drink and a plate of food. Murmuring a soft thank you, she ate and drank while he leaned against the wall, silently watching her. As the silence stretched out between them, it made her uncomfortable as she waited for him to say something. It set her on edge being under such scrutiny when he gave away nothing. Finally, she couldn't take it anymore . "What did you do to me?"

"I tied your life force to Eros. In doing so, you felt all the pain—heart, body, and soul—that Eros is feeling, and he felt yours."

"Why did you do that? Isn't that dangerous to him? What about the baby?"

Anteros sighed. "The baby is safe. I would never harm her. Should it become necessary, I can make sure she survives outside your womb until she is full term. And it is not dangerous to Eros. He is a god, an immortal. You—on the other hand— as a mortal, are at risk. Should you fail, your soul will drain from your body in order to heal Eros. If that happens, he lives, and you die."

Psyche stared at Anteros. It took her a few minutes to process what he said. There was something he was hiding from her. She repeated what he had told her in her mind, looking at it from every angle, trying to figure out what he wasn't telling her. He loved his brother; she had no doubt on that score. That love seemed to extend to her daughter, as well, since she was his blood. At least she could rest her mind that her child would be safe. "If he is immortal, how did my stabbing him cause such damage? Shouldn't he have healed almost instantly? I thought only gods could wound and kill each other? I'm mortal; I shouldn't be able to hurt him like that."

Anteros glared down at her. "Eros said you were intelligent. Apparently you are also too clever for your own good."

Psyche simply waited. She couldn't force him to reveal the answer to the question that had been plaguing her since that horrible day. How had she wounded Eros so badly? The blade had been the one she'd carried with her to the island. It was nothing special. By all accounts, she should be powerless against a god… Unless? "Am I a demigoddess? Is that why I was able to harm Eros? And how is it that I can control animals?"

The hair on the back of her neck rose in fear at the menacing growl that filled the chamber. Anteros' eyes swirled red with rage. "No, you are not a demigoddess. Nor are you fully human. You are you, and that makes you a danger to Eros, and everything he cares for."

Psyche gathered her courage. "So that makes me a threat to you, as well, since you are his twin, and he loves you." She braced herself, sure that he would strike out at her for her impudence. The blow never came; instead, she watched the sinister smile that twisted his lips.

"Let us see how much of a threat you truly are to us, then. Tomorrow, Aphrodite will arrive to oversee the next phase of your punishment. She will believe that the trials she tasks you are of her own making, but in fact, they will be mine. She is a rather easy mark for manipulation. You will be given a series of four tasks, each harder and more dangerous than the last. Each one you will dedicate and do in honor of Eros. By each successful act of trust and faith on your part, he will heal. Succeed, and the two of you will be reunited. Fail, you will die so that he may live."

CHAPTER 53

"Wake up, harlot!"

Psyche was violently shaken out of her sleep. Looking up, she saw the servant that had been one of the ones charged with whipping her looming over her. Seeing that she was awake, the woman flung the blanket off her, exposing her naked body and flinging a gown at her, along with her knapsack. "Get dressed; the goddess demands your presence."

Psyche felt awful. It reminded her of the time when she had been sick as a child with a very bad fever that had lasted a week. She had been left weak and aching with fatigue and body pain once the fever had broken. There was a dull ache in her chest. She looked down, startled to see welts covering her body. She gently ran her finger over a particularly angry one on her thigh, but all she felt was smooth skin. She felt no pain at all from them, just muscle pain and fatigue.

"Hurry up, or there will be more where that came from."

Psyche lifted the garment over her head, bracing herself, but no real discomfort came with her movements, just soreness. The coarse gown settled against her skin. The material was designed to scrape and irritate skin that had been whipped, but she felt nothing. Illusion. Her welts were fake. Anteros must have put them there to hide the fact that she had not been whipped. She sent a silent prayer of thanks to him.

She stood up slowly, her body stiff and feeling weak. She followed the servant, careful to keep up the illusion of true pain. It would not do for them to know that she was only sore and fatigued from what Anteros had done to her, and not from being whipped.

She entered the main chamber of the temple to find Aphrodite sitting on her throne. The room was a mess; the floor was covered with various types of grains and seeds. It was ankle deep, and there was a single, clear path. Psyche took care to stay on it and not trample on what were obviously votive offerings. She knelt down in front of the goddess and bowed her head.

"Well, you are not so pretty now, are you? I must say, I do love the sight of welts on you. I must remember to keep them fresh; it wouldn't do for them to fade away," Aphrodite said, laughing.

When Psyche said nothing, the goddess smirked. "I had quite an interesting conversation with Anteros. He is Eros' twin brother, by the way—the god of unrequited love—and so enjoys punishing people who reject love. He has been in such a state since you harmed Eros. He has requested to be the one to come up with your punishments, and I agreed to his request. He is such a deliciously evil genius when it comes to devising them."

Psyche stayed silent. She couldn't afford to tip off the goddess that she had escaped her punishment, or that she had already had this very conversation with Anteros. He had been very insistent that Aphrodite stay in the dark about the previous night's events.

"Demeter told me you cleaned her temple. Since you love to play the pious maid, you have until sunset to clean *my* temple. You must sort all the grain and seeds, and put them into their respective bins. If you fail, last night's whipping will seem like child's play."

Laughing in delight, Aphrodite disappeared, leaving Psyche alone in the temple. She looked at the seeds and harvested grain that blanketed the floor. There were at least a dozen type of each scattered and mixed, and it would take a small army months to sort them out. There was no way that she could complete this task in the allotted time all by herself.

She slumped over in despair. She would fail on the first task given to her. "Eros," she whispered, "I pray to you. I dedicate this labor in your honor, to show you my love and trust in you. I wish you could help me."

Psyche felt a soft stirring in her mind before she heard the whisper of a voice.

Psyche?

"Eros? Eros, please. Speak to me. Where are you?"

Psyche...been unconscious...weak...baby...you...safe?

Psyche wanted to cry. He still cared for her even after everything that had happened. She wanted to lie and reassure him that she was safe, but she knew better. "I am in Aphrodite's temple. Anteros is in charge of my punishment for stabbing you. He has set four tasks for me to complete in your name to help heal you. I am so sorry for everything. You must believe me. I never meant to hurt you," she pleaded tearfully.

PSYCHE...NO...WHY...GET OUT...

She cried out, collapsing from a sudden sharp stabbing pain in her chest. She looked down and pulled aside her gown, certain she had been stabbed. Seeing nothing but smooth skin, she realized she was feeling his pain and terror.

It was horrible. “I can’t leave. I am sorry. I had no choice. Anteros has given his word that our baby will be safe. Please do not hurt yourself further; I will do my best to complete these tasks. I will make this right.”

Psyche...show me...see...through...your...eyes...

“What do you mean? What do you want to see?”

Task...show task...let me in...open mind...see...

Then Eros broke off abruptly, his energy spent. She could feel his weariness and struggle to stay awake on her end of their link. The threads that tied them together were fragile. She thought over what he said. He said to open her mind. But how?

She thought over the dilemma. Looking around the temple, her gaze fell upon the locked double doors. An idea came to her. She didn’t know if it would work, but she had to try.

Closing her eyes, she took several deep breaths. With each one, the chaos in her mind slowly settled until she could think clearly. Her heart settled into a steady rhythm. Once her heart and mind were calm, she started to build the image of a temple in her mind. She was meticulous, building it brick by brick, imagining that the temple housed her very essence. When it was complete, she pictured herself standing in the center of the building, facing the locked door. The temple was impenetrable; the only way for someone to enter was if she opened the doors.

Focusing on the locked door, Psyche imagined the doors slowly unlocking. With each imaginary turn, the locks opened one by one, slowly unbolting the doors to her mind. Finally, the last lock gave way. She imagined the doors being pushed opened.

At first, all she could see was endless darkness outside the doors of her mind. She thought of her husband, pieced together a picture of him, and called out to him. In the distance, she saw a shadow separate itself from the darkness. At first it was just a little flicker, but gradually, it took shape. As time ticked on, the image became crisper, more defined. She could make out the ghostly form of a male with large wings.

It moved slowly, its steps halting, so unlike the normal gait of her husband that she feared she had summoned another. Panicking, she prepared to slam the doors shut, but just at the last moment, the winged figure came into focus. Phanes. No, Eros.

She let out a sob at the sight of him. He looked so pale and defeated, so unlike the confident and strong man she knew her husband to be. Looking down, she shuddered at the stab wound that still looked fresh, blood dripping down in slow rivers past the salve that did nothing to heal him. Guilt flayed her soul; she had done that to him. She had harmed her husband, the father of her child, the love of her life, the man who had given her love, protection, happiness, and pleasure beyond her wildest imaginations. She deserved to be punished. She didn't deserve his help.

Stop it...guilt...useless

Psyche locked eyes with Eros; he stood still several yards away from the entrance to her mind. He swayed. She rushed to him, determined to catch him, only to be knocked back by an invisible force when she tried to go through the door. She slammed her hands against it, but it held, keeping her trapped inside the temple, and Eros locked out.

"Eros. Please come closer."

Can't...barrier...too strong...time running out...show me task...now

Psyche reluctantly stepped back and gestured to the interior of the temple. She brought up the image of the scattered seeds and grains. "I only have a few hours to clean and sort them into their correct piles. There is no way that I can complete this task by myself. It would take an army."

Yes...you have an army...use them...call them to you...command them...

Frowning, Psyche turned back to Eros. He was beginning to fade away. "I don't understand. I don't have an army. Eros, that makes no sense."

Your powers...use them...creatures big and small...temple has hidden army...use them..

"Eros—"

Sorry...too weak...can't stay awake...please...Psyche...use...

In a blink of an eye, Eros disappeared. A cry of grief ripped from her and echoed throughout the temple of her mind, the force of it knocking her back into her body and causing her to fall to the cold stone ground of Aphrodite's temple.

She lay there, tears dripping, as she tried to make sense of what Eros was trying to tell her. An army. There was a hidden army in Aphrodite's temple. Surely their loyalty would be to the goddess, not to her. Doubt crept in. Eros must be delusional to suggest such a thing. His wound had to be affecting his judgment. He must not know what he was saying.

No! Doubt and lack of faith were what had got her into this mess. She refused to let them take hold of her again. Eros had said there was a hidden army in the temple, and that she should use her powers to command them. But where would they be hidden?

Movement in the corner of her eye caught her attention. Blinking to clear her vision, she watched a lone ant pick up a seed three times its size. It turned around and walked to her, stopping just in front of her. It stayed there, looking at her as it easily held the seed.

Realization dawned on her. The temple—like so many

buildings—*did* have a hidden army. Only this army was made up of ants. If there were enough of them, they could easily help her sort the grain and seeds in the allotted time. If she could command them, that is.

Focusing on the ant, she felt the familiar rush of adrenaline flood her body. "Little ant, gather your colony and help me sort the seeds and grains into the storage bins before nightfall."

The little ant dropped the seed and scurried away, disappearing into a small crack in the floor. She pushed herself up into a sitting position, waiting for it to reappear. Seconds passed like honey flowing in winter. Nothing happened. Right before she could chastise herself for her foolishness, a swarm of ants invaded from every corner of the temple. There had to be hundreds of thousands of them, a living moving sea of them. She watched in astonishment as they quickly grabbed a seed or a grain. There were so many ants that before long, at least a quarter of the grain and seeds were held by an ant before all movement stopped.

The ants stood frozen. Psyche looked at them, wondering what she had done wrong. It was then that she realized they were all looking at her. Staying very still, she gave her next command. "The bins need to be filled. All the ants with lentils, put them in the green bin. The faro goes in the blue bin, the wheat berries go into the yellow bin."

She watched in astonishment as the ants followed the rest of her commands on where to place the harvest. They worked quickly and efficiently. Within four hours, the floor was clean and the bins filled with their respective seeds. The ants disappeared as quickly as they had appeared.

Psyche finally stood up, watching where she stepped so as not to accidently step on any stray ant that remained behind. She carefully inspected and cleaned the rest of the temple, making sure that not a grain was left forgotten, but the ants had left nothing on the floor. By the time night fell, the temple was back in order.

Psyche did not have long to wait before Aphrodite made her appearance. The front doors suddenly opened and the goddess strutted in. Dropping to her knees, Psyche bowed her head, waiting for Aphrodite to speak. Hearing nothing, she dared to take a peek at the goddess through the veil of her hair.

Aphrodite stood in the center of the temple, a dumbfounded expression on her face. She looked at the various bins, expertly sorted. She scoured the floor, looking for an errant grain or seed. She found nothing. Anger and hatred filled her face. She marched over to Psyche, grabbed her hair, and yanked her head back. "Which god did this?"

Psyche fought to keep her hands at her side. She dared not strike back. "No god did this. I swear, my lady."

"Impossible. You cheated. You had to use only your own abilities to sort the harvest. This was an impossible task. You will pay for this. Now give me the name of who helped you!"

"Aphrodite."

Both women froze when they heard Anteros' voice. He suddenly appeared beside them. "She did not cheat. She used only her own abilities to complete this task. I watched her the entire time. Let her go. She passed this one. We will see if she can pass the next one tomorrow. Besides, Ares is waiting for you."

Aphrodite glared at Anteros. "If I did not know better, I would think *you* helped her. Very well. Let us see if she can survive the next task on your list."

Once her hair was released, Psyche slumped back onto her knees.

Flinging a small piece of bread at her feet, Aphrodite smirked at her. "Here is your reward. We mustn't let the mongrel in your belly starve." She turned to Anteros before disappearing. "See to it that she makes it back to the dungeon. Make sure to make it as uncomfortable as you can."

Anteros waited until he was sure that the temple was empty before helping Psyche to her feet. He nodded to her. "You did well today."

Gathering her courage, she dared to enquire further. "Thank you. Please tell me, how is Eros? I saw him for a moment, and he looked so bad."

Anteros stared at her. Never had she seen eyes that cold, or that looked like death. She fought to maintain eye contact. She couldn't let him go without knowing if Eros would heal.

"That depends on you. Today's show of faith and trust helped. We will see if you are strong enough. Now let's get back to your dungeon."

Turning his back on her, he headed toward the dungeon only to stop after several steps when he realized that she was not following. Swearing under his breath, he turned around, ready to force her to move when he stopped dead in his tracks at what he saw.

Psyche was still kneeling on the floor, but this time, she was surrounded by the ants that had answered her call. He watched as she quietly thanked them, giving them all the bread that was to be her dinner, apologizing to them for the poor reward for their efforts on her behalf.

The ants reluctantly took the bread, only tearing it apart when she implored them to take it. Whatever the ants said to her brought a tearful smile to her face before she sent them back to their underground home with the bread.

She did not move to follow him until the ants were gone, and even then she kept her eyes on the ground, making sure not to step on any of them.

Anteros reached out and stopped her as she went to step around him. "That was your dinner."

"I know, but they earned the meal. I just wish I could have given them more for their help."

Something in him refused to let the matter go. "Do you expect me to provide you with more food?"

"No. I expect only that you will protect Eros and our child. I am expendable compared to them." With that, she gently pulled her arm from his grasp and went straight to the dungeon.

He followed her and watched as she walked over to the pallet of blankets on the floor. She lay down, and quickly fell asleep.

Anteros stood over her for a long time, not sure what to make of what he had just witnessed. A part of him wished he could trust the innate goodness that he sensed in her, but then he would have sworn his own soul mate had the same characteristic, and look how that had turned out.

Swearing, he left.

Appearing next to Eros, who was lying asleep in his bed, Anteros bent over him, checking his wound. It still looked bad, but if he was not mistaken, the bleeding had stopped. Not wanting to trust his eyes, he turned to Pax. "How is he? Have you seen any improvement?"

Pax looked at him with tired eyes. "His coloring has improved slightly. I believe that is because the wound finally stopped bleeding today."

"How long has it been since the bleeding stopped?"

"At least a few hours. It didn't start bleeding again even after we cleaned and rebandaged it. I think your plan is working."

"Let us hope so, for all our sakes."

CHAPTER 54

The smell of freshly baked bread and honey roused Psyche from her sleep. It triggered her hunger, making her stomach growl, further drawing her from the blissful arms of slumber. Taking a deep breath, she let the sweet smell fill her nostrils. It lured her from the comfort of sleep with the promise of sating her hunger.

Rolling over, the smell became more powerful. She opened her eyes to see a tray full of various foods and drink set beside her. It drew her from the last vestiges of sleep. Then her stomach growled again, making its need loud and clear. Finally awake, she pushed herself up with a groan and reached over for the tray, pulling it over to her. She dug into the food and drink, famished.

Attacking the food, she made short work of eating almost everything on the tray. She had not eaten anything since the previous morning. Not knowing when her next meal would be, she wrapped up the little food she could not finish and put it into her travel bag. Better to conserve than to waste.

"Well, at least your appetite is unchanged."

Turning around toward where the voice had come from,

she spied Anteros in the farthest corner of the room in the shadows, leaning against the wall.

"How long have you been here? Why are you hiding in the shadows? Is Eros alright?"

Anteros shook his head, choosing to ignore her questions for the moment. "I am happy to see you are not one of those annoying women who barely eat or enjoy their food. That at least you have in your favor."

Shaking her head at his avoidance of her questions, she tried again. "Anteros, please. Tell me, how is Eros?"

The minutes ticked by as he stayed silent. It was slowly driving her mad, and she had to restrain herself from lashing out at him, demanding that he tell her how her husband was doing. She would bet her last breath that he was enjoying her torment. He was a god who liked to punish people, and he was well suited for it.

"Eros is doing slightly better. He was the one to demand that I feed you. You will need your strength. Today's task has been set. Be ready."

With that warning, he—and the tray of food —disappeared.

Before Psyche had a chance to call him back, the door to her prison opened, and one of the priestesses of the temple came in. "Get up. You have five minutes to make yourself presentable for the goddess."

Psyche quickly washed up and took care of her needs before gathering her meager belongings and following the priestess out of the dungeon. Aphrodite was seated, smirking as she watched Psyche drop down to her knees before her.

"Well, look what the cat dragged in. I must say, you look a little worn at the edges. Beauty is so fleeting in mortals."

When Psyche made no reply, Aphrodite narrowed her eyes. "Being the goddess of beauty is such a demanding role. The countless prayers, parties, personal favors, and what-not. It is quite exhausting. There is a feast planned for the end of the month, and I must simply look my best. So today, you will go and collect the wool from the golden sheep of Helios beyond the river from my temple. You will collect enough so that a gown can be spun from its threads, and I will wear it to the feast. Do not even think of trying to escape."

Then Aphrodite waved her off, a cunning smirk on her face that Psyche did not trust. After the goddess left the temple, she was grateful to be away from the oppressive atmosphere.

Psyche followed the river until she came to a spot where it narrowed just enough for her to safely cross. It was then that she spotted one of the golden sheep in the distance. It was a magnificent creature. Its wool looked like spun gold in the early morning light. Shading her eyes, she raised herself on her tiptoes, trying to spot the rest of the flock. It was difficult at first, but she soon spotted the sheep lying in the shade among all the shrubs in the field.

Dropping back down, Psyche checked to make sure she had the sack and the knife in her knapsack to collect and store the wool. It was going to be a difficult day to get the amount of wool she would need, and she had never done this type of work before, though she had seen it done by the men of her father's kingdom.

"Hear me, Eros. I dedicate this labor in your honor. Please accept my humble efforts to heal the wound that I caused."

Psyche then stepped to the river's edge, gathering her gown, and started to cross it when the lone sheep suddenly became alerted to her presence. Its ears dropped back against its head and it let out a shrill sound before charging at her. Gasping in fear, she fell back, landing on her backside.

Holding up her hand, she yelled "Stop!"

The sheep skidded to a halt on the other side of the shore.

It stalked back and forth along the edge, snorting and stamping the ground.

"Rejoin the flock and leave me alone," Psyche ordered.

It trembled in rage, barely held back by her command. It fought the compulsion to obey, but in the end, it had no choice.

She watched as the sheep finally turned around and rejoined the rest of the flock. She stayed on the ground, waiting for her racing heart to slow down. Her powers barely kept the one sheep from attacking her. How could she control a whole flock? Little wonder Aphrodite had a smirk on her face; she knew that the sheep would attack. It left no doubt in Psyche's mind that the goddess hoped that she would be severely injured, if not mauled to death.

Closing her eyes, Psyche repeated the steps she had created to open her mind to Eros. It took far less time to complete the temple and open the doors this time. She sent a call out to her husband, hoping he was well enough to answer. If he didn't, she was determined to figure out a way to get the wool, Aphrodite be damned.

Psyche?

Joy burst in her heart at the sound of his voice. "Eros, my love. How are you?"

Feeling better...where...are...you? Baby? Aphrodite?

"The baby and I are fine. Aphrodite sent me on my second trial. I have to collect enough wool from a flock of golden sheep to make her a gown, but the sheep are too wild. I was barely able to control one. I don't know what to do."

Alarm shot through their link. She could feel his agitation even before he spoke. *Helios' flock? Too dangerous...they will... kill you. Must not approach...them...your powers...aren't enough...*

Despair gripped her hard. How could she approach the sheep if they were vicious killers? What use were her powers if she could not use them to accomplish this one task? Her self-doubts began to crowd in on her; they clawed at her, trying to drag her down and drown her in her own fears and feelings of worthlessness. She was going to fail if she couldn't figure this out. Look what she had done to the man that she loved. She was weak. Maybe she really was nothing more than a pretty face.

Psyche...STOP! You are everything...to me...you are enough... intelligent...kind ...strong...stop punishing yourself...I forgive you... please listen...

She felt faint. *He forgave her.* She could feel the truth of his words through their link. He could not lie to her when their minds were connected, tenuous as the bond was. He really believed she was all those things. Since he truly believed in her, she would have to, as well.

Taking a deep breath, she pushed the negative thoughts out of her mind. She had to believe in herself, not just in Eros. She had to believe in the two of them. "What do you suggest I do, then?"

Send thoughts...to sheep...make them scratch themselves more... on briar patch...at noon they...will sleep in...the cave...safe for you to cross river...collect wool from the branches...will be enough...promise...

"I will do as you say. I promise. Now please, get some rest. I can feel how exhausted you are. I will contact you again. I love you."

Love you too.

Psyche felt the break in their connection. It left her feeling more alone then she had ever felt in her entire life. Soon they would be together again, she promised herself. She would complete her penance, thereby healing his wound, and then be reunited with her husband. She just had to keep faith in herself and Eros. And Anteros, as well, if truth be told. Though he was a wild card in all of this.

Pulling herself together, Psyche looked over at the field

where the sheep had gathered. They were near the briar patch. Some of them were already rubbing themselves against the branches, trying to scratch an itch.

Settling herself into a more comfortable position, she concentrated on the sheep. She sent out waves of encouragement. The briars felt good. They could reach the most elusive of itchy skin. *The briars felt good.*

She kept repeating those thoughts, over and over, projecting them onto the flock. She watched as they responded to her suggestions. For several hours, the entire flock rubbed themselves against the briars. She could see tuffs of golden wool everywhere they rubbed. Soon the entire briar patch looked like flowering bushes, their golden petals glistening in the sunlight.

Psyche ate the leftovers of her breakfast while she waited for the sheep to make their way to the cave to escape the noonday heat. After finishing, she gathered her belongings and scanned the pasture. It was completely empty.

Gathering her gown, she waded across the river. Reaching the briar patch, she was amazed at the amount of wool that clung to its barbs. There was so much that it could easily make several gowns.

Opening the large sack, she spent the next few hours gathering every clump of wool that littered the field. It was tiring and backbreaking work as the sun beat down on her. By the time she had picked off the last bit of wool, she was drenched in sweat. Exhausted and weary, she tied the sack tightly and slung it over her back.

She had just made it across the river when the sheep meandered out of the cave, back into the field. She splashed water over her face, neck, and arms, cooling off before setting off for Aphrodite's temple.

The sun was getting ready to set when she finally made it back. She carried her heavy burden to the dais, where

Aphrodite sat. She set the large sack in front of the goddess and opened it, revealing the golden wool, before sinking to her knees in supplication.

"I have gathered the golden wool as you commanded, my lady."

Psyche had to fight to keep her expression bland at Aphrodite's shocked look. It was glaringly obvious that the goddess had not only expected her to fail, but to possibly die in the effort. That she succeeded unscathed seemed to set her temper on edge.

"Let me see that," she snapped.

Her two attendants took the sack and emptied it out into a box. The amount and quality of the wool soon became apparent. It was worthy of being used to make a gown fit for a goddess. Even Aphrodite could not find fault with it.

"Very well. Let us see how well you do on your third task." She turned to her two attendants and snarled, "Take her back to the dungeon. *Now.*"

Psyche inclined her head and rose to her feet. She followed the two attendants and was grateful when they left her alone, locking the door behind her.

She was so tired that she staggered to her pallet and sank down. She was asleep within minutes.

CHAPTER 55

Anteros stood guard over Psyche while she slept. He watched from the shadows, unseen to the eyes of mortals and immortals alike. It was a good thing he had little need for sleep, for he had gotten precious little over the last few weeks.

Eros was getting better with each show of trust that Psyche made. With this last show of faith, Eros' wound had finally begun to heal. Today's trial—should she succeed, which he had very little doubt that she would—should heal the stab wound almost to completion. It was the reason why he divided himself between the two.

It was the final trial that he was most concerned about, however. That was the most dangerous leap of faith of them all. It was also the one that would hopefully unlock the door to Psyche's memories and powers from where she had hidden them within herself. If she failed, then Eros and Psyche would never truly be reunited, and the primordial gods —along with their soul mates—would be forever separated.

Eurynome. He shuddered when her name slipped past his

defenses. Anteros' inner drakon stirred at the thought of their soul mate. Just her name had the power to bring him to his knees. Love, hate, rage, lust, sorrow—it all threatened to break free. It was only his hard-won self-control that kept him from lashing out.

She was out there, lost to him, but not for long.

He glanced over at Psyche. She was the key to finding her. And when he did, he planned on finishing what Eurynome had started all those centuries ago with her betrayal. They would fight, and one—if not both of them—would die. But before all of that, he had to make sure that Eros was safe, and that meant making sure he reunited with Psyche, heart, body, and soul.

His beast snorted. *Is she strong enough?*

Anteros shook his head. "She has to be. I will make sure of it."

Psyche stirred, the sound of his voice pulling her from her sleep. It was still a few hours before dawn.

Really looking at her, Anteros noticed that even now, with exhaustion still gracing her features, the beauty of her soul still shown through. He had doubted the truth of that beauty, but he was slowly changing his mind.

Waving his hand, he sent Psyche back to sleep. He used his powers to clean her and her clothes, making the pallet more comfortable, and providing a filling meal for when she woke up. He told himself it was for the baby's sake.

Right. For the baby. Keep telling yourself that.

"Shut up," he snapped at his drakon.

His beast laughed at him before settling back down. With one last look at Psyche, he left to make the final arrangements for her last two tasks.

* * *

PSYCHE WOKE up to the pressing needs of her body. She could swear she felt her daughter bouncing on her bladder. Glancing down at her stomach, she murmured, "That's enough, little one. Mama can only take so much play." She felt a wave of love from her daughter before she subsided and settled down. It made Psyche smile when she had had precious little to smile about.

Stretching, she muffled a yawn before sitting up. Getting out of the pallet, she groaned, her body sore. She quickly took care of her needs. Splashing water on her face from a wash bucket, it helped push the cobwebs from her mind. She was surprised to see her gown was clean when she went to use it to dry her face. She took a closer look and realized that not only was her gown clean, but she was, as well. She distinctly remembered collapsing on the pallet last night, too exhausted to wash up. Only a powerful immortal could have accomplished such a task without waking her.

She looked around, trying to see if anyone was in the room with her. "Anteros? Eros? Pax? Is anyone here?"

Silence. She was alone. She suspected that Anteros had taken pity on her; though she had a feeling that if she thanked him, he would simply deny it. How she was so certain, she could not say. It was just that she felt like she knew him.

She was pulled from her thoughts by the rumbling of her stomach. She was starving again. Looking over at the pallet, she noticed the tray laden with food and drink. Knowing her time was short, she quickly ate at much as she could stomach before secreting the rest of it in her knapsack.

The tray disappeared just as the door to her cell opened. One of her female guards stood in the doorway. "Get up. Aphrodite is here."

Psyche followed her back to the main floor of the temple. She dreaded what was in store for her today. Even though

Anteros had said he was devising her trials, she couldn't help but suspect that Aphrodite was adding her own spin on them in the hopes of destroying her.

She knelt down and waited for the goddess to give her the next task. A large crystal flask appeared beside her. It piqued her curiosity, and she wondered what her new task would be. She did not have long to wait.

"If I didn't know any better, I would think you have had someone helping you accomplish your tasks. Anteros has assured me that is not the case. He is such a vicious god when it comes to protecting those he considers his. Poor Eros, I hear that he is suffering quite a bit, no thanks to you."

Aphrodite laughed when Psyche made no comment. "Today's task should be quite easy. You are to take this crystal vessel and fill it with the spring water that feeds the rivers Styx and Cocytus. If you should break it, you fail, and I get to choose your next punishment myself. Hurry along now, I do not want to be kept waiting."

Psyche picked up the flask and hurried to get out of the oppressive presence of the goddess. She followed the path that led away from the temple and headed toward the mountains, a few miles away.

It took her a few hours to reach the base of the mountain. It was approaching high noon when she made it to where a waterfall of violently gushing black water carved itself into the side of the mountain. The water poured out from the top of the mountain and disappeared about halfway down it. There had to be a basin somewhere. She looked to find the pool beneath the waterfall, but she couldn't find it from where she stood.

Psyche carefully climbed to the top of a large outcrop of rocks. She couldn't keep the groan of despair from escaping her lips. There was no basin; the waterfall just disappeared into the side of the mountain halfway down. There was no way that she could get any of the water from where she stood. She would have to climb to where the water was. She looked around, trying to see if there was a path. Again, she couldn't find one. It was a straight vertical climb to get to the water. How was she supposed to get to it? She would have to either sprout wings or turn into a goat. Neither was going to happen. Frustrated, she kicked a loose rock, sending it flying. The sound of the rock hitting something echoed throughout the field.

Immediately, twin roars let loose, sending a rush of fear throughout her body. Movement caught her attention. She spied two drakons coming out of twin caves on either side of the water. They were enormous, and from the looks of them, very angry at being disturbed.

"Drakons. The water is guarded by drakons. Of course it is. You wouldn't happen to be related to Eros and Anteros by any chance?" she quipped nervously.

Both beasts stared down at her. *Stay away. Danger. Do not approach. Or perish.*

Hearing the beasts' thoughts gave Psyche some comfort. At least she could communicate with them. However, it was obvious they were the guardians of the spring.

"I need to fill this flask with the water. It is just a little bit. Will you let me fill it? Or better yet, can you fill it for me?" she asked.

No.

"Seriously? You cannot help me get just a small flask of water?" she demanded.

No. Mortal cannot touch water.

With one last look, the drakons settled down and closed their eyes. She wasn't fooled into believing that they were asleep.

Psyche sat down. She reached into her mind, opening the line of communication with Eros. Perhaps he could help her reason with the stubborn drakons. For all she knew, they could be distant relatives of her husband.

"Eros? Can you hear me? I need your help."

She felt a stirring in her mind.

Psyche? What is it, my love?

"You sound stronger, Eros. How are you?" she asked, joy and gratitude racing through her body.

Better. Stronger. Thanks to you. Do you have need of me?

"Yes. I need your help." She quickly told him of her trial and the obstacles that she was facing. "What can I do?"

Need wings to get water. Call for Zeus' eagle. He will help... owes me a favor. Be careful. Water is dangerous to mortals. Don't touch.

"Thank you, my love. Rest now. I can feel how tired you are. And I promise to be careful." Eros left their link. She wanted to call him back to her, but she could tell how tired he was, but she was also able to tell that he was much better than before.

"Hear me, Eros. I dedicate this task to you. May my offer of service speed you in your recovery," she prayed. "And I can't wait until we are reunited again."

Psyche scanned the area, looking for an eagle's nest. She saw a giant one sitting on a mountaintop; that had to be it. She concentrated on sending her thoughts only to the eagle. "Please, I need your help. I am the bride of Eros and I am calling in the favor you owe to my husband. Please, come to me. Help me."

Over and over she sent the message. Before long, the air was rent by a piercing scream. An enormous eagle emerged. Then it took flight, coming at great speed in her direction.

Psyche was nearly pushed off the rocks that she was sitting on by the wind generated by the flapping of its wings. She had to brace herself and cover her face from the flying debris as it landed in front of her.

Opening her eyes, she saw an eagle the size of a small cottage standing in front of her. She watched in helpless fascination when it bowed before her.

"Greetings, bride of Eros. What favor would you have me do in order to pay back my debt?"

"Hello. Thank you for coming. I need to fill this flask with the source water for the rivers Styx and Cocytus. And I need to bring it to Aphrodite. Can you help me reach the water so that I can fill it?"

"You ask for a dangerous favor. This is the water that the gods swear by. It is very dangerous to one such as you, especially in your condition. I will get the water for you. The drakons will not bother me, though they would attack you. Give me the flask."

Psyche gladly handed it over. The eagle took it with its beak and launched itself into the sky. She watched as it flew to the water, only to hover in front of it, thrusting the open flask so that it filled with the precious water. Once it was filled, he flew back to her, landing a few feet away from her.

"Take a piece of cloth and wrap it around the flask so that you may close it without touching the water. Be careful that it does not break and spill on you."

Doing as the eagle said, Psyche took a piece of cloth out of her knapsack and carefully took the crystal vessel from the eagle. She made sure not one drop of water touched her skin while she closed the top. Wrapping it up, she then carefully stepped off the rocks and dropped to the ground, careful to keep her bundle safe. "Thank you so much for your help. Your debt to my husband has been paid."

The eagle inclined its head before launching itself back into the air. Psyche traveled carefully back to Aphrodite's temple. She watched every step; the last thing she needed was to trip and break the fragile vessel, which she was sure was what the goddess intended by giving her such a delicate container.

Once she was safely in front of the dais, she gingerly knelt in front of Aphrodite and held the flask up to her. "I have brought you the source water for the Styx and Cocytus, as you have requested, my lady."

"Impossible!" Aphrodite snapped, jumping up from her throne and marching to stand in front of Psyche. "You lie! No mortal can approach that water, let alone get a flask filled with it. Give it to me!"

Snatching the vessel from her hands, Aphrodite opened it.

Silence. Psyche dared to take a quick look.

Her face red with rage and disbelief, Aphrodite glared down at her. "What sorcery is this? You must be a witch to have accomplished such a feat. Tell me how you did this! Who is helping you?" She pulled back her arm, clutching the crystal vessel, ready to smash it against Psyche's face.

Reflexively, Psyche threw up her arms and braced herself against the blows that the goddess was preparing to rain down upon her.

Before the goddess could land a single strike—or spill any of the water on her, however—Anteros caught Aphrodite and spun her away from Psyche. "You are not to touch her. That was the agreement. You do not want to break your vow to me," he warned, his voice hard with barely restrained rage.

"Anteros! She is cheating! You *must* see that."

"She has not cheated once this entire time. Now take the water and leave. Tomorrow, she will be given the final task. Ares is looking for you."

Aphrodite snatched her arm back from him, and with one last hate-filled look, she disappeared into thin air, leaving the two of them alone.

"Thank you, Anteros. She would have killed me if you had not arrived."

Instead of answering, he held out his hand and helped her

to her feet. Silently he turned away, and she followed him to the dungeon. After escorting her in, he made sure that she had plenty of food and drink for the night before disappearing.

"Rest. Tomorrow is the final trial. Succeed, and you and Eros will be reunited. Fail, and I will have no choice but to do what is necessary to save my brother's life."

CHAPTER 56

Psyche spent a restless night, tossing and turning, in her pallet. She barely got any sleep, since her mind racing with thoughts of being reunited with Eros, as well as curiosity as to what her final trial would be. She finally fell asleep in the wee hours of the morning.

She was shaken awake by Aphrodite's servant. "Get up and prepare yourself for the goddess. And be quick about it."

It took her a few minutes to take care of her needs before she was brought out to the goddess' throne room. Aphrodite was lounging on a chair, swinging a small box in her hand, a predatory gleam in her eye. She sent a knowing smirk toward Psyche as she approached, sending shivers down her spine. Whatever the final trial was, it was one that the goddess seemed sure would end in failure for her.

"Well, well, well. If it isn't the little witch who has somehow passed every trial so far. It seems Nike favors you. We'll see how you fare with this last and final one. I do so *love* a challenge," she said mockingly.

Psyche said nothing. She had learned it was best not to engage the goddess when she was in such a mood. She could not count on Anteros stopping an attack from her if he was off taking care of Eros.

A hard gleam in her eyes, Aphrodite waved the box in the air, drawing Psyche's attention to it. "Your last task is quite important. With all the stress you have caused me, it has had a dreadful effect on my complexion. Therefore, you will go to see the goddess Persephone and ask her for a little bit of her beauty. You will carry it in this box. Succeed, and your trials are over. Fail...well, the underworld will then have a new resident."

Laughing, Aphrodite tossed the box to her. Psyche barely caught it before it hit the ground. When she looked back up, the goddess was gone, leaving her to fulfill the impossible task.

Psyche wandered out of the temple, distraught by the monumental challenge in front of her. How could she accomplish such a task when the heroes of legends and demigods had failed countless times before her? What could Anteros be thinking? Maybe he really was trying to kill her for stabbing Eros.

She walked for over an hour in a daze, with no real direction in mind. Seeing an abandoned tower, she sat down, leaning against it as she dreaded contacting her husband. What would he say about this last task? If this was what was needed to complete his healing, she would gladly do it. She just did not have any confidence that she would survive its completion.

Closing her eyes, she created the temple and opened the doors wide, sending out a call to Eros. He appeared just outside the temple doors. Crying out, she ran to him, but as soon as she tried to leave the temple, she was pushed back. Eros tried to enter when he saw her fall, but he too was blocked from entering.

He cursed, hitting the barrier still separating them with

his fist. *Psyche, my love. Why are you crying? What has happened?*

She sat on the floor sobbing, hugging her legs to her chest. "My last task is to travel into the Underworld and fill a box with some of Persephone's beauty for Aphrodite. No mortal has ever succeeded in a journey to Hades' realm. I'm scared that I will fail you, that I will fail us. I'm so sorry. I don't know what to do."

By Ouranos' balls!

While Eros alternated between cursing and threatening Aphrodite, Anteros, and the universe in his rage, Psyche was able to look at his wound. It was much improved, though she noticed that his anger was slowly pulling the wound back open. Blood began to appear along the edges, and it was only a matter of minutes before it would start bleeding again; she was sure of it. "Eros, please stop. Calm down. Your wound is starting to tear again."

He stopped at her plea, looked down, and he saw that she spoke true. All at once, the anger left him and he slid down to sit on the ground, his energy spent, leaning against the invisible barrier. She crawled to him, stopping when she too met the invisible barrier that kept them apart. She leaned against it, as well. Placing her hand against it, she watched as Eros mirrored her actions. They were so close, yet still so far apart. It broke her heart. They sat there in silence, both lost in the moment.

"It isn't fair," she whispered. "We came so close. This final task will seal our fate. No mortal has ever returned from the Underworld." Psyche placed her hand over her stomach. "Will you tell her about me?"

*STOP...We do not give up...we are stronger than this...*you *are stronger...*

She took a deep breath, letting it out slowly. This was a test of trust and faith, she sternly reminded herself. It was the only way to heal the wound between them, so she had to have faith in not just her husband, but in herself, as well. If they worked together, they could overcome the impossible. Anteros loved his brother, and he would never intentionally do anything to harm him. "I believe in you. We can do this, if we work together. Tell me what to do."

Eros nodded. She could feel his determination and pride in her through their shared link. *Alright...here is what you will do.*

Psyche listened to the instructions that Eros laid out so that she could accomplish this last task. It was a daunting list, so she paid careful attention to all the details. He then made her repeat his instructions back to him until he was satisfied that she would not deviate from them. By the time they were finished, Eros was spent.

"Go my love. I will do this. We will be together again soon. Now please rest. If I need you, I will call to you. I promise."

Eros nodded reluctantly. He did not want to let her out of his sight, but time was slipping away. If they were to do this, he had to let her go while it was still daylight. *Be careful. Do what I have said and you will be fine. Remember, I love you.*

"And I love you. Now go and rest. I will be fine," she said, giving him a small smile, trying to reassure not just him, but herself, as well. She watched as he slowly faded away, his strength spent.

Snapping her eyes open, Psyche allowed herself a few minutes to gather her courage before setting off for the land of the dead. Opening her knapsack, she found several new items that had not been there before today. She carefully went through it, sending a quick prayer of thanks to both Eros and Anteros. She made sure that she had all that she needed before heading off to the cave that Eros had told her was one of the entrances to the realm of Hades.

Psyche found the path leading to the cave, but before she set foot on it, she prayed. "Here me, Eros and Anteros. I dedicate this last task to my husband, to prove my love, faith, and trust in him. Please let this last act of devotion heal the wound that I caused with my lack of trust and faith. May we then be reunited at last."

Taking a deep breath before stepping onto the path, she followed it, careful not to stray from the road, the noonday sun beating down on her. Before long, she came upon the first obstacle that Eros had warned her about. A lame man and horse were on the road, carrying a load of firewood. The old man turned to her. "Please, my lady. Can you help an old man? Can you please pick up the wood that has fallen off my cart?"

She said nothing, not responding to the old man's pleas, even though everything in her wanted to help him. She had been warned it was one of the traps set out for mortals on their way to the underworld. If she stopped to help him, she would be caught up in the vicious cycle of picking up the fallen wood, and for every piece she picked up, another would fall, taking its place. She would soon lose track of time, and she would eventually die, trapped repeating the same pattern over and over until she collapsed from exhaustion and hunger.

Avoiding the old man, she neither looked at him nor responded to his pleas. She skirted around him and hurried down the path, fighting the compulsion to turn back with everything in her. It wasn't until she was out of earshot that the compulsion finally released her from its deadly grip.

She continued on until she came to the entrance to the cave. She opened her sack and pulled out a coin and two barley cakes. Putting the coin in her mouth, she closed the sack and walked in.

The cave was pitch black, save for a few flickering lights

in the distance. She had to be careful as she picked her way down, as the path was jagged with rocks, and the declining slope made it difficult to navigate. The further in she went, the colder it became. Her only source of light was the eerie glowing figures in the distance. The air was still, and the only sound she could hear other than the beating of her own heart and her rasping breath was the drip, drip, dripping sound of water dropping from the stalactites on the ceiling.

All of a sudden, a low wail echoed throughout the chamber, causing her hair to stand on end. The misery contained in it pierced her to her very bones. She swore she could feel its pain in her soul.

It wasn't long before she came upon the source of the sound. On the shore of an underground river stood dozens of shades, the souls of the dead, waiting for Charon to ferry them across the River Styx. Before long, she saw him in the distance, a heavily cloaked figure pushing his boat toward the shore. The closer he came, the more animated the shades became, his presence drawing them to an outcrop of rocks that formed a natural dock.

Pulling up beside the dock, he got off the boat. Psyche couldn't see anything of the man beneath his robe; all she could see was a tall figure wrapped in blood-red cloth. She watched in fascinated horror as the dead lined up, one by one, in front of him. To each he said but one word, "Coin," in a low, rasping growl. The dead then opened up their mouth, allowing Charon to take the coin, payment for their passage to the kingdom of Hades.

Psyche braced herself and joined the dead, becoming the last in line to board the skiff. One by one, the line got shorter until it was just her left. Stepping up, she raised her head and opened her mouth. It was then that she finally got a good look at Charon. She had to swallow back the scream that welled up in her core at the sight of him. He was a nightmare come to life.

Paper-thin skin was stretched over his bones, and he looked like a corpse dug up from the grave after many months. He was nothing but skin and bones, and it was as if his insides had been sucked out. And yet, there was no smell of rotting flesh. Instead, the subtle fragrance of fresh-cut flowers filled her nose. Glowing red eyes peered out at her from their sunken sockets, and she feared that he could see into her very soul.

They stood there facing each other, neither moving nor saying anything. Panic gripped her at his continued silence. What if he refused to give her passage? She was alive, not a shade like his other passengers. How would she get across if he refused her?

"Living flesh, you seek passage into the land of the dead. Is this what you truly desire?"

Psyche nodded and opened her mouth, offering up her coin. Charon reached out with his withered hand and took the coin from her mouth. "Get on board, little mortal. If you dare."

She stepped into the boat and took a seat farthest away from the shades. Charon joined them and pushed off from the shore, guiding it toward the kingdom of Hades. Psyche huddled against the side of the boat, trying to stay as still as possible so as not to draw any more attention to herself. The gently rocking lulled her into a meditative state, lowering her guard. It was then that she became aware of a low murmur of voices. They grew louder and more urgent as time went on. She tried to ignore them, but she made the mistake of glancing at the water.

She gasped in horror at the number of souls trapped in the water, all of them reaching out and begging to be pulled into the boat. Men, women, and children all pleading for help. Her heart broke at their misery and suffering. She saw an elderly man reach out to her, and the suffering in his eyes made her reach out to him, but at the last moment, she saw the barley cakes clutched in each of her hands. Their presence reminded her of all the warnings that Eros instructed her to be on guard for. She cursed herself for her foolishness.

Pulling back her hand, she murmured a soft apology and averted her eyes from the water. She hunched over and squeezed her eyes shut, refusing to look at anything. After what seemed like an eternity, the boat came to a standstill. "All souls depart. Including you, living flesh-and-blood mortal."

Psyche opened her eyes, and stood up. She followed the shades as they left the boat and started traveling deeper into the underworld. Eros had warned her to stay on the path. So far she had avoided all the traps, but soon she stumbled across another one, the group of seemingly harmless elderly women weaving on their loom. "Come here and join us, child. We have room for another weaver in the group."

Clutching the barley cakes, Psyche fought off the temptation to join the women. It seemed everything on this journey was designed to trap her. She continued to follow the shades until she reached the formal gates to the entrance of the land of the dead. The souls passed through the gate easily, but it was not the gates that gave her pause, but the monstrous three-headed beast that guarded them. Cerberus. Hades' guard dog stood to one side, his three heads missing nothing.

One of the heads sniffed the air, letting out a low growl before turning its glowing red eyes in her direction. The other two heads turned, as well, spying her standing just a few yards away. With a vicious howl, the beast leapt forward, charging at her, its three mouths gaping open, ready to tear her to pieces.

"Stop, please!" she cried out, using all her powers on the

rampaging hound. At the last minute, he slid to a stop right in front of her. She looked up at the beast that easily was the size of a house. It dropped all three heads down to smell her.

Psyche stood still, letting all three heads sniff her. All of a sudden, the center head let out a whine, nuzzling one of the barley cakes in her hand.

"If you want one of the cakes, you must sit down," she commanded.

Cerberus sat down at once, looking down at her with pleading eyes. Tucking one loaf under her arm, she carefully ripped the other cake into three equal parts and fed one to each head. After taking the pieces and eating them, they laid down, putting their heads on their two front paws and wagging their tail.

She laughed at the playful display and spent several minutes petting each head, playfully telling them what a good dog they were, and that she would give them the other barley cake when she came back.

Psyche then walked through the gates and quickly followed the line of the dead who were entering the palace of Hades. She soon found herself at the massive doors of a great hall where the dead were judged and sentenced to one of the three domains of the underworld: the Elysian Fields for the righteous; the Asphodel Meadows for the indifferent; and Tartarus for the truly wicked.

High up on a dais stood two thrones, both occupied by the rulers of the underworld. When she stepped into the room, a hush fell among the crowd. Psyche froze when all eyes turned upon her.

Hades stood up. "A mortal enters the kingdom of the dead. Come here, child, and tell us who you are and why you have dared to make such a perilous journey."

Psyche hurried forward, dropping to her knees at the foot of the dais. "Forgive me, my lord, my lady. My name is

Psyche and I have come on a mission from the goddess Aphrodite herself."

"Psyche? The young princess whose beauty rivals that of Aphrodite herself? The one I hear that Eros has pledged his heart to? Are you that Psyche, by any chance?" a soft feminine voice inquired.

"Yes, my lady. I am she, though I never claimed that my looks could rival the goddess of beauty herself; that was a claim others made. I swear on my life that I have never dared think of myself in any way an equal to the gods, let alone claim to be superior to them."

"You may raise your eyes to us, my child. Though I am the final judge of mortal souls, I can see the truth and purity of your heart. We know you speak the truth. Please, let us offer you a place to rest, and some refreshments after such a long journey," Hades offered, his voice infinitely kind and genuine.

Psyche raised her eyes, but stayed where she was on the ground. She took a moment to study the famed couple. To say she was surprised at the appearance of the god of the dead was an understatement. Unlike his brethren, he was rarely depicted in works of art, so it was a shock to see what he truly looked like. Before her stood a god of infinite masculine beauty. He was tall and muscular, with a closely cropped head of hair and beard made up of multiple shades of browns and reds. Dark brown eyes stared down at her. He looked to be no older than in his early thirties, with lightly tanned skin that belied a life spent underground.

Beside him, holding his hand, stood his wife, Persephone, the goddess of spring and fertility. She was as beautiful as her husband was handsome. She had golden blonde hair that fell in waves down her back. Deep, emerald-green eyes shone with a kindness that was genuine in nature. She had a lush figure that was a compliment to her husband's warrior build, and her fair skin gleamed in the light. They made a striking couple, and it was clear in their body language that they were deeply in love with each other.

Psyche opened her knapsack and took out the box given to her by Aphrodite, turning to Hades. "I thank you for your kind hospitality, but I regret that I must decline. I have been given a task and a short time to accomplish it. Please, I must ask your wife to fill this box with a little bit of your wife's beauty. Aphrodite needs it."

Hades and Persephone exchanged a troubled look. "I see. If Aphrodite needs it, I will of course give her what she asks for."

The box floated out of Psyche's hands and traveled the short distance to land in the palm of Persephone. The goddess opened the box, and Psyche watched as she waved her hand over it before shutting and locking the lid before returning it to her. "Here, take this back to Aphrodite with my blessings, but please be careful with it."

"Thank you my lady, my lord. If it pleases you, I will not take up any more of your time as I must get this back to Aphrodite."

Hades waved his hand. "Of course you may go, but have a care as you travel back to the mortal realm. You are a very brave young lady, and I would be very upset if you were to enter my kingdom again before your time is up. Good luck and safe travels."

Bowing her head once more, Psyche murmured her thanks and got up, quickly making her way out of the palace and retracing her steps out back to the gates of the underworld. Here, she gave the other barley cake to Cerberus, who proceeded to lick her hand and face in thanks for the treats.

After much laughter, she broke away and all but ran the entire length of the path back to the River Styx to wait for Charon to dock. She was in luck; Charon was just pulling in when she arrived on the shore. While she waited for the dead to disembark from the boat, she took out another coin and placed it in her mouth, eager to get back to the mortal realm.

Stepping up to Charon, she parted her lips.

"Back again, living, flesh-and-blood mortal. Come along," he said, after plucking the coin from her mouth.

Climbing into the skiff, she sat in the center, closing her eyes and humming to herself to keep from being tempted by the pleadings of the dead. It seemed like it took forever for them to cross to the other side, but soon enough, they docked on the shore.

Psyche all but leapt out of the boat, and briskly followed the path through the cave, heading towards the daylight that spilled into it from the entrance. Stepping out into the sunlight, she walked away from the cave and proceeded to head back to Aphrodite's temple. It wasn't until she put some distance between herself and the first trap leading to the cave that she stopped to sit down and catch her breath.

Psyche finally let herself relax. She had done it. She could hardly believe it. She had managed to travel to and from the heart of the underworld, and had lived to tell the tale of it. Clutching the box to her chest, she allowed a few tears to escape. "I did it, my love. The last task completed to finally heal your wound. Now we can be together forever."

"I am afraid it is not that simple."

Startled, Psyche whipped around to find a hooded figure standing in the shadows. "Who are you? Show yourself."

The mysterious person stepped forward, but they did not pull back their hood. Power filled the air with an oppressive strength; whoever this person was, they were not only immortal, but an extremely powerful and ancient being. How Psyche knew that, she could not say. All she knew was that she was in the presence of a being of immeasurable strength and power, so much so that it bled off them in waves.

"I am afraid the time is not yet right to reveal myself to you. Though I will say this: I am sorry for the pain you are about to experience."

Psyche scrambled to her feet and started to back away. "What are you talking about? Stay away from me."

The cloaked figure waved their hand, sending a blast of power directed at the box that Psyche held protectively in her arms. It suddenly opened, allowing the black mist it held to escape its confines. The box held not the beauty of the flesh, but that of death, and it swirled around her, enveloping her in its cold embrace.

Shock and pain radiated throughout her body as the mist clung to her. With every breath she took, she inhaled more and more of it, making her feel like she was inhaling shards of glass. She started to choke, unable to get air into her lungs. She felt like she was drowning. Icy tendrils of cold seeped into her veins, spreading out and leaching the warmth from her body, turning her skin blue. Her vision blurred, then dimmed.

Psyche railed against the injustice of it all. To be so close, only to die right before she could be reunited with Eros. Her baby was frantically kicking, making her cry out in anguished rage. Her heart broke. Her soul wept.

Collapsing, unable to breathe, Psyche finally lost consciousness, sending her into the sweet arms of death itself.

The hooded figure took one last look before disappearing, leaving Psyche on the ground.

CHAPTER 57

Psyche groaned before opening her eyes and pushing herself up off the ground. She took in her surroundings. She was back in the land of the mists, surrounded by the shadow people. But something had changed since the last time she had been here. There was a new addition to the landscape, and she could now make out a temple in the distance. "What is happening? Why am I here again?"

Terrified as the memory of what happened after she left the Underworld came back to her, she cried out, "Eros!"

"I'm afraid Eros cannot hear you. No one can."

At the sound of the feminine voice behind her, Psyche scrambled to her feet and turned to face her. It was the mysterious figure who had forced open the box, sending her back here. She stood a little ways from her, and the mists swirled around her transparent form.

"Who are you? What do you want?"

The hooded figure gestured around them. "Who I am is not important right now. What is important is for you to finally release all the souls who are trapped here."

"You are insane. No one can release the shades from Hades' realm. The dead cannot be brought back among the living."

Startled laughter met her statement. "We are not in the land of the dead. You have just visited the Underworld. While I will admit there are some similarities, can you not tell the difference now that you have been to both places?"

Psyche took a good look around. She had to admit, now that she had been to both, it was very apparent that they were not the same place, but two very different spaces. "Then where are we?"

"We are in the Vault of Souls. It is a realm that exists between life and death, and only the primordial goddess who created it can undo it and release the souls of the immortals trapped here."

"Then what am I doing here? I am just a mortal woman. I may have some small power to communicate with animals, but I am definitely not a goddess."

Psyche could swear she felt the shock coming off the woman at her question.

"You really don't remember, do you? You have no idea who you really are. You not only locked the others here, but you locked yourself away, as well. How you and Eros must have suffered from the separation."

Psyche could scarcely believe what she was hearing. "You make no sense. You have mistaken me for someone else. Is this why you keep dragging me here?"

"I do not have the power to drag you here. This is your domain, not mine. You control this realm because you created it. The only reason I was able to enter was because I followed you in through our bond. Even now, I am split between this world and the living."

She held up her hand, stopping Psyche from interrupting her. "My time here is running out, so listen. I know you have no reason to trust me, but I swear to you, I am your friend, not your enemy. You must go to the temple, which is where you will find the answers you seek, but hurry, time is running out. You are dying. You must remember who you are before it is too late."

Before Psyche could question her further, the woman disappeared. She debated with herself on what to do. She tried to leave, but nothing she did worked. She turned to face the temple. It was letting off a soft, pulsating glow, drawing her attention to it. Her heart started to beat in time with it. A compulsion to go to it filled her, and before long, she found herself walking toward it as if in a trance. The shadow people slowly materialized on either side of the path, silently watching her.

She stopped in front of the steps of the temple. Her heart was pounding so hard she thought it would rip itself from her chest. Fear and excitement filled her. The building was enormous, an exact copy of the temple that she had created in her mind to communicate with Eros. The giant doors in front of her slowly opened, beckoning her to enter. Steeling herself, she went up the steps and entered the temple, the doors closing and locking silently behind her.

* * *

EROS WAS RIPPED from the healing sleep that Pax had put him in by a burning sensation that raced across his chest. Sitting up, he pulled aside the bandage that covered his stab wound and looked down in shock as the wound sealed itself, leaving nothing behind. Smooth, unblemished skin met his eyes; there was not even a faint pink line to show that anything had happened.

His strength was returning, as well. Psyche had done it.

She had accomplished the impossible. Now they could finally be together forever.

Opening his mind, he searched for their connection. He refused to be without her for another second. He followed the familiar path, but instead of finding her, he found nothing but a cold dead end. There was no life, just a cold emptiness. Disbelief and rage tore through him. His beast fought him, clawing at his insides, trying to get out. Leaping from the bed, Eros threw back his head and roared to the heavens in wild, savage grief.

The door to his bedroom slammed opened and several people rushed in. Khloris, Zephyrus, Pax, and Anteros all stopped dead when they saw him. Anteros was the first to reach him. Grabbing hold of him, he demanded, "What has happened?"

Eros—his eyes glowing red—slammed his brother against the wall, cracks appearing like spiderwebs behind him. "What have you done? Where is she?"

Anteros stayed very still, shocked at the rage, grief, and heartache that poured off of Eros. It threatened to consume him, and everyone around them. The building shook from his grief. "What do you mean? I just got word before you woke that Psyche succeeded in her last act of faith. She is unharmed and heading back to Aphrodite's temple even as we speak."

"LIES!" Eros and his beast roared together, shaking and slamming Anteros against the wall again, threatening to bring the cave down on their heads with his returning strength. "She is dead! I can't feel her through our bond. What have you done?"

Shocked gasps echoed behind him. Anteros' usually tanned skin paled at his accusation. "I swear to you, O adelfós mou, I have no idea what you are talking about. She succeeded. You are completely healed. She—"

Eros snarled, hatred poisoning his heart and soul. "You hated her. You wanted her to fail so you could punish her. You can't find your soul mate to punish, so you used Psyche in her place. Hear me well, brother. I will destroy everything and everyone if she is gone, including you, this I swear."

With the gauntlet thrown down between them, Eros threw Anteros aside before he disappeared. Anteros rose up from the floor. Guilt and shame filled him. If he was being honest, a small part of him had been punishing Psyche as a substitute for Eurynome, but only in the beginning. With each task she completed, he had the chance to get to know the person she had become, and with this last task, he could honestly say that he was beginning to trust her when he trusted so few, thanks to all the betrayals. That he should be the one to betray his brother's trust made him sick to his stomach. He turned to look at the others, who all could barely keep their shock and fear from their faces. "I will follow him and find out what is going on."

"What can we do to help?" asked Khloris.

"Pray," said Anteros. "If we have lost Psyche, Eros will become a monster who will destroy the universe in his rage." Leaving them with that warning, he vanished.

CHAPTER 58

Eros flew along the path Psyche would have followed back to Aphrodite's temple after leaving the Underworld. Desperately, he searched for her, screaming her name, all the while trying to reconnect the telepathic link between them, but it kept coming back cold and lifeless.

He nearly dropped out of the sky when he spotted a crumpled body lying face down next to the road. *Please let it not be her,* he prayed over and over again as he landed. Dropping to his knees, he groaned in anguish when he turned the crumpled figure over. It was Psyche.

Gathering her up in his arms, he gently rocked her back and forth, silent tears running down his face, pleading with her to wake up. She was so cold to the touch that he wrapped his wings around her. "Please, little butterfly, come back to me. I can't lose you again."

A shadow fell over him, and looking up, he saw Anteros holding an open box. "Eros, draw the mist from her now and place it back in the box. Hurry."

Eros looked down at Psyche, noticing for the first time the blackish mist that clung to her lips. Putting his lips against hers, he inhaled deeply, drawing the mist from her lungs. Anteros held the box out and Eros exhaled the mist back into it. He did this several times, until he was sure he had removed every last trace of the deadly mist from her. Snapping the box shut, Anteros held on to it tightly.

Eros put his lips against Psyche's and pushed air into her lungs. He repeated the process until she suddenly took a shuddering breath on her own. Her skin was losing its bluish tinge. He pulled back and monitored her chest to ensure that she was breathing on her own.

Moving his hand over her stomach, he was relieved to see that their child was unharmed and doing well. She was as healthy and hale as always, though he could feel her emotional distress as she too tried to connect with Psyche.

"What madness possessed her to open the box? I repeatedly warned her not to open it. Why did she not listen to me?" Eros demanded in despair.

"She didn't open it."

Eros looked up at Anteros, anger and suspicion heavy in his voice as he demanded, "What do you mean, she didn't open it? How do you know this?"

Anteros knelt down next to them. He held out the cursed box for Eros to inspect. "Look at the lock. I made it so only a powerful immortal could open or close it. Psyche is still mortal; she couldn't open it even if she wanted to. I made sure of that. Someone else forced it opened. You can still feel the power lingering from where it was hit."

Eros focused his attention on the box. The fading power of an immortal still clung to it. It had a unique taste and feel that was undeniable, even as the one who it belonged to tried to hide it. The signature teased along the path of their minds, leading to ancient memories long buried. An immortal had opened the box, and not just *any* immortal, but an ancient one, but which one was the question.

"Chaos take it. How can they hide themselves from us?"

"I don't know, brother, but we will find out. After Psyche wakes up she may be able to describe them to us."

Turning their attention back to her, they watched with bated breath as the color slowly returned to Psyche's face, and the warmth to her body. The tenuous thread between Eros and Psyche's soul gave off tiny sparks, but it still remained mostly closed off. With this last act of trust, it should have opened fully on her side, but it was still as fragile and closed off as ever, barely there at all. However, that was the least of Eros' concerns. Psyche was comatose.

"Why is she not waking up?" Anteros asked.

Eros shook his head. "She is trapped somewhere just beyond life. I don't know where she is, but I must follow her and pull her out before it is too late. I trust you to guard us."

Before Anteros could protest, Eros separated his consciousness from his body and followed the thin thread that connected him to Psyche. It brought him to a strange shadow world. A land of perpetual darkness, a place made up of the muted colors of the night. Landing in the middle of what could pass for a field made up of mist and shadows, Eros called out, "Psyche! Where are you?"

In the distance, he saw the vague outline of a temple; it looked similar to the one that held Psyche's conscious mind, the one she had constructed. It was the only tangible structure that he could make out in this strange world. He decided to head over to it to see if she could be there.

He alternated travel by foot and air, searching for Psyche among the mists and shadows. Along the journey, vague figures appeared in the darkened grey void. They were part of the shadows and they were ever changing, going from a vaguely human outline to being absorbed back into the shadows, though he noticed none of them were focused on him. They all seemed focused on the temple. It gave him both hope and fear that it was Psyche drawing their attention. This place was a mystery, even to him. He could tell it was an ancient place, born many eons ago, and inhabited by mysterious beings.

After what seemed like an eternity, he arrived at the steps of the temple. Up close, he could feel the temple pulsating with power. The age of it rattled his very bones. It suddenly became clear to him that it was the source of the power that held this strange world together. Its roots ran deep, vibrating with raw power. If he was not mistaken, he would swear it was as old as he was, and he had been one of the first beings to emerge out of Chaos. How he could not know of its existence was a mystery for another time. He had to find Psyche.

He ran up the steps, and grasping the door, he tried to open it. It refused to budge. He tried using his powers, but it had no effect. In frustration, he hit the door, screaming, "Psyche!"

Just as he was about to go mad, the doors opened and a blazing light came out, temporarily blinding him in its intensity. The light quickly subsided enough so that he could see Psyche standing in front of a central firepit in the floor of the building. It suddenly came roaring to life, the flames shooting up into the rafters of the temple.

He tried to go in, yet even with the doors open, he could not enter the building. "Psyche!" he called out desperately. "Come to me now!"

She did not move or acknowledge his presence. She simply continued to silently watch the flames. They swirled and danced, as if they had a life of their own. It was then that he noticed the flames were rapidly changing shape.

"Is this the secret that you kept from me?" she asked.

He could scarcely believe what he was seeing. The flames were telling their life story. The first image was the nothingness of the universe before the explosion of life from Chaos.

Then came the primordial gods and goddesses: Gaia, Ouranos, Tartarus, himself. He had forgotten what the two of them had looked like when they had been conjoined as one being. Most of the time, they had assumed the body of a hermaphrodite, but he had forgotten how they had seamlessly transformed into male and female figures whenever the mood struck them.

He watched the birth of the Titans, and then the Olympians. Then the wars. So much fighting among the gods for the throne of Olympus: the Primordialomachy, the first war between the primordial gods and their allies; the Titanomarchy, the Titans against the Olympians; the Gigantomachy, the Giants pitted against the Olympians; and so on. The moment when the Olympians were cursed. So many wars, so much senseless betrayal, pain, and destruction, that it made him sick to his stomach.

He relived the horror of the Olympians gods declaring war on the humans, his greatest creation. He watched as Zeus and the other Olympians sliced his children in half, forever physically separating them from their soul mates and scattering them far and wide, forcing them to search for their missing half. Many dying of a broken heart.

He saw himself before the separation from Thesis. He watched the happy memories of Ophioneus and Eurynome before she betrayed them, and then Eurynome attacking Ophioneus with a viciousness that broke the first serpent's heart, starting the metamorphosis of his rebirth as Anteros.

It all played out in front of him. Finally the flames replayed that cursed night, when he and Thesis were torn from each other. Only this time, he was finally seeing what happened to Thesis after he fell to the sea once they were torn apart.

She lay on the ground, in shock from the pain and trauma of being ripped from her other half. Even wounded, she was defiant against their enemy who held the scythe against her heart. Now he would finally learn what really happened.

"Why?" Thesis cried as she asked the one question that even he did not know the answer to.

"Why? You dare to ask me that? I have been made to suffer unlike any other immortal. Pain, betrayal, separated from the ones I love the most, yet could not protect. That is why. All because of love. What good is love if it causes such pain and heartache? It drives you mad. Better that love dies than to suffer from it. You don't understand what I have suffered, all because of you. But you will. My only consolation is that at least now you will understand a small portion of my agony before I send you back to the void."

Thesis shook her head. "If you kill love, all will be lost. There will be only barrenness and death in the world. Is that what you want? Do you really wish to feel nothing for yourself, for your loved ones?"

"You know nothing of suffering. You made me love a monster. To bear his children. You—who have never known fear, or been helpless, hopeless—who have never had children, will never be able to truly understand what you have done to me and the others. I hate you. Once I send you back to Chaos, I will hunt down and destroy all the bonds between the primordial gods. There will be no more soul mates, no more love, and no more children."

"You are right," Thesis said. "I have never experienced what fear, being helpless and hopeless feels like, so I cannot understand it, but I will. But I will not let you destroy love. Without love, there is no life, no purpose in being. I will protect my brethren and the humans with my last breath. This war has just begun, I swear it. I sacrifice myself for love. I am the seal and protector of the primordial gods and their soul mates. My sacrifice is their salvation. They will return when love is reunited with his soul. Then I will come back wiser, stronger, and more powerful, and you will be defeated. This I swear," she vowed, before impaling her heart on the scythe,

releasing her powers, locking herself and the primordial gods away from their enemy.

Eros saw the blast created by her sacrifice. He cried out and dropped to his knees in agony. She had done it to save them all. She had used her powers to heal and reshape both him and Anteros so not only could they live, but so that their enemy could not find them in their new forms. Now he understood why she had chosen to be reborn a mortal, so that she could not only escape detection, but to learn and grow, and evolve into her own being. To become her own person, independent of him, and to give herself a chance to heal and let her powers grow.

Eros thought the flames had no more secrets to reveal, but he was wrong. What he saw next was truly shocking. Psyche had sacrificed her physical being, but a drop of her blood had been preserved through the centuries, lying dormant until the time was right, finding root in the womb of a queen, allowing her to find a way to be reborn.

Her soul had been weakened by the blast. Even with her releasing the majority of her powers into the world, there was still enough left over to plant the seed for the creation of a new one. This was the realm she created at the time of the blast. This was where she locked away the primordial gods to protect them. They were the shadow figures, caught between wakefulness and sleep, controlled by her subconscious mind in the mortal world.

Their power had fueled the regrowth of hers. But this place was more than that. This temple not only anchored this place, it housed her new powers and memories. How to unlock it without harming her was the question.

"Psyche. Please my love, turn around. Look at me," he begged.

"Psyche? Or is it Thesis? Who do you truly want?" she asked, not turning around.

"I want *you*. Who you are, who you choose to be, in whatever form you want to be. I love you. Please, look at me."

Finally, she responded to him. She looked at him over her shoulder. "Phanes. Eros. You're here."

"Yes, I'm here for you."

She looked at him as if seeing him for the first time, and in a way, she was. He could see hints of both Thesis and Psyche in her gaze. "We are both changed. We are not who we were, nor are we who we thought. It is all very strange to me. Do you not find it so?"

"Yes, though I have always had my memories of you, of us. You lost yours. We have both changed. We are not who we once were, and yet we are. How do you feel, now that you know?"

She slowly walked around the fire, trailing her fingers along the edge of the flames before answering him. "I feel split in two. Broken. Two pieces of a sword that must be put into the forge and be welded back together again."

"Please, let me in. Let me get you out of here," Eros begged. He was terrified of what she might do in her confused state. Having both Thesis and Psyche's memories had to be overwhelming her, confusing her.

She gave him a sad smile. "I'm afraid I can't do that. I finally know what I must do. I must reclaim myself. I have to destroy this prison and release the others. I just hope you and Ophioneus can contain the blast this time."

Psyche stepped into the fire. Horrified, he watched the flames engulf her. He was helpless, unable to stop or protect her. An earthquake violently shook the entire realm, and the temple began to crumble as the light from the flames shot out in all directions, blinding him and piercing the shadow people, breaking the bonds that tied them to this world.

He had just enough time to send a warning to Anteros before the temple completely exploded, releasing Thesis' memories and powers in a cataclysmic eruption that tore the realm to pieces, releasing the primordial gods back into the world. The violence was greater than the explosion that had birthed the primordial gods from Chaos.

Eros' conscious mind was sent hurtling back into his body. He tried to contain the blast, but it was too powerful, even with Anteros lending his strength to his. The seismic waves rippled across the universe, sending shock waves felt by every living being, mortal and immortal alike. There was no way to hide what was happening from their enemies, or their allies.

All around the world, the Primordial gods awoke, their powers and memories rushing back to them, hitting them like a tsunami. Eros and Anteros felt them. They sent out a desperate call to their brethren—both enemy and ally alike—to help them contain the explosion of power before it ripped apart the very fabric of the universe. If that happened, the consequences would be dire.

The Primordial gods and goddesses answered their call. It took their combined efforts, but they managed to contain the blast until the power receded back. Once the danger was over, the ancient gods broke away, not yet ready to face the world after being caged for so long. But they would be back.

Eros and Anteros found themselves on the ground, unable to move until the last wave stopped. The two brothers lay there panting, hurting from the blast. Eros went to move his arms, only to realize that they were pinned under the weight of another. Looking down, he gave a shout of triumph. Psyche was in his arms, and she was alive. He was grateful for small miracles. He sat up and ran his hands over her, confirming that she was unharmed.

Groaning, Anteros called out, "Eros? Are you alright?"

"I think so. What about you?"

"I'll live. Where is Psyche? Are she and the baby alright?"

"I'm right here, Ophioneus," she answered. "The baby and I are fine. Though you don't have to shout all the way to Olympus to be heard."

Eros looked down. Psyche was awake in his arms, glowing from the power that radiated from her core. She had retained the outer shell that was Psyche, but now she was no longer mortal. But more importantly, he saw the knowledge of who she was in her eyes. The bond between them was fully open. Their souls reunited at last. It threatened to drown him in the love and happiness that he felt coming from her through their bond. They were finally reunited: heart, mind, and soul. She was back, memories of both lifetimes, powers, and all. Yelling in joy, Eros pulled her into a tight embrace. "You're back!"

"Yes, my love, I'm finally back."

Running his hands down her back, he felt something protruding. Scared that she had been injured, he gently turned her so that he could get a better look. What he found instead stunned him.

Wings. She had wings, and not just any type, but those of a butterfly. They were beautiful, composed of all the colors of the rainbow. "You have wings."

Psyche laughed. "I know. Aren't they pretty? I am a primordial goddess, so why shouldn't I have wings of my own?"

Eros smiled. "And what are you the goddess of? Desire? Love? Motherhood?"

Psyche grinned. "I am the primordial goddess of souls."

"Perfect," he murmured. "You are definitely my soul."

Not able to resist anymore, he pulled her into his embrace, taking her lips in a searing kiss. He poured everything he felt for her into it. He started out gentle, but it soon became rough and hungry with passion. Desire gripped him hard, and he struggled to keep control of himself. It didn't help that Psyche was just as desperate and hungry for him. He reluctantly broke off their kiss. Though he desperately wanted to make love to her, now was not the time.

Anteros loudly cleared his throat. "Far be it from me to interrupt your reunion, but it will have to wait. There is no way that blast went unnoticed, and we need to leave before we are discovered. Plus, Psyche needs to deliver this box to Aphrodite. We cannot have anyone suspecting who we really are just yet."

Eros reluctantly pulled the two of them to their feet. "As much as I hate to admit it, Anteros is correct. The seal is broken, and the primordial gods have been awakened and released back into the world. War will come, and we need to be prepared."

Psyche nodded. "I know. I wish it could be otherwise, but I know that our time to prepare is short."

She turned to face Anteros. Before anyone could guess what she was about, she stepped up to him, pulling him into a hug. At first he was hesitant, but then he returned her embrace. "Thank you for all that you have done for us. You are a true brother to us both," she murmured.

Anteros patted her on the back before stepping back and said gruffly, "I am glad you are back, Thesis."

She furrowed her brows before stating, "I'm Psyche. Thesis is from another time, another life. Just as Phanes is Eros."

"Yes, but before we leave, I need to know the identity of the one who forced open the box. There was no way you as a mortal could have. I felt their power, but I can't identify who it was."

Psyche reached out and cupped his cheek. She was reluctant to hurt him any more than he had already suffered, but he had to know the truth. "I'm sorry, Ophioneus, but it was Eurynome."

A terrifying growl escaped from deep within his chest. It sent a shiver of fear down her spine at the terrible rage she felt coming off him in waves. He stepped back, breaking their connection. "I am Anteros. Ophioneus is dead, and so is she, when I find her."

CHAPTER 59

Psyche entered the temple of Aphrodite, her wings and her powers carefully concealed so that she could not detect the immortal goddess that had been unleashed within her. After her terrible revelation, the three of them went their separate ways, each to accomplish the next part of their mission. Eros to Mt. Olympus, Anteros to scour the world for the reawakened primordial gods, and she to Aphrodite's lair. They were to regroup in a few hours' time.

Stepping in front of the dais, Psyche dropped to her knees. "I have accomplished my last task for you. I have brought back some of Persephone's beauty."

Aphrodite screamed in fury. "Impossible! No mortal has ever come back from the Underworld. You cheated! Who did you have go in your place? Tell me!"

"My lady, I went myself. You have only to ask Hades and Persephone to confirm that it was I who made the journey. I have done as you and Anteros bade me to do. I am free now to make my appeal to Eros, to ask him to take me back as his bride. I thank you for the opportunity to prove myself to him."

Aphrodite flung the box against the wall. "You will never have him! He is mine. You should have died a dozen times, but you returned every time. No matter. I will still take my revenge, and he will eventually forget about you."

Psyche kept her head slightly averted. She was more than ready to teach the petty goddess a thing or two about revenge. Sh*e could easily make her forget about the trouncing after the fact,* she told herself. Unfortunately, Eros chose that very moment to appear.

"Aphrodite. Enough," he commanded. "You will not touch her."

Eros reached down and helped Psyche up. He wrapped his arm around her, tucking her front into his side. He gently tilted her face up to receive his kiss. "Hello, my love, I've missed you so much," he whispered against her lips, ignoring Aphrodite.

"Eros! How dare you! She is my prisoner. I have the right to punish her for her insult to me. Now leave!"

Eros laughed. "Actually, that is where you are wrong. I have just had an interesting conversation with Zeus. He agrees that Psyche would make me an excellent wife, so he has granted permission for her to become immortal. The wedding will take place within the hour on Mt. Olympus. You are welcome to attend. In fact, Zeus insists that you come and bless our union."

Both he and Psyche winced at the shrill scream that threatened to shatter their eardrums at his revelation. If he did not know better, he would swear Aphrodite was having some sort of fit, what with the amount of twitching she was doing. It was quite the sight. Her lips kept moving, but she could only make choking sounds.

"Are you alright, Aphrodite?" Psyche asked solicitously.

She was finally able to choke out, "You cannot marry her! You swore to make her fall in love and marry her to a wretched beast."

Eros snickered. "I did keep my promise. You love to tell everyone what a wretched beast I am. Perhaps you should be more specific next time."

"And I do love him," Psyche added.

Aphrodite became so enraged that she launched herself at them. Eros quickly subdued her, pinning her against a wall. His beast raged to be let out, but luckily for Aphrodite, Psyche had a calming effect on him. Besides, he had a much more malicious punishment in mind for her.

Eros waited until Aphrodite tired herself out trying to break his hold before he spoke. "That is the last time you will ever attack me or mine again, Aphrodite. I still have to collect the debt you owe me. So, here it is. You will swear now on the River Styx that you will never in word, deed, conspiracy, or machination ever cause harm in any way, shape, or form to me or to those I consider mine ever again on pain of death. And you will dance at our wedding."

It was almost comical how easy it was to outmaneuver the spiteful goddess, and in the end, she had no choice but to give her vow to him.

Stepping back, he swept Psyche into his arms and flew her to Mt. Olympus, leaving the crazed Aphrodite behind.

* * *

PSYCHE RESTED her head against the side of the bath. It had been a beautiful second wedding. All the gods had attended their ceremony, even Aphrodite, who did indeed dance, though it was clear to everyone in attendance that it pained her to do so. It had been a magical evening. The funniest part was when Psyche had been offered ambrosia and nectar by

Zeus, and she had "transformed" into a winged goddess, none the wiser to her true nature.

Eros joined her in the whirling bath. He had insisted that their wedding night be back at their island home, where they had had an intimate dinner with their friends and family before retiring for the evening.

Right now she was enjoying the foot massage he insisted that she needed. She smiled. "I have been thinking on a name for our daughter."

Eros arched a brow. "Really? What name do you have in mind?"

"Hedone."

"You wish to name her pleasure?"

Psyche nodded. "She is a pleasure, and I believe that is her calling as a goddess. She loves to bring joy and pleasure to others; she hates it when anyone is sad. What do you think?"

"I think that my beast and I will be very busy when she comes of age, killing off all her unworthy suitors, but I love the name, so Hedone it is. Speaking of pleasure," Eros said as he pulled her onto his lap. "I believe it is customary that we dedicate ourselves to making love all night long. What do you think?"

She snorted in laughter. "I believe you are correct, my love. Especially since once the baby arrives, we will have precious little time to ourselves."

"Well then, let us not waste another minute," he said.

Eros moved to stand between her legs, trailing kisses down her throat. He loved the taste of her, and it had been too long since they had last touched each other. He needed to reconnect with her in the most primal way possible. That it should happen where he first introduced her to the pleasures of the flesh all those months ago seemed like fate was finally on their side.

Psyche moaned in pleasure/pain when he lightly bit her

nipples. They were more sensitive to his touch now. She slid her hand in his hair, gripping it hard as she urged him to give her more. She loved being able to finally see her husband as they made love. It drove her mad with lust and spurred her passions to greater heights.

Heading toward where he really wanted to put his mouth, he was momentarily stopped by the swirling water that covered his ultimate goal. Smiling in wicked delight, Eros looked up at Psyche's lust-filled eyes. "We are going to put your wings to the test tonight, my love. You are going to use them to keep yourself upright while I have my dessert."

Using his strength, he lifted her above him while he stood in the middle of the bath. "Drape your legs over my shoulders. I need to taste you," he growled.

Psyche followed his instructions, draping her legs over his shoulders, opening herself up to him. Immediately, Eros fastened his mouth over her sex, licking and nipping the folds of her labia like a starving man before a feast. She cried out, arching her back. Her wings beat frantically, keeping her from falling over, though she knew her husband would never let that happen.

It didn't take long before she was crying out as her orgasm ripped through her. Eros kept licking her, driving her passions up again. Right before she could reach her pleasure a second time, he stopped, earning him a growl of protest from her.

He chuckled roughly. "I love it when you growl at me. I think you have been taking lessons from my drakon."

"I will do more than growl if you do not finish what you have started," she threatened.

Eros laughed. "Oh, I will finish, have no fear. Fly above me for a moment, little butterfly."

Psyche used the power of her wings to rise above him. She hovered in place, just out of reach of her husband. Two could play that game. Every time he beckoned for her to come down, she flew within a few inches of his reach, only to dart away at the last minute, stroking his body as she passed him by.

On the fourth time, Eros leapt into the air, causing her to shriek in mock fright and fly away. At that moment, the chase was on throughout the large bathing chamber. Each time he caught her, he stroked her passions higher before releasing her. The first time, he ran a slow caress down her backside. The second time, he licked the back of her neck. The third time, he slipped his finger into her tight sheath and pumped several times, bringing her right back to the edge before pulling away. He licked his finger, groaning at the taste of her passions. "Delicious."

Psyche had had enough of his teasing. She landed, and sauntered over to one of the reclining chairs. After laying back on it, she slid her hand down to her sex and began to stroke herself. Eros quickly landed beside her. He pulled her hand away and quickly came down on top of her. He then entered her, causing her to cry out in pleasure.

He set a slow pace, staring into her eyes as they made love. It was a melding of the two. Their coming together a healing of sorts. They were finally reunited, and though there was a war coming their way, they knew that as long as they were together, they would be unstoppable.

EPILOGUE

A cloaked figure stood on the cliffs overlooking the sea. It had been many eons since they had last seen the full moon's light sparkling over the water like jewels. After being locked away in a small cell in the depths of Tartarus, the world felt too big. Too overpowering. They felt too exposed.

It wouldn't be long now. The primordial gods had been awakened and released back into the world. Soon they would rise. War was coming, and new factions would form. Who would betray whom in this new life? they wondered.

Eros and Psyche were reunited. They were a force unlike any other. The power that she now wielded was immense. So too were the powers of Eros and Ophioneus. All three had grown in power and strength. They would be a worthy opponent. But they were not the only ones who had grown in power and strength over the eons.

They too had become a force to be reckoned with. So powerful even Tartarus could not imprison them any longer. They had been forged in the very depths of hell, and the world would soon feel their wrath.

War was coming, and those who had betrayed them would soon learn. They had no idea what had been unleashed when they escaped, but they would soon learn, and they would pay.

They would all pay. It was time.

KEEP READING FOR AN EXCERPT FROM THE NEXT PRIMORDIALOMACHY SERIES NOVEL BY E.X. ALEXANDER.

The Wind and the Flower

AVAILABLE 2022 FROM 11TH MUSE PUBLISHERS, LLC

ISLE OF THE BLESSED

Khloris sat back on her hunches and ran a critical eye over her work. The beds of flowers that she had painstakingly planted were finally beginning to take root. With a little more care, and this patch would soon flourish.

Satisfied with the work she had accomplish, she gathered up her tools, and placing them in her basket, stood up. She took a moment to stretch out the kinks in her neck and back. Tilting her head back, she rubbed her lower back for a few minutes until the stiffness loosened up, letting out a sigh of relief when the knot that had formed while she worked suddenly relaxed.

Bending down, she was about to grab her basket when a hand suddenly shot past her and picked it up. Startled, she looked up to see the last person she ever expected to see on the Blessed Island.

"My lord Eros," she greeted softly.

With the sun directly behind the god of Love, it created a glow that surrounded him, little sparks of light reflecting off his pure white wings and blond hair. Feeling the power that radiated off him set her teeth on edge. She could feel the weight of his age and the presence of a predator in her very bones. It raised the hair on the back of her neck in warning, urging her to run. He was far more powerful and ancient then anyone thought, she suddenly realized, and it baffled her how she and the gods of Olympus had failed to see the predator that walked among them.

Grasping her hand and helping her to stand, Eros carefully - though firmly - guided her hand to rest in the crook of his arm, refusing to release her until he was assured that she would leave her hand where he had place it.

All of a sudden, the terrible weight of his age and power disappeared. Leaving her feeling slightly disoriented. Blinking rapidly, she found herself walking, escorted by Eros with no memory of when he had arrived, let alone how she came to be holding his arm as they meandered through the field she had been cultivating.

Realizing that she had missed what Eros was saying, her cheeks turned rosy with mortification. "Forgive me my lord, but I am afraid I haven't been paying attention. Would you be so kind and repeat what you have said?"

Chuckling kindly, "There is nothing to forgive, my dear. I fear you have been in the sun too long. You seemed to have developed a touch of sun illness from working in the gardens for most of the day. I said that we must get you to some shade and drink, as I fear that you may faint."

Stiffening in consternation, she snapped, "I am a nymph, my lord. We do not get sun illness, nor do we faint."

Laughter erupted from him, "Well, that puts me in my place, doesn't it? And here I thought I was being heroic, helping the poor maiden in distress."

Before she could give a retort, they were at one of the many stone benches that dotted the landscape of the island; a large olive tree sheltered this particular one, providing much needed shade, though she was loath to admit it. After they took a seat, Eros set her basket to the side and pulled out a flask. Handing it to her, she gratefully took several long sips from it, pleasantly surprised that it contained pomegranate juice. When she tried to hand it back to him, not wishing to drink it all – though she secretly wished to - he motioned for her to continue drinking. Grateful, she took several more long sips, the flask never emptying. Giving it a puzzled look, she glanced at Eros, her question clear on her face.

"Enchanted, it will always replenish itself," answered Eros.

"I'm surprised you drink pomegranate juice, I thought for sure it would be filled with wine."

Smiling, "We'll let this be our little secret."

For several moments, they sat in companionable silence, a cool breeze gently blowing, offering a welcome respite from the relentless heat of the day. "Why are you here my lord? It is rare to see one of the gods here on the island."

Arching a brow at how forward she was, he could not help but admire her straightforward approach. It was a refreshing change from his dealings with other immortals. "I came here specifically to see you."

"Me?"

"Yes, you."

Confused, for what could a god need help from a nymph such as herself, "But why me, my lord?"

"Call me Eros, Khloris. I have an important matter and I need your help. There is no one else I can trust with this problem."

Turning to fully face Eros, she was taken aback by the pain she glimpsed in his eyes before he quickly hid it. "What do you need me to do?"

"I need you to go to my brother's island of Antipaxos and see what is causing the death of several species of rare flowers."

Khloris could not stop from laughing. The very notion so ridiculous she felt sure he was jesting. "Funny, Eros. I never realized you had such a sense of humor."

When Eros did not join her in laughing, she realized he was deadly serious, and her laughter died away into an awkward silence. "You surely jest."

Shaking his head, "No, I wish I was jesting. However, you are the only one who I believe can solve this problem before it is too late."

"Eros, I am a nymph, not a goddess. My powers are nothing compared to the pantheon. Surely Demeter, or-"

"No," interrupted Eros, "none of the goddesses have the ability to solve this problem. We need you Khloris, no one else. Besides, no goddess is allowed to step foot on our islands without the express permission of the primordial goddesses and ourselves, and you know we rarely ever give that permission."

"While nymphs who swear allegiance to you and your brother are the sole exception to that rule, I believe. Which still doesn't answer why you need me specifically when there are so many more accomplished and wiser nymphs than myself; so tell me, what is so important about these flowers?"

Smiling at the intelligence of such an observation, Eros reached forward and took hold of both of her hands in his, the urgency of his quest clear in the tension of his body. "I will need you to make that oath to Anteros and myself before I can tell you anymore."

"But…if I swear allegiance to you I could be forced to leave the island. I would be bound by my oath to you forever. I want to help you, Eros, truly I do, but this is my home, this is all I know, I do not want to lose it and everyone I love. "

"I swear to you Khloris, if this were not a matter of grave importance I would not ask this of you. Though if it eases your mind, I can swear that you will be able to return and live here on the island for as long as you desire. My brother and I will never make you do anything you truly do not want to do. You will not lose your home, that I swear to you on the River Styx."

Letting go of the breath she had subconsciously been holding, she let out a sigh of relief, "Fine, as long as once this task is over I can return here, than I can give you my oath. I swear my allegiance to you Eros, and to your brother Anteros."

Bringing one of her hands to his lips, he flipped it over, pressing a soft kiss to her pulse. Her racing pulse called to him, however, while he felt a mild interest in her, she was not the one he truly wanted. Releasing her hands, he sat back. Taking a look around, he saw that the souls of the heroes who inhabited the island were off in the distance. Sending out a wave of his power, he ensured that no one – alive or shade – could hear this part of their conversation.

Turning back to Khloris, he locked eyes with her before answering her question, "The flowers are important because they are the origin of ambrosia and nectar. Without them, the bees of our islands cannot make the food of the gods, and they will weaken. Should that happen, they will die at the hands of our enemies not long after that. So Khloris, will you help me now?"

ACKNOWLEDGMENTS

I wish to thank the following people who have helped me on this path to publishing my first novel.

First and foremost, to my parents and brothers. Especially to my youngest brother for the constant encouragement and gentle reminders to keep on writing. Thank you for being my greatest supporter.

To all my friends (you know who you are) who have encouraged me and shown me unwavering support as I pursued my dream of becoming an author.

To LK Shaw for all the help writing my blurb.

To the beta readers and editors who have helped point out where my story worked and where it needed help.

And lastly to you, the readers who took a chance on reading my debut novel.

Thank you all.

ABOUT THE AUTHOR

E.X. Alexander is a romance author who loves to tell a good romance story: the hotter, the better. A proud Greek American (no My Big Fat Greek Wedding jokes or she'll be forced to pull out the Windex ;) who loves to spend time with her family and friends. There is no better way to relax than to curl up with a steamy romance novel with purr babies under a blanket. Okay, a spa day would be a close second. If she is not reading or writing she can usually be found in her car listening to heavy metal and rock music in pursuit of her two favorite fruits: coffee and chocolate. (Yes, they are fruits.)

Visit her website and join her newsletter to keep up with the latest news: www.exalexander.com